D0437243

Three Daughters of Eve

Three Daughters of Eve

ELIF SHAFAK

B L O O M S B U R Y

NEW YORK • LONDON • OXFORD • NEW DELHI • SYDNEY

Bloomsbury USA
An imprint of Bloomsbury Publishing Plc

1385 Broadway
New York
NY 10018
USA

50 Bedford Square
London
WC1B 3DP
UK

www.bloomsbury.com

BLOOMSBURY and the Diana logo are trademarks of Bloomsbury Publishing Plc

First published by Penguin Random House UK 2016
First U.S. edition by Bloomsbury USA 2017

ISBN HB: 978-1-63286-995-1
ePub: 978-1-63286-997-5

Library of Congress Cataloging-in-Publication Data is available.

4 6 8 10 9 7 5

Typeset by Westchester Publishing Services
Printed and bound in the U.S.A. by Berryville Graphics Inc., Berryville, Virginia

What will you do, God, when I die?
When I, your pitcher, broken, lie?
When I, your drink, go stale or dry?
I am your garb, the trade you ply,
You lose your meaning, losing me.

– R. M. Rilke, from *The Book of Hours*

Would you come if someone called you
by the wrong name?
I wept, because for years
He did not enter my arms;
then one night I was told a secret;
perhaps the name you call God
is not really His,
maybe it is just an alias.

– Rabia, the first woman Sufi saint,
eighth century, Iraq

Contents

Contents

Contents

PART ONE

The Handbag

Istanbul, 2016

It was an ordinary spring day in Istanbul, a long and leaden afternoon like so many others, when she discovered, with a hollowness in her stomach, that she was capable of killing someone. She had always suspected that even the calmest and sweetest women under stress were prone to outbursts of violence. Since she thought of herself as neither calm nor sweet, she had reckoned that her potential to lose control was considerably greater than theirs. But 'potential' was a tricky word. Everyone once said that Turkey had great potential – and look how that had turned out. So she had comforted herself that her potential for darkness, too, would amount to nothing in the end.

And thankfully Fate – that well-preserved tablet upon which was engraved everything that happened, and was going to happen – had, for the most part, spared her from wrongdoing. All these years she had led a decent life. She had not inflicted harm on a fellow human being, at least not deliberately, at least not lately, except for engaging in an occasional bit of gossip or bad-mouthing, which shouldn't count. After all, everyone did it – and if it was such a monumental sin, the pits of hell would be full to the brim. If she had caused anguish to anyone at all, it was God, and God, though easily displeased and famously capricious, was never hurt. To hurt and to be hurt – that was a human trait.

In the eyes of family and friends, Nazperi Nalbantoğlu – Peri as she was known to all – was a *good* person. She supported charities, raised awareness about Alzheimer's and money for families in need; volunteered at retirement homes where she competed in backgammon tournaments, losing intentionally; carried treats in her handbag for Istanbul's copious stray cats and, every so often, had them neutered at her own expense; kept a close eye on her children's performance in school; hosted elegant dinners for her husband's boss and co-workers; fasted on the first and last days of Ramadan, but tended to skip the ones in between; sacrificed a hennaed sheep every Eid. She never littered the streets, never jumped the queue at the supermarket, never raised her voice – even when she had been treated rudely. A fine wife, a fine mother, a fine housewife, a fine citizen, a fine modern Muslim she was.

Time, like a skilful tailor, had seamlessly stitched together the two fabrics that sheathed Peri's life: what people thought of her and what she thought of herself. The impression she left on others and her self-perception had been sewn into a whole so consummate that she could no longer tell how much of each day was defined by what was wished upon her and how much of it was what she really wanted. She often felt the urge to grab a bucketful of soapy water and scrub the streets, the public squares, the government, the parliament, the bureaucracy, and, while she was at it, wash out a few mouths too. There was so much filth to clean up; so many broken pieces to fix; so many errors to correct. Every morning when she left her house she let out a quiet sigh, as if in one breath she could will away the detritus of the previous day. While Peri questioned the world without fail, and was not one to keep silent in the face of injustice, she had resolved some years ago to be content with what she had. It would therefore come as a surprise when, on a middling kind of day, at the age of thirty-five, established and respected, she found herself staring at the void in her soul.

It was all because of the traffic, she would later reassure herself. Rumbling, roaring, metal clanking against metal like the cries of a thousand warriors. The entire city was one giant construction site. Istanbul had grown uncontrollably and kept on expanding – a bloated goldfish, unaware of having gobbled more than it could digest, still searching around for more to eat. Looking back on that fateful afternoon, Peri would conclude that had it not been for the hopeless gridlock, the chain of events that awakened a long-dormant part of her memory would never have been set in motion.

There they were, inching along a two-lane road half blocked by an overturned lorry, trapped among vehicles of all sizes. Peri's fingers tapped on the steering wheel, switching radio channels every few minutes, while her daughter, earphones in, sat with a bored expression in the passenger seat. Like a magic wand in the wrong hands, the traffic turned minutes into hours, humans into brutes and any trace of sanity into sheer lunacy. Istanbul didn't seem to mind. Time, brutes and lunacy it had aplenty. One hour more, one hour less; one brute more, one lunatic less – past a certain point, it made no difference.

Madness coursed through this city's streets, like an intoxicating drug in the bloodstream. Every day millions of Istanbulites downed another dose, not realizing that they were becoming more and more unbalanced. People who would refuse to share their bread shared their insanity instead. There was something inscrutable about the collective loss of reason: if enough eyes experienced the same hallucination, it turned into a truth; if enough people laughed at the same misery, it became a funny little joke.

'Oh, stop picking at your nails!' Peri said all of a sudden. 'How many times do I have to tell you?'

Slowly, very slowly, Deniz pulled her earphones down around her neck. 'They are *my* nails,' she said, and took a sip from the paper cup placed between them.

Before setting out on the road they had stopped at a Star Börek – a Turkish coffee chain that had been repeatedly sued by Starbucks for using their logo, their menu and a distorted version of their name but was still, because of legal loopholes, in business – and bought two drinks: a skinny latte for Peri, a double chocolaty chip crème frappuccino for her daughter. Peri had finished hers, but Deniz was taking forever, sipping gingerly like an injured bird. Outside the sun was melting into the horizon, the last rays painting the roofs of shanty homes, the domes of the mosques and the windows of skyscrapers in the same dull shade of rust.

'And this is *my* car,' Peri said under her breath. 'You are dropping skin flakes on the floor.'

As soon as the words escaped her mouth she regretted them. *My car!* What a terrible thing to say to one's child – or to anyone, for that matter. Had she become one of those materialistic fools whose entire sense of self and place lay in the possessions she owned? She hoped not.

Her daughter did not seem taken aback. Instead Deniz shrugged her bony shoulders, glanced outside and furiously moved on to the next fingernail.

The car lurched forward, only to stop again with its tyres screeching. It was a Range Rover in a shade named Monte Carlo Blue, according to the dealer's catalogue. There were other colour options in the brochure: Davos White, Oriental Dragon Red, Saudi Desert Pink, Ghana Police Gloss Blue or Indonesian Army Matt Green. Peri imagined, with pursed lips and a shake of the head, the frivolous marketing types who invented these names, and wondered whether drivers were aware that the sleek and swanky cars in which they flaunted themselves were associated with the police, or the military, or sandstorms in the Arabian peninsula.

Whatever their colour, Istanbul teemed with deluxe vehicles, many of which looked out of place, like high-born, pedigree dogs that, though destined for lives of comfort and ease, had somehow lost their way and wandered into the wilderness. There were racing convertibles that roared with the frustration of having nowhere to gather speed, off-roaders that, even with the deftest of manoeuvres, could not be wedged into diminutive parking spaces – if, by chance, any were available – and pricey sedans designed for wide-open roads that existed only in faraway lands and TV commercials.

'I read it's been ranked the worst in the world,' Peri said.

'What?'

'The traffic. We are number one. Worse than Cairo, imagine. Even worse than Delhi!'

Not that she had ever been to Cairo or Delhi. But, like many Istanbulites, Peri held a firm belief that her city was more civilized than those remote, rough, congested places – even though, 'remote' was a relative concept and both 'rough' and 'congested' were adjectives often applied to Istanbul. All the same, this city bordered on Europe. Such closeness had to amount to something. It was so breathtakingly close that Turkey had put one foot through Europe's doorway and tried to venture forth with all its might – only to find the opening was so narrow that, no matter how much the rest of its body wriggled and squirmed, it could not squeeze itself in. Nor did it help that Europe, in the meantime, was pushing the door shut.

'Cool!' Deniz said.

'Cool?' Peri echoed incredulously.

'Yeah. At least we are number one in something.'

That was the thing about her daughter: lately, whatever opinion Peri expressed on any subject, Deniz took the opposite position. Every remark Peri made, no matter how apt or logical, her daughter received it with a hostility that verged on hatred. Peri was aware that Deniz, having reached the delicate age of twelve and a half, had to break free of her parents' – especially the materfamilias's – influence. She understood that. What she couldn't get her head around was the amount of fury involved in the process. Her daughter seethed with a boiling rage that Peri had never experienced at any stage in her life, not even in adolescence. She herself had sailed through puberty with an innocent confusion, almost naivety. How different a teenager she had been compared with her daughter, even though her mother had not been half as thoughtful and understanding as she was. In some circuitous way, the more Peri suffered from her daughter's random outbursts, the more maddened she was with herself for not having been angry enough in the past with her own mother.

'When you are my age you won't have the patience left for this city,' Peri murmured.

'*When you are my age . . .*' Deniz mimicked bitterly. 'You never used to talk like that.'

'That's because things are getting worse!'

'No, Mum, it's because you're making yourself old,' Deniz said. 'It's the way you talk. And look at what you are wearing!'

'What's wrong with my dress?'

Silence.

Peri glanced down at her purple silk dress and beaded, embroidered chiffon jacket. She had bought the ensemble from a boutique in a shining new shopping centre nestled within a larger shopping centre – as if the one had just given birth to the other. It was too expensive. When she objected to the price, the clerk had said nothing, a tiny smile forming in the corner of his mouth. *If you can't afford it, lady, what are you doing here?* the smile said. It had vexed Peri, the condescension. 'I'll take it,' she had heard herself say. Now she felt the tightness of the fabric against her skin, saw the wrongness of the colour. The purple that had appeared to be bold and confident under the shop's fluorescent tubes looked garish and pretentious in daylight.

Useless thoughts these were, since she had no time to go home and change. They were already running late for a dinner at the seaside mansion of a businessman who had made a colossal fortune in the last few years – not that there was anything unusual about that. Istanbul abounded with the old poor and the nouveau riche and with those who yearned to pole-vault from the former to the latter category in one quick leap.

Peri disliked these dinner parties, which went on late into the night and often left her with a migraine the next day. She would rather stay home and, in the witching hours, be immersed in a novel – reading being her way to connect with the universe. But solitude was a rare privilege in Istanbul. There was always some important event to attend or an urgent social responsibility to fulfil as if the culture, like a child scared of loneliness, made sure everyone was at all times in the company of others. So much laughter and food. Politics and cigars. Shoes and dresses, but above all, designer handbags. Women paraded their handbags like trophies won in faraway battles. Who knew which ones were original, which ones fake. Istanbul's middle-to-upper-class ladies, not wanting to be seen purchasing counterfeit goods, instead of visiting dubious stores in and around the Grand Bazaar, invited shopowners to their houses. Vans full of Chanel, Louis Vuitton and Bottega Veneta, their windows blackened, their number plates obscured by mud (though the rest of the vehicles were utterly spotless), zipped back and forth between the affluent quarters, and were admitted into the private garages of villas through back gates, as in a *film noir* or spy movie. Payments were made in cash, no receipts issued, no further questions asked. At the next social gathering, the same ladies would furtively inspect one another's handbags not only to identify the luxury brand, but also to judge the authenticity – or the quality of the knockoff. It was a lot of effort. Optical effort.

Women stared. They scanned, scrutinized and searched, hunting for the flaws in the other women, both manifest and camouflaged. Overdue manicures, newly gained pounds, sagging bellies, Botoxed lips, varicose veins, cellulite still visible after liposuction, hair roots in need of dyeing, a pimple or a wrinkle hidden under layers of powder . . . There was nothing that their penetrating gazes could not detect and decipher. However carefree they may have been before they arrived at the party, too many female guests became, by and by, both victim and perpetrator. The more Peri thought about the evening ahead, the more she dreaded it.

'Need to stretch my legs,' said Deniz as she popped out of the car.

Immediately, Peri lit a cigarette. She had quit smoking more than a decade before. But lately she had given in to carrying a packet of cigarettes around and lighting up every now and then; though satisfied after a few puffs, she never finished any of them. Each time she threw away what was left with guilt and something akin to disgust. She chewed mint gum afterwards to mask the odour, though she disliked the taste. She had always suspected that if chewing-gum flavours were political regimes, peppermint would be Fascism – totalitarian, sterile, stern.

'Mum, I can't breathe,' said Deniz, now back in. 'Don't you know it'll kill you?'

Deniz was at that age when children treat smokers like vampires on the loose. At school she had given a presentation on the harmful effects of smoking, featuring a poster showing Day-Glo arrows pointing from a newly opened cigarette packet to a freshly dug grave.

'Okay, okay,' said Peri, as she waved a hand in dismissal.

'If I were the President, I'd lock up parents who smoke next to their kids. Seriously!'

'Well, I'm glad you're not running for office,' Peri said, before pressing the button to lower her window.

The smoke she exhaled outside swirled in the air and then slowly, unexpectedly, entered the open window of the car next to them. That was the one thing one could never get rid of in this city: proximity. Everything was adjacent to something else. Pedestrians wound their way through the streets as a single organism; travellers sat squashed on ferries or stood shoulder to shoulder on buses and subways; bodies sometimes collided and clashed, and sometimes coexisted weightlessly, brushing gently against each other like dandelion spores in the breeze.

There were two men in the car beside them. Both grinned at her. Remembering that the *Advanced Learner's Guide to Patriarchy* defined the act of a woman blowing smoke into the face of an unfamiliar male as an open sexual invitation, Peri paled. Though easy to forget at times, the city was a stormy sea swollen with drifting icebergs of masculinity, and it was better to manoeuvre away from them, gingerly and smartly, for one never knew how much danger lay beneath the surface.

Whether driving or walking, a woman did best to keep her gaze unfocused and turned inward, as if peering into distant memories. When and wherever possible, she should lower her head to convey an unambiguous message of modesty, which was not easy, since the perils of urban life, not to mention unsolicited male attention and sexual harassment, required one to be vigilant at all times. How women could be expected to keep their heads down and simultaneously have their eyes open in all directions was beyond Peri. She threw away the cigarette and closed the window, hoping the two strangers would soon lose interest in her. The traffic light changed from red to green, but it didn't matter. Nothing was moving.

That was when she noticed a tramp walking down the middle of the road. Tall and gangly with an angular face, he was thin as a whisper, his forehead creased beyond his years, his chin covered in a rash and his hands in weeping patches of eczema. One of the millions of Syrian refugees who had fled the only life they knew, she first thought – though there was an equal chance that he was a local Turk or a Kurd or a Gypsy or a bit of everything. How many people in this land of endless migrations and transformations could say with certitude that they were of one pure ethnicity, unless they were lying to themselves – and to their children? But, then again, Istanbul amassed deceptions galore.

The man's feet were caked with dried mud, and he wore a ragged coat with the collar turned up, so dirty that it was almost black. Having found her lipstick-smudged cigarette, he was smoking it nonchalantly. Peri's gaze travelled from his mouth to his eyes, surprised to see that he had been watching her with an amused expression. There was a swagger in his manner, a challenge almost; he seemed not so much a tramp as an actor playing the part of a tramp and, confident of his performance, he was waiting for applause.

Having now three men to avoid, the two in the car plus the tramp, Peri turned aside brusquely, forgetting that there was a coffee cup there. The frappuccino tipped over, sending its frothy contents into her lap.

'Argh, no!' Peri shrieked as she gaped in horror at the dark stain spreading on her expensive dress.

Her daughter whistled, clearly enjoying the disaster. 'You can say it's a piece by a new crazy designer.'

Ignoring the remark and cursing herself, Peri blindly grabbed her handbag – a lavender ostrich Birkin, perfect in every detail other than the misplaced accent on the word 'Hermès', for there was nothing the city's bootleggers couldn't counterfeit except proper spelling – which she had tucked between her legs. She took out a packet of tissues, even though she knew, or a part of her knew, that wiping would only worsen the stain. In her distraction, she made a mistake no veteran driver in Istanbul ever would: she tossed her handbag into the back seat – and the doors unlocked.

She could see something fluttering out of the corner of her eye. A beggar girl, no older than twelve, was coming towards them, pleading for coins. Her clothes flapping about her skinny frame, her palm extended forward, she walked without moving her body from the waist up, as if through water. She stayed in front of each car for about ten seconds before proceeding to the next. Perhaps, Peri thought, she had figured out that if one could not inspire mercy in that brief amount of time, one would never do so. Compassion never came as an afterthought: it was either spontaneous or absent entirely.

When the girl reached the Range Rover, both Peri and Deniz automatically glanced in the opposite direction, pretending not to have seen her. But the beggars of Istanbul were used to being invisible to others and came well prepared. Exactly in the spot where mother and daughter had turned their heads stood another child of around the same age, waiting with an open palm.

To Peri's immense relief the light turned green and the traffic shot forward like water out of a garden hose. She was about to put her foot on the accelerator when she heard the back door open and close, as fast as a switchblade. In the mirror she saw her handbag being scooped out of the car.

'Thieves!' Her voice hoarse from the effort, Peri screamed. 'Help, they stole my bag. Thieves!'

The cars behind her honked frantically, oblivious to what had happened, eager to go. It was obvious nobody was going to help. Peri hesitated, but only for a moment. With a dexterous spin of the steering wheel, she swerved the car to the kerb and left her emergency lights flashing.

'Mum, what are you doing?'

Peri didn't respond. There was no time. She had seen the direction in which the children had scampered off, and she needed to follow them at once; something inside, an animal instinct for all she knew, assured her that if she could find them she would get back what rightly belonged to her.

'Mum, let it go. It's just a bag – and fake!'

'I've got money and credit cards in there. And my phone!'

But her daughter was worried, embarrassed even. Deniz did not like to attract attention, only wanted to blend in, a drop of grey in a sea of grey. All her rebelliousness seemed to be saved for her mother.

'Stay here, lock the doors, wait for me,' Peri said. 'For once, do as I say. Please!'

'But, Mum . . .'

Without thinking, not thinking at all, Peri dashed out of the car, forgetting for an instant that she was wearing high heels. She took off her shoes, her bare feet hitting the asphalt heavily. From inside the car, her daughter gaped at her, eyes wide with astonishment and mortification.

Peri ran. In her purple dress, carrying the weight of her years, her cheeks aflame, the wife-housewife-mother-of-three, in front of dozens of eyes, was painfully aware that her breasts were hopping frantically and she was unable to do anything about it. Even so, tasting a strange sense of freedom, trespassing in a forbidden zone she could not name, she sprinted across the road towards the inner streets, while drivers laughed and seagulls swirled above her head. If she hesitated, if she so much as slowed for a second, she would have been horrified at what she was doing. The possibility of stepping on rusty nails, broken beer bottles or rat urine would have terrified her. Instead she charged ahead. Her legs, almost independently, as if with a memory of their own, kept going faster and faster, remembering the time long ago at Oxford when she would jog three to four miles every day, rain or shine.

Peri used to love running. Like other joys in her life, that, too, was no more.

The Mute Poet

Istanbul, 1980s

When Peri was little, the Nalbantoğlus lived on Mute Poet Street, in a lower-middle-class neighbourhood on the Asian side of Istanbul. Amidst the decaying days, a mixture of scents – fried aubergine, ground coffee, freshly baked flatbread, simmering garlic – emanated from the open windows, so strong that it permeated everything, seeping into gutter drains and manhole covers; so sharp that the morning wind immediately changed its direction. But the locals did not complain. They never noticed the smell. It was outsiders alone who picked it up – although very few outsiders ever had reason to come to this area. Houses leaned higgeldy-piggeldy like headstones in an unkempt graveyard. A fog of boredom hovered over everything and only lifted momentarily when the shouts of children, cheating at a game, pierced the air.

Rumours abounded as to the origin of the street's peculiar name. Some believed that a renowned Ottoman poet who had resided in the area, unhappy with the meagre baksheesh granted him after a poem he had sent to the palace, swore not to open his mouth again until he was suitably rewarded by the Sultan.

'Surely the Master of the Lands of Caesar and Alexander the Great, the Ruler of Three Continents and Five Seas, the Shadow of God on Earth, would bestow his unbounded generosity on his humble subject. But if he doth not, I shall take it as a sign of the inferiority of my poems and I shall stay mute till the day I die, for a dead poet is preferable to a failed poet.' Such were his last words before he fell as silent as midnight snow. It wasn't pretension; he revered, feared and obeyed whatever in his mind he imagined a ruler to be. Still, being an artist he could not help but crave more attention, more praise, more love – and a few more coins would not be so bad either.

When the incident reached his ears, the Sultan, amused by such impudence, promised to make amends. Like all despots, he had mixed feelings about artists: while he disapproved of their unpredictability and unruliness, he also enjoyed their presence, provided they knew their limits. Artists had an unusual way of looking at things, which could be entertaining, except when it was not. He liked to keep a few of them in his court, under a tight rein. They were free to say whatever they pleased so long as they didn't criticize the state and its rules, the religion and the Almighty, and, above all, the sovereign.

As fate would have it, that same week, following a plot in the seraglio to overthrow the Sultan and put his eldest son on the throne, the sovereign was murdered – strangled with a silk bowstring so as not to spill his noble blood. In death, as in life, the Ottomans liked to keep everyone in their places, everything meticulously regulated, unambiguous. While royals were strangled, thieves were hanged, rebels decapitated, highway robbers impaled, local dignitaries pounded in a mortar; concubines dropped into the sea in weighted sacks; every week a new set of severed heads was displayed on the gibbets in front of the palace, their mouths stuffed with cotton if they were high-ranking officers, with straw if they were nonentities. That was exactly how the poet felt. Bound by his oath, he remained silent till the day he breathed his last.

Others had a different version of the story. When the poet demanded to be compensated generously, the Sultan, angered at such effrontery, ordered his tongue to be cut out, chopped up, fried and fed to the cats of seven neighbourhoods. But, having uttered so many sharp words all these years, the poet's tongue had an acrid taste, even after it was sautéed with sheep's-tail fat and fresh onions. The cats all walked away. The poet's wife, who had been watching the scene from behind a latticed window, secretly gathered up the pieces and sewed them together. She had barely placed her creation on the bed and gone to look for a surgeon who could put the tongue back in her husband's mouth when a seagull swooped through the open window and stole it. Hardly surprising, given that the seagulls of Istanbul are notorious scavengers and feast on whatever comes their way, regardless of taste. A bird that can peck out and gobble up the eyes of animals twice its size can devour anything. Hence the poet remained as silent as a fisherman's lamp. Instead a white avian, circling above his head, cawed the poems he could no longer recite to the entire city.

Whatever the truth behind its name, the street on which the Nalbantoğlus lived was a quaint, sleepy lane where the most cherished virtues were modelled on the three states of matter: to obey Allah – and the imams – with unswerving compliance, ultimate surrender and unbroken stability (solid); to accept the Divine River of Life no matter how much mud and debris it might sweep along (liquid); and to forgo ambitions since all possessions and trophies would eventually vanish into thin air (gas). Around here every destiny was seen as preordained, each suffering unavoidable, including those the residents of the street inflicted on each other, such as football fights, political brawls and wife-beating.

Theirs was a two-storey house, the colour of sour cherries. Throughout the years it had been painted several different hues: salted-plum green, walnut-jam brown, pickled-beet purple. The Nalbantoğlus rented the ground floor; their landlord lived upstairs. Although the family was not at all rich – all wealth is relative by the standards of time and place – Peri had grown up without feeling deprived. That would come later and, like all things deferred, it would arrive with such force that it seemed to be making up for lost time. She would learn to see the faults of the household in which she had once been so protected and beloved a daughter.

She was the Nalbantoğlus' last child, her conception one big surprise, since her parents, having already raised two boys into their late teens, were deemed too old. Sheltered, cosseted, her every need not only satisfied but also anticipated, Peri led a life of acquired ease in these early years. Even so she was aware of a breeze of tension at home, which grew into a full-blown gale whenever her father and her mother happened to be in the same room.

They were as incompatible as tavern and mosque. The frowns that descended on their brows, the stiffness that infused their voices, identified them not as a couple in love, but as opponents in a game of chess. On the faded board of their marriage they each pushed forward, strategizing the next moves, capturing castles, elephants and viziers, aiming to deliver the ultimate defeat. Each side saw the other as the tyrant in the family, the intolerable one, and longed to say, someday, 'Checkmate, *shah manad*, the sovereign is helpless.' Their marriage had been so deeply woven with mutual resentment that they no longer needed a reason to feel wronged and frustrated. Even at that young age Peri sensed that love was not, and probably never had been, the reason why her parents were together.

In the evenings she watched her father slumped at the table with plates of mezes distributed around a bottle of raqi. Stuffed grape leaves, mashed chickpeas, grilled red peppers, artichokes in olive oil and his favourite, lamb's brain salad. He would eat slowly, sampling each dish like a fastidious connoisseur, even though the food was no more than a necessity so as not to drink on an empty stomach. 'I don't gamble, I don't steal, I don't accept bribes, I don't smoke and I don't go around chasing women; surely Allah will spare His old creation this much misdeed,' Mensur was fond of saying. Ordinarily, he would have a friend or two join him for these lengthy suppers. They would rattle on about politics and politicians, depressed about the state of things. Like the majority of the people in this land, they talked most about the things they liked least.

'Travel the world, you'll see, everyone drinks differently,' Mensur would say. He himself had moved around a fair amount in his youth as a ship's engineer. 'In a democracy, when a man gets drunk, he cries, "What happened to my sweetheart?" Where there is no democracy, when a man gets drunk, he cries, "What happened to my sweet country?"'

Soon words would melt into melodies and they would be singing – bouncy Balkan tunes at first, revolutionary Black Sea songs next, and gradually, inevitably, Anatolian ballads of heartbreak and unrequited love. Turkish, Kurdish, Greek, Armenian, Ladino lyrics would mix in the air, like coiling wisps of smoke.

Sitting by herself in a corner, a heaviness of heart would come over Peri. She often wondered what it was that made her father so sad. She imagined sorrow sticking to him like a fine layer of black tar under the sole of his shoe. She could neither find a way to lift his spirits nor stop trying, for she was, as everyone in the family would testify, her father's daughter.

From the ornate picture frame on the wall, Atatürk – the father of the Turks – would glance down at them, his steel-blue eyes flecked with gold. There were portraits of the national hero everywhere; Atatürk in his military uniform in the kitchen, Atatürk in a redingote in the living room, Atatürk with a coat and kalpak in the master bedroom, Atatürk with silk gloves and flowing cape in the hall. On national holidays and commemorative days Mensur would hang a Turkish flag with a picture of the great man outside a window for everyone to see.

'Remember, if it weren't for him, we'd have been like Iran,' Mensur often said to his daughter. 'I'd have to grow a round beard and bootleg my own booze. They'd find out and flog me in the square. And you, my soul, would be wearing a chador, even at your young age!'

Mensur's friends – schoolteachers, bank officers, engineers – were just as devoted to Atatürk and his principles. They read, recited and, when inspiration struck, wrote patriotic poems – many of which were so similar in rhythm and repetitive in essence that, rather than separate pieces, they felt like echoes of the same call. Even so, Peri enjoyed lingering in the living room, listening to their amiable chatter, the tones and cadences of their voices, rising and falling with each new glass topped up to the brim. They did not mind her presence. If anything, her interest in their conversation seemed to rejuvenate them, filling them with hope for the youth. Thus Peri stayed around, sipping orange juice from her father's favourite mug, which had the signature of Atatürk on one side and a quote from the national leader on the other: *The civilized world is ahead of us; we have no choice but to catch up.* Peri loved this porcelain cup, the smooth touch of it against her palm, though it made her slightly regretful each time she finished her drink, as though the chance of catching up with the civilized world had also disappeared.

Peri would be up and down like a yo-yo. Ice buckets to refill, ashtrays to empty, bread to toast; there was always some task to be done – especially since her mother absented herself on such evenings.

As soon as Selma placed the food on the table, quietly sighing to herself, she would retreat to her bedroom and not emerge until the next morning. Sometimes she wouldn't reappear until midday or later. Depression was a word unheard of in the house. *Headaches*, she would explain. She often suffered from severe headaches that left her debilitated and in bed, her eyes almost closed, as if squinting against perpetual sunlight. When the body was weak, the mind was purified, she claimed – so pure that she saw omens in everything: a pigeon cooing outside her window, a bulb that suddenly burned out, a leaf swimming in her tea. Cloistered in her room, she would lie prostrate, listening and accounting for every single sound. It was impossible not to hear: the walls were as thin as sheets of rolled-out dough. But there was another wall between Selma and Mensur, erected decades earlier, rising higher with every passing year.

Some time ago Selma had joined a religious circle led by a preacher famous for the eloquence of his sermons and the rigidity of his views. They called him Üzümbaz Efendi, for he was known to claim that wherever he saw signs of idolatry and heresy he would crush them, like trampling grapes underfoot. It didn't bother him in the least that his soubriquet brought to mind the making of wine – a sin no less grave than the drinking of it. Neither juicy grapes nor bottled wine piqued the man's interest nearly as much as the act of crushing itself.

Under the preacher's influence Selma had changed visibly. She now not only declined to shake hands with the opposite sex, but also refused to sit on a bus seat that had last been occupied by a man – even if he had vacated it for her. Although she did not wear a niqab, as some of her close friends did, she covered her head fully. She no longer approved of pop music, which she found corrupt and corrupting. She banished from the house all kinds of confectionery and snacks, ice cream, potato chips and chocolate products – even foodstuffs labelled halal – ever since Üzümbaz Efendi had told her that they might contain gelatine, which might contain collagen, which, in turn, might contain pork. Such was her fear of coming into contact with any pig extract that instead of shampoo she used raw olive-oil soap; instead of toothpaste a miswak stick; and instead of a candle, a wad of butter with a wick inserted. In her suspicion that glue from pig bones might have been used in their manufacture, she refused to wear foreign-brand shoes and advised everyone to do the same. Sandals were safest. For years, on the instructions of her mother, Peri would go to school wearing camel-leather sandals and goat's-wool socks – only to be ridiculed by her classmates.

With a circle of like-minded spirits, Selma organized trips to beaches in and around Istanbul, trying to convince women sunbathing in bikinis to repent of their ways before it was too late for their souls to be saved. 'Every inch of flesh you show today will scorch you in hell tomorrow.' The group distributed flyers written with poor grammar and worse spelling, abounding in exclamation marks, lacking in commas; they harped on about how Allah did not wish to see Eve's granddaughters half naked in public spaces. Later in the evenings, when the beaches were deserted, the same flyers could be seen flapping in the wind, ripped and stained, the words 'debauchery', 'sacrilege', 'eternal damnation' scattered in the sands like strands of dried seaweed.

Animated though she always was, Selma had become even more talkative and argumentative in this new stage of her life, keen to bring others, especially her husband, to the path of the righteous. Given that Mensur had no intention of being corrected, the Nalbantoğlu household was divided into *her zone* and *his zone* – *Dar al-Islam* and *Dar al-harp* – the realm of submission and the realm of war.

Religion had plummeted into their lives as unexpectedly as a meteor, and created a chasm, separating the family into two clashing camps. The younger son, Hakan, irredeemably religious and excessively nationalistic, took his mother's side; the elder son, Umut, in his effort to diffuse the conflict, remained for a while neutral, though it was clear from everything he said and did that he leaned towards the left. When he finally came out as a leftist, he would do so as a fully fledged Marxist.

All of that put Peri, the youngest child, in an awkward position, with both parents striving to win her over; her very existence became a battleground between competing worldviews. The thought that she had to make a choice, once and for all, between her mother's defiant religiosity and her father's defiant materialism almost paralysed her. For Peri was the kind of person who, if possible, tried not to offend anyone. Surrounded by warriors who rebelled against one another, fighting wars to no end, she settled on compulsory complaisance, forcing herself into docility. Without anyone knowing, she quenched the fire in her, turning it to ashes.

The gulf between Peri's parents was nowhere more apparent than in one particular corner of the living room. There were two shelves above the TV stand, the first of which was reserved for her father's books – *Atatürk: The Rebirth of a Nation* by Lord Kinross, *The Great Speech* by Atatürk himself, *Things I Didn't Know I Loved* by Nâzim Hikmet, *Crime and Punishment* by Dostoyevsky, *Doctor Zhivago* by Boris Pasternak, an entire collection of memoirs (by generals and common soldiers) on the First World War, and an old edition of *The Rubáiyát of Omar Khayyám*, its cover tattered from multiple readings.

The second shelf was a different world altogether. For years it had been occupied by porcelain horses of all sizes and colours – ponies, stallions and mares with golden manes and rainbow tails, frolicking, galloping, grazing. Gradually, books began to arrive: *Hadiths* compiled by al-Bukhari; *Disciplining the Soul* by al-Ghazali; *Step-by-step Guide to Prayer and Supplication in Islam; Stories of the Prophets; The Good Muslim Woman's Handbook; The Virtues of Patience and Gratitude; The Islamic Interpretation of Dreams*. The right corner was reserved for Üzümbaz Efendi's two books: *The Import of Purity in an Immoral World* and *Sheitan is Whispering in Your Ear*. As new titles were added, the horses were relegated, inch by inch, to the end of the shelf, where they perched precariously as if on the edge of a cliff.

The deluge of words and emotions coursing through the corridors of the house baffled Peri's innocent mind. She knew, from all that she had been taught, that Allah was the one and only. Yet she could not for a moment believe that the religious teachings her mother held sacred and her father railed against belonged to the same God. Surely they did not. And if they did, how could that God be seen in such diametrically opposite ways by two people who shared a wedding ring – if no longer a bed?

Alert and compliant, Peri was a witness to the vendettas, watching how her loved ones would tear each other to pieces. Early on she learned that there was no fight more hurtful than a family fight, and no family fight more hurtful than one over God.

The Knife

Istanbul, 2016

Before long, Peri caught sight of the beggars who had snatched her handbag. Although they had escaped as fast as their feet could carry them, she was quicker than they were. She couldn't believe her luck – if luck it was. She raced after them into a cobbled alleyway – its stone walls rising from the shadows – her chest burning with each breath.

The children were there, standing on either side of a man – the tramp who had smoked the rest of her cigarette. Peri took a step towards them, but could not speak. She had acted without thinking, and, now that she was thinking, she felt disorientated.

The tramp smiled serenely, as if he had been expecting her. Up close he looked different, the gaunt lines of his cheekbones perfectly symmetrical, a youthful glow from the inky depths of his eyes. Were it not for the wretchedness of his appearance, one might have said there was a hint of the dandy about him. On his lap he held her handbag reverently, caressing it like a long-lost lover.

'That's mine,' Peri said, her voice tight as she swallowed the knot that rose in her throat.

At this he opened the clasp and held the handbag in the air before turning it upside down. Its contents spilled out: house keys, lipstick, eyeliner, a pen, a miniature bottle of perfume, a mobile phone, a pack of tissues, a pair of sunglasses, a hairbrush, a tampon . . . And a leather wallet. This he picked up gingerly. From inside, he pulled out a wad of banknotes, credit cards, a woman's pink ID, a driving licence, family photos of favourite memories. Whistling all the while, he pocketed the money and the phone, ignoring the other items. It emitted a carefree, chirpy melody that sounded like a tune from an old music-box. Just as he was about to throw away the wallet, something caught his eye. A

Polaroid, which had partially slipped out from a compartment where it had been carefully tucked away, hidden from view. A relic from a time long gone.

Raising an eyebrow, the tramp studied the Polaroid. There were four faces there: a man and three young women. A professor and his students. Wrapped in coats, hats and scarves, they stood with their backs to the Bodleian Library in Oxford, huddled together for warmth or out of habit, forever trapped inside one of the coldest days of that winter.

The tramp lifted his head and grinned at Peri as if he had recognized Oxford from a film or a newspaper clipping. Or he might just as well have noticed that one of the girls in the snap was the woman now standing in front of him. She had gained weight and wrinkles, her hair was shorter and straighter, but her eyes were the same, barring the hint of sadness. He tossed the photo aside.

Peri watched for a few seconds – no more – the Polaroid fly into the air, then flutter to the ground. She flinched as though the photo were alive and might have been hurt in the fall.

Panicking, she shouted to the tramp that people were on their way to help her: the police, the gendarmerie, her husband. She waved her hand to show her wedding ring, painfully aware in that moment that the girl she once was would have mocked her for flaunting this symbol of her marital status as if it were an amulet. But there were enough reasons the man would not believe her, not least the catch in her voice. The alley was deserted, the light draining from the sky. How far had she strayed from the main road? She could still hear the sound of traffic but it was muffled, as though coming from behind a glass wall. Suddenly she was afraid.

The tramp was motionless for an awkward moment. So still was the air that Peri thought she could make out the scuttle of a mouse in the pile of rubbish nearby, rushing, rummaging while its heart, no bigger than a pistachio, drummed in its tiny chest. The alley felt outside the realm of Istanbul's cats, outside the city borders and, in that instant, outside this world.

Calmly, the man fished for something in his coat pocket and pulled it out. It was a plastic bag containing a tiny tube of solvent. He took the tube and squeezed the entire contents into the bag. Next he blew air into it, making a small balloon. He smiled at his creation, an idyllic snow globe in which every flake of snow that ever fell was either diamond or pearl. Placing it over his nose and mouth, he inhaled heavily; once, twice, then a longer third time. When he raised his head again, his expression had altered, there and not there. He was a glue addict, Peri understood. Only now did she notice the broken blood vessels in his eyeballs, like cracks on scorched earth. A voice inside told her to go back to her daughter and her car, but she stood so still the adhesive might just as well have been spilled on to her feet, fixing her to this spot.

The tramp offered the plastic bag to one of the children, who, in her excitement, almost snatched it from him. She huffed noisily while the other girl waited her turn, impatient and irritated at being the last. Glue, the favourite treat of street children and underage prostitutes; the magic carpet that carried them, as light as feathers, over the roofs and domes and skyscrapers into a far-off kingdom where there was no fear and no reason for fear; no pain, no prisons, no pimps. They stayed in that Eden for as long as they could, sucking golden grapes off the stalks, nibbling on juicy peaches. Safe from hunger and cold, they chased ogres, jeered at giants and stuffed genies back into the bottles from which they had escaped.

Like all sweet dreams this one, too, came with a price. The glue dissolved the membrane of their brain cells, attacked their nervous systems, destroyed their kidneys and livers, devouring them, inch by inch, from inside.

'I'm calling the police,' Peri yelled, louder than needed. *Not the right thing to say,* she thought to herself and added, even louder: 'My daughter's already called. They'll be here any minute.'

As if that were his cue, the tramp rose to his feet. His moves were slow and deliberate, perhaps to give her enough time to change her mind, or else to make it clear that none of what was about to happen was his fault.

The two children were nowhere to be seen. When they had left and where they had gone, Peri had no idea. They followed the orders of the tramp. He was the Sultan of the backstreets, the Emperor of uncollected rubbish and open cesspools, of everything unwanted and abandoned; the magnanimous collector of it all. Not his features but the intensity with which he carried himself reminded Peri of someone – someone she thought she had left locked in the past, someone she had loved like she had loved no one else.

Tearing her gaze away from the man, for a second or so, Peri glanced at the Polaroid on the ground. It was one of the few photos from her time at Oxford that she had kept over the years – and the only photo of Professor Azur. She could not afford to lose it.

When she looked back, she was startled to see that the tramp's nose was bleeding. Thick drops of blood splattered his chest, a scarlet so bright it resembled paint. Still shuffling towards her, he didn't seem to be aware of it. Peri heard a gasp – her own voice unfamiliar to her ears – as she caught sight of a glint of steel.

The Toy

Istanbul, 1980s

They came late on a Friday night. Like owls, they waited for the evening to throw a black mantle over the city before seeking their prey. Peri's mother, who had gone to bed past midnight, after cooking one of her specialities – slow-roasted lamb with mint leaves – was the last to hear the pounding on their front door. By the time Selma was up and awake the police were already inside the house, ransacking the room her sons shared. After the raid, as though incapable of forgiving herself, Selma would never again have a full night's sleep – she would become a nocturnal creature herself.

Although the police were examining every last item, it was clear from their behaviour that they were here for the older son – Umut. They made him stand alone in a corner, and forbade him to exchange even a glance with his family. Seeing him in this state, seven-year-old Peri felt a sadness so pure that it bordered on despair. This she had never voiced aloud, but Umut was her favourite brother. Large, hazel eyes that crinkled around the corners with every smile, a wide forehead that made him look wiser than his years. Like her, he had a tendency to blush easily. Unlike her, he was full of good spirits, as befitted his name – hope. Despite the age gap between them, Umut had always been close to Peri, playing along with her silly games for no reason but love; pretending to be a kidnapped prince aboard a pirate ship or a scheming wizard atop the Mountain Kaf – whatever the story of the day called for.

At university – chemical engineering – Umut had become somewhat withdrawn. He grew a luxuriant, walrus-like moustache, and put up on his walls pictures of people Peri had never seen before: a grandfather with a hoary beard; a man with round wire spectacles and an open face; another with wild hair and a dark beret. There was also a woman with pinned-up hair and a white hat. When Peri had asked who they were, her brother had explained, 'That is Marx, the other, Gramsci. The one with the beret is comrade Che.'

'Oh,' Peri had said, clueless as to what he was talking about but affected by the ardour in his voice. 'How about her?'

'Rosa.'

'I wish my name were Rosa.'

Umut had smiled. 'Your name is more beautiful, believe me, but, if you wish, I'll call you Rosa-Peri. Maybe you'll be a revolutionary.'

'What's a revolutionary?'

Umut had paused, searching for an appropriate answer. 'Someone who wants every child to have toys and no child to have too many.'

'O-kay . . .' Peri had said guardedly – she had liked half of what she had heard, disliked the other half. 'How many is too many?'

Laughing, Umut had ruffled her hair, her question lingering in the space between them, unanswered.

Now it was the same posters that the police were ripping off the walls. When there was nothing left to shred, they checked the books, all of which belonged to Umut, as Hakan was not much of a reader. *The Communist Manifesto* by Karl Marx, *The Condition of the Working Class in England* by Friedrich Engels, *The Permanent Revolution* by Leon Trotsky, *Of Mice and Men* by John Steinbeck, *Utopia* by Thomas More, *Homage to Catalonia* by George Orwell . . . Flicking through the pages with a look of irritated frustration, they seemed to be hunting for personal letters and notes. Though they uncovered none, they still confiscated the books.

'Why are you reading this shit?' The police chief grabbed a book – *The Kiss of the Spider Woman* – and shook it in Umut's direction. 'You are a Muslim Turk. Your father is a Muslim Turk, your mother is a Muslim Turk. Seven generations, the same. What is it to you, huh, all this foreign crap?'

Umut stared at his bare feet – his toes, round and clean, pressed against one another as though for safety.

'If they have a problem, damn Westerners, it's their problem,' the man said. 'In our country everyone is happy. We don't have classes over here. We don't even know what the word means. Did you ever hear someone ask, "Hey, what's your class?" Of course not! We are all Muslim and we are all Turks. Full stop. Same religion, same nationality, same everything. Which part of that don't you get?'

The inspector moved close to Umut, leaning forward as if to sniff him. 'This country had three military takeovers to put an end to such bullshit. Now it's cropping up again! You think we'll allow it? Your books are full of lies. They're written in venom! Maybe you've been poisoned, have you?'

Umut said nothing.

'I'm asking you a question, imbecile,' the man yelled, his nostrils flaring. 'Have you been poisoned, I said!'

'No,' Umut replied, his voice barely a whisper.

'Hmm, I think you have,' said the man, nodding in agreement with himself. 'You certainly look like you have.'

The mattresses, the wardrobe, the drawers, even inside the wood-burning stove . . . No nook, no cranny went uninspected. Whatever they were looking for they seemed unable to find, which made them angrier.

'They're hiding it. Search the rest of the house,' ordered the police chief. He was smoking one cigarette after another, flicking the ashes on the floor.

'Excuse me . . . hiding what exactly?' Mensur ventured – his thinning hair tousled, his striped pyjamas rumpled, slippers on his feet – from the opposite corner of the room where the rest of the family had been made to wait.

'I'll shove it up your arse when we find it,' the police chief replied. 'As if you don't know.'

Wincing at the harshness of the words, Peri held her father's hand. But her eyes were fixed on her brother. She worried for Umut, whose face had turned as pale as a waning moon.

The police riffled through the other bedrooms, the bathroom, the toilet, the pantry where they kept the okras they had dried and the cucumbers they had pickled. From inside the kitchen came the sounds of drawers being opened, boxes grubbed about in, cutlery tossed around.

Where once had been neatly ordered shelves with lace trim, now there was disarray. An hour passed, maybe more. Outside, the faintest strip of light broke through the leaden sky, like a baby tooth cutting through raw flesh.

'What about the girl?' asked the police chief. He flicked the cigarette butt on to the carpet and crushed it with the heel of his shoe. 'Did you check her toys?'

Selma, her gaze fixed on the carpet she had cleaned earlier in the day, interjected, 'There must be a misunderstanding, efendim.* Ours is a decent family. We are all God-fearing people.'

Ignoring the comment, the man turned to Peri. 'Where are your things, child? Show us.'

Peri's eyes widened. Why was everyone interested in her toys – not that she had too many – the revolutionaries, the police? 'I'm not telling you.'

Mensur, still holding Peri's hand, pulled his daughter back and murmured, 'Hush. Let them look, we have nothing to worry about.' Then, directing his words at no one in particular, he said, 'She keeps them in a trunk under her bed.'

A few minutes later, when the police chief re-emerged with his men behind him, it was the expression on his face more than the object he held between his fingertips that alarmed Peri.

'Well, well . . . what do we have here?'

Peri had never seen a gun before. In contrast to those on TV this one seemed so small and cute that for a moment she wondered if it were made of chocolate.

'Hidden inside a cradle. Under a dolly! How convenient!'

'I swear on the Holy Quran, we know nothing about this,' said Selma, her voice brittle.

'Of course you don't, woman, but your son does.'

'It's not mine,' Umut said, his cheeks flushed. 'They asked me to keep it for a few days. I was going to return it tomorrow.'

'Who are they?' asked the police chief. He sounded happy.

* *efendim*: 'sir'.

Umut took a ragged breath, sinking into silence.

Outside rose the incantation of the muezzin calling from a nearby mosque, '*There is no God but God. Prayer is better than sleep.*'

'All right, off we go,' ordered the police chief. 'Take him in.'

Mensur, whose face had frozen at the sight of the gun, said, 'Please, there must be an explanation. My son is a good boy. He'd never hurt anyone.'

The police chief, who had taken a few steps towards the door, turned back on his heels. 'Always the same crap. You don't keep an eye on your children; they mingle with godless communist bastards, they get themselves into all sorts of shit. When it's too late, you wail and beg. Wah-wah. Why do you make babies if you won't take care of them, you fucking morons? Can't control your dicks?'

With an abrupt move the police chief grabbed Mensur's pyjama bottoms and pulled them down to his knees, revealing crisp white, though slightly worn, underwear. A couple of policemen chuckled at the sight. Others feigned indifference.

Peri felt the energy in her father's hand ebb; his fingers grew light and bloodless, the hand of a cadaver waiting to be dissected. Her father's silence, her father's shame, her father whom she had adored, revered, loved and idolized since the day she had uttered her first word. By the time Mensur, trembling, had pulled up his pyjama bottoms, the police officers were through the door, taking Umut with them.

The family would not see Umut for seven weeks, during which he remained in solitary confinement. Charged with membership of an illegal communist organization, he had confessed to owning the gun – after he was stripped naked, blindfolded, strapped on to a metal bedframe and given electric shocks. When the electrodes were attached to his testicles and the voltage was doubled, he admitted to being the leader of a cell that was plotting a series of assassinations of state officials. The acrid smell of charred flesh, the coppery smell of blood, the tart smell of urine and the cinnamon smell of the chewing gum of his chief torturer – an officer named 'Hose' Hassan, so called because of his inventive torture techniques with a garden hose.

Each time Umut passed out he was revived with cold water and soaked with buckets of salt water to increase the conductivity. In the mornings, the same police officers would apply medicinal ointment to his injuries so that they could continue the abuse in the afternoon. As he rubbed the balm into Umut's wounds, Hose Hassan would complain about his low salary and lengthy working hours, and how his daughter had eloped with an older man who was a father to a child and a husband to another woman. The lovebirds had returned, six months later, stone broke and scared. He could have killed them there and then; instead, he had spared their lives. Like many professional torturers, he was kind to his relatives, respectful to his superiors and cruel to everyone else.

In between sessions, Umut was made to listen to the screams of other prisoners, just as they were made to listen to his own. Again and again, the national anthem would blare out over loudspeakers. Once, during an electric shock, they forgot to put a towel in his mouth, a simple oversight, and he bit through his tongue, almost severing it in two. For a long, long time eating was a wretched experience; he could taste food only when he swallowed it.

Torture, widely practised in prisons, detention centres and young offender institutions across the country in the aftermath of the 1980 coup d'état, was said to have slowed down by then, but it carried on just the same. Old habits died hard. Not that there were no changes. Falaka, the beating of the soles of feet, was, for the most part, replaced by suspension by the arms for hours – a cleaner method that left fewer marks. Burning with cigarettes and the extraction of nails or healthy teeth were also outdated. Shocks were quick, efficient and left almost no traces. So was forcing prisoners to eat their own excrement, drink each other's urine or spend hours in septic tanks. No visible signs of maltreatment. Nothing for nosy journalists or Western human rights activists to detect, should they appear without warning.

Eventually, Umut was sentenced to eight years and four months without parole.

After the verdict was announced, the Nalbantoğlus paid regular visits to the prison on the outskirts of Istanbul. They arrived in varying combinations, depending on the day – Mensur with his younger son, Selma with her daughter, Mensur with his daughter, but never Mensur and Selma together. With dozens of other people they would sit at a wide, plastic table, whose surface bore the marks of hundreds of anxious, painful encounters. They would keep their hands visible, as instructed, to make sure nothing was exchanged. In this state, they would try to mend the hole of silence with smiles that did not reach their eyes and words that snapped and slipped out of their grasp.

On one occasion, when Umut stood up to leave, Mensur noticed a stain of blood on the lower back of his son's prison uniform. A blot the size and shape of a willow leaf. It had a name, the torture method that had caused it – 'Bloody Coke'. Beaten and stripped, the inmates were forced to sit on a Coca-Cola bottle. It was said to be a 'cocktail' served to a select few: political prisoners, suspected gays and transsexuals rounded up from the streets.

Mensur stared at the stain, dazed. He let out a gulping cry, gasping for breath, despite a desperate effort to keep himself composed. Fortunately, Umut, already back in his ward, had not heard him. But Peri, whose turn it had been to accompany her father on that day, certainly had. She witnessed the entire scene, though for some reason it was only images – as if she were watching a silent film – that would stay with her. After that day, Mensur forbade Peri to visit prison. She should sit at home instead and write letters to her brother. She should tell him heart-warming, touching stories, small details of joy to give him faith in the human spirit. This Peri did for as long as she could. She composed letters with a delight she did not feel, about people she had barely met and incidents that had not quite happened in the way she described. Umut, as if he could see through the deceit, never responded.

He would often appear in her dreams, however, from which she would wake up in the middle of the night, screaming. Sometimes she would manage to go back to sleep. Other times, she would slip out of bed, climb into her wardrobe and close the door from inside, trying to imagine what a prison cell must feel like. As she listened to her heart beating in that dark, confined space, and fearful that the oxygen was slowly running out, she would pretend her brother was beside her, breathing, breathing.

The horror of having Umut behind walls, instead of uniting the Nalbantoğlus, distanced them from each other to the point of mutual enmity. Mensur blamed his wife. He was at work all day long, he argued; it was Selma who was supposed to have kept an eye on their son. Had she spent less time with fanatical preachers who promised her the scent of paradise and been more attentive to what went on under her nose, she might have prevented the calamity that had befallen them. Reticent, sullen, resentful, Selma, meanwhile, held her husband responsible. It was Mensur who had sowed seeds of godlessness into the mind of their son. All his soliloquies on materialism and freethinking had led to this disaster.

Over the years, Mensur and Selma's marriage had hardened into a hollow husk. Now the shell cracked wide open and they found themselves on separate sides of the rift. The air inside the house turned stifling, heavy, as if it had absorbed the sadness of its inhabitants. It seemed to young Peri that no sooner had the bees and the moths entered through the open windows, than they rushed in panic to fly out. Even those insatiable mosquitoes no longer sucked the Nalbantoğlus' blood, for fear of ingesting their unhappiness. In the cartoons and movies that Peri watched, ordinary mortals were bitten by spiders, stung by hornets, after which they would transform into superheroes and lead exciting lives. In their case it was the other way round. Fleas and bugs, after coming into contact with the Nalbantoğlus, metamorphosed into the ways of humans, crushed by the weight of feelings for which they had no use.

It was around those days that Peri began to reframe her relationship with Allah. She stopped praying before going to sleep, contrary to the way her mother taught her, but she also refused to remain indifferent towards the Almighty, contrary to her father's advice. Instead, all the anguish and hurt she dared not to voice within earshot of her parents, she turned into a cannonball of words and hurled headlong at the skies.

She began to quarrel with God.

Peri argued with Him about everything, asking questions to which she knew there were no easy answers, asking all the same, in a lowered voice, so that no one could hear. How irresponsible of Him to allow terrible things to happen to those who didn't deserve it. Could God see and hear through prison walls and across cell bars? If He could not, He was not all-powerful. If He could, and still did nothing to help those in need, He was not merciful. Either way, He was not what He claimed to be. He was an impostor.

The anger Peri couldn't direct at her mother and her master Üzümbaz Efendi, the frustration she couldn't hold against her father and his drinking habits, the sorrow she couldn't convey to her elder brother and the weariness she felt towards her other brother, she mixed them all into a gooey batter and poured it into her thoughts on God. There it baked, in the furnace of her mind, rising slowly, cracking in the middle, burning around the edges. While her friends seemed as uncomplicated and light as the kites they flew, playing in the streets, joking around at school and taking every day as it came, Nazperi Nalbantoğlu, an unusually intense and introverted child, was busily searching for God.

God, a simple word with an obscure meaning. God, close enough to know everything you did – or even considered doing – yet impossible to reach. But Peri was determined to find a way. For she had come to believe through some twisted logic of her own that if she were to bring together her mother's Creator and her father's Creator, she might be able to restore harmony between her parents. With some kind of agreement as to what God was or was not, there would be less tension in the Nalbantoğlu household, even across the world.

God was a maze without a map, a circle without a centre; the pieces of a jigsaw puzzle that never seemed to fit together. If only she could solve this mystery, she could bring meaning to senselessness, reason to madness, order to chaos, and perhaps, too, she could learn to be happy.

The Notebook

Istanbul, 1980s

'Come and sit with me, love,' Mensur said to his daughter one rare evening when he was alone at the dinner table.

Peri immediately did as told. She had missed him terribly. Although in the same house, he had been distant, absorbed in his own thoughts, a mere shell of the man he used to be ever since the day Umut was arrested.

'Let me tell you a story,' Mensur said. 'Once, there lived a reed-flute player in Istanbul; a Sufi but of the maverick kind. Whenever he saw a bottle of raqi or wine, he'd scold those around him. "Don't you know a drop of this liquor is a sin?" Then he'd open the bottle, dip his finger inside, wait a few seconds, and take his finger out, dripping. "I removed that sinful drop," he'd say. "Now we can drink in peace."'

Mensur chuckled at his own words – a low, sad laugh.

Peri studied her father, sensing in his question a lonely rebellion, but against what or whom? Tentatively, she asked, 'Baba, may I try it?'

'What? You want to drink raqi?'

Peri nodded. She had never given it a moment's thought before, but, now that she said she wanted it, she really did. It was a way of bonding with her father.

Mensur shook his head. 'You are only seven. No way!'

'Eight,' Peri corrected him. 'I'll be eight this month.'

'Well, I've always said better to have your first taste of alcohol at home with your parents than secretly outside. You shouldn't really drink before you're eighteen,' Mensur mused. 'By that time, who knows if it'll be allowed, thanks to those religious fanatics. Maybe they'll put a bottle or two on display somewhere. The Exhibition of Degenerate

Objects! Just like the Nazis and modern art, eh? Yes, maybe you should take a sip before it's too late.'

Thus saying, Mensur filled a glass with water and added a generous splash of raqi. While Peri watched the alcohol disperse in the water, her father watched her with a tender expression.

'See these drops? That's me and my mates. We dissolve in a sea of ignorance.' Mensur raised his glass, and said, '*Sherefe!*'*

Thrilled to be treated like an adult, Peri smiled. '*Sherefe!*'

'If your mother sees us, she'll skin me alive.'

In haste, Peri took a mouthful. Her face instantly twisted in disgust. It was dreadful. It was worse than anything she had ever tried. The bite of anise, sharper even than its smell, burned her tongue, tickled her nose, brought tears to her eyes. How could her father drink this awful stuff every evening with such relish?

'Promise me,' Mensur said, paying no heed to his daughter's reaction. 'Never buy into old wives' tales, if you know what I mean.'

'Yes, yes,' Peri said, after she had knocked back a glass of water and gulped a slice of bread to get rid of the taste in her mouth. 'Like when they say, don't jump over a child, he'll stop growing. If you crack your knuckles, you'll break an angel's wings. Whistle in the dark, you'll invite Sheitan. That kind of thing.'

'That's right, all that nonsense. Listen, there's a rule I've come to respect and I advise you to do the same. Never believe anything you haven't seen with your eyes, heard with your ears, touched with your hands and grasped with your mind. Promise?'

Eager to please her father, Peri chirped, 'I promise, Baba.'

Pleased, Mensur beat his index finger in the air to accentuate his words. 'Education will save us! It's the only way forward. You must go to the best university in the world.' He paused as he considered which university that might be. 'You are the only one among my children who can do this. Work hard. Save yourself from ignorance, bigger promise?'

'Bigger promise.'

* *Sherefe*: 'To your honour'.

'There is one problem, though,' Mensur said. 'Men don't want women to be too clever or too educated. I wouldn't want you to die a spinster.'

'It's okay, I'm never going to get married. I'll stay with you.'

Mensur burst into laughter. 'Trust me, you don't want to do that. Just don't give your heart to anyone who doesn't care about science . . . knowledge. Biggest promise?'

'Biggest promise.' Peri slid down in her chair as a new thought entered her mind. 'What about God? We can't see Him, can't hear Him, can't touch Him . . . but should we still believe in Him?'

Mensur looked rueful. 'I'll let you in on a secret. When it comes to the Almighty, grown-ups are no less confused than kids.'

'But is God real?' Peri insisted.

'He'd better be. When I meet Him in the next world, before He has a go at me, I'll ask Him where He's been all this time. He's left us to our own devices for too long!' Mensur popped a slice of cheese into his mouth and chewed vigorously.

'Baba . . . Why didn't Allah help Umut? Why did He let all this happen?'

'I don't know, my soul,' Mensur said, his Adam's apple bobbing up and down.

They fell quiet. Peri curled her toes and pressed her slippered feet on the carpet, sensing it would be wiser to change the subject. The mention of her elder brother had darkened the already dim mood, like a cloud that drifts across the pale moon. 'What about heaven and hell?' The trials and tribulations of hell had been a constant refrain throughout her education. The idea that her father might find himself in the abode of the damned with its boiling cauldrons, its punishing flames and its dark angels called zabanis terrified her.

'Well, I'm not really heaven material, no? There are two possibilities: if God has no sense of humour, I'm doomed. Express train to hell. If He has one, there's hope, I might join you in paradise. They say they have rivers flowing with the best wine!'

A wave of alarm swept over Peri. 'But what if Allah is as stern as Mother always says He is?' she whispered.

'Don't fret, we'll have a plan B,' said Mensur. 'Make sure you put a pickaxe in my grave. I'll dig a tunnel out of wherever I end up!'

Peri's eyes widened. 'Hell is so deep, if you throw a pebble it takes seventy years for it to reach the bottom. Mother told me.'

'I'm sure she did.' A silent sigh. 'Here's the good thing: a year on earth is only a minute in the afterworld. One way or another, I'll come and find you.' His face brightened. 'Oh, I almost forgot. I've got something for you!'

From his leather bag Mensur produced a wrapped package – a silvery box tied up with a golden bow.

'For me?' Peri studied the package.

'Aren't you going to open it?'

There was a notebook inside. A beautiful, hand-stitched turquoise notebook with sequins and a mirrored mosaic on the cover.

'I know you're curious about God,' Mensur said pensively. 'I can't answer all your questions. No one can, frankly, including your mum and that cuckoo preacher of hers.' He downed the rest of his raqi in a single swallow. 'I have no sympathy for religion, or for the religious, but you know why I'm still fond of God?'

Peri shook her head.

'Because He is lonely, Pericim, like me . . . like you,' Mensur replied. 'All alone up there somewhere, no one to talk to – okay, maybe a few angels, but just how much fun can you have with the cherubim? Billions pray to God, "Oh give me victory, give me money, give me a Ferrari, do-this-do-that . . ." Same words over and over, but hardly anyone goes to the trouble to get to know Him.'

Mensur topped up his glass, a flash of sadness in his eyes. 'Think how people react when they see an accident on the road. Straight away they say, "Oh, heaven forbid." Can you believe it! Their first reaction is to think of themselves, not the victims. So many prayers are carbon copies of one another. Protect *me*, love *me*, support *me*, it's all about *me* . . . They call it piousness; I call it selfishness in disguise.'

At this, Peri cocked her head to one side, eager to console her father but without a clue as to how. The house sank into a quiet so delicate a puff of air would have tipped it over. Peri wondered if her mother, behind walls and from her bed, was listening to this conversation and, if so, what was going through her mind.

'From now on when you have a thought about God – or about yourself – write it down in your notebook.'

'Like a diary?'

'Yes, but it'll be a special one,' said Mensur, perking up. 'A lifelong diary!'

'But there won't be enough pages.'

'Exactly, the only way is to erase previous writings. Do you get it? Write and erase, my soul. I can't teach you not to have dark thoughts. Never really figured it out myself.' Mensur paused. 'But I was hoping you could at least rub them out.'

'So that I can have new dark thoughts?'

'Well, yes . . . new dark thoughts are better than old dark thoughts.'

That same night, as she sat up in bed, Peri opened her diary and wrote down her first entry: *I think God comes in many pieces and colours. I can build a peaceful God, all-loving. Or I can build an angry God, punishing. Or maybe I'll build nothing. God is a Lego set.*

Put up and pull down. Write and erase. Believe and doubt. Was that what her father really meant? In the end it hardly mattered, for that was what Peri, harking back to that day years later, decided she had heard. Her father's teaching would solidify what she already suspected about herself: that, while some people were passionate believers and others passionate non-believers, she would always remain stuck in between.

The Polaroid

Istanbul, 2016

The tramp lunged at Peri, swinging the knife so swiftly and recklessly it was a miracle she was able to dodge it. The blade missed the side of her abdomen by inches but sliced her right palm open. She let out a piercing wail, her voice cracking with pain. Blood streamed down her wrist, dripping on to her purple silk dress.

Her heart pounding in her ribcage, sweat pouring down her forehead, she pushed the man with all her might. Not expecting resistance he lost his balance, swaying momentarily – a respite Peri used to knock the knife from his hand. Enraged, he hit her in the chest with such force that for a horrible moment she couldn't breathe. She thought of her daughter, waiting in the car. She thought of her two young sons, watching their favourite TV show at home. An image of her husband swam into her head: at the dinner party surrounded by other guests, checking his watch every few minutes, sick with worry. The realization that she might never again see her loved ones brought tears to her eyes. How stupid it was to die like this. People faced death defending their countries and their flags and their honour; she, defending a fake Hermès bag with a misplaced grave accent. But maybe it was all equally meaningless.

The tramp punched her again, this time in the stomach. Felled, Peri coughed, nearly all her strength drained out of her.

She summoned up a last reserve of willpower. 'Stop it! I tell you, stop now!' Peri shouted as though reprimanding a misbehaving child. She was trembling; her body seemed to refuse to listen to the orders from her brain not to panic. 'Look,' she whispered hoarsely, 'if you hurt me, you'll be in serious trouble. They'll put you in jail. They'll break your . . .' She wanted to say 'your spirit', but instead she said 'your bones'. 'Trust me, they will do that.'

The tramp sucked upon his teeth. 'Whore,' he said. 'Who do you think you are?'

Nobody had ever called Peri a whore before and the word pierced her like a splinter of ice. She made another attempt, opting for reconciliation. 'Keep the bag, okay? You go your way, I go mine.'

'Whore!' he repeated, stuck inside the oath.

His expression darkened; his eyes became thin fissures in his face. He drew in his breath, aroused by his own thoughts. Beyond the alley, a car approached the opening, its headlights briefly carving a tunnel of escape. Peri wished to shout for help, but it was already too late. The car had disappeared. They were plunged into shadows again. She took a step back.

Catching Peri by the neck, the tramp shoved her down. Her hair came loose; the pin that had been holding the bun ricocheted off the ground. A tiny, metallic sound. When she fell backwards, her head hit the asphalt from the impact. Strangely, it didn't hurt. From down here the sky seemed impossibly far and resembled a sheet of bronze, unmoving, solid, cold. She tried to get up, her hand leaving bloody prints. In a flash, he was on top of her, struggling to tear off her dress. A sour smell emanated from his mouth – of hunger, cigarettes, chemicals. It was the stench of decay. Peri retched. The flesh trying to penetrate her flesh was that of a corpse.

It happened all the time in this city that encompassed seven hills, two continents, three seas and fifteen million mouths. It happened behind closed doors and in open courtyards; in cheap motel rooms and five-star luxury suites; in the midst of the night or plain daylight. The brothels of this city could tell many a story had they only found ears willing to listen. Call girls and rent boys and aged prostitutes beaten, abused and threatened by clients looking for the smallest excuse to lose their temper. Transsexuals who never went to the police for they knew they could be assaulted a second time. Children scared of particular family members and new brides of their fathers- or brothers-in-law; nurses and teachers and secretaries harassed by infatuated lovers just because they had refused to date them in the past; housewives who would never speak a word, for there were no words in this culture to describe marital rape. It happened all the time. Canopied under a mantle of secrecy and silence that shamed the victims and shielded the assailants, Istanbul was no stranger to sexual abuse. In this city where everyone feared outsiders, most assaults came from those who were too familiar, too close.

In the ensuing minutes in the quiet of that alley, as though waking from a dream only to find herself ensnared in someone else's nightmare, Peri's perception of the events splintered into disparate layers. She fought back. She was strong. He was too, unexpectedly so from his gaunt frame. He headbutted her, knocking her unconscious for a few seconds. She could have given up, so sharp was the pain, so irresistible the urge to let despair take over.

That was when she saw a silhouette out of the corner of her eye. Soft and silken, too angelic to be human. She recognized it – *him*. The baby in the mist. Rosy cheeks, dimpled arms, sturdy, plump legs; wispy, golden hair that had not yet turned dark. A plum-coloured stain covered one cheek. A cute little infant, except he wasn't. A jinni. A spirit. A hallucination. A figment of her wired, fearful imagination – although this was not their first encounter.

Unaware of the apparition behind him, the tramp swore under his breath as he grappled with his trousers. Impatiently, he tugged at the rope around his waist that served as a belt. He must have knotted it too tightly; he was unable to untangle it with one hand while holding Peri with the other.

The baby in the mist gurgled with delight. Through his innocent eyes Peri saw the folly she had been sucked into, the laughable misery. She chuckled. Loud and bold. Her reaction puzzled the tramp, who paused for a fleeting second.

'Let me help you with that,' Peri said, nodding towards the cord.

His eyes sparkled – half disorientated, half distrustful. A flicker of condescension crossed his face. He had managed to scare her and he knew, from past experiences, fear was all it took to bring someone, anyone, from their lofty position down to their knees. He pulled away – merely an inch or two.

With all her might, Peri launched herself at the man. Caught by surprise, he tumbled rearwards and fell on his back. Lithe and agile, she jumped and kicked him in the crotch. He keened like a wounded animal. Peri felt nothing – no pity, no rage. One always learned from others. Some people taught beauty, others cruelty. She couldn't tell whether it was because the intoxicant he sniffed earlier was working its way through his body, weakening him, or because she was fortified by some wild and unknown energy, but she felt powerful. Unhinged. Dangerous.

She rammed her foot into his face, all her strength focused on that single action. A sickening sound rang out – the crack of a nose being broken. The sight of his blood, this time in abundance, instead of terrifying her goaded her to hit him harder. Before she knew it, she was kicking and punching him everywhere.

The tramp clutched his stomach, his coat rolled up, revealing an emaciated torso underneath. Listless and light, he endured the beating as if he were tired of the chasing, the stealing, the struggle and the pettiness of it all.

'You son of a bitch,' Peri said under her breath. In all these years she had never cursed aloud, not since Oxford, and it felt – like the last time – surprisingly easy, sweet.

The baby in the mist glided past. As evanescent as a whisper; a figurine made of the finest silks and gauzes. He was not smiling any more; his features, carved from honey-coloured wax, were unmoving. Nor did he seem to judge what was happening. He was beyond such things, from outside this realm. Swiftly, and once again having helped Peri, he vanished. The vapour dissolved into the evening's gathering darkness without a trace.

All at once, Peri stopped hitting the tramp. A rising breeze stirred her hair, a shrieking seagull – perhaps a distant descendant of another seagull that had in the aeons of time swallowed a poet's tongue – circled above, angry at something or someone in this city of crowds and concrete.

The man was panting, every breath like a sob. He had blood all over his face and his upper lip had split.

I'm sorry, Peri thought and almost said it aloud, the words catching in her throat. In that instant, as though conditioned, she recalled a voice, loving and reprimanding at the same time. *Are you still apologizing to everyone, my dear?*

If Professor Azur had been transported to Istanbul, that's what he would have said to her now, most likely. How bizarre it was that the past came flooding in at the very moment disorder breached the banks of the present. Random memories, repressed anxieties, untold secrets, and guilt, plenty of guilt. All her senses dimmed, the world became a blurry backdrop. Engulfed by a feeling of placidity, almost a kind of numbness, that separated her from everything else, including the pain from a place in her body she couldn't locate, Peri remembered things from her life that she thought she had forever left behind.

The tramp started to weep. Gone was the Emperor of the streets, the beggar, the addict, the thief, the rapist . . . all his roles had been stripped away, leaving behind a boy crying in the dark for a comforting touch that would never come. Now that the effect of the glue had fully worn off, physical pain had replaced hallucinations.

Peri approached him, the blood pulsating in her ears, horrified at what she had done. She would have offered him help had her daughter not arrived just then.

'Mum, what happened?'

Fast as an arrow, Peri turned back. She composed herself, trying her hardest to gather her thoughts. 'Sweetheart . . . why didn't you wait in the car?'

'How much longer could I wait?' Deniz said, but whatever reprimand she had in mind instantly vanished. 'Oh my God, you are bleeding. What on earth happened? Are you okay?'

'I'm fine,' Peri said. 'We had a bit of a scuffle.'

The tramp, now deadly quiet, staggered to his feet and stumbled over to a corner, showing no more interest in them. Mother and daughter picked up the handbag and as many of its scattered contents as they could find.

'Why can't I have a normal mother like everyone else?' Deniz muttered to herself, as she scooped up credit cards off the ground.

It was a question Peri could not answer, and therefore did not try.

'Let's go,' Deniz said.

'Just a second.' Peri's eyes cast around for the Polaroid, but it seemed to have disappeared.

'Come on!' Deniz yelled. 'What's wrong with you!'

Leaving the alley, they hurried back to their car. The Monte Carlo Blue Range Rover was waiting for them, miraculously unstolen.

The rest of the ride continued in silence: the daughter picking at her fingernails, the mother with her eyes fixed on the road. Only later would it occur to Peri that they had not retrieved her mobile phone. Maybe the tramp still had it in his pocket; maybe it had fallen out during their struggle, and somewhere in that alley it was flashing and ringing – yet another cry that went unheard in Istanbul.

The Garden

Istanbul, 1980s

The first time Peri saw the 'baby in the mist' she was eight years old. The encounter would change her forever, intertwine itself through her life like a vine through a young tree. It would also be the beginning of a series of experiences that, though familiar because of their similarity, would become no less frightening over the years.

Unlike most houses in the vicinity, the Nalbantoğlus' was surrounded by a lush garden on four sides. It was at the back that they spent most of their time outside. That was where they hung red peppers and aubergines and okra on strings to dry in the sun, prepared jar upon jar of spicy tomato sauce, and steamed sheep's heads in cauldrons on Eid al-Adha. Peri would try hard not to look at the sheep's eyes, open and unblinking. Her throat would tighten at the thought that whoever ate those eyes would also ingest the horror they had witnessed seconds before being slaughtered. The idea was doubly disturbing, since she knew it would be her father who would consume the delicacy that evening at his raqi table.

It was also here that they piled up raw wool; then aired, washed and beat it with sticks before stuffing it into mattresses. Occasionally, a bit of fluff would break free from the rest and gently fall on to someone's shoulder like a feather from a shot pigeon.

When Peri had confessed to her father that the raw wool reminded her of dying birds and that the eyes of sheep stared at her accusingly, Mensur had smiled and given her a peck on the cheek. 'Don't be so sensitive, canimin içi,* don't take life too seriously' – as if he himself were any different.

* *canimin içi*: 'core of my soul'.

A wooden, unpainted fence – with posts so wide apart that it resembled a mouth with missing teeth – separated their property from the outside world. Of all the activities in the garden, Peri's favourite, after the games she played with other children, was the day of communal carpet washing. How she longed for that time to arrive, which would happen every few months. The weather had to be clement – neither too dry nor too damp, the carpets sufficiently dirty, and everyone in the right mood.

One such day, all the carpets and rugs had been rolled up and dragged outside, where they were laid out on the grass, side by side. Hand-knotted, flatwoven or factory produced, there were about twelve of them to wash. Thrust into a universe of symmetrical knots, central medallions and hidden symbols, the children of Mute Poet Street leaped back and forth with squeals of laughter, sailing across oceans and into ports on their flying carpets.

Meanwhile, in a separate corner, an uncovered cast-iron cauldron boiled on an open fire. Bowls of water were drawn from it and poured on to the rugs to soften the fabric. Next each would be soaped, brushed, scrubbed and rinsed. Again and again. Not all the women took part in the drudgery. Peri's mother, for one, stood to one side, finding the job too tedious and too messy for her taste. Others, the brave and the diligent, had already turned up their shalwars and skirts, their faces flushed with the importance of their mission, their hair no longer contained by their headscarves, their bare feet flattening the deep shag-pile of the rugs as though trampling through a field of young barley.

Over the ensuing hours the children built castles from mud; trapped flies using matchboxes smeared with jam; ate apricots (and crushed the kernels) and watermelon (and dried the seeds); made wreaths from pine needles; and chased a tawny cat that was either overweight or heavily pregnant. Then they ran out of things to do but so far only a third of the carpets had been thoroughly cleaned. One by one Peri's friends went home, to return later in the day. This being her garden, her house, she stayed.

A beautiful day it was, bright and warm. Spilling, splashing – the wind was saturated with the sounds of water. The women gossiped, chuckled and sang. Someone made lewd jokes, which Peri could not work out but guessed must have been naughty by the scowl on her mother's face.

In the afternoon the carpet-cleaners took a break to have lunch. They carried out the food that had been prepared beforehand – stuffed cabbage leaves, börek with feta, pickled cucumbers, cracked bulgur salad, grilled meatballs, apple cookie rolls . . . A large round tray was brought out on which each dish was placed amidst stacks of flat bread and glasses of ayran,* white and foamy like dollops of cloud from the hands of a generous god.

Feeling ravenous, Peri snatched a börek from the plate. She had barely bitten into it when a desperate shriek pierced the air. Her mother, in her haste and distraction, had bumped into the boiling cauldron, remarkably managing not to knock it over on to herself. But her left arm was burned from elbow to fingertips. Dropping whatever they were doing, the other women rushed to Selma's help.

'Pour cold water on her arm,' said someone.

'Toothpaste! Smear it all over the burn.'

'Vinegar, that's how we healed my aunt's burns. Hers were worse,' said someone else.

With everyone scampering inside to attend to Selma in the best way they knew how, Peri was left alone in the garden. A strip of sunlight fell across her face; an insect hummed its drowsy way nearby. Under a fig tree on the opposite side of the road she spotted the tawny cat, its jade eyes narrowed to mere slits. It occurred to her to feed the animal. Grabbing a meatball, she climbed over the fence. In a flash, she was outside.

'What's your name, little girl?'

Peri turned to find a young man in a red-and-white-check shirt and blue denims that appeared never to have been washed. The beret he wore seemed about to slide off his head. She didn't respond at first, for she knew better than to talk to strangers. But she didn't walk away either. The beret intrigued her, reminding her of the poster in Umut's room. Maybe this stranger was a revolutionary. Maybe he had heard about

* *ayran*: 'cold yoghurt drink'.

her brother – and his fate. She decided if she didn't tell him the truth, it wouldn't quite be giving him information. So she said, 'I'm Rosa.'

'Oh, I never met a Rosa before,' he said, his face tilted towards the sun. 'And a very pretty one too. You'll break hearts when you grow up.'

Peri said nothing, though something stirred inside her, a tiny swell of sensuality, a force not yet awake, half thrilled, half repelled by the compliment.

'You like cats, I can see,' he said.

His voice was small, brittle. Later on, though not at that moment, Peri would liken it to the bean she kept inside moist cotton wool by the window ledge. Just like that bean, the stranger's voice was hiding, changing, germinating.

'I saw a furball around the corner,' he said. 'She has given birth to five kittens, apparently. They are so cute and teeny, like mice. They have pink eyes.'

Feigning indifference, Peri offered the cat the last piece of meatball.

The man came a step closer: he smelled of tobacco, of sweat, of damp soil. He crouched down and smiled at her. They were now at the same eye level. 'It's a pity their mother will drown them.'

Peri held her breath. Down in the field, where stray dogs roamed and a few goats grazed, there was a reservoir no one used because whenever it rained more than three inches it became contaminated with sewage. She glanced in that direction, half expecting to see feline bodies floating on the water.

'Cats do that,' the man said with a sigh.

Peri couldn't help asking, 'But why?'

'They don't like pink eyes,' he replied. His own were light brown with hollowed skin underneath, and closely set on his angular face. 'They fear they have given birth to strange creatures, like fox cubs. So they kill them.'

Peri wondered if fox cubs had pink eyes and, if so, what their mothers thought about that. In her family she was the only one with green eyes and felt lucky that no one had seen this as a problem, so far.

The man, observing her bewilderment, stroked the cat's head before he stood up. 'I better go and check on the kittens. They need looking after. Would you like to join me?'

'Who? Me?' she said – only because she didn't know what else to say.

He pursed his lips, taking his time to reply, as though it were she who had suggested coming with him. 'You can, if you want. But they are very small. Do you promise to be careful not to hurt them?'

'Promise,' she said airily.

A window opened somewhere; a woman yelled into the wind, threatening her son if he did not come home for lunch this very minute she would break both his legs. The man, suddenly nervous, looked left and right. His face narrowed as he said, 'We mustn't be seen together. I'll walk ahead, you keep behind me.'

'The kittens. Where are they?'

'They're not far, but it's better if we drive. My car is just around the corner.' He gestured vaguely before quickening his footsteps.

Peri started to follow the man, who had a distinct limp. Though a part of her had qualms about what she was doing, this was the first decision she had made without her parents, and the closest she had come to a sense of freedom.

Soon, with an evasive glance over his shoulder, he reached his car and got into the driver's seat, waiting for her.

Peri stopped, alerted by something less intuitive than physical. She shuddered as though an icy wind had touched her bare skin. But what startled her the most was the mist that had descended from nowhere. A curtain of fog – layers upon layers of grey, like rolls of cloth unfurled in a draper's store. The fog confused her, momentarily, as to where she was going and why. She could detect the milky silhouette of a tree nearby, but the world beyond that was not visible any more – including the man, only a few feet away.

Inside the cloud of grey, Peri beheld the strangest sight: a baby – his face round, open, trusting. A purple stain extended from one cheek down to his jaw. He had some liquid dribbling from the corner of his mouth, as if he had just thrown up a little.

'Peri, where are you?' Her mother's voice, laden with panic, wafted from the sour-cherry-coloured house.

She couldn't answer. Her heart pulsed in the hollow of her throat as she blinked in bewilderment at the baby in the mist. *It must be a spirit, a jinni,* she thought. She had heard of them – creatures made of smokeless fire. They were here long before Adam and Eve were sent tumbling down from the Garden of Eden; so, historically speaking, the earth belonged to them. Humans were the latecomers, the invaders. The jinn lived in remote areas – snowy mountains, dark caves, arid waste lands – but they often found their way into the city to inhabit stinking toilets, grimy cellars, fusty vaults. Since they wandered freely, one had to tread with care; stepping on one of them by mistake was sure to end badly, probably in paralysis. Perhaps that was what had happened to her too. She could barely move.

'Peri! Answer me!' Selma shouted.

The baby in the mist recoiled as if he had recognized the voice. The greyness began to dissolve. So did the baby himself, bit by bit, like a morning haze under rays of the rising sun.

'Here, Mother!' Peri turned and ran back as fast as she could towards their garden.

She would ask around, afterwards, if anyone in the neighbourhood knew about any kittens with pink eyes. No one did.

Later, much later in life, Peri understood she had missed by a hair's breadth becoming another item in a newspaper. Nameless, save for her printed initials, N. N.; her photo with a black band over her eyes. She could have been there, next to the reports about a deadly attack on a mafia leader in Istanbul; the clash between the Turkish Army and the Kurdish separatists in a town along the south-east border and the court decision to ban Henry Miller's *Tropic of Capricorn*. The whole nation would read the details of her abduction, knocking on wood, shaking their heads, clucking their tongues, thanking God that it was someone else's child and not theirs.

She called her saviour 'the baby in the mist' and left it at that, neither able nor willing to grasp from where it had sprung. But the vision kept returning, at unexpected intervals throughout her life. It appeared not only when she was in danger but during ordinary moments as well. Indoors or outdoors, morning or night, the fog could descend at any time and anywhere, hedging her in on every side as if it wanted her to acknowledge, once and for all, how lonely she really was.

Years later, it was this secret she would carry in her suitcase when, at the age of nineteen, she travelled to Oxford University for the first time. You were not allowed to bring meat or dairy products into England from outside European countries, but no one said you couldn't bring along your childhood fears and traumas.

The Hodja

Istanbul, 1980s

A week later Peri mustered the courage to reveal her secret to her father.

'You are seeing things, did you say?' Mensur asked, with a newspaper crossword folded on his lap.

'Not things, Baba. Just one thing,' Peri said. 'An infant.'

'Where is this infant exactly?'

Peri blushed. 'In the air, sort of floating.'

For a moment, his expression gave nothing away. 'You are my clever daughter,' he said finally. 'Do you want to turn into your mother? If so, go ahead, fill your head with foolishness. I'd have expected better of you.'

Her heart sank. Determined never to disappoint him, she yielded. It wasn't that hard. After all, she had not touched the apparition, and, even though she had seen it, and later on she would also hear it, she could not trust her senses, given the oddness of the experience. By her father's rule of thumb, the baby in the mist did not exist. It was all inside her head, she concluded, but as to why it was inside her head, she could think of no plausible explanation.

'The civilized world, Pericim, was not built on unfounded beliefs. It was built on science, reason and technology. You and I belong in that world.'

'I know, Baba.'

'Good. Drop this subject. And do not, ever, mention it to your mother.'

It was inevitable, though. If her father's physics had its universal rules, so did human psychology. The moment one was told not to enter the fortieth door or not to peek into a chest, that door was bound to be unlatched, that chest had to be prised open. To be fair, for as long as she could, Peri kept her promise, but the next time the baby in the mist appeared, she went running to her mother for help.

'Why didn't you tell me before?' Selma said, her forehead creased with concern.

Peri swallowed hard. 'I told Dad.'

'Your father? What does he know?' Selma said. 'Listen, this sounds like the doing of a jinni. Some are well behaved, others pure evil. The Quran warns us against the danger. They'd do anything to possess a human being – especially a girl. Women are especially vulnerable to their attacks; we must be careful.'

Selma leaned forward and moved a lock of her daughter's hair behind her ear. The gesture, simple and affectionate, set off a rush of tenderness inside Peri. She asked, 'What should I do?'

'Two things. First of all, always tell me the truth. Allah sees through every lie. And parents are the eyes of Allah on earth. Secondly, we must find an exorcist.'

The next morning the two of them went to see a hodja famous for his powers to cleanse one of demonic possession. A portly man with a tiny, dark moustache and a wheezy voice. In his hand he held an onyx rosary, which he thumbed slowly. His wide head was out of proportion to the rest of his body – as if it had been planted in haste, an afterthought; and his shirt had been buttoned all the way up, so tightly that it had swallowed his neck.

Gazing at Peri searchingly, he asked questions about her eating, playing, studying, sleeping and toilet habits. Under his scrutiny, an uneasiness came over the child, but she stayed put in her chair, doing her best to reply in earnest. He asked her if she had recently killed a spider or a caterpillar or a lizard or a cockroach or a grasshopper or a ladybird or a wasp or an ant. This last one made Peri hesitate; who knew, maybe she had stepped on an ant – or, worse yet, an anthill. The hodja confirmed that the jinn, elusive as they were, could take the form of insects, and if one crushed them without uttering the name of Allah, one would be possessed there and then.

Thus saying, the hodja turned to Selma. 'Had the child learned not to go out without reciting the Fatiha,* this wouldn't have happened. I've got five kids, none of them were ever bothered by jinn. Why? Simple, because they know how to protect themselves. Did you not teach her anything, sister?'

Selma's gaze darted from the man to her daughter and back. 'I try, but she doesn't listen. Her father is a bad influence.'

'It's nothing to do with him . . .' protested Peri. Then, quietly, 'What happens now?'

In lieu of an answer, the exorcist held the child by the shoulders, leaned in close to her face for what felt like eternity and hissed, 'Whatever your name, I'll find it out. Then you'll be my slave. I know you are one of the unholy. You spiteful, wicked thing. Abandon this innocent girl. I warn you!'

Peri squeezed her eyes shut. The man's fingers loosened around her shoulders. He sprinkled rosewater on her head, reciting prayers to ward off the evil. He asked her to swallow tiny papers with Arabic letters on them, the ink dyeing her tongue a blue so bright that it would last for days. Nothing happened. That night, upon the hodja's instructions and her mother's insistence, Peri spent an hour alone in the garden, flinching at every little sound, a silhouette of fear in the faint light of a street lamp. The next morning they sent her to chase a pack of stray dogs. The dogs chased her instead.

'Oh, jinni, I give you one last chance,' said the exorcist when they went to see him a second time. In his hand he held a long stick made from a dead willow branch. 'Either you come out willingly, or I'll give you a severe beating.'

Before Peri could grasp what she had heard, the man hit her on her back. The child screamed.

Selma paled. 'Is this necessary, efendim?'

'This is the only cure. The jinni needs to be scared. The longer it stays in her body, the more powerful it gets.'

'Yes, but . . . I can't allow this,' said Selma, her lips drawn into a thin line. 'We must leave.'

* Opening chapter of the Quran.

'Your choice,' said the hodja flatly. 'Let me warn you, sister. This child is prone to darkness. Even if you get rid of this jinni now, she can be taken captive by another, easy as breathing. Keep an eye on her.'

Mother and daughter, more scared by the exorcist than by any conceivable jinni, exited the house in a hurry – though not before Selma made a hefty payment.

'Don't worry, I'm going to be fine,' said Peri, when they reached the bus stop. She held her mother's hand, feeling guilty. 'Mother, what did he mean when he said I was prone to darkness?'

Selma looked unsettled, not so much by her daughter's question as by her own inability to provide an answer. 'Some people just are, by birth. That explains, I guess, the things you did when you were little –' She stopped herself, her eyes tearing up.

Not knowing what her mother meant, Peri feared that she must have done something very, very wrong. 'I'll be good, I promise.'

Yet another promise she would do her utmost to keep from that day forth. Obediently, she would adhere to what was expected of her, tracing her steps back to where she had veered away from the routine, ever so careful not to cause surprises, no shocking incidents. She would be as unremarkable and unthreatening as she possibly could be.

Selma planted a kiss on her forehead. 'Canim,* let's hope this thing is over, but beware! It might return. And if it does, you must tell me. The jinn are vengeful.'

It did return, but, having learned her lesson the hard way, Peri mentioned it to no one. Her mother was too superstitious and her father too rational for either of them to be of any help to her in so surreal a matter. Anything remotely uncanny, even if only slightly out of the ordinary, Selma would attribute to a religious cause; and Mensur, to downright insanity. Peri, for her part, preferred to commit to neither.

The more Peri considered her options, the more she was convinced that she had to keep her visions to herself. Deeply unsettling though they were, she accepted them as a peculiarity of life, like an eye floater, something that didn't go away and only bothered her when she was

* *Canim*: 'My life.'

aware of it, leaving her no choice but to learn to live with it. Thus the baby in the mist – whether a jinni or something else altogether – was stowed away in the recesses of her mind, a riddle unresolved.

Years later, not long before she left for Oxford, she would write down in her God-diary: *Is there really no other way, no other space for things that fall under neither belief nor disbelief – neither pure religion nor pure reason? A third path for people such as me? For those of us who find dualities too rigid and don't wish to conform to them? Because there must be others who feel as I do. It is as if I'm searching for a new language. An elusive language spoken by no one but me . . .*

The Fish Tank

Istanbul, 2016

It was quarter to nine in the evening when mother and daughter reached the seaside konak. Wrought-iron balconies, white marble steps, mosaic fountains, high-tech security cameras, electric gates, barbed-wire fencing. The estate resembled less a house than an island, a palatial citadel that had locked itself out of the city, if not the other way round. Every security measure had been taken to ensure that no hawkers, no burglars, no criminals and no unwelcome lifestyles crossed its threshold.

Peri kept her injured right hand close to her chest, holding the steering wheel with her left. On the way they had stopped by a chemist's and had the pharmacist, a middle-aged man with a grizzled moustache, attend to the gash. When he inquired how this had come about, Peri had said briskly, 'Chopping vegetables. This is what happens when you cook in a hurry.'

He had laughed. The pharmacists of Istanbul were a wise breed. They would neither let a lie go undetected nor pursue uncomfortable truths. Prostitutes with injuries caused by customers, pimps or self-mutilation; women battered by their husbands; drivers thumped by other drivers – they could all walk into chemists' shops and blurt out their lies, safe in the knowledge that even if they were not believed, at least they would not be questioned.

Peri checked the bandage, grimacing as she saw the crimson stain that had seeped through the gauze. She would have preferred to take it off before entering the party to avoid difficult questions, but the pain, the blood and the risk of infection were enough to change her mind.

As soon as they stopped at the gate, a burly security guard in a dark suit and a cloud of aftershave appeared. While he parked the car, Peri and Deniz passed through the manicured garden with vine-covered trellises. A gentle wind ruffled the leaves of the plane trees.

'Darling, I shouldn't have chased that man. What was I thinking?' said Peri, breaking the silence. With her good hand she touched her daughter, ever so lightly, as though the girl were fragile, her anger made of glass. They used to be so close; in the past they'd had their own codes. It was hard to believe now that this was the same girl who used to shake with laughter at her silly jokes and hold her hand when a Disney character shed tears. That sweet child had disappeared, leaving this stranger in her place. The transformation – for she had no other word – had caught Peri unprepared, even though she had read scores of articles on how puberty came earlier and earlier – especially for girls. She had always been determined to have a far better relationship with her daughter than the one she'd had with her mother. In the end, wasn't that the only real aspiration to be fulfilled in life: to do a better job than our parents, so our children might be better parents than we were? But what we often discover instead is how we unwittingly repeat the same mistakes as the previous generation. Peri also knew that anger all too often masked fear. She said softly, 'I'm sorry if I scared you.'

'Mum, you did scare me,' said Deniz. 'You could have been killed!'

Her daughter was right. Back in that alley she could have lost her life to the tramp. But what Deniz did not know was that the opposite was just as true, if not more so – she could have killed the tramp.

'I'll never do such a thing again,' Peri said, as they reached the stairs to the house.

'Promise?'

'Promise, sweetheart. Just don't say anything to your father; it'll make him worry.'

Deniz paused – an instant of hesitation that disappeared as quickly as it had come. She shook her head. 'He has a right to know.'

Peri was about to say something in return but the huge oak door, carved with flowers and foliage, opened from inside. A maid in a black skirt and white chiffon blouse stood at the entrance, smiling. From behind her rose the sounds and smells of a dinner party in full swing.

'Welcome, come on in, please.'

The maid spoke with a striking accent – probably Moldavian or Georgian or Ukrainian, one of the many foreign women who worked in Istanbul households, while back home their children were raised by relatives and friends, and their spouses waited for monthly payments to arrive.

'Why did you bring me here?' Deniz hissed loudly.

'I told you, your friend's going to be here. Come on, let's enjoy the evening.'

No sooner had they taken a step inside than Peri saw her husband pushing through the guests towards them, his expression a mixture of apprehension and irritation. Slim-cut nut-brown jacket, crisp white shirt, blue-and-fawn tie, shoes polished to the lustre of glass – Adnan had taken care with his appearance. A self-made man, he had worked his way up from humble beginnings to accumulated wealth through property development. He often said he owed his success to no one but Allah the Almighty. Peri, much as she respected her husband's hard work and business acumen, was unclear why the Creator would have favoured him over others. Adnan was seventeen years older than Peri, but it seemed to her that the age difference became most apparent whenever he was upset and the lines in his forehead deepened – as they did now.

'Where have you been? I called you fifty times!'

'I'm sorry, darling, I lost my phone,' Peri said, in the most soothing voice she could muster. 'Long story, let's not talk about it now.'

'You know why we're late, Dad?' Deniz said, her eyes lit up at seeing her father. 'Because Mum was busy chasing thieves!'

'What?'

Deniz pushed a strand of hair out of her eyes. She had her father's nose, long and slightly bulbous, and his confidence. 'Ask her,' she said, before walking towards a girl her own age, who was looking bored among the older guests.

But there was no time to explain. The owner of the mansion, having interrupted his conversation with a well-known journalist, strode over to them. He was a broad-shouldered, stockily built man with a bald head and the ruddy complexion of a heavy drinker. Not a single wrinkle lined his face, every inch of which had absorbed the latest anti-ageing treatments. When he smiled his features remained stock-still, save for the merest twitch at the corners of his lips.

'You made it!' the businessman boomed. His blue eyes, glittering with mischief, sized her up. 'What happened to your hand? Did someone try to kidnap you? It's your fault. You shouldn't be so beautiful!'

Peri smiled, even though the joke made her blanch. She hoped neither he nor anyone else would comment on the state of her dress: torn at the hem, spattered with frappuccino. Mercifully, the stains of blood were disguised as uneven brownish marks. She said, 'We had a little accident on the way here.'

Adnan's brow furrowed with concern. 'An accident?'

'Nothing important, believe me,' Peri said, as she touched her husband's elbow – a signal not to ask further. She turned to the businessman, amiably. 'What a gorgeous house you have.'

'Thank you, my dear. Unfortunately, we have enough reason to suspect we've been struck with the evil eye. One calamity after another. First, our pipes burst. The ground floor was flooded to our ankles. Then lightning struck, a tree fell on to our roof, can you imagine? All in the course of these past few months.'

'You should have a nazar boncugu,'* Adnan suggested.

'Well, we have something even better. Tonight we've invited a psychic!'

'Oh, really?' Peri inquired, not because she was interested in the subject but because she knew she was expected to say something. She had a feeling that lately public interest in mediums and fortune-tellers had rocketed. Perhaps it was no coincidence that in a country where instability was the norm, there was such a craze for prophecies and predictions – mostly expressed by women, though pertinent to both sexes. Amidst chronic political ambiguity and lack of transparency, the crystal-gazers, whether fake or genuine, served a social function by shifting uncertainty into some semblance of certainty.

'Everyone says he's terrific,' the businessman said. 'This guy doesn't

* *nazar boncugu*: 'evil-eye bead'.

just talk to the jinn. He commands them. Whatever he orders them to do, they obey, apparently. He has jinn wives – a full harem!' He snorted on the last word, but, noticing Peri was not joining in, he fixed his eyes on her. 'What's wrong? You look like you've seen an apparition yourself.'

Peri instinctively recoiled. There were times when she had wondered whether people could read her face and know she had visions, things they couldn't see. Fortunately, the businessman had no wish to listen to anything other than his own voice. 'I know brokers who consult this guy before buying stocks. Crazy, isn't it? Psychics and stock markets.' He laughed. 'My wife's idea. Don't blame her. Poor thing, she lost it a bit after the crash.'

It had been all over the news. About six months ago, a dry-cargo vessel, 335 feet long and sailing under the flag of Sierra Leone, had run aground and straight into the waterfront residence. It had destroyed the seawall and the elaborate south-facing balcony, which dated back to the last century of the Ottoman Empire.

It was on this balcony that Kaiser Wilhelm II had had tea with a pasha known for the scale of his ambitions and his admiration for German culture and military prowess. That same pasha had then spread rumours that the Kaiser was a Muslim, he having had the opening lines of the Quran whispered into his ear at birth, even before he was placed on his mother's breast: his real name was Hajji Wilhelm, lifelong friend and adamant guardian of Islam – a convenient label when the day arrived for the Ottomans to enter the war on the side of Germany.

It was also on this historic balcony that a young Turkish heir, besotted with a White Russian dancer who had escaped to Istanbul after the Bolshevik Revolution – having failed to persuade his family to accept his beloved – had put a pistol to his head and shot himself. The bullet, after travelling through his brain and smashing his skull, had exited behind his left ear and pierced the wall behind him, where it would stay undiscovered for three decades.

In its stormy history the mansion had seen heroes rise and fall, empires soar and collapse, maps expand and shrink, dreams turn into fine dust. But never before had it been rammed by a ship. The vessel's prow had sliced through the wall, demolished a painting by Fahrelnissa Zeid and miraculously stopped just short of the Murano chandelier. Now, in memory of that day, a miniature toy ship dangled from the same chandelier, giving the hosts a chance to relate the story, again and again.

'Oh, there you are! We thought you'd never come,' a voice cried from behind them.

It was the businessman's wife. She had spotted Peri as she left the kitchen, after pelting the cook with orders. She wore an emerald green designer cocktail dress with a high collar and open back, cinched at the waist. On her finger a ring of a similar colour flashed bright, the stone as big as a swallow's egg. Her lips were tinted bright crimson and her hair was pulled up into a bun so tight it reminded Peri of the goatskin stretched on a darbuka.*

'The traffic . . .' said Peri, as she kissed her hostess on both cheeks.

That was the one excuse that won forgiveness no matter how late you were. Once the word was uttered it rendered any other explanation redundant. Peri scanned the faces of her hosts, seeing with relief that it had worked. They looked convinced, although her husband clearly was not – but she would have to deal with him later.

'Don't you worry, honey; we all know what it's like,' said the hostess as she eyed Peri's dress, taking in every rip and stain.

'I didn't have time to change,' said Peri. True, she felt naked under the scrutiny, but she also derived a secret satisfaction – at a party full of designer bags and overpriced dresses – from shocking everyone just a tiny bit.

'Relax, you are among friends,' said the hostess. 'Would you like to borrow one of my dresses?'

Peri entertained an image of how, given her record so far this evening, she would probably spill tomato sauce on the woman's dress. She shook her head. 'I'll be fine; thank you for offering.'

'Well, then, come and eat, you must be starving,' the woman said.

'What can I get you to drink? Red? White?' asked the businessman.

'So kind, but I must use the ladies' first,' said Peri.

* *darbuka*: 'Middle Eastern goblet drum'.

She followed a maid into the depths of the mansion, all the while feeling her husband's eyes burning a hole in her back.

Inside the bathroom, Peri locked the door, closed the toilet lid and sat down. Gulping in a lungful of air, she massaged one temple with her fingertips, overcome with exhaustion. She had neither the energy nor the will to go out and face all those people, and yet she knew in a little while she must. If only she could slip away through the toilet window.

Carefully, she unwrapped the bandage. The knife had sliced her palm from one end to the other; it wasn't too deep a cut, no stitches had been required. Even so, at the slightest movement, it hurt like hell and started to bleed again. Now, as the wound throbbed with each beat of her heart, she could not help trembling. The gravity of what had happened was finally dawning on her. Her mouth was dry as dust. She wrapped up her hand again.

When Peri stood up to wash her face, her eyes widened with surprise. Right across from her was a massive reef aquarium, on which the sink had been set. Inside the glass tank swam dozens of exotic fish, all of them shades of yellow and red, the colours of the football team the businessman supported. Everyone knew he was a huge fan, had a private box in the team's stadium and enjoyed being photographed with the football players on every occasion. Someday soon he intended to become the President of the club and had been manoeuvring actively behind the scenes with this goal in mind.

Peri watched the fish in their artificial universe, pristine and protected. On both sides of the sink were silver hamam bowls with repoussé motifs, in which were stacked perfectly rolled, perfectly starched hand towels. All around on the floor, candles burned with tall flickering flames. A blend of aromas caught her nose, sweet and syrupy. Underneath she detected a sharp synthetic smell of detergents – an ugly reminder of the tramp's glue.

A strong urge to do something unexpected and bold took hold of her. She wanted to smash the aquarium to pieces, shards of glass flying every which way while the fish were sent skidding across the marble floor. Off they would go, flipping their tails, gasping for air, the thrill of escape coursing through their being; they would skate along the corridor, zigzag in and around the feet of the guests, the light from the chandelier reflecting off their scales; they would glide out of the back door, slide from one end of the terrace to the other and, just when they feared death was imminent, plunge into the deep sea, where they would find old friends and relatives that had stayed in the same waters, bored and unchanged.

The new arrivals would tell the other fish what it felt like to live in that big mansion above the sea, relinquishing the vastness of the blue in exchange for not having to worry about their next meal. Soon the fugitive fish would be swallowed up by large predators, for how could those used to the pampered habitat of a rich man's aquarium survive in dangerous waters? All the same, they would not trade a single minute of freedom for all the years in captivity.

If only she could find a hammer . . . Sometimes her own mind scared her.

The Breakfast Table

Istanbul, 1990s

Umut's imprisonment, like a torch shone into dark corners, exposed the weaknesses and failings the Nalbantoğlus had been hiding, as much from themselves as from others. Anyone who observed them would have noticed the hole Umut's absence had opened up in the midst of their lives, but they chose to pretend it wasn't there, that hungry hollow. It was no more than a coincidence that Mensur began to drink more heavily; a coincidence too that Selma's cheeks turned an anaemic yellow from lack of sleep after nights of praying and lack of proper food after days of fasting.

Increasingly, Peri's dreams became more disturbing, her screams louder. She slept with the lights on and kept an amber necklace by her bed, having read that amber drove the demons away. Nothing helped. In her dreams she saw schools that looked like jails, and wardens who bore a strange resemblance to her mother or father. She found herself covered in maggots and faeces, her hair shaved to the scalp, arrested and imprisoned for a crime she did not know she had committed. From these nightmares she always woke with a galloping heart, and needed several extra seconds to rejoin the real world.

Mensur had changed. Gone was the man who would down a few with his friends in the warmth of old ballads and lively political debates. He now preferred to drink alone, silence his faithful companion. For a long while his body, strong and sound, showed no signs of deterioration – save for the half-circles under his eyes, dark crescents in a pallid sky.

Then came the inevitable. In the mornings Mensur would wake up sweating and aching, looking worn out, as though he had been breaking stones in his sleep. He was often confused, nauseous. Trying hard to hide the trembling that invaded his body, he stood distant, buried in silence, or he spoke too much, uncontrollably. The company he worked for decided to give him early retirement when it became obvious he was in no state to work. Without a daily job he spent more time in the house – a change unwelcome to his wife and younger son. Apprehensive, frazzled and easily flurried, he resembled an overstretched empire fighting on two fronts: the old Eastern frontier, the battle with his wife; and the newly opened Western one, the battle with Hakan. He was losing on both sides.

They quarrelled constantly, viciously, father and son, a jumble of male voices, hurtful accusations rising above the breakfast table, like shoals of dead fish floating to the surface after a dynamite explosion. Outwardly, it was over the pettiest issues – a comment about a tasteless shirt or the slurping of tea – yet, inside, the rift went deep.

Always, without exception, Selma stood behind her younger son. She was feistier fighting for her offspring than for herself. Fierce and vigorous, a falcon defending her chick against the enemy raptor. That made two against one. An equation that forced Peri to take sides and rush to her father's aid, if only for the sake of balance. However, she didn't really want to win. All she wanted was some sort of ceasefire. A temporary suspension of pain.

Soon after, Hakan, who had never really seen the value of a good education, announced he was dropping out of university and had no intention of going back to that *useless cowshed*. Overnight, to the chagrin of his parents, he ended his student days, his mind sealed before it had been opened. They could see in his eyes how much he abhorred his life and those whom he held responsible for its misery.

Many days a month Hakan would come home solely to fill his stomach, change his clothes and catch some sleep. As directionless as a balloon in the wind, he tried his hand at several jobs without success – until he found a cause through a set of friends he called Brothers. Mates who had big opinions about America, Israel, Russia, the Middle East, and saw conspiracy theories and secret societies everywhere. They greeted each other by knocking their temples together and splashing out high-sounding words – such as 'honour', 'allegiance' and 'righteousness'. In their company, Hakan proved to be a quick learner. The cynicism and pessimism of his new circle suited him. With the help of the Brothers he landed a position at an ultra-nationalist newspaper. Shamelessly careless when it came to grammar and spelling, he nonetheless had a knack for words, a talent for incendiary rhetoric. Under a pseudonym he began to write columns that became increasingly shrill and thuggish in their messages. Every week he revealed the traitors of the nation – the rotten apples that, if not taken care of, could putrefy the entire basket: Jews, Armenians, Greeks, Kurds, Alevis . . . there wasn't a single ethnic group that a Turk could trust, other than another Turk. Nationalism, like a bespoke suit, fitted his mood. Nationalism assured him that he had been born into a superior nation, a worthier race, and was destined to do great things, not for himself but for his people. Clad with this identity, he felt strong, principled, invincible. Observing her brother's transformation, Peri would come to understand that nothing swells the ego quite like a cause motivated by the delusion of pure selflessness.

'You think you have only one son in jail? In this house I'm just as much a prisoner,' Hakan shouted at his father after another breakfast quarrel. 'Umut is lucky, he doesn't have to listen to you haranguing us every day.'

'You call your brother lucky, you miserable wretch?' Mensur shouted back, his voice shaking worse than his hands.

Peri listened, her head down, her shoulders stiff. There was something about a family row that resembled an impending avalanche: one wrong word and it threatened to turn into something so huge it brought down everyone.

'Let him be. He's just a young man,' Selma muttered to her husband.

'An irresponsible young man who lives off his father's money,' said Mensur.

'Oh, you don't want me to eat your food, right? Fine, from now on I won't.' Hakan flung the empty breadbasket against the wall, where it bounced like a rubber ball, the crumbs scattering around. 'Anyway, who wants the bread of an alcoholic?'

Never before had the word actually been spoken. Unthinkable. Unretractable. Irreparable, to call the head of the house an alcoholic, and yet it was done. Hakan, unable to shoulder the silence that ensued, stormed out.

Selma began to cry. In between sobs, her voice rose and fell in a litany of laments. 'We've been cursed. The whole family! Yes . . . it's a curse.'

In her elder son's misfortune she saw a punishment and a warning from Allah, she said. As they had paid no heed to the divine message, she was certain there would be more damnation to come.

'That's the stupidest thing I've heard,' Mensur said. 'Why would God want to destroy the Nalbantoğlus? I'm sure He's got better things to do.'

'Allah works on us in all sorts of ways. He wishes to teach us . . . teach *you* . . . a lesson.'

'And what lesson is that?'

'See the error of your ways,' Selma said. 'Until you get it, none of us will have peace.'

Mensur sat tight in his chair. 'If you really believe what happened to Umut is God's doing, and that God needs prisons and torturers to carry out His teachings, there's something wrong with you, woman, or else, dammit, there's something wrong with your God.'

'Tövbe, tövbe . . .'* Selma murmured.

To balance out Allah's wrath, Selma went days, sometimes weeks, without eating much; content with bread, yoghurt, dates and water. Votive offerings; visceral negotiations with the Almighty. At nights she slept little, spending her time doing the only two things that quieted her mind: praying and cleaning. From her bed, she could spot a layer of fine dust on every piece of furniture; she listened to the termites eating away at the wooden cabinets – why couldn't the others hear them? Crushed aspirin, white vinegar, lemon juice, baking soda. She scrubbed, rinsed, brushed, waxed and wiped. In the mornings the family woke up to the smell of detergents.

Selma washed her hands so frequently, and with such intensity, that they smelled of antiseptic all the time. The skin was cracked, bleeding

* *Tövbe, tövbe*: 'Repent, repent'.

in places, which increased her fear of contamination and led her to wash them again even harder. To hide the state of her hands, she began to wear black gloves with her hijab and a long, dark, loose coat that reached almost to her heels. One evening, as Selma and Peri were returning from the bazaar, Peri looked back and, for a fleeting second, she could not see her mother – so thoroughly had she blended in with the night.

Mensur, mortified at his wife's appearance, wished not to be seen with her any more. He shopped alone; so did she. Her outfit epitomized everything that he had always despised, loathed and confronted in the Middle East. The benightedness of the religious. The presumption that their ways were the best – only because they had been born into this culture and swallowed unquestioningly whatever they had been taught. How could they be so certain of the superiority of their truths when they knew so little, if anything at all, about other cultures, other philosophies, other ways of thinking?

For Selma, Mensur's manners embodied all that set her on edge: the condescension in his eyes, the finality in his voice, the righteousness in the tilt of his chin. The arrogance of the secular modernists. The pompous and pretentious ease with which they placed themselves outside and above society, looking down on centuries-old traditions. How could they call themselves enlightened when they knew so little, if anything at all, about their own culture, their own faith?

Rigid with the dread of having to converse, husband and wife slipped past each other, untouching. What they lacked in love, they made up for in resentment.

Meanwhile, Peri found solace in literature. Short stories, novels, poems, plays . . . she devoured whatever she could lay her hands on at the limited library at school. When there was nothing else to be found, she read encyclopaedias. Devouring everything from Aardvark to Zombie, she came to know about things that, though of no current use in her life, might someday come in handy, she hoped. But even if they were never to have a function, she would still keep reading, propelled by her hunger for learning.

Books were liberating, full of life. She preferred being in Story-land to being in her motherland. Refusing to leave her room on weekends, munching on apples and sunflower seeds, she finished one borrowed novel after another. She discovered that intelligence, like a muscle, needed to be exercised with increasing levels of stress, if it were to grow to its full potential. Unsatisfied with the rote learning at school, she developed verbal and visual methods of her own to store information – names of plants in Latin; lines of poems in English; the dates of wars, peace treaties and more wars, of which there were far too many in Ottoman history. She was determined to excel in every subject, from literature to maths, from physics to chemistry. She imagined different subjects as tropical birds kept in separate cages side by side. What would happen if she cut holes in the wire mesh and the birds could fly into the next cage and then the next? She longed to see maths keeping company with literature, physics with philosophy. Who had decided they could not mingle, anyway?

Peri understood that her obsession with studying kept her apart from her peers and earned her their envy and animosity. It suited her just fine. Like all Nalbantoğlus, she had a natural proclivity for loneliness. She didn't mind that the other children called her teacher's pet; she didn't mind that she wasn't invited to popular girls' birthday parties or asked out to films by popular boys. That life was about enlightenment or ideals or love – that made sense to her. But fun – that was never her thing.

Like every outcast she would soon discover that she was not alone. In every class there were a few who, for a variety of reasons, remained out of sync with everyone else. They would recognize each other immediately. It took one untouchable to know another: a Kurdish boy ridiculed for his accent; a girl with facial hair; another girl in a lower class who could not control her bladder when she got nervous in exams; a boy whose mother was rumoured to be a wanton woman . . . With them she became good friends. But her true companions were always books. Imagination was her home, her homeland, her refuge, her exile.

Hence she read and studied, and finished at the top of her class, term after term. Whenever her self-confidence needed a boost, she ran to her father. And Mensur always gave the same counsel: 'Education, my soul. Education will save us. You're the pride of our joyless family, but I want you to be educated in the West. Plenty of good schools in Europe but you must go to Oxford! You'll fill your head with knowledge and then you'll come back. Only young people like you can change the fate of this tired old country.'

Back in his youth Mensur had met a student from Oxford, a backpacker, a pale-skinned hippie with whom he had felt an instant rapport. The man was planning to travel through Turkey all alone on his bike. He had boasted that he kept all his money inside his sock to thwart pickpockets and hotel thieves. Worried that something might happen to this naive foreigner, Mensur had insisted on accompanying him. The two of them had traversed the Anatolian peninsula, after which the fair-haired Brit had crossed into Iran. What happened to him Mensur did not know. But he had never forgotten his own bafflement at seeing his country through the eyes of a Westerner. It was the first time he had realized that what was ordinary to him was not necessarily so to outsiders. It was the first time he had realized there was an 'outside world'. Now he wanted his daughter to be educated *there*. It was his most fervent wish. Peri – and hundreds of youngsters like Peri – would become an educated, idealistic, forward-thinking graduate who would rescue this country from its backwardness.

Peri understood and accepted that some daughters were born with a mission: to fulfil their fathers' dreams. In doing so, they would also be redeeming their fatherland.

The Tango with Azrael

Istanbul, 1990s

The summer Peri turned eleven years old, her mother, fulfilling a long-awaited dream, went on pilgrimage to Saudi Arabia. Her elder brother still in prison, her other brother squatting in God knows whose house, she and her father were left in charge at home. They prepared their own food (kofte and chips for lunch, kofte and spaghetti for supper), washed the dishes (simply rinsed) and watched any TV programme they fancied. It was like being on holiday, except better.

On the day of the local bazaar, Peri woke up, feeling queasy. She held her stomach with a sneaking feeling that all that kofte and spaghetti had finally got to her. She would have to remind her father to change the menu. But a surprise awaited her in the bathroom: stains on her underwear. Too dark and yet she knew it was blood. Her mother had warned her this would happen and, when it did, she would have to be all the more careful with boys. *Don't let them touch you.* It was too soon! At school, she had eavesdropped on older girls complaining about it: 'My aunt is back!' they would say airily. 'Could you check my back?' they would ask each other, hurrying their steps. In her classroom, there was one girl who claimed she had had her period, though everyone knew it was a lie. That left Peri as the first among her peers. She had grown too fast this past year, no matter how much she'd tried to hide it. She had been told enough times that she was pretty to understand this was what people thought of her. Her own perception of herself was acutely different. How she wished she had hair black as night, instead of a mousy light brown; instead of her newly beginning curves, a confident flatness. She would have loved to have been born as the third son of the Nalbantoğlus. Wouldn't life be easier had she been a boy?

She found a clean old bedsheet, cut it into strips. If she used it sparingly, wisely, she would not have to say anything to her mother. She could wash, dry and reuse them, the way she knew many women did in this country. That way, she could conceal the truth until she was about fourteen, the age she regarded as fitting for her first period. God had made a mistake in His divine calculation. She was determined to correct it.

Two weeks later Selma returned, sunburned and thinner. She plopped down on the sofa and began to relate her journey to Mecca, her words galloping along as her porcelain horses would have done, had they a breath of life in them.

'Last year, a stampede inside a pedestrian tunnel in the holy city killed more than a thousand pilgrims. Now the Saudis are cautious,' she explained. 'But they can't prevent diseases. I got so sick I thought I was going to die. Right then and there!'

'Oh, I'm glad you didn't,' Mensur said. 'Good to have you back.'

'Thank Allah, I'm home,' Selma said with a sigh. 'If I hadn't made it, I'd have been buried in Medina, close to the Prophet, peace be upon him.'

'The cemeteries in Istanbul have a better view,' Mensur quipped. 'We've fresh sea air. Buried in Medina, you'd have been mulch for a date palm. In Istanbul, you can fertilize mastic, linden, maple . . . Jasmine would be great. You'd be bathed in perfume all year round.'

Selma shrank away from her husband's words as if they were hot cinders spat sizzling from a fire. Worried that they might lock horns again, Peri butted in, 'What's in your suitcase, Mum? Did you bring us anything?'

'I brought you the whole of Mecca!' came the answer.

Peri and Mensur perked up, their faces beaming – two expectant kids. One by one packages were unwrapped: dates, honey, miswak, colognes, prayer mats, musk, rosaries, scarves and Zamzam in tiny bottles.

'How do you know this is sacred water – did anyone authenticate it?' Mensur inquired, shaking a bottle. 'They might as well have sold you tap water.'

At which Selma grabbed the bottle, opened it and drained it in one swallow. 'This is pure Zamzam but your mind is filthy!'

'Fine.' Mensur shrugged.

Pointing at a box, Peri asked, 'What's that, Mum?'

That turned out to be a mosque-shaped bronze wall-clock – 20 × 18 inches – with a swinging pendulum and minarets on both sides. Selma explained it could be programmed to show prayer times in a thousand cities worldwide. Then she hung it up on a nail in the living room, in the Qibla direction, across from the portrait of Atatürk.

'I'm not having a mosque under my roof,' said Mensur.

'Oh, really? But I have to live with an infidel under mine,' riposted Selma.

'Well, right now half of my sins are yours. If you hadn't bought that thing, I'd have never blasphemed. Take it down!'

'I won't,' Selma shouted. 'I chose it, paid for it, carried it all the way from the holy land. I got sick there, almost died. I'm a haji, show me some respect!'

It was the first time Peri heard her mother yell at her father. Coming from a woman whose main rebellion for years had been either stoical silence or barbed words at low decibels, it sounded like an explosion. The wall-clock stayed where it was, albeit muted – a concession that made neither party happy.

During the rest of the day, Mensur was locked in a deep sulk. The same evening there was a power cut that went on for hours. Mensur took his place at the raqi table earlier than usual, between Atatürk and the prayer clock, his pale face cast in shadows by a lit candle; he said he was feeling unwell. Bringing his hand to his heart, as if to salute an invisible being, he tilted his head to one side and collapsed.

It was a heart attack.

For as long as she lived Peri would never forget how the night grew darker by the minute. As she observed with horror, her father slumped over like a lifeless mannequin, his forehead hitting the table; he was picked up by neighbours, who had come when they heard Selma's cries, and carried to the sofa. Then, as he was placed on a stretcher, tucked into an ambulance, rushed into the A & E department and pushed into an operating theatre with machines beeping on all sides, the only thing she could think of, over and over, was whether it was a punishment from God. The question was so intimidating that it could not be expressed aloud; it had to be swallowed down. She would have liked to ask her mother, weeping by her side, but was terrified of the answer Selma might provide. Was this the way of Allah? First, He allowed you to utter profanities and joke without inhibition. Next, He made you pay the price? It was almost as if He waited for you to sin so that He could smack you with His wrath. Was the way of God one of camouflage, a trick to disguise calculated revenge?

Another persistent thought gnawed away at her. Deep down in her mind, Peri was convinced that her father's heart attack was, through some circuitous chain of causation in the universe, instigated by her period. Why had she bled so early and while her mother was away? It was wrong of her to try to become the woman of the house. Wrong also because, as she now reckoned, the faster she grew, the sooner her father might die.

In the waiting room at the hospital, Peri and Selma sat on the worn-out sofa. A shaft of moonlight pierced through the windows, only to be engulfed by the intrusive glare of the fluorescent lamps. The TV was on, though silent. On the screen, a woman in a red sequined dress turned the wheel of fortune and was disappointed to see it land on 'bankrupt'. The caretaker on duty, a hefty man with a bushy moustache and the only person watching the programme, laughed gleefully.

'I'll go and pray,' Selma said.

'May I come with you?'

Selma stared at her daughter, half expecting this question. 'That'd be good, actually. Allah listens to children's prayers.'

Peri nodded, as a dutiful daughter should. Save for a few invocations learned by rote at school, she had never performed the Salah, given her wish to side with her father in all matters related to faith. Mensur, unlike his wife, kept his prayers succinct and non-ceremonial. He rarely used the word 'Allah', preferring the more secular-sounding 'Tanri'. Now Peri was ready to do things her mother's way. She would do anything to save her father's life, even betray him.

Inside the lavatory they performed their ablutions – rinsing their mouths, washing their faces, hands, feet. The water was chilly but Peri did not complain, regarding the ritual as a preamble to a conversation with God. There were no prayer rooms in this wing of the hospital and they used a corner of the waiting room instead – the TV still on, the red-sequined-dressed woman still determined to win.

Having no prayer rugs, they spread their cardigans on the floor. Whatever her mother did, Peri imitated, like an echo. Thus, as Selma crossed her hands over her chest, so did Peri. Selma bent down, stood up and then prostrated herself, her forehead touching the ground; so did Peri. There was, however, one vital difference. Her mother's lips were constantly moving, whereas Peri's were still. It occurred to her that this might not sit well with God. A silent prayer was tantamount to an envelope with nothing inside. Since no one, not even the Creator, would care to receive such an envelope, she figured out she would have to say something. And this, after some deliberation, was what the child uttered:

Dear Allah,

Mother says You watch me all the time, which is nice, thank You; it's also a bit spooky because sometimes I want to be alone. Mother says You hear everything – even when I talk to myself. Even the thoughts inside my head. You also watch all that happens. Can You see the baby in the mist? No one notices it but me, though I am sure You do too.

Anyway, I was thinking, our eyes are small and it takes us about a second to blink. Now, Your eyes must be huge, so it must take You at least an hour to shut Your eyelids, and maybe in that time You can't gaze at my father.

When I get cross at someone, Dad tells me, 'You are not a little child, you can forgive.' If You are angry with my father, please forgive him and make him well again. He is a good man. From now on, please can You blink every time my father sins?

I promise I'll start praying again. I'll pray every night for the rest of my life.

Amin

Peri, perched on her cardigan, saw her mother turn her head right and left, and rub her hands over her face, thus ending the prayer, all of which she imitated, sealing her confidential letter.

The next morning Mensur was propped up in bed with pillows, teasing his visitors, and a few days later he was out of hospital with a fat bill and a battery-operated pacemaker in his heart. He was advised to give up drinking and to stay away from stress – as if stress were an obnoxious relative one could simply stop inviting to dinner. In any case, Mensur would not listen. Having danced a tango with Azrael, the angel of death, he claimed he had nothing to be afraid of any more.

This, too, would penetrate Peri's dreams, the ghostly sight of her father dancing a disjointed jig with a skeleton – that turned out to be his own.

The Poem

Istanbul, 2016

Inside the bathroom of the seaside mansion Peri stood still, staring at herself in the ornate mirror. The semblance of composure she had maintained with her daughter had now vanished, replaced by disquiet. The loneliness of the fish in their tank made her think of the figures in cartoons, hopelessly marooned on a desert island, yet never thinking of escape. Could *she* swim away? Daily habits were altered, personalities reformed, allegiances renounced, friendships broken, even addictions spurned, but the hardest thing to change in this life was one's attachment to a place.

A ripple of laughter arose from the other side of the door. The businessman was telling a joke, his voice soaring above the din. Peri missed the punchline, which, by the sound of the reaction, was crude, salacious.

'Oh, you men!' a female voice was heard, half reprimanding, half teasing.

Peri pursed her lips. She had never been one of those women who could say for all to hear, and certainly not in such a flirtatious tone, 'Oh, you men!'

Whether men or women, it was always people with rough journeys in their pasts, uncertainty in their eyes and invisible wounds in their souls that intrigued her. Generous with her time and loyal to the bone, she befriended these select few with an unflagging commitment and love. But with everyone else, who constituted pretty much the majority, her interest quickly morphed into boredom. And when bored all she wanted was to escape – to free herself from that person, from that conversation, from that moment. She had a hunch that tonight, boredom would be her consort at the bourgeois dinner, and to counterbalance it she promised herself to find little games to play, amusements for her eyes only.

Hurriedly, she splashed water on her face. Had her lipstick not been crushed and her eyeshadow palette lost in the alley, she would have liked to retouch her makeup. Giving her hair a quick comb with her fingers, she checked herself in the mirror one more time. The face looking back at her was pale, restless – as if a troubled spirit had passed through her unawares. She opened the door. To her surprise, her daughter was waiting outside.

'Dad was wondering where you were.'

'I needed to wash up a bit.' Peri paused. 'What did you tell him?'

Peri saw in Deniz's eyes a twinkle of affection before indifference took over. 'Nothing,' she said.

'Thank you, my love. Let's go back.'

'Wait, you forgot this,' said Deniz, holding out something in her hand.

Peri didn't need to take a closer look to know it was the Polaroid. She had searched for it everywhere in that airless alley. But Deniz must have spotted it first and slipped it into her pocket. Now her daughter demanded, 'How come I've never seen this before?'

There were four figures in the snapshot. The professor and his students. Happy and hopeful and ready to change the world, and joyously unaware of what tomorrow held for them. Peri remembered the day the photo was taken. *The worst winter in Oxford in decades*. She remembered it all – bone-chilling mornings, frozen pipes, heaped snow banks, and the intoxicating elixir of falling in love coursing through her body. She had never felt more alive.

'Who are these people, Mum?'

Keeping calm – too calm – Peri said, 'It's an old picture.'

'Is that why you carry it in your wallet? Next to your children's photos?' said Deniz, her voice laden with disbelief and curiosity. 'So who are they?'

Peri pointed to one of the girls. She wore a magenta headscarf wrapped neatly in a turban style and her hazel eyes were outlined with thick kohl that curled all the way up to her eyebrows. 'That's Mona. An Egyptian-American student.'

Intent and silent, Deniz studied the girl.

'The other girl is Shirin,' Peri said. Her gaze landed on a striking figure with voluminous black hair, full makeup and high-heeled leather boots. 'Her family was from Iran, but they had moved around so much she didn't feel like she belonged anywhere.'

'How did you meet them?'

It was a moment before Peri answered. 'University friends. We shared the same house, were in the same college. We took the same seminar, but not all of us at the same time.'

'What was the seminar about?'

Peri smiled a faint smile, the memory etched in every line of her expression. 'It was about . . . God.'

'Wow,' Deniz said, her usual response to things she had no interest in. She tapped a finger on the tall man standing in the middle. His brown-blond hair was unruly and long enough to curl; his eyes seemed to glow from under a flat cap; his chin was strong and well defined; his expression tranquil, though not altogether peaceful.

'Who is he?'

A frisson of discomfort passed across Peri's features, so subtle as to be almost unnoticeable. 'He was our professor.'

'Really? He looks like a rebellious student.'

'He was a rebellious professor.'

'Is there such a thing?' asked Deniz. 'What was his name?'

'We called him Azur.'

'That's a weird name. Where is this place anyway?'

'England . . . Oxford.'

'What? How come you never told me you went to *Oxford*?' Deniz uttered the last word with an exaggerated lilt.

Peri hesitated, unsure what to say. Why she had never shared it with anyone, including her children, she had an idea, but this was neither the time nor the place to reveal it. 'Only for a while,' she said, her voice tailing off. 'I didn't finish.'

'How did you get in?'

She sounded impressed, but Peri also detected a note of envy tinged with resentment in her remark. Her daughter had started stressing about university exams, though they were still several years away. The education system, geared to make young minds ever more competitive, might have been fine for students like Peri, but for free spirits like Deniz it was unmitigated misery.

'You might not believe it, but I had top grades all the way through school. Father always wanted me to get the best education ... in Europe. He helped me with the application, and I met the requirements.'

'Grandpa?' asked Deniz, finding it hard to reconcile the image of the doddering old man in her mind with this forceful agent of change.

Peri smiled. 'Yes, he was proud of me.'

'Grandma wasn't?' Deniz asked, detecting a conflict.

'She was worried that I'd get lost in a foreign country. It was the first time I was leaving home. Not easy for a mother.' Peri drew her breath, surprised at her own statement, surprised that she empathized with her mother.

Deniz gave this some thought. 'When was all this?'

'Around 9/11, if that means anything to you.'

'I know what 9/11 is,' Deniz said. Her face lightened with a fresh realization as she said, 'So this was before you met Dad. You drop out of Oxford, return to Istanbul, get married, give up on your education, have three kids in a row and become a housewife. How original, bravo!'

'I wasn't trying to be original,' Peri said.

Ignoring the remark, Deniz chewed her bottom lip. 'Why did you leave?'

That was the one question Peri was not prepared to answer. The truth was too painful. 'It was too hard for me: the classes, the exams ...'

Wordlessly, Deniz gave her mother a sidelong glance, her incredulity apparent. For the first time it crossed her mind that the woman who had given birth to her, the woman she had seen every day of her life and expected to cater to her every need and whim, might have been a different person before she and her brothers were born. It was an uncomfortable thought. To this day her mother had been a *terra cognita* where Deniz knew each blissful valley, each placid lake and each wintry mountain. She didn't like the possibility that there might be parts of that continent still unmapped.

'May I have the photo now?' Peri asked.

'Wait a second.'

Her eyelashes catching the light from the ceiling lamp, Deniz brought the Polaroid closer to her face and squinted, almost cross-eyed, as though expecting to discover a secret code in it somewhere. On impulse, she turned over the photo and saw the inscription on the back in the stilted handwriting of someone making an effort to be neat: *From Shirin to Peri with sisterhood / Remember, Mouse, 'I can no longer call myself a man, a woman, an angel or even a pure soul.'*

'Who is Mouse?' Deniz said with a chuckle.

'That's what Shirin used to call me.'

'That'd be the last nickname I'd call you!'

'Well, I guess I changed,' Peri said. 'Come on, we must go.'

Deniz still looked quizzical. 'What does this "no longer a man, a woman, an angel . . ." mean? What kind of nonsense is this?'

'Just a poem . . . Sweetheart, give the photo back to me.'

From the drawing room erupted the sound of clapping and cheering. Someone was being teased or dared to do something. Curious, Deniz, after the briefest hesitation, returned the photo to her mother and headed back into the party.

Alone in the corridor, Peri held the Polaroid tight, and was surprised to feel the warmth it radiated, as if it were alive. How strange it was, when you came to think of it, that while moments withered, hearts stiffened, bodies aged, promises perished, and even the strongest convictions faded, a photograph, a two-dimensional representation of reality and a lie, remained unchanged, forever faithful.

She tucked the Polaroid away in her wallet, careful not to look at any of the faces in the shot, resistant to the gaze of the past, resistant to the judgement of a younger Peri about the woman she had become. She straightened her back, ready to meet the other guests, many of whom were, in truth, no more than strangers, and walked slowly back to the party.

The Covenant

Istanbul, 1990s

In secondary school Peri went through seasons of faith, seasons of doubt. Unknown to her father she had remained loyal to the oath she had made to God. Every night before she went to sleep, in words carefully chosen, ever so passionately, she prayed. She tried hard. If she sacrificed her disbelief on the altar of love and became as pious as all those preachers proselytizing under Istanbul skies, Allah would be more pleased with her family and less stern with her father, she hoped. An irrational covenant, for sure, but wasn't every covenant with the Almighty bound to be so?

The problem with praying, however, was that it had to be pure, monophonic. One consistent voice from beginning to end. But when she talked to God, her mind fragmented into a plethora of speakers, some listening, some making witty remarks, others expressing objections. Even worse, unwanted images flooded her mind – of death, darkness, violence, genocide but especially sex. She closed her eyes, opened her eyes, struggling to erase the naked bodies writhing in her imagination. Mortified by her inability to control her brain and worried that these thoughts tainted her prayers, she would start over and over, rushing to finish before impure ideas took hold once again. Readying for prayer was like shoving into a cupboard all the junk and clutter, before God came to visit the house of her mind. While she wanted to look her best, she remained acutely conscious of what she'd concealed from His gaze.

If, instead of praying alone at home, she prayed amidst a congregation, she might quell the voices consuming her, she thought. With a few like-minded friends, she fell into the habit of visiting local mosques. She treasured the plentiful light from the high, arched windows, the chandeliers, the calligraphy, the architecture of Sinan. It troubled her, however, that the women's sections were either tucked away at the back or lodged upstairs behind curtains, always secluded, separate, small.

In one neighbourhood a middle-aged man followed them into the mosque, and afterwards into the courtyard.

'Girls should pray at home,' he said, his eyes travelling over the contours of their breasts.

'This is Allah's House, it's for everyone,' said Peri.

He took a step towards her, thrusting out his chest. His body was a reminder, a warning, a frontier. 'This mosque is not big enough. Even men have to spill out on to the pavement. There's no room here for schoolgirls.'

'So mosques belong to men?' Peri said.

He laughed, as if surprised that she could have thought it was any other way. Peri was disappointed that the imam, who had overheard the conversation in passing, said nothing to defend them.

Another time, in Üsküdar, upstairs in the women's section, she opened the curtains so that they could see the beauty of the mosque while they were praying. Instantly, an older woman, dressed head to toe in black, pulled the curtains closed, murmuring angrily under her breath. It wasn't only men who wanted women to be out of sight. Some women, too, were of the same mind.

Yes, she had tried. But there was always a gap between her and the ways of the religion printed on her pink ID card. Whose idea was it to have a religion box on ID cards anyway? Who decided whether a newborn baby was Muslim or Christian or Jewish? Certainly not the baby itself.

Had Peri been allowed to fill in the religion box herself, she would probably have written: 'Undecided'. That would be more truthful. If her mother was going to end up in heaven and her father in hell, her abode should be the purgatory somewhere in between.

She refrained from talking about these issues with the pious, because once they noticed her vacillating between doubt and faith, they insisted on trying to win her over. The few atheists she had met were not so different. Whether in the name of God or science, there was no satisfaction for the ego quite like the satisfaction of converting someone to your side. But being proselytized was the last thing Peri wanted. Did these people not understand that she did not want to reach a decision about their code of belief? All she wanted was to be on the move. If she came down on one side or the other, she feared she would turn into someone else and it would be the end of her.

She wrote in her God-diary: *I'm perpetually in limbo. Maybe I want too many things at once and nothing passionately enough.*

The day Peri graduated from school at the top of her year, she and her father prepared breakfast together. Dicing tomatoes, chopping parsley, whisking eggs, they made a menemen so spicy that every bite would burn a hole in their tongues. They worked side by side, their actions coordinated, effortless. Peri watched her father slice an onion, noticing with relief that the tremor in his hands seemed to have calmed down. But he sweated profusely, a thin film of perspiration covering his forehead. She knew that if he were alone in the kitchen he would have already poured himself a glass.

Afterwards, Mensur drove his daughter to an educational agency that helped Turkish students to apply to schools abroad. They had visited the stuffy, dimly lit office several times in the past months, queuing alongside hopeful teenagers, unable to take their eyes off the beaming faces filling the brochures of Western universities. From their shiny pages popped up a wild diversity – a seeming United Nations – of students, all without exception looking happy.

On the way, they stopped at the traffic lights beside an Ottoman mosque famed for being built on the sea. Seagulls were settled around the circumference of the dome, like a string of pearls.

'Baba, how come you were never religious?' Peri asked, staring at the mosque.

'Heard too many bogus sermons, seen too many fake gurus.'

'What about God? I mean, do you still believe He exists?'

'Sure I do,' Mensur said a tad half-heartedly. 'That doesn't mean I understand what He is up to.'

A tourist couple – Europeans by the look of them – were taking pictures in the courtyard of the mosque. The woman had covered her head with one of the long scarves provided at the entrance. Someone – perhaps a passer-by – must have warned her that her dress was too short; she had tied another scarf around her waist to cover her legs above the knee. The man, by contrast, had sandals and Bermuda shorts apparently no one had seen as a problem.

Pointing at the couple, Mensur remarked, 'If I were a woman, I'd be twice as critical of religion.'

'Why?' Peri asked, even though she guessed the answer.

'Because God is a man . . . They've made us believe so, all those godly people.'

A car pulled up next to them, playing a song by Santana at full blast.

'You see, my soul,' Mensur continued. 'I'm fond of the Bektashi or Mawlawi or Melami Sufi traditions with their humanism and humour. The Rind were free of all kinds of prejudice and intolerance – how many people remember them today? That ancient philosophy has disappeared in this country. Not only here. Everywhere across the Muslim world. Suppressed, silenced, erased. What for? In the name of religion they are killing God. For the sake of discipline and authority, they forget love.'

The light turned green. Seconds earlier – not after – the cars behind them had begun honking their horns. Mensur slammed his foot on the accelerator and murmured to himself: 'How did these idiots wait in their mothers' wombs!'

'Baba, doesn't religion give you a sense of security – like a protective glove?'

'Maybe, but I don't want an extra skin. I touch the flame, I burn; I hold ice, I'm cold. The world is what it is. We'll all die. What's the point of safety in crowds? We are born alone, we die alone.'

Peri leaned forward, about to say something, but her father's voice carried on. 'When you were little you asked me if I was scared of hell.'

'And you told me you'd tunnel your way out of it.'

Mensur's face broke into a grin. 'You know why I'm not that keen on heaven?'

'Tell me.'

'I look at the people who'll go there, those who pray and fast and seem to do everything they're supposed to do. So many of them are full of pretension! I say to myself, if these chaps are headed for heaven, do I really want to be there? I'd rather burn peacefully in my own hell. Hot it is, but at least there's no hypocrisy.'

'Oh, Baba, I hope you won't speak like this around others. You're going to get yourself in trouble.'

'Don't worry, my tongue loosens only when I'm next to you. Or after I've had a few. Those fanatics will never sit with me at a raqı table. I'm safe.' He chuckled.

In a little while they reached the Dolmabahçe Palace, with its triumphal arches and clock tower. Mensur asked, 'Do you know the story of the black fish?'

He said it was not far from here that Sultan Murad IV had one stormy night sat down to read *Arrows of Misfortune* – a collection of satirical poems by the great Nefi. Barely had he begun when lightning struck a chestnut tree in the palace gardens – an omen, for sure. Deeply agitated, the Sultan not only threw the book into the sea, but also signed a letter granting Nefi's enemies permission to chasten him any way they chose. A few days later, the poet, strangled with a noose, was plunged into the very same waters in which his poetry had disintegrated, verse by verse.

'You see, what a toxic cocktail is ignorance and power. The world has suffered more in the hands of the religious than in the hands of people like me – whatever funny word you call my kind!'

Peri looked out of the window towards the silver-tipped waves shimmering in the afternoon sun, hoping to catch sight of a fish or two dimpling the surface. She knew, now that she had learned about the poet's fate, that she would never forget this story. She took on the sorrows of others as though they were her own and hung them around her neck, just like the pine-needle necklaces she used to make as a child. They would prick her skin and hurt, but she would refuse to take them off until they dried and crumbled into particles fine as dust.

Mensur followed her gaze. 'That's why the fish in this part of the

Bosphorus are black. They've swallowed too much ink. Poor things, they still search for words from poems and flesh from poets . . . the same thing, when you think about it.'

Peri loved her father's tales. She had grown up with them. Yet the melancholy with which they were infused pierced her soul, like a splinter under her skin that had become an organic part of her. Sometimes she imagined she had splinters all over – both in her body and in the recesses of her mind.

'Why am I even talking about these things?' said Mensur with a new intensity. 'Aren't you excited about Oxford?'

They had applied to several universities in Europe, the US and Canada. Places with names so strange that no tongue could pronounce them. But it was Oxford that Mensur kept raving about.

'It's not certain I'm going.'

'Oh, you are,' declared Mensur. 'Your English is the best. You've worked hard to get it right. You've passed the exams, done the interview and now you've got an offer.'

'Baba, how are we going to afford it . . .' said Peri. Her voice tailed off.

'Stop worrying, I've taken care of that.'

He was selling their car as well as the only investment they'd ever had – a field not far from the Aegean Sea, where he had planned to grow olive trees someday. It weighed heavily on Peri's conscience that her father was giving up his dreams for her. Still, when their eyes met in shared understanding, she smiled. Although she tried not to talk about it, the truth was that she could not wait to go to England.

'Baba, are you sure Mother will be okay with this? I mean, have you spoken with her?'

'Not yet,' Mensur said. 'I will at some point. How can she not want her daughter to go to the best university in the world? She'll be thrilled!'

Peri nodded, even though she knew he was lying. Neither of them would tell Selma her daughter was leaving, not until the last possible minute.

The Last Supper

Istanbul, 2016

Upon walking into the spacious dining room, Peri found everyone settled at the table, clustered in separate conversations. Adnan was chatting with a family friend, the CEO of a global investment bank. By the looks on their faces they were either talking about politics or football – the two subjects where men freely displayed their emotions in the presence of others. At each end of the table sat one of the hosts. To those around him the businessman was recounting a holiday anecdote with the suave confidence of a man accustomed to being listened to, while his wife watched indifferently from a distance. Peri took a step forward, knowing that, in a flash, all heads would turn towards her. For a second she considered tiptoeing sideways until she reached the oak door entryway, where she could make her escape.

'Darling, why are you standing there?' The businessman's wife had spotted her. 'Come and join us.'

Peri forced a smile as she slid into the empty chair reserved for her. While she had been in the bathroom, most, if not all, the guests had heard about the accident. Now everyone was staring at her with sympathetic curiosity, eager to hear the story.

'Are you all right?' asked a woman who ran a PR agency. Her hair was coiffured into an elaborate pompadour held in place by a large rhinestone hairpin that made Peri think of a kebab skewer. It gave the woman a dangerous look. 'We were worried for you.'

'Yes, what happened to you, dear?' added the CEO.

Peri caught Adnan's eyes, detecting a trace of concern in her husband's generally affectionate gaze. In front of him were an empty soup bowl and a tumbler of water. He was a teetotaller – both for health and religious reasons. Adnan was a believer.

'Nothing worth mentioning at such a lovely table,' Peri said, turning to the CEO. 'I'm more interested in what you were talking about so passionately.'

'Oh, bribery and corruption in the premier league,' said the CEO. 'Well, some teams seem bent on losing their matches. If I didn't know better, I'd say they were being paid to do it.' He threw a puckish glance at his host.

'Bullshit,' the businessman said. 'If you're trying to run down my team, I can assure you, my friend, we'll win by the sweat of our brows.'

Peri sat back, relieved at having turned the conversation away from herself, though for how long she couldn't tell.

The others had already finished their soup, and a maid appeared with a bowl for Peri – beetroot-and-carrot broth with a dollop of goat's cheese. Someone filled her glass without asking. Napa Valley, red. Before taking it to her lips, she sent a silent salute to the soul of her father.

Peri glanced around the room as she slowly began to eat. Italian furniture, English chandeliers, French curtains, Persian carpets, and a plethora of ornaments and cushions with Ottoman motifs; it was a house – though more sumptuous than the average – decorated in the same style as so many other Istanbul homes, half Oriental, half European. On the walls were paintings by well-known and upcoming Middle Eastern artists, many of which Peri guessed would have been under- or overpriced, as the region's art scene, perhaps not unlike its politics, was still in a state of flux.

In the past, Peri had been to more dinner parties than she could count where conservative Muslims had seen no harm in mingling with liberal drinkers. They would politely raise their glasses of water in a toast, joining in the gesture. Religion, in this part of the world, had been a collage of sorts. It had not been that uncommon to consume alcohol all year round and repent on the Night of Qadr, when one's sins – so long as one was genuinely remorseful – were erased wholesale. There were plenty of people who fasted during Ramadan both to renew faith and to lose weight. The sacred dovetailed with the profane. In a culture of hybridity, even the most rational gave credence to the jinn and kept nearby a blue glass charm – esteemed throughout the land as a protector against the evil eye. Meanwhile, even the most devout had enjoyed entering the New Year watching TV, clapping to the rhythm of a belly dancer. *A bit of this, a bit of that. Muslimus modernus.*

But things had changed dramatically over the last years. Colours congealed into blacks-and-whites. There were increasingly fewer marriages in which – like that of her mother and father – one spouse was devout and the other not. Nowadays the society was divided into invisible ghettoes. Istanbul resembled less a metropolis than an urban patchwork of segregated communities. People were either 'staunchly religious' or 'staunchly secularist'; and those who had somehow kept a foot in both camps, negotiating with the Almighty and the times with equal fervour, had either disappeared or become eerily quiet.

Tonight's gathering, therefore, was unusual in that it brought together people from opposite camps. Grand and palatial, Peri likened the setting to a Renaissance painting. Had she been the artist, she would have called it *The Last Supper of the Turkish Bourgeoisie*. She counted the people around the table. Sure enough, there were thirteen, including herself.

'Oh, she is not even listening,' said the PR woman.

Realizing they were talking about her, Peri smiled. 'What were you saying?'

'Your daughter told me you went to Oxford.'

Peri's face closed. Her eyes searched for Deniz, but she was eating with her friend in the next room.

'Really, darling, you are so tight-lipped!' said the businessman's wife. 'Why didn't you tell us?'

Peri said, 'Maybe because I didn't graduate . . .'

'Who cares?' quipped the journalist. 'You're still entitled to show off.'

'My brother does!' said the PR woman. '"When I was at Oxford . . ." That's the first thing he tells people.' She turned to Peri. 'Which years were you there?'

'Around 2001.'

'Oh, same as my brother!'

Peri felt a sinking sense of unease, which deepened when she heard her husband join in: 'Deniz mentioned you had a photo; why don't you show them?'

He was doing it deliberately, Peri understood, prodding and provoking her in front of others. It hurt him to learn that she still carried that Polaroid. He knew, of course. Not everything, but most of the story. It was he, after all, who had picked up the pieces after she'd left Oxford.

'Come on, show us!' someone enthused.

Hard as Peri tried to change the subject, it didn't work. Not this time. They were determined to see how she looked in her university years – and how much she had changed since then.

She pulled the Polaroid out of her bag and placed it on the table. In the candlelight four figures could be discerned, smiling faces from a discarded past, standing in the snow-covered Old Schools Quadrangle of the Bodleian Library; icicles dangled from the cornices of the entrance tower behind them. Each guest took a good look at the snap and passed it on to the next, but not before making a comment.

'Oh, you were so young!'

'Wow, look at that hair. Was it permed?'

When the photo reached the PR woman, she put on her glasses. She studied it carefully. 'Wait' – she said, her eyebrows rising – 'this man looks familiar.'

Peri tensed up.

'I used to visit my brother every year. I'm sure he showed me this man's photo . . . where was it . . .'

Peri's expression froze.

'Oh, yes, I remember now! It was in a newspaper. This man was a famous professor . . . he was disgraced . . . forced to resign from Oxford! Everyone was talking about him. There was a scandal.' She directed her gaze at Peri. 'Surely, you must have heard about it?'

Peri sat still, unable to fabricate a lie, unwilling to tell the truth. To her immense relief, the maids marched in just then carrying the starters. Appetizing smells filled the air. In the interruption as the dishes were served, Peri managed to retrieve the Polaroid. By the time she put it back in her bag, her hands were trembling so much she had to keep them under the table.

PART TWO

The University

Oxford, 2000

The day Nazperi Nalbantoğlu, fresh out of school, arrived at Oxford she was accompanied by her anxious father and her even more anxious mother. Her parents' plan was to spend the day together; after seeing their daughter settled in to her new life, they would board the train back to London in the evening. From there, the couple would take the plane to Istanbul, where they had spent most of their thirty-two years of firmly unstable married life, like an old staircase that, though rickety, still stood against the ravages of time. But things proved to be more complicated than expected. Twice Selma broke down sobbing, her mood swinging through cycles of perturbation, self-pity and pride. Every now and then, the woman grabbed an end of her headscarf, seemingly to wipe her face but in reality to dab away a tear. A part of her was delighted with her daughter's achievement. No one in their extended family had won a place at any foreign university, let alone Oxford. The possibility had not even entered their minds, so far removed was 'here' from 'there'.

Another part of her, however, found it impossible to accept that her youngest child, a girl at that, would be living a continent away, alone, in a place where everything was foreign. It hurt her profoundly that Peri had applied without her knowledge or approval. She sensed her husband's shadow behind the fait accompli. The two of them had informed her only when everything was done, and all she could do was murmur a feeble objection, lest she risk alienating her daughter, probably for the rest of their lives. She wished they had a relative, or a relative of a relative, anyone – as long as they were Muslim and Sunni and Turkish-speaking and God-fearing and Quran-reading and easy to reach by phone – in this strange city to whom she could entrust Peri. But she knew of no one who fitted the description.

Mensur, meanwhile, though he yearned to see his daughter excel academically, was no less despairing about letting go of her. Outwardly composed, he spoke in a halting, disconnected way, in the same tone he might have used to talk about a distant earthquake: accepting but with an undercurrent of pain. Peri understood, and to some extent shared, her parents' uneasiness. Never before had they been separated; never before had she been away from her family, home and homeland.

'See, how beautiful it is here,' Peri said. Undeterred by the pressure building in her chest, she could not help feeling excited, ready for her life to soar.

The sun sent out shafts of warm light from between the clouds, giving the feeling that summer had returned despite the occasional flicks of chilly autumn wind. With its cobbled streets, crenellated towers, cloistered arcades, bay windows and carved porticoes, Oxford resembled a place out of a children's picture book. Everything in the compass of their gaze was redolent of history – so much so that even the coffee shops and department stores felt part of this centuries-old endowment. In Istanbul, ancient though the city was, the past was treated like a visitor who had overstayed his welcome. Here in Oxford, it was clearly the guest of honour.

The Nalbantoğlus spent the rest of the morning sauntering, admiring the gardens tucked within the time-worn, ivy-clad walls of the quadrangles, their feet crunching tentatively on the gravel, unsure of whether they were allowed to enter these spaces and with no one to ask. Some parts of the town felt so empty that the flaking limestone walls lining the ancient lanes seemed to ache for human attention.

Tired and famished, they spotted a pub on Alfred Street, a place with low ceilings, creaking wooden floorboards and clamorous customers. Timidly, they settled at a snug table by the window. Everyone was drinking beer in glasses fit for the hands of giants. When the waitress, a girl with a piercing in her bottom lip, arrived, Mensur ordered fish and chips for each and a bottle of white wine.

'Imagine, this place goes back centuries . . .' said Mensur. He stared at the oak panelling as if it contained a code he might decipher if he tried hard and long enough.

Selma nodded – notwithstanding, she had noticed other things when she looked around: students guzzling beer in a corner, a woman in a skimpy dress that might as well have been a camisole, a tattooed man fondling his girlfriend, whose cleavage was deeper than the rift between Selma and her husband . . . How would she be able to leave Peri all alone amidst these people? Westerners might be advanced in science and education and technology, but what about their morals? It irked her that she had to keep her thoughts to herself, lest she annoyed her husband and daughter. Her mouth was turned down, a sign of the caustic remarks that she held back. It was unfair to have to be the principled one, the boring parent all the time.

Unaware of his wife's concerns, but not entirely naive about her views, Mensur said, 'We are proud of you, Pericim.'

It was the second time Peri was hearing this from her father and she enjoyed it as much as the first time. With their modest resources, he had invested well beyond their means in her education. She was determined not to fail him.

'We must toast,' Mensur declared as their wine arrived. 'To our brilliant daughter!'

Selma's face closed. 'You know Allah prevents me from joining you.'

'That's fine,' Mensur said. 'I'll be the sinner. When I die, send me a pass from heaven.'

'If only it were that simple,' said Selma. 'You'll have to work your way up in Allah's eyes.'

Mensur chewed the inside of his mouth for a moment. Listening to his wife preach her smartly arranged words had the same effect on him as seeing a row of neatly standing dominoes. He couldn't suppress the urge to tip one over. 'You speak as if you know first-hand what Allah thinks. Did you enter His mind? How do you know what He sees?'

'Because He tells us in the Quran, if you only cared to read,' Selma said.

'Oh, please, can't you two manage not to quarrel for a day?' Peri pleaded. To change the subject and ease the tension, she added, 'So I'll be back in Istanbul soon for the wedding.'

Hakan was about to get married. Even though Umut – who had

retreated to a town by the Mediterranean after being released from prison – was still unmarried, Hakan had refused to wait his turn, defying the family order. At first, everyone had suspected that behind his impatience there might be an embarrassing explanation, a bump too obvious for the bride to hide, but it had then become clear that the only reason for the rush was the groom-to-be's personality.

They finished the rest of their lunch, mostly in silence.

As they waited for the bill, Selma took her daughter's hand and said, 'Stay away from those who are no good.'

'Yes, I know, Mother.'

'Education is important, but there's something far more important for a girl, you understand? If you lose that, no diploma will redeem you. Boys have nothing to lose. Girls need to be extra careful.'

'Right . . .' Peri said, as she averted her gaze.

Virginity, that shibboleth that could only be alluded to and not spelled out. It loomed large in many a conversation between mothers and daughters, aunts and nieces. A subject to be tiptoed around, like a moody sleeper in the middle of the room no one dared to disturb.

'I trust my daughter,' chimed in Mensur, who had ended up drinking most of the wine on his own and now sounded just a bit tipsy.

'I do too,' Selma said. 'It's the others I don't.'

'That's a stupid thing to say,' Mensur said. 'If you trust her, why care so much about other people?'

Selma's lips puckered into a grimace. 'A man who drinks himself to death every day can't call anyone but himself stupid.'

Listening to her parents cross swords again, their battles never won, the tally never settled, all Peri could do was stare out of the window into the heart of the town that was to become, at least for the next three years, her university, her sanctuary, her home. Apprehension churned in her stomach. Dark thoughts circled in her mind. She recalled the expensive saffron – not the fake spice but the real deal – sold inside delicate glass tubes in Istanbul's bazaars. Such was her optimism – limited, confined, perishable.

The Map

Oxford, 2000

'Hello!' a voice called out from behind them, seconds after they had reached the front lodge of her college, where a second-year student appointed to show them around was waiting.

Turning back they saw a tall, young woman with the bearing of the Sultana she might have been in another time, another land. She wore a skirt as pink as the rosewater meringue Peri had treasured as a child. Her black hair fell in loose curls down her back, which she held perfectly straight. She had painted her lips a glossy carmine and rouged her cheeks. But it was her eyes, dark and set wide apart, outlined with a purple pencil and shaded with the brightest turquoise, that were the most striking. Her makeup was like the flag of an unstable country, declaring not only its independence but also its unpredictability.

'Welcome to Oxford,' she said with a grin, as she extended a manicured hand. 'My name is Shirin.' She pronounced it with as many vowels as she could possibly pack in: Shee-reen.

Although with her large, arched nose and her noticeable chin she was not, in any conventional sense, pretty, she had such a powerful aura that she could be perceived as beautiful. So taken was Peri by her appearance that she smiled broadly as she stepped forward towards the girl.

'Hi, I'm Peri – and these are my parents.' She thought to herself, *We'll pretend to be a normal family for a day.*

'Wonderful to meet you all. I hear you're Turkish. I was born in Tehran, but I've never been back,' Shirin said with a casual wave of her hand, as if Iran were just around the corner, waiting. 'I guess that's why they asked me to show you round. They like to lump us all together. Are you ready for a tour?'

Peri and Mensur nodded enthusiastically. Selma looked disapprovingly at the girl's short skirt, high heels, heavy makeup. To her eyes, Shirin didn't look like a student. And she surely didn't look Iranian.

'What kind of a student is she?' Selma murmured in Turkish.

Peri, seized by an irrational concern that the British-Iranian girl might actually understand Turkish, hissed back, 'Mother, please.'

'Let's go!' Shirin exclaimed. 'Normally, we'd start with our own college and then see the rest of the town. But I never do anything in the right order. It's against my nature. So follow me, folks!'

Thus saying, Shirin launched into a long discourse on the history of Oxford. As she chattered, she guided them deeper into the crooked lanes of the old city. Lively and good-humoured, she talked so fast that her words gushed out in a wild torrent, which the Nalbantoğlus found hard to catch – especially Selma, who saw no resemblance between the old-fashioned grammar-based English she had learned years ago in school – and forgotten with the speed of lightning afterwards – and the gibberish that she heard right now. To help her out, Peri assumed the role of translator – if rather loosely. She softened, rephrased and, where need be, censured anything that might irritate her mother.

Meanwhile, Shirin explained that all the colleges in Oxford were autonomous, self-governing foundations that controlled their own affairs – a fact Mensur found confusing. 'But there has to be President, authority above everything,' he objected in his broken English, and glanced around, as though he feared the town might descend into anarchy.

'I have to disagree,' Shirin said. 'In my experience, authority is like garlic: the more you use it, the heavier the smell.'

Mensur, who had spent most of his adult life longing for a central authority, strong and solid and secular enough to stop the rise of religious fundamentalism, looked up in alarm. Authority for him was a binder – the mortar that held the pieces of a society together in perfect order. Without that, the bricks would fall down, the structure would come apart.

'Surely not all authority bad,' Mensur insisted. 'What about women's rights, what do you say when a strong leader defends women?'

'Well, I'd say, thank you very much, I can defend my own rights just fine. We don't need a higher authority to do that for us!'

As she said these words, Shirin glanced at Selma, taking in her headscarf and long, shapeless coat. Peri, ever sensitive to other people's negativity, realized that her mother's dislike of Shirin was mutual. The British-Iranian girl seemed to harbour a disdain for women who covered their heads – a disdain she felt no need to hide.

'Come, Mother.' Peri gently pulled Selma by the arm – the one with the burn scar, a souvenir from a carpet-washing day years before. The two of them fell behind.

On the steps up to the entrance of the Ashmolean Museum, mother and daughter spotted a couple kissing passionately. Peri blushed as if she herself had been caught in the boy's arms. Out of the corner of her eye she saw Selma scowl. This was the same woman who had taught her absolutely nothing about sex. She still remembered when, as a child one day in the hamam, she had asked about the thing she saw dangling in between a boy's legs. Selma's response had been to storm off towards the boy's mother and launch a tirade that did not quite carry over the noise of the running water from the marble fountains, but, judging by her gestures, must have been harsh. Peri had felt mortified, and guilty too, for being curious about something she clearly had no right to be curious about.

Over time curiosity had yet again got the better of her. She once asked her mother if she had ever considered having an abortion, given the long interval in years between Selma's first pregnancies and her very last. Her parents might have considered that their family was already complete and chosen not to have her.

'Well, it was embarrassing. I was forty-four when you came along,' Selma had said.

'Why didn't you terminate it?' Peri had pushed.

'It was illegal back then. Although there would have been ways. But of course it would have been a sin, surely. I said to myself, sin in the eyes of Allah is worse than shame in the eyes of neighbours, so I carried on.'

Peri had never told her mother how she loathed this reply. She had expected her to say something gentler. *I never thought of ending the pregnancy; I already loved you so much* or *I had arranged to see a woman who would help, but the night before I saw you in my dream, a little girl with green eyes* . . . But, as things stood, Peri concluded she was a sandwich baby born between Sin and Shame: two layers of doom.

Together they visited the college where Peri would be in residence. Her accommodation was in a front quad, a magnificent Grade I-listed building that, to the Nalbantoğlus' eyes, looked less like a dormitory than a museum. As impressed as Peri was with the high ceilings, oak panelling and the timelessness of tradition, she was also silently disappointed by the size and simplicity of her room. A sink, a wardrobe, a bureau, a bed, a desk, an armchair and a cupboard. That was it – a surprising contrast with the spectacular exterior – but then there was the exhilarating freedom of living alone for the first time.

As they went down the narrow staircase, moving aside for other students to pass, Shirin turned and winked at Peri. 'If you want to make friends fast, leave your door open. That way, people will pop in and say "Hello". A closed door means, "Back off, I don't want to be disturbed."'

'Really?' Peri whispered, not wanting her parents to catch any of this. 'But how can I study with interruptions?'

Shirin chuckled as if the mention of studying were the funniest thing she had heard that day.

During the rest of the afternoon, Shirin showed the Nalbantoğlus the circular Radcliffe Camera, the Sheldonian Theatre, and the Museum of the History of Science with its early scientific instruments. Their next stop was the Bodleian Library. Shirin explained that 'the Bod', as students and dons called it, had over a hundred miles of underground shelves. At one time you had to take an oath not to steal the books. In some college libraries there were still chained books, as in medieval times.

Mensur pointed at an inscription on the coat of arms on the wall. 'What does that mean?'

'*Dominus illuminatio mea*, "The Lord is my Light"', said Shirin, pointing her eyes to the skies, either inadvertently or mockingly, it was hard to tell.

Recognizing the gesture more than the words, Selma elbowed her husband in the ribs. 'See, if a Turkish university had a similar sign on its wall about Allah, you'd be riled. You'd regard it as a retreat for fanatics! A terror camp for suicide bombers! But here you have no problem with religious inscriptions!'

'That's because in Europe religion has a different nature,' said Mensur dismissively.

'How so?' said Selma. 'Religion is religion.'

'Not true. Some are more . . . *religious*,' said Mensur, sounding, even to his own ears, like a surly child. 'Look, in Europe religion doesn't try to dominate everything and everyone. Science is free!'

'Science bloomed in al-Andalus,' said Selma. 'Üzümbaz Efendi explained it to us, Allah bless his soul. Who do you think invented algebra? Or the windmill? Or the toothbrush? Coffee? Vaccination? Shampoo? Muslims! When Europeans were barely washing themselves, we had gorgeous hamams scented with rosewater. We are the ones who taught hygiene to Westerners, now they are selling it back to us.'

'Who cares who invented what a thousand years ago?' said Mensur. 'Ask yourself, woman, who has made the most of science!'

'Dad, Mum, enough,' muttered Peri, mortified that a stranger was witnessing her parents' confrontation.

Shirin, whether because she had picked up the tension and wanted to fan the flames a little, or out of sheer coincidence, went on to explain that many of the oldest colleges in Oxford had evolved from Christian monastic foundations. Peri translated none of this into Turkish for her mother.

As they climbed the stairs in the Bodleian Library, Peri stopped to read the names of the patrons inscribed on a brass board. Since time immemorial, without interruption, the wealthy and the mighty had supported this magnificent collection. It saddened her to think that had this library been built in Istanbul, say around the same period, it would have been razed to the ground, probably more than once, and rebuilt on each occasion with a different architectural style and a new name depending on the dominant ideology of the times – until one day, it would have been converted to military barracks and then, most probably, to a shopping centre. She heaved a sigh.

'Are you okay?' asked Shirin, standing right beside her.

'Yeah, I just wish we had such lovely libraries in Turkey,' said Peri.

'Keep wishing, sister. Europe has been printing books since the Middle Ages. I don't know when exactly the Middle East started doing it, but I know, for a fact, we are all doomed – I mean, Iran, Turkey, Egypt. Okay, I get it, rich cultures, lovely music, good food. But books are knowledge, knowledge is power, right? How can the gap ever be closed?'

'Two hundred and eighty-seven years,' Peri said quietly.

'What?'

'Sorry,' Peri said. 'Gutenberg's press dates from around 1440. A few Arabic books were published in Italy in the 1500s. But it was with Müteferrika in the Ottoman Empire that Muslims started printing – under heavy censorship, of course. Anyway, that adds up to a difference of about two hundred and eighty-seven years.'

'You're a weird one,' said Shirin. 'You'll definitely survive at Oxford.'

'You think so?' Peri smiled.

Feeling thirsty, they stopped for coffee in the Covered Market nearby. While Peri and Shirin looked for a table, Mensur and Selma went in search of lavatories, walking apart from each other.

'Speaking of gaps, there seems to be quite a large one between your parents,' said Shirin suddenly. 'Your father's kind of leftist, right? And your mum –'

'I wouldn't call him a leftist, but yes, he's a secularist . . . Kemalist, if you know anything about Turkey. And Mum is –' Just like Shirin, she, too, left the sentence hanging in the air. Slowly, Peri picked an invisible piece of lint off her sleeve and rolled it between her fingers. She had never met anyone so blunt and intrusive, but she wasn't half as offended as she felt she ought to be. Still, she changed the subject. 'So you were born in Tehran?'

'Yes, the oldest of four girls. Poor Baba! He desperately wanted a boy, but Sheitan sneaked into his bed. Baba smoked like a chimney, ate like a bird. *It's killing me* – that's what he used to say. He meant the regime, not us. Finally, he found a way out. Madarjan didn't want to leave but, out of love, she agreed. We were spirited to Switzerland. Have you ever been there?'

'No, this is the first time I've left Istanbul,' said Peri.

'Well, Switzerland's nice, far too nice, bathing-in-melted-caramel-nice, if you know what I mean. Four years of my life in sleepy Sion. Believe it or not, I once overheard a girl complain to her father that the supermarket didn't stock her favourite variety of berries! I mean, hello, the world is boiling, the Berlin Wall has fallen, and you're talking about berries? Though I was a child, even I could feel something exciting was in the air. I love it when walls come down. Okay, life was good in Switzerland, but a bit too slow for my taste. Ever since then I've been rushing to make up for lost time.'

Peri listened, her face changing from curiosity to delight.

'Afterwards we went to Portugal. I liked it there, but not Baba. Still smoking, complaining. Two years in Lisbon, just when I've learned enough Portuguese, bam! Pack up, kids, we're going to England, the Queen's waiting! I was fourteen for God's sake. When you're fourteen, you should be dealing with your own drama, not your family's. Anyway, the year we arrived Baba died. Doctor said his lungs had turned to coal. Don't you think it's kind of bizarre for a physician to use a metaphor – does he think he's a poet or what?' Shirin drummed her fingers on the table and examined her manicure. 'England was Baba's dream, not mine, and here I am as British as a treacle tart but as out of place as a stuffed date cake!'

'Where do you see as home?' said Peri.

'Home?' Shirin sucked her teeth in disapproval. 'I'll tell you a universal rule: home is where one's granny is.'

Peri smiled. 'That's nice. Where is yours?'

'Six feet under. She died five years ago. She adored me, her first grandchild. Neighbours said till her last breath she hoped we'd come back. That's home for me! Buried with Mamani in Tehran. So, technically speaking, I am home-less.'

'I'm . . . uhh . . . sorry,' said Peri, sensing in her own hesitation an inability to keep up with extroverts, of whom Shirin was clearly one.

'You know what they call the cemetery over there? Zahra's Paradise. Pretty cool, eh? All graveyards should be named "paradise". No need to trouble the Almighty with the Day of Judgement and boiling cauldrons and hair-thin bridges and whatnot. You die, you go to paradise, end of story!'

Peri stood still, charmed and puzzled in equal degree. It seemed to her that her new friend, though of the same age, had lived twice as much as she and seen more of the world than her entire family had in total. Peri had never heard anyone speak like this about the afterlife. Not even her father, who frequently expressed his distaste for all matters of faith.

In a little while Mensur and Selma returned. By now, the couple had finally found something to agree upon: Shirin. For different reasons, yet with equal intensity, the girl had rubbed each of them up the wrong way. Separately, they were both planning to tell their daughter to stay away from the British-Iranian girl. Surely, she would be a bad influence.

About an hour later, having walked in dizzying circles, they finished their tour in front of the Oxford Union. Before parting, Shirin gave Peri a hug as if they were long lost friends. Her perfume was heady and musky, and so overpowering that for a second Peri felt disorientated, her head swimming.

Shirin said that the English, though polite and well mannered, could be too reserved and too cautious for a lonely foreigner in a new country, and Peri would be better off hanging around with other international students or those from a mixed cultural background – like herself.

'So, I guess I'll see you around?' Peri said.

She meant it. For, even as she was slightly intimidated by Shirin's personality, she could not help but be drawn to her endless chatter, self-assurance and audaciousness. One always yearned for what one lacked.

'See me around?' echoed Shirin, as she kissed Selma and Mensur on both cheeks, even though they held themselves rigidly. 'You bet you will! Forgot to tell you, we're in the same quad.'

'Really?' asked Peri.

'Yup.' Shirin beamed from ear to ear. 'Actually, you're just opposite me. And if you dare to make noise, I'll raise hell . . . just kidding. Turkey and Iran, neighbours, just like on the map. We'll be great friends. Or great enemies. Maybe we'll start a war. World War Three! Because you know that's what's going to happen, right? There'll be another fucking war because the Middle East is totally screwed up – oops, excuse my bloody language.'

Then, turning to Peri's startled parents, and mispronouncing their surname, Shirin announced, 'Mr and Mrs Nawbawmtlooo, don't you worry about your daughter. She's in good hands. From now on, my job will be to keep an eye on her.'

The Silence

Oxford, 2000

After her parents left for the train station, with a sickening sense of loneliness Peri returned to her staircase in the front quad of her college. Thrilling though it was to be free of their quarrels and bickering for once, at least they were familiar to her, and in their absence she was left with an unsettling feeling, as if a carpet had been pulled out from underneath her feet and she was forced to walk on rough terrain. Now that the pride and the excitement of the day had dissipated, she was overcome by a profound disquiet. She realized she was not as ready for the next big stage in her life as she had liked to imagine. Holding herself tense against the wind, so unlike the salty breeze of a late afternoon in Istanbul, she took a breath and slowly let it out. Her nose searched for habitual smells – deep-fried mussels, roasted chestnuts, sesame bagels, grilled sheep intestines blended with the aromas of Judas trees in spring, daphne plants in winter. Like a demented sorceress who had forgotten the formulas of her potions, Istanbul mixed unlikely aromas in the same cauldron: rancid and sweet; stomach-churning and mouth-watering. Here in Oxford, however, the resinous odour hanging in the air seemed unwavering, reliable.

She climbed the dark wooden staircase to her room, where she opened her suitcases, took out her clothes and hung them in the wardrobe, organized her drawers, arranged family photos on the desk. She placed her God-diary beside her bed.

She had brought along a few of her favourite books, some in Turkish, others in English – Sadegh Hedayet's *The Blind Owl*, Alice Munro's *The Love of a Good Woman*, Zadie Smith's *White Teeth*, Michael Cunningham's *The Hours*, Arundhati Roy's *The God of Small Things*, Oğuz

Atay's *Tutunamayanlar,* Italo Calvino's *Invisible Cities,* Kazuo Ishiguro's *An Artist of the Floating World.*

'Why do you always read Western writers?' the only boyfriend she had ever had once asked.

She was in school back then, in her final year, and he, three years older, was already at university, studying sociology. The hidden accusation in the question had caught her by surprise. In truth, Peri read both local and world literature. Her tendency was to lose herself in any book that captured her imagination and awakened her curiosity, regardless of the nationality of its author. Yet, compared with her boyfriend, whose shelves displayed Turkish titles – and a few Russian and South American novels, which he said were *uncorrupted* since they were not written through *the distorted lens of cultural imperialism* – her reading list was too European.

'When I look at you, I see a typical Oriental intellectual in the making,' he had said. 'In love with Europe, at odds with her roots.'

Why roots were rated so highly compared with branches or leaves, Peri had never understood. Trees had multiple shoots and filaments extending in every direction, under and above the ancient soils of the earth. If even roots refused to stay put, why expect the impossible from human beings?

Even so, besotted with him, Peri had felt a stir of guilt. Although she was a more avid reader than he, it seemed as if she had wasted her time roaming the side streets and back lanes in the City of Books, tempted by its flairs and flavours. She had tried, for a while, not to spend any money on Western titles, but her new resolution had quickly collapsed. A good book was a good book and that was all that mattered. Besides, for the life of her, she could not comprehend the reactionary attitude to reading. In many parts of the world you were what you said and what you did and, also, what you read; in Turkey, as in all countries haunted by questions of identity, you were, primarily, what you rejected. It seemed that the more people went on about an author, the less likely it was that they had read their books.

Eventually, their relationship, undermined less by their diverging taste in literature than their differing attitudes to intimacy, had come to an end. There was a type of boyfriend in the Middle East who became irritated if you rejected his sexual advances; yet, at the same time, the moment you began to respond passionately to his desires, you lost your value in his eyes. Doomed if you said 'no', doomed if you said 'yes'. Either way, it was a no-win situation.

Once she finished arranging her room, Peri opened the leaded window looking out on to the pristine lawns of the college garden. A sense of emptiness hovered in the air, blurring the outlines of every perceptible shape in the distance. Staring at the shadows of the trees nearby, she shuddered as if a spirit or a jinni, pitying her loneliness, had brushed up against her ever so softly. Could it be the baby in the mist? She did not think so. She had not seen him in a long while. An English ghost, probably. Oxford seemed like a place where ghosts, uninhibited and not necessarily frightening, could move around at will.

The first thing that struck Peri about Oxford was the silence. That was, and would remain for months to come, the one peculiarity she found hard to get used to – the absence of noise. Istanbul was unashamedly boisterous, day and night; even when one pulled down the shutters, drew the curtains, put in earplugs and pulled the blanket up to one's chin, the din, barely weakened, would penetrate through the walls, seeping into one's sleep. The last cries of street-hawkers, the rumbling of late-night lorries, the sirens of ambulances, the boats on the Bosphorus, the prayers and the profanities, both of which multiplied after midnight, would hang in the wind, refusing to disperse. Istanbul, just like nature, abhorred a vacuum.

As she sat on her bed, Peri felt a knot in her chest. Her parents' anxiety seemed to have caught up with her, though for reasons of her own. She felt like an impostor. She feared she might never succeed here, among students who were surely far better educated and more articulate than she. The English she had learned at school, and refined through long nights of reading on her own, might not be enough to keep up with some of the advanced courses in the Philosophy, Politics and Economics degree. Though she took pains to hide it as best as she could, Peri's fear of failure was profound. Her throat constricted. She was surprised at how fast her eyes welled up. The tears, when they came, felt warm and familiar and somehow not sad at all.

A knock jolted her back to the moment. Without waiting for an answer, the door was pushed open and Shirin walked in.

'Hello, neighbour!'

Peri sniffed involuntarily and smiled as she tried to compose herself.

'Told you to leave your door open.' Shirin stood in the middle of the room, arms akimbo. 'Is it a boy?'

'What?'

'You're crying. Did you break up with your boyfriend?'

'No.'

'Good, you should never shed tears over a man. What then? You broke up with a girlfriend?'

'What? No!'

'O-kay, easy,' Shirin said, throwing up her hands in mock apology. 'I can see you're as straight as dried spaghetti. I'm more the fresh pasta type.'

Peri's eyes widened.

'If those tears are not for a sweetheart, you must be homesick,' Shirin said with a tilt of her head. 'Lucky you!'

'Lucky me?'

'Yup, if you are homesick, it means you have a home somewhere.'

Shirin planted herself down on the armchair by the desk and produced out of her pocket a bottle of nail varnish – a red so bright that several creatures might have been slaughtered in the making of it. 'Do you mind?'

Once again without waiting for a reply, she took off her slippers and began to paint her toenails. A pungent chemical smell infused the air.

'So now that your parents have left, can I ask you a few things?' Shirin said. 'You religious?'

'Me? Not really . . .' said Peri painstakingly, as though revealing something it had taken her a while to understand. 'But I care about God.'

'Hmm. I need more than that. Like, for instance, do you eat pork?'

'No!'

'What about wine, do you drink?'

'Yeah, sometimes, with my father.'

'Aha, I thought so. You are a half and half.'

Peri frowned. 'What do you mean?'

But Shirin was not listening any more. She seemed to be looking for something else in her pockets. Unable to find it, she screwed up her nose, stood and headed to her room across the staircase, wobbling on the bottom of her heels so as not to smudge her freshly painted toenails.

Curious and slightly irritated, Peri followed Shirin into her room, its door wide open. She stopped dead, struck by the mess she saw. Makeup kits, face creams, lace gloves, perfume bottles, half-eaten apples, sweet wrappers, empty crisp bags, crumpled Coke cans, books and pages torn from magazines were scattered around. Some of these pages had been stuck up on the walls, next to a poster of Coldplay and a black-and-white picture of a dark-haired sultry-looking woman that read *Forough Farrokhzad*. From the other end of the room a huge poster of Nietzsche, with his copious moustache, glared at her. Next to it was what looked like an enlarged, colourful photocopy of a Persian miniature, its frame glittering gold. Underneath it stood Shirin, fumbling inside her backpack.

'What did you mean by that?' Peri repeated.

'Half Muslim, half modern. Can't stand the sight of pork, but content with wine – or vodka or tequila . . . you get the drift. Loosey-goosey when it comes to Ramadan, fasts here and there, yet eats on days in between. Won't abandon religion, for you never know if there's life after death, better to play it safe. Doesn't want to let go of freedoms either. A bit of this, a bit of that. The great fusion of the times: *Muslimus modernus*.'

'Hey, I feel offended,' said Peri.

'Of course you do. A *Muslimus modernus* always does.' With that Shirin pulled out from her backpack a pellucid bottle – topcoat for her nails – and exclaimed, 'Found it!'

Peri glared at Shirin. 'If I am who you say I am, what about you?'

'Oh, sister, I'm just a wanderer,' said Shirin. 'I don't belong anywhere.'

As she applied the topcoat to her toenails, Shirin went on to inveigh against bigots and hypocrites and conformists and what she called ignoramuses. Like a river her ideas gushed, words of liquid, seething, splashing, searching. She said people who believed or disbelieved with a sincere passion were equally worthy of respect in her eyes. What she couldn't tolerate were those who didn't think. The copycats, she called them.

In the hush that followed, Peri was pulled in two opposite directions. A part of her disliked Shirin's argumentative swagger. She could sense the girl's anger, but at what exactly – her motherland, her father, her religion, the mullahs in Iran – she could not be certain. Another part enjoyed listening to Shirin, catching in her soliloquy echoes of her own father's voice. Either way, this was not the kind of conversation she had expected to find herself engaged in on her first evening away from home. She wanted to chat about the classes, the dons, where to go for coffee, where to get the best sandwiches, the particulars of everyday life in Oxford.

It began to rain; a soft, steady patter filled the room. The sound must have had a soothing effect on Shirin, for when she spoke again, her voice, though still suffused with emotion, was calmer. 'Sorry to bombard you with my personal crap. It's up to you what you choose to believe in, none of my business. Don't know why I got carried away like that.'

'It's okay,' Peri said. 'I'm just glad my mother isn't here.'

Shirin laughed – an airy giggle, almost childish.

'Tell me about the other students,' said Peri. 'Are they all very smart?'

'You think everyone in Oxford is fucking Einstein?' Shirin snorted on the last word. 'Look, students are like milkshakes, they come in flavours. There are about six kinds of students around here, I'd say.'

First, there were the social-environmental-justice types. Talkative, serious, peppery, immersed in campaigns like saving rainforests in Borneo or persecuted Buddhist monks in Nepal, Shirin explained. They were easy to identify, with their baggy sweaters, beaded necklaces, bad haircuts, turned-up jeans, purposeful expressions, and ballpoint pens and pads – always equipped to collect signatures. They organized night-time vigils, and during the day put up flyers everywhere, and got themselves into one heated debate after another. They loved making you feel guilty for not being part of something larger and more meaningful than your petty life.

Second, there were the Eurotrash. They came from wealthy European families who somehow all seemed to know one another; over the holidays they went skiing at the same resorts and came back flaunting their tans and parading their snaps. Practising a sophisticated form of endogamy, they dated only among themselves. At lengthy breakfasts they consumed loaves of bread with wads of butter and still managed to stay slim. They liked to complain that the croissants were stale and the cappuccinos were fake, and they never stopped talking about the weather.

Third, the public school crowd. Selective socializers. They established cliques at warp speed, choosing their friends mostly on the basis of the schools they had been to. With abundant energy and confidence, they launched into a series of extra-curricular activities. They rowed, canoed, fenced, acted; played cricket, golf, tennis, rugby, water polo and did t'ai chi or karate in their spare time. All that action must have left them thirsty, for they gathered in 'drinking societies' where they made the most of dressing in black tie and drowning in alcohol, revelling in the exclusion of those who lacked the social background to become members of their clubs. One had to be nominated to join, and any prospective candidate could be blackballed.

Then there were the international students: Indians, Chinese, Arabs, Indonesians, Africans . . . Most of them fell into two subgroups. Those who, like magnets drawn to each other, cast about for the familiar. They dined, studied, smoked and hung around in clusters where they could speak their mother tongue. And then there were those who did the exact opposite, aiming to distance themselves as far as possible from their compatriots. The latter had the most volatile accents, which changed dramatically in their attempts to sound more British or, at times, American.

Fifth, there were the nerds. Serious, studious, intelligent, inquisitive, worthy of respect but impossible to befriend. In mathematics, physics, philosophy, they sprang up like wild mushrooms, preferring their quiet, shady corners to open sunlight. They studied their subjects with a passion that verged on neurosis. You could spot them even amidst a crowd, walking briskly from the library to their tutorials, eager to discuss issues with dons in the cloisters, but otherwise perfectly content in their solitude; in truth, they were more comfortable in the company of their books than next to their peers in the college bar or the Junior Common Room.

As she kept listening to Shirin, Peri felt an excitement laced with anxiety. She was both ready and afraid to discover this new world into which she needed the strength to walk. 'How do you know all this?'

Shirin laughed. 'Because I've dated guys – and girls – of each group.'

'You dated . . . girls?'

'Sure. I can love a woman, I can love a man. I don't give a damn about labels.'

'Oh,' Peri said uneasily. 'Well . . . uhm, what about the sixth category?'

'Aha!' Shirin said, her dark eyes lit with flecks of amber. 'Those are the ones who arrive here as one thing and then become something else altogether. They thrive. Ugly ducklings transformed into swans; pumpkins into coaches; Cinderellas into heroines. For some students Oxford works like a magic wand, it touches you and ta-da! You change from frog to prince.'

Peri shook her head. 'How so?'

'Well, it happens in several ways, but usually it's thanks to someone . . . a tutor, probably. Someone who challenges you and makes you see yourself for who you are.'

Something in Shirin's tone intrigued Peri. 'Is that your experience?'

'Yep, you got it! I'm a type six,' Shirin said. 'You wouldn't have recognized me a year ago. I was a ball of anger.'

'And what happened?'

'Professor Azur happened!' said Shirin. 'He opened my eyes. He taught me to look within. I'm a calmer person today.'

If this was her calmer self, Peri didn't want to know what the other Shirin might have been like. She asked, 'Who's Professor Azur?'

'You don't know?' Shirin smacked her lips as if she had something sweet on her tongue. 'Azur is a walking legend around here!'

'What does he teach?'

A smile flashed across Shirin's face. 'God.'

'Really?'

'Really,' said Shirin. 'He's a bit like God himself. He's published nine books, and he's always on a panel or conference. Quite a celebrity, I must tell you. Last year *Time* magazine named him among the one hundred most influential people in the world.'

Outside a wind was picking up, slamming a window open and shut somewhere in the building.

'It was fucking hard to be his student!' Shirin continued. 'Hell, he made us read so much! It was insane! All kinds of weird stuff: poetry, philosophy, history. I mean I like these things, don't get me wrong, why would I be in the humanities if I didn't like them, huh? But he'd find these texts that no one knew a jot about and ask us to debate them. Still, it was fun. By the time I finished I was not the same person.'

Once Shirin started talking, Peri noticed, she kept going on and on, like a car with bad brakes, unable to slow down, much less stop, unless by an outside force. Now she was saying, 'You should consider taking his seminar as an option. Well . . . if Azur allows you to, that is. Hard to convince him. Easier to make a camel jump a ditch.'

Peri smiled. 'We have the same proverb in Turkey. Why is it so hard to get on to his seminar?'

'You need to be eligible. That means you need to discuss it with your academic adviser, et cetera. If he approves, you go to Azur. That's a bit tricky. The man is hard to please. He asks you the weirdest questions.'

'About?'

'God . . . good and evil . . . science and faith . . . existence and mortality . . .' Shirin frowned, searching for more words. 'Everything. It's like an academic audition. I've never understood what he's looking for. In the end, he chooses only a handful.'

'It seems like you've made the cut twice,' said Peri, feeling something like envy creeping into her throat, for no reason at all.

'That's right,' Shirin said. The pride in her voice was impossible to miss.

A brief silence ensued.

'I still see him for advice at least once a week,' Shirin babbled, unable to keep quiet for more than a minute. 'Actually, I'm a bit potty about him. He's ridiculously handsome. No, not just handsome. He's hot!'

Peri sat tight on her chair, not knowing how to respond. On the surface, they both came from Muslim countries, similar cultures. Yet how different from her was this girl, who seemed in every respect perfectly at ease with herself and her sexuality.

'Wow, it sounds like you have a crush on your professor,' Peri said. She couldn't help adding, 'Isn't that wrong?'

Shirin tossed back her head and gave out a hoot of laughter. 'Oh, it's very, very wrong. Detain me at Her Majesty's pleasure!'

Embarrassed by her naivety, Peri shrugged. 'Well . . . the seminar sounds cool. But I need to focus on other things.'

'You mean you're too busy being a mortal,' Shirin said, fixing her sharp stare on her new friend. 'God will have to wait.'

Though it was meant to be a joke, Shirin's remark was so unexpected and forceful, it perturbed Peri. She glanced away towards the window and the slate-grey sky from which the last light was fading. The wind, the rain, the banging of a window shutter, the winter chill in the air, even though it was only the beginning of autumn – she would remember it all for many years to come. It was a defining moment in her life, though she would not understand this until it was gone.

The Pastime

Istanbul, 2016

The hors d'œuvres vanished amidst effusive compliments to the chef. Smoked aubergine purée, Circassian chicken with garlic and walnuts, artichoke with broad beans, stuffed courgette flowers, grilled octopus in lemon butter sauce. When she saw the latter, a shadow passed across Peri's face. She had long stopped regarding octopus as food and pushed it away with her fork, gently.

Having thrashed out the intrigues of the football world, the guests turned their conversation to the next favourite topic of Istanbul dinners: politics. And the inevitable question asked each time more than three Turks came together was asked inevitably: 'Where are we heading?'

Peri thought there was something hypocritical about the capitalist class in this part of the world. On the outside they were professedly conservative and for the status quo; inside they seethed with fury and frustration. With little crossover between their public and private personas, the elite – especially the business elite – spent a lifetime looking over their shoulder. Publicly they kept their thoughts to themselves, she could see, refraining from talking politics – unless they had to, in which case they made a few innocuous comments, no more. They sauntered through society with an air of indifference, like customers strolling past shops without apparent interest. When they came across something that bothered them, which happened often, they closed their eyes, plugged their ears, sealed their mouths. Within the walls of their homes, however, the mask of insouciance fell away; and they went through a metamorphosis. Their apathy turned into brazenness, their mumbling into shouts, their discretion into rashness. At private parties, the Istanbul bourgeoisie could hardly rant enough about politics, as if to compensate for their silence outside.

At Oxford, Peri had studied how the bourgeoisie in the West, with its liberal, individualistic values and opposition to feudalism, had played a progressive role in the course of history. Over here the capitalist class was an afterthought, an epilogue to a chronicle yet to be told. In the eyes of Marx, the bourgeoisie had created a world after their own image. Had the *Communist Manifesto* been written in and about Turkey, that thesis might have been somewhat different. Notoriously evasive, the local bourgeoisie had yielded to the culture that surrounded them. Like a pendulum that knew no rest, they oscillated between a self-approving elitism and a self-effacing statism. The State – with a capital *S* – was the beginning and the end of everything. Like a thundercloud in the sky, the authority of the State loomed over every house in the country, whether a grand villa or a humble shack.

Peri glanced at the faces around the table. The rich, the wannabe-rich and the ultra-rich were all equally insecure. Much of their peace of mind depended on the whim of the State. Even the most powerful worried about losing control, even the most affluent dreaded hardship. You were expected to believe in the State for the same reason you were expected to believe in God: fear. The bourgeoisie, despite its glamour and glitz, resembled a child afraid of its father – the eternal patriarch, the Baba. Amidst uncertainty, unlike their counterparts in Europe, the local bourgeoisie had neither audacity nor autonomy, neither tradition nor memory – squeezed between what they were expected to be and what they wished to be. *Not so unlike me*, Peri thought to herself.

The mingling smells of candles and spices, like a dense bank of fog, lay above them. The air in the room felt heavier and warmer, in spite of a cool wind blowing through from the terrace, where a few men had stepped out to smoke. That there was tension among some of the guests was not lost on Peri. Politics transformed friends into foes. The opposite was also true: politics united people who otherwise had little in common, making comrades out of adversaries.

In the next quarter of an hour, as the starters were consumed, postures changed, faces hardened, smiles grew serious. With exclamation marks punctuating their assertions, they conversed about the future of Turkey. Since the future of Turkey was tied up with the future of the globe, they also talked about America, Europe, India, Pakistan, China, Israel, Iran. Clearly they mistrusted all, though some more than others. Sinister lobbies and their puppets machinated against Turkey, imperialists manipulated their lackeys, hidden hands that controlled everything from afar. They discussed international relations with the kind of watchfulness they reserved for glue sniffers and dope addicts on the streets, expecting at any moment to be assaulted and mugged.

Peri listened quietly, though deep inside she was seized by a tangle of emotions. She longed to be home, alone under a blanket, reading a novel. A part of her was embarrassed for not knowing how to enjoy the evening, the delicious food, the fine wine; and for not being enough fun, as her daughter often reminded her. The other part, however, wanted to get drunk, go back to the bathroom and smash the fish tank. She still remembered vividly her father's story – shoals of pitch-black fish nibbling the verses of a poem and the eyes of a poet.

This is how she felt tonight – Istanbul was gnawing at her soul.

The Runner

Oxford, 2000

Being a student at Oxford had two immediate effects on Nazperi Nalbantoğlu. The first was cinematographic. With its ancient quadrangles and tranquil gardens, soaring spires and crenellated battlements, formal dining halls and dignified chapels, Oxford evoked a sense of openness and beauty and purpose, as though every detail were part of a well-designed panorama – a filmic story, in which she, the fresher, starred. A feeling of exhilaration. An expectation that something important was going to happen with her at its centre.

Many mornings, Peri would wake up elated, bursting with energy and ambition, as if there were nothing she could not accomplish as long as she tried hard enough. After graduating, she planned to stay in academia or to find a job at a top international institution. She would make a lot of money and buy her parents a big house by the sea – they would each occupy one floor and never have to quarrel. Determined to make her father proud, she could already see her degree certificate framed, polished and hanging on the wall of their living room, next to the portrait of Atatürk. In the evenings, when Mensur raised a toast to the national hero, he would also salute his daughter's achievements.

The second effect Oxford had on Peri was the opposite of the first. It was claustrophobic. A particular way of shutting inwards, almost evasion; the place was too much to take in and could be deciphered only piecemeal. On such mornings Peri became withdrawn, trapped inside her head, intimidated by the difficulty of her tutorials or the ways of the dons and the formality they claimed was essential to academic study.

She soon learned it wasn't cool to own sweatshirts and teddy bears with the name of the university emblazoned all over them; they were only for tourists, though she couldn't resist getting a mug. When she went home for her brother's wedding, she planned to take it with her and give it to her mother as a present. Selma would probably display it on her shelf, next to her porcelain horses and books of Islamic prayers.

One morning, the moon still high in the sky, Peri watched from her window a female student – wearing earphones, her cheeks flushed – running through the quad. She herself had tried it a few times back in Istanbul, despite the obstacles the city peppered along her trail. Here it was a privilege, of sorts, not to have to worry about broken pavements, potholes in the roads, sexual harassment, cars that did not slow down – even at pedestrian crossings. The same day, she bought herself a pair of trainers.

After a few trial-and-errors she found her ideal route. She would cross the High Street near Magdalen Bridge, run along Merton Field, through Christ Church Meadow, and back round Addison's Walk, depending on her stamina. Sometimes the cobbles seemed to roll out beneath her feet and she had the feeling that at the end of one of those quaint little streets she would find a portal to another century. Getting into a rhythm was the hardest part, but once she did she could keep on going for almost an hour. After she had run for a good long while, her hair clinging damply to her neck, her heart galloping to the point of pain, she would feel as though she had entered another space, a threshold between the living and the dead. She was aware that she thought about death far too much for a person so young.

Many went running at Oxford – academics, students, staff. One could easily tell those who enjoyed it for the exercise and those who saw it as a burden, doing it only because they had promised someone – their doctor, their partner – a fitter version of themselves. Peri envied the runners who were clearly better than she was, but mostly she was content with her performance – weekends and weekdays without fail. When she had to work in the mornings, she ran after dusk. If evenings were full, she forced herself out of bed at sunrise. A few times, too sporadically to turn into a habit, she went on late runs to clear her head, the night so silent she could hear nothing but her rasping lungs as she ran full-pelt through the centre of town. Such iron self-discipline, she assured herself, would do her good, not only physically but also emotionally.

Occasionally, when she fell into sync with another runner, she wondered what he or she might be thinking about. Maybe nothing. For Peri, this was the only time she could quiet her anxieties and dispel her fears. Speeding across the meadows, inhaling the moist air, which, at any moment, might turn to rain, she felt a lightness of being that she had never before experienced, as though she – Peri, Nazperi, Rosa – had not saved her worries all these years the way others collected golden wrappers and foreign stamps; she felt like a blithe spirit, as though she had no past and no memory of the past.

The Fisherman

Oxford, 2000

Freshers' Week, they called it. Before the Michaelmas term began in earnest that October, a cornucopia of social events and fun had been jam-packed into a few days to help fresh-faced undergraduates get to know the university, the town and its surroundings, make new friends – and possible enemies – and shed their nervousness as fast as a gingko tree drops its leaves at the first frost. Barbecues, meetings with tutors, cooking and eating competitions, afternoon teas, dances, karaoke and a fancy-dress party . . . Clad in her fresher T-shirt, Peri wandered casually around and conversed with students and staff members. The more she talked to people, the more she was convinced that everyone knew what they were doing, everyone but her.

Peri had learned that the university – intent on changing its image as the preserve of a privileged few and creating a diversity of intake and environment – had recently announced a bursary scheme to encourage candidates from disadvantaged backgrounds to apply. She now scanned the faces around her, observing a range of ethnicities and nationalities – but their economic circumstances were harder to discern.

She noticed that underneath the frantic buzz, there was a subtle traffic of glances. One boy in particular seemed interested in her. Tall, firm-jawed with close-cropped blond hair, powerful shoulders and a triumphal posture – from swimming or rowing, she guessed – he smiled at Peri as a gourmet might smile at an exotic dish.

'Stay away from him,' a voice spoke into Peri's ear.

Instantly, Peri turned around. She saw a headscarved girl, her eyebrows bow-shaped and her eyes rimmed with the darkest kohl. She wore a nose stud in the shape of a miniature silver crescent.

'University Boat Club, extremely popular,' said the girl. 'He's fresher-fishing.'

'Excuse me?'

'That guy, he does the same thing every year, apparently. Then he goes around boasting about how many fish he caught in one week. Someone told me he's trying to break his record from last year.'

'You mean, the fish are . . . girls?'

'Yes, the irony is, some girls have no problem with being treated like stupid glittering fish, all dolled up.' A teasing note crept into her voice. 'It's hard to break our chains when some of us love being shackled.'

Peri's eyes widened as she tried to picture what a fish in chains might look like.

'Ask people around here, who needs feminism?' the girl went on. 'They'll say, "Oh, women in Pakistan, Nigeria, Saudi Arabia, but not Britain, we are so over it! Surely not Oxford, huh?" But the reality is different. Did you know that women students do unusually badly here? There's a massive gender gap in exam results. A freshwoman in Oxford needs feminism just as much as a peasant mother in rural Egypt! If you are with me, sign our petition.' She offered a pen and a paper that read 'Oxford Feminist Squad' at the top.

'Hmm . . . and you are a feminist?' Peri asked cautiously, finding it hard to match the term with the girl's outlook.

'I sure am,' said the girl. 'I am a Muslim feminist and if some people think that's impossible, it's their problem. Not mine.'

As Peri put down her signature, she had a sudden memory of her ex-boyfriend in Turkey. He was not only against reading European literature but also against all kinds of Western ideologies, of which he said feminism was threat number one. *A red herring to steer our sisters away from the real issue: class conflict.* There was no need for a women's separate movement, since the demise of economic exploitation would automatically end all sorts of discrimination. The emancipation of women would come with the emancipation of the proletariat.

'Thank you,' said the girl, as she took back her pen and paper. 'My name is Mona, by the way. What's yours?'

'Peri.'

'Good to meet you,' said Mona. Her smile was radiant.

Peri learned that Mona was Egyptian-American. Born in New Jersey, she had moved with her family to Cairo when she was about ten. 'The children should be raised in Muslim culture,' her father had said. Several years later, having discovered that life in Egypt was tougher than they had expected – or that they were after all true Americans – they had gone back to the States. It was her second year at Oxford, and she was changing disciplines to focus on philosophy. Her mother was covered, she said, but not her older sister. 'We have made different choices in life.'

Besides championing feminism, Mona was involved in a series of volunteer activities: Aid to the Balkans Society, Friends of Palestine Society, Sufi Studies Society, Migration Studies Society; and the Oxford Islamic Society, where she was one of the leading members. She was also about to launch a 'hip-hop society' because she loved the music. Drawing on her encounter with diverse cultures, she wrote lyrics, hoping that one day someone would rap them.

'Wow, how do you find time for all that?' Peri asked.

Mona shook her head. 'It's not about finding time. It's simply about time management. That is why Allah gave us five prayers a day – to structure our lives.'

Peri, who had never adhered to the five prayers – not even to one, not even in her religious phase after her father's heart attack – pursed her lips and said softly, 'You seem at home with religion.'

'I guess you might say I am at peace with who I am,' said Mona, and checked her watch. 'Need to go, but I'm sure I'll see you around. I'm always collecting signatures for one good cause or another.'

Before they parted they shook hands – firmly, that was Mona's style.

That same night Peri wrote in her God-diary: *Some people want to change the world; others, their partners or friends. As for me, I would love to change God. Now that would be something. Wouldn't everyone in the world benefit from that?*

Back in Istanbul, Peri had tried, often unsuccessfully, to behave like an extrovert when she was not, and had socialized more than she cared to. At Oxford, with the cultural pressure off her shoulders, she enjoyed, no, she *treasured*, the solitude. Introversion was not the only reason she shunned most of the excitement of Freshers' Week. She found out that, although certain events (student common room teas, gatherings with dons) were free, others (vegan cupcakes, halal marshmallows, vegetarian pizzas) required money. She would be better off on her limited budget if she avoided the hullabaloo. Instead, she concentrated on her to-do list: getting her student ID; purchasing textbooks, if possible second-hand; opening a student bank account. Bent on figuring out the cheapest way to survive, she compared prices in shops and supermarkets.

Peri was probably one of the few students who was thrilled when the week, with all its fun and frolic, came to an end. The term started right away. Relieved, she settled into a routine of lectures, tutorials, reading lists and essays. In an environment that was totally new to her, studying was a solid rope to hold on to and she did so with all her might.

Shirin came and went at different hours, leaving a trail of perfume lingering in the air. Heady molecules of magnolia and cedar. Although the rhythms of their daily lives were driven by incompatible habits, increasingly they had breakfasts and lunches together, conferring about the lectures, the dons and, sometimes, that subject of perpetual interest – boys. Peri, who did not have much experience in this field, would listen to Shirin jabber non-stop about the art of dating the male of the species, her spirits sinking lower and lower. In the company of experienced friends who effortlessly flirt, there's a despondency that descends on a relative novice, a feeling of being left so far behind as to become a mere spectator.

Peri searched for the seminar Shirin had mentioned. She located it on a list of optional seminars offered by the Philosophy Department, some with impressive and elaborate titles: 'The Atomists' Critique of Creationism'; 'Holism in Stoic Psychology and Epistemology'; 'Plato's Philosopher Kings, The Good Life and the Noble Lie'; 'Aquinas: His Medieval Critics and Fellow Scholastics'; 'German Idealism and Kant on Philosophy of Religion'; 'Philosophical Issues in the Cognitive Sciences'.

Towards the bottom of the list a short title stood out: 'GOD'. Next to it was a description: *By drawing on sources from antiquity to the present day, from philology to poetry, from mysticism to neuroscience, from Eastern philosophers to their Western counterparts, this seminar explores what we talk about when we talk about God.*

In brackets was the name of the instructor: Professor Anthony Zacharias Azur. Underneath was a note: *Limited space, speak to the instructor first. Caution: This may or may not be the right class for you.*

Peri found the description intriguing, the arrogance behind it as beguiling as it was off-putting. She thought about inquiring further, but in the frenzy of those early days she soon forgot about it.

Shirin was right. 'God' would have to wait.

The Black Caviar

Istanbul, 2016

The main course – wild-mushroom risotto and roasted lamb with saffron and honey-mint sauce – was served on large silver platters garnished with grilled vegetables at the edges. The sight of maids in their starched uniforms marching in and lifting the covers on heaps of steaming meat was so theatrical that some of those present applauded with delight. Their spirits swelled by the delicacies and the wine, the guests became more cheerful and increasingly louder and bolder.

'Frankly, I don't believe in democracy,' said an architect with a crew cut and perfectly groomed goatee. His firm had made huge profits from construction projects across the city. 'Take Singapore, success without democracy. China. Same. It's a fast-moving world. Decisions must be implemented like lightning. Europe wastes time with petty debates while Singapore gallops ahead. Why? Because they are focused. Democracy is a loss of time and money.'

'Bravo,' said an interior designer who was the architect's fiancée and prospective third wife. 'I always say, in the Muslim world democracy is redundant. Even in the West it's a headache, let's admit it, but around here, totally unsuitable!'

The businessman's wife agreed. 'Imagine, my son has a master's degree in business. My husband employs thousands. But in our family, we have only three votes. Our driver's brother in their village has eight children. I'm not sure if they've ever read a book in their life; they'll have ten votes! In Europe, the public is educated. Democracy cannot harm. The Middle East is a different story! Granting an equal vote to the ignorant is like handing matches to a toddler. The house could burn down!'

Stroking the hair on his chin with the knuckle of his index finger, the architect said, 'Well, I'm not suggesting we should abandon the ballot box. We couldn't explain that to the West. A controlled democracy is just fine. A cadre of bureaucrats and technocrats under a smart, strong leader. So long as the person at the top knows what he's doing, I'm fine with authority. How else will foreign investors come?'

Everyone turned and looked at the only foreigner at the table – an American hedge-fund manager visiting the city. He had been trying to follow the conversation with the help of sporadic translations whispered in his ear. Thrust into the spotlight, he fidgeted uncomfortably in his chair. 'Nobody wants a destabilized region, for sure. You know what folks in Washington call the Middle East? The Muddle East! Sorry, guys, but it's a mess.'

Some of the guests laughed, a few grimaced. Mess it was, but it was their mess. *They* could criticize it to their heart's content, but not a rich American. Sensing the negative energy, the hedge-fund manager compressed his lips.

'All the more reason to support my thesis,' the architect said between mouthfuls of risotto. An apolitical man for many years, and though half Kurdish by blood, lately he displayed chauvinistic tendencies.

'Well, the entire region is coming to the same realization,' the bank CEO conceded. 'After the Arab Spring fiasco, any sane person has to recognize the benefits of strong leadership and stability.'

'Democracy is passé! I know it might sound shocking to some, but so be it,' said the architect, pleased that his views were gaining acceptance. 'I'm all for benevolent dictatorship.'

'The problem with democracy is it's a luxury, like Beluga caviar,' said a plastic surgeon who owned a clinic in Istanbul but lived in Stockholm. 'In the Middle East, it's unaffordable.'

'Even Europe doesn't believe in it any more,' said the journalist, stabbing his fork into a piece of lamb. 'The EU is in tatters.'

'They behaved like a pussycat when Russia turned into a tiger in the Ukraine,' said the architect, now in his pomp. 'Like it or not, this is the century of tigers. Sure, they won't love you if you're a tiger. But they'll fear you, and that's what matters.'

'Personally, I'm glad we weren't allowed into the EU. Good riddance,' mused the PR woman. 'Otherwise we could have been like Greece.' She gently pulled her earlobe, made a tsk-tsk sound, and knocked on the table twice.

'The Greeks? They are hankering for the Ottomans to come back, they were happier when we ruled over them . . .' remarked the architect with a chuckle, which he cut short when he noticed Peri's expression. He turned to Adnan, with a wink. 'I'm afraid your wife doesn't like my jokes.'

At which Adnan, who had been listening with one hand under his chin, gave a smile – half sombre, half sympathetic. 'I'm sure that's not true.'

Peri's eyes fell on the risotto congealed on her plate. She could have let the comments pass; a bit like other people's cigar smoke, unwanted but tolerable to an extent. But she had promised herself, years ago, right after she left Oxford, never to be silent again.

With a tight nod, she said to her husband, 'But it is true, I don't like this kind of talk. Democracy as black caviar, states like tigers . . .' As this was the first time she had spoken in a while, all heads turned towards her and she returned their gaze. 'You see, there's no such thing as benevolent dictatorship.'

'Why not?' asked the architect.

'Because there's no such thing as a small god. Once somebody starts playing God, sooner or later, things will get out of hand.'

All the while her mind raced with thoughts about Professor Azur. *He's a bit like God himself.* Might things not have gone so wrong had he only acknowledged that he, no less than his students, was only human?

'Get real,' cut in the architect. 'This isn't your fancy Oxford! We're talking about realpolitik. Our neighbours are Syria, Iran, Iraq. Not Finland, Norway, Denmark. You'll never get Scandinavian-style democracy in the Middle East.'

'Maybe not,' Peri said. 'But you can't stop me from wishing for it. You can't stop us all from desiring what we are denied.'

'Desire! What a word!' said the architect, as he leaned forward, his palms flat on the table. 'Now you're entering dangerous waters.'

Peri shook her head, aware that according to the *Advanced Learner's*

Guide to Patriarchy, members of the Decent Turkish Ladies' Club could not defend in public the merits of 'desire'. But she sorely wished to cancel her membership – and if she could not resign, she should be sacked. She thought of Shirin. Her feisty friend would surely have given this man a piece of her mind. Animated by this thought, Peri said, softly, 'If you're telling me I should accept things as they are . . . that nations, like obedient good wives, should also give up their dreams . . . their fantasies . . . then your grasp of international relations – and women for that matter – is weaker than I thought.'

There was a brief silence, palpable, when no one knew what to say. Into the leaden moment the businessman lifted his chin, squared his shoulders, clapped his hands, like a flamenco dancer about to take centre stage, and roared, as jovial as before, 'Where on earth is our next course?'

The swinging door between the kitchen and the dining room was pushed open and the servants came scurrying in.

The Celebration

Oxford, 2000

It was Shirin's twentieth birthday, which she was celebrating at the Turf Tavern – a centuries-old, half-timbered pub down a narrow alley under the old city walls. Peri, late to the party, walked purposefully with a present tucked under her arm. Having agonized over what to get her friend, she had settled on something she knew Shirin would love: a jean jacket studded with brightly coloured sparkling beads. It had cost her a small fortune.

When Peri entered the oak-panelled pub, a warm humidity of alcohol and laughter enveloped her under the low ceiling. Given Shirin's popularity, she had expected a large crowd, and so there was. A knot of noisy friends surrounded the birthday girl, whose new boyfriend was next to her, his arm on her shoulder. Her previous boyfriend – a second-year Physics student, clever and kind – had overplanned their encounters to the point of exasperation, according to Shirin. 'I decided to dump him after I saw his weekly schedule.' Times for morning lectures, library hours, gym, tutorials were all blocked off. The 4.15–5.15 p.m. slot had her name entered. On Friday evening there was another spot reserved for her. 'Can you believe it, Mouse, he's squeezed me in between 7.30 and 10.30 p.m.? Dinner, film, sex.'

Shirin's loud voice jolted Peri out of her thoughts. 'Hey, here's my neighbour. Hi, there!'

Looking stunning in a pearl-and-sequin-embellished top and white, tight-fitting, low-slung jeans, Shirin grabbed her present and gave Peri a kiss and a hug. 'Where have you been? You missed the guest of honour. He just left.'

'Who?'

'Azur,' Shirin said, her eyes beaming. 'He was here. I can't believe he came. So cool! He just stopped by, gave a toast and left.'

Shirin seemed to want to say more but someone pulled her by the arm to blow out the candles on the cake. Peri glanced around, not expecting to know any of Shirin's gregarious friends, who were standing, drinking and talking loudly. To her surprise, however, she saw a familiar face: Mona. In an orange long-sleeved tunic over trousers and a matching headscarf, the girl was sitting at a corner table, sipping a glass of cola.

'Hi, Mona.'

'So happy to see you,' said Mona, looking relieved to have someone to talk to.

'I didn't know you were friends with Shirin,' said Peri, as she sat down next to her.

'Well, not exactly friends, but she invited me and I thought . . .' said Mona, her voice trailing away.

Peri realized what the girl did not express aloud. You didn't easily turn down an invitation from one of the most popular students in college. So Mona – outgoing and self-confident – had come, not knowing quite what to expect. Now, among dozens of uninhibited, rollicking party-goers swaying to a rhythm only they themselves could hear, she felt an unease she dared not show.

The two of them plunged into a conversation – over slices of birthday cake – while Shirin and her friends had rowdy fun.

'May I ask you something?' said Peri. 'When we first met you said you and your sister had made different choices in life. So does that mean . . . you *prefer* to cover your head?'

'Of course. My parents always gave me the option. My hijab is a personal decision, a testimony to my faith. It gives me peace and confidence.' Mona's face darkened. 'Even though I have been bullied for it, endlessly.'

'You have?'

'Sure, but it didn't stop me. If I, with my headscarf, don't challenge stereotypes, who's going to do it for me? I want to shake things up. People look at me as if I'm a passive, obedient victim of male power.

Well, I'm not. I have a mind of my own. My hijab has never got in the way of my independence.'

Peri listened intrigued, finding in this girl a younger version of her own mother. The same outspoken defiance, the same resoluteness. It was a feeling she knew only too well. She was accustomed to people prattling on fervently, self-assuredly. What it was about her that inspired others to pour out their emotions, she couldn't fathom. It seemed peculiar for someone as ambivalent as she to be inundated by the certainties and passions of others.

'These hip-hop lyrics you write . . . are they about religion?'

Mona laughed. 'Hip-hop is about love. Poetry. Maybe a bit of anger too – against injustice and inequality. It's empowering –'

A burst of laughter in the background cut short her reply. Someone had challenged Shirin's boyfriend to a yard-of-ale contest. A two-foot-tall glass with a large bulb at one end was filled with beer, which the boy was now chugging as fast as possible. He managed to finish the drink, his face plastered with a cheesy grin and his shirt soaking. To the cheers of the crowd, he gave Shirin a long, wet, happy kiss, but suddenly stopped to rush outside, having been overcome by the need to vomit.

Mona said, 'I think I'd better leave.'

'I'll come with you,' Peri said.

Not that she was bothered by the alcohol or the suggestive behaviour in the way Mona seemed to be. Peri's discomfort was of a different nature. When confronted with others' exuberance and unable to keep up, she always shrank, a hedgehog rolling herself into a ball – self-protection from joy.

When Peri and Mona left the pub, unnoticed, it was full moon. Passing under the Bridge of Sighs, they wound their way through the dimly lit side streets.

'I don't get it,' said Mona. 'Why did Shirin invite me?'

Peri had been wondering the same thing herself. 'Well, she likes to make new friends.'

Mona shook her head. 'No, there's something else. I can't put my finger on it. We've known each other for some time but I've always had the feeling she doesn't like me because of . . . my headscarf, probably.'

Remembering how Shirin had stared at her mother, Peri fell quiet.

'If that's the case, fine, I don't care. But why does she try to befriend me?' Mona said, her face fierce with pride. 'Do you think I'm being paranoid?'

'No,' Peri said. 'I mean, yes, a bit. I'm sure you can be friends.'

'Well, we'll see,' Mona said. 'Shirin always tells me I should take Professor Azur's seminar.'

'Really?' Peri tensed as if her body had sensed a danger her mind was yet to grasp. 'She does the same thing to me. Go to Azur, she says.'

'So I'm not the only one . . .' Mona said distractedly. She pointed towards Turl Street. 'Anyway, I'm this way.'

'Okay, well, have a good night.'

'You, too, sister,' said Mona. 'We must meet more often.'

With that she gripped Peri's hand firmly in both her own, shook it vigorously and disappeared into the night.

Alone again with her thoughts, Peri turned on to Broad Street. Ahead in the dark she noticed a figure illuminated by the sodium-yellow street lights: a bag lady pushing a rusty pram, piled with clothes, cardboard, plastic bags – a perennial traveller from here to nowhere. Peri scrutinized her. Her clothes were soiled and clung damply to her body; her hair was matted with dirt and what looked like dried blood. Little by little, Peri could pick out more details: calluses on her palms, a bruise that discoloured her right cheekbone, puffiness around the eyes. In Istanbul one spotted down-and-out faces all the time. Some huddled in corners to hide from strangers' eyes; most begged for attention, food and money. In Oxford there were vagrants too, just not as many as in Istanbul, but somehow, seeing a homeless person was disconcerting, because of the stark contrast with the exquisite serenity of the town.

Feeling oddly drawn to the woman, who moved with short, deliberate steps, Peri began to follow her. A foetid smell entered her nostrils when the wind momentarily changed direction. A mixture of urine, sweat and excrement.

The bag lady was talking to herself, her voice strained. 'How many times do I have to tell you, dammit?' she asked. Her face hardened as she waited for an answer. She chuckled with glee but her rage was quick to rise. 'No, you fucker!'

Peri felt a heaviness of heart so sharp it verged on melancholy. What separated her – an Oxford student with a promising future – from this woman who had nothing to her name? Was there an edge over which polite society feared to fall – like the brink of the flat world that had once filled ancient sailors with dread? If so, where was the boundary between sanity and madness? She recalled what the hodja had said when she and her mother had visited him. Perhaps he was right. Perhaps she was *prone to darkness*.

The woman stopped and turned around, her gaze cutting through Peri. 'Were you looking for me, darling?' she cackled, revealing a set of nicotine-stained teeth. 'Or were you looking for God?'

Peri paled. She shook her head, unable to answer. Stepping forward, she opened her fist to offer the coins she had prepared. The woman's hand extended from her coat-sleeve and grabbed them as deftly as a lizard's tongue taking an insect off a leaf.

Peri instantly swung round, setting off towards her college, almost running, scared without knowing why, hoping that each step would take her further from the bag lady and the creeping suspicion that the two of them belonged in the same place.

That night Peri stayed up late, reading. Had she kept an eye on the lawn outside, she might have seen Shirin, having misplaced her late key, slip off her wedge heels, get a leg up from an equally inebriated friend over the twelve-foot-high stone garden wall – split and stain her tight white jeans in the process – drop into a flower bed, scramble to her feet and knock on a random window of a ground-floor room, all the while giggling and singing a lilting Persian melody.

The Dictionary

Oxford, 2000

Oxford had no shortage of pubs and eating places suitable for a student budget, yet Peri seldom crossed the threshold of any of them. And, while there were more than a hundred clubs and societies she could have joined, she shied away from every single one, including the Feminist Squad. She had to stay on course, she reminded herself; anything else would take her mind off her studies. This included boys. Falling in love was messy; falling out of love was even messier. All the emotions and the back and forth; the lunches, suppers and walks; then the quarrels over petty issues and the reconciliations. In short, placing another human being, if not at the centre of your life then somewhere close to it, was a lot of effort. She had no time for that. Likewise, friendships could be just as demanding, labour-intensive. Every now and then she would come across a student with whom she would instantly hit it off, but then avoid deepening the bond. There was something rigid and robotic, almost dogmatic, in the way Peri disciplined herself around one single motto during those early weeks in college: study, study, study.

Accustomed to success all her school life, she was painfully aware of her newly gained academic weaknesses. She had no trouble following the lectures. Participating in the tutorials – the debates and writing assignments – proved more difficult. Putting her thoughts on paper in a language other than her mother tongue was challenging. Determined not to fail, she pushed hard, unsatisfied with herself.

She understood that for her to excel at Oxford she had to improve her English. Her brain was in need of words to express itself fully, the way a sapling was in need of raindrops to grow to its potential. She purchased stacks of coloured Post-it notes. On them she wrote the words she chanced upon, fell in love with and intended to use at the earliest opportunity – just as every foreigner did, one way or another:

Autotomy: The casting off of a body part by an animal in danger.

Cleft stick: (from Tolkien, The Lord of the Rings*): To be in a difficult situation.*

Rantipole: (from the Legend of Sleepy Hollow*): Wild, reckless, sometimes quarrelsome person.*

In her first Political Philosophy essay, she wrote: *In Turkey, where daily politics is rantipole, each time the system is in a cleft stick, democracy is the first thing to be severed and sacrificed in an act of autotomy.*

When it was her turn to read her essay aloud to her tutor, he stopped her halfway through, looking both perplexed and amused. 'Was that even English?'

Peri was mortified. The sentence that had sounded smart and sophisticated and stylish to her ears was no more than gibberish to a native speaker. How could the foreigner and the local hear the same words so differently? Refusing to be discouraged, obsessed with nuances, she kept on collecting dazzling words. They reminded her of the spiral shells and pink corals, smoothed by countless tides, she had picked up as a child when her family went to the seaside. Except, unlike those pretty but motionless keepsakes, words were breathing, alive.

A sense of direction not being her strong suit, Peri occasionally got lost when she was exploring Oxford. On one of these outings she discovered a bookstore called Two Kinds of Intelligence. Its uneven floorboards creaked in fancied sympathy as she walked across the front room; bookshelves rose to the ceiling on every wall; there was a fireplace in the corner, above which were old prints of Oxford; a flight of wooden stairs led to two small rooms, each packed with hand-picked volumes reflecting the owners' peculiar tastes in philosophy, psychology, religion, the occult. With framed photographs on the walls, pastel bean bags on the floor for customers to sit on and a coffee machine that served free coffee all day long, it instantly became a favourite spot.

The owners (she was Scottish; he, Pakistani) were impressed with her when they realized she knew the origin of the store's name. It was the title of a poem by Rumi. Peri even remembered a few verses: *There are two kinds of intelligence, one acquired, as a child in school memorizes . . . from books and what the teacher says . . . the other . . . intelligence . . . fluid . . . a fountainhead from within you, moving out.*

'Well done,' said the woman. 'Come and read here whenever you like.'

'To further nourish your intelligence. Both kinds!' said the man.

This Peri did. Soon it became a habit. She would grab her coffee, put a coin in the tip box and plant herself on a bean bag, reading until her back hurt and her legs felt stiff. She also visited the Bodleian a lot. She would find a remote carrel, pile up more books than she could possibly read, surreptitiously open a package of pretzel sticks and bury her head in waves of words.

She bought postcards with pictures of Oxford. The sunlit medieval streets, the honeyed limestone buildings, the shaded college gardens . . . A few of these she sent to her parents, but the rest were reserved for her brother Umut. She wrote to him all the time, though his answers were irregular, curt. Still, she never gave up. She kept her postcards light, even mirthful. No need to mention her fears, her migraines, her nightmares and the loneliness, which by now, she knew, was both a curse and a companion. Instead, she talked about the oddly engaging ways of the British, their pragmatism, their unspoken confidence in their institutions, their quirky humour.

Umut wrote back with messages on lined paper, scraps torn from biscuit boxes, calendars or grocery bags. But once he sent a postcard. An indigo sea, a red fisherman's boat, the calming breeze of the Mediterranean, and a sand soft as promises . . . as though, he, too, were trying his hand at the art of feigning happiness.

During 'Formal Hall' – in a great hall dating back centuries – surrounded by portraits of former presidents of the college, Peri would sit at the ancient oak benches, the tables adorned with the college silver, served by white-jacketed scouts and feel translated into another dimension. She was a figure in a painting, surreal and romantic at once. There were parts of the college that had not changed for centuries, and she loved the touch and the smell of history, continuity. On many days she would visit the old library just to breathe in the heady aroma of the stacked bookshelves. She would go down into a basement where she would wind a handle to move the shelves in order to reach the books she needed. Amidst thousands of titles, each of which was a refuge, she felt complete. Strangely, there was one recurrent thought that would surface in her mind when inside that vastness of knowledge: God.

It puzzled her that this was so, since, among all the attributes she might claim for herself, none would come close to 'religious' or even 'spiritual'. This she would never dare tell her mother, but there were moments when she doubted if she believed in anything at all. Culturally, she was a Muslim, of course. She loved the Ramadan and the Eids, each of which filled her heart with warmth and her mind with visceral recollections of smells and tastes. Islam, for her, was reminiscent of a childhood memory – so very familiar and personal but also somehow vague, far removed in space and time. Like a cube of sugar dissolved in her coffee, there and not there.

It had always struck her as odd that so many Turks memorized Arabic prayers without having the slightest idea what they were saying. Whether English or Turkish, Peri *loved* words. She held them in her palms like eggs about to hatch, their tiny hearts beating against her skin, full of life. She inquired into their meanings – hidden and manifest; she studied their etymologies. But for countless believers, the words in the prayers were holy sounds one was expected less to penetrate than to imitate – an echo without a beginning or an end, in which the act of thinking was subsumed by the act of mimicking. In the sheltered bosom of faith, one found the answers by letting go of the questions; one advanced by surrendering.

blind faith

Into her God-diary Peri wrote: *Believers favour answers over questions, clarity over uncertainty. Atheists, more or less the same. Funny, when it comes to God, Whom we know next to nothing about, very few of us actually say, 'I don't know.'*

The Angel

Oxford, 2000

Ever since she arrived at Oxford, Peri had regularly spoken on the phone with her father, deliberately calling at hours when she knew he was more likely to pick up the phone. Today, however, when she called Istanbul, it was her mother who answered.

'Pericim . . .' Selma said lovingly, but quickly changed her tone. 'You *are* coming to your brother's wedding?'

'Yes, Mother. I told you I would.'

'She's an angel, I'm telling you.'

'Who?'

'The bride, of course, silly.'

Anxious because of the preparations, Selma praised her future daughter-in-law's virtues with an exaggeration that was not lost on Peri.

'That's great, we could do with an angel in the family,' said Peri. She could taste the insinuations wrapped inside her mother's compliments, like sweets hiding something rancid inside shiny packaging. The bride was the daughter Selma had never had – pious, easy-going, obedient.

'What's wrong with you?' asked Selma.

'Nothing.'

Selma sighed. 'You must be here for the henna night.'

Unlike the wedding, which was regarded as the groom's responsibility, the henna night fell under the bride's family's duties.

'Mum, we talked about this. I can only attend the wedding.'

'That won't do. People will gossip. You must come earlier.'

Peri rolled her eyes. The speed at which her mother could ruin her mood still astonished her – as if Selma, and only Selma, knew exactly where in her daughter's heart to squeeze to speed up the flow of her blood.

'I can't afford to miss more lectures,' Peri said firmly.

Their conversation turned sour, each side blaming the other for being selfish. After she hung up, Peri felt a seething resentment at all that had been said and left unsaid, at all that was broken between them and could not be mended.

That same night, Peri slept fitfully. She woke up with a pounding headache, on the verge of a migraine. She checked the drawers but could not find any painkillers. Massaging her temples, she pressed the bottom of a metal can against her throbbing right eye, which always helped. She crawled back into bed and curled into herself. She didn't expect to fall asleep but before she knew it she was dreaming.

A garden with gnarled trees. Alone, wearing a dress that fluttered in the breeze, Peri sauntered. Beside a stream, she saw a massive oak. There, dangling from one of the branches, was a baby in a basket, a dark stain covering half of its face. Peri noticed in horror that the tree was on fire, flames licking its trunk from the ground up. She grabbed a bucket and began to draw water from the stream. Soon there was water everywhere, churning and eddying around her feet. When she looked up again, the baby was no longer on the tree; it had been carried away by what had now become a rowdy river. Peri screamed as it dawned on her that she had done something terribly, irretrievably wrong.

There was a tapping somewhere, soft yet persistent. Peri tried to open her eyes, unsure whether this, too, was part of her dream.

'It's me, Shirin, you scared the shit out of me,' came a voice from the other side of the door. 'You all right?'

Peri sat up, blinking in confusion. 'I'm fine,' she said. Her throat felt parched and dry, like dead leaves. She was horrified that she had screamed loudly enough to be heard from the room opposite.

'I'm not leaving unless I see you with my own eyes.'

Slowly, Peri got out of bed and opened the door. Shirin had on peach-coloured silk pyjamas with a matching eye mask, which she had pulled up to her forehead. Her eyes, free of makeup, and circled with a thick layer of cream, looked darker and smaller.

'Shit, you sounded like a woman in a horror film,' Shirin said. 'One of those dumb heroines who runs upstairs when she sees a psycho instead of opening the front door and getting the hell out of there.'

'Sorry if I woke you up.'

'Don't worry about me,' Shirin said, as she folded her arms across her striking bosom. 'You always have nightmares?'

'Sometimes . . .' Peri admitted. She stared down at the fitted carpet, spotting a stain she hadn't noticed before. 'Just silly dreams.'

'Recurring?'

'Sort of, yes.'

Shirin pushed a strand of hair behind her ear and said, in a voice that brooked no opposition, 'I've seen enough madness in my family, and God knows I'm a bit cuckoo myself. I can recognize it when I see it.'

'You mean I'm crazy?'

'Not certifiably nuts, but the scream I heard was quite something. If you have a psychological problem, you've got to deal with it.'

'I don't have a psychological problem!'

'Argh!!!' Shirin unleashed an excruciating sound, like a wild animal being pierced by an arrow. 'I get so upset when people are offended by the word "psychological"! I bet you wouldn't have been offended if I said you were haemorrhoidical.'

'Haemorrhoidal,' Peri corrected.

'Whatever,' said Shirin, glancing at the Post-its on the walls. 'You're the dictionary girl.'

'Look, it's very kind of you to come to check on me, but I'm fine.' Through the leaded window the moon cast a distorted rectangle of light on to her face. 'I'll be going home for my brother's wedding. I can't afford to miss lectures but family obligations come first. I feel a bit stressed out.'

Shirin nodded. 'Fine, go to that wedding, but when you come back you need to get out more. It's okay to have a bit of fun; you're young, did you forget?'

'I'm not like you,' Peri said quietly.

'You mean you enjoy misery?'

'Of course not!'

'There are two ways of dealing with melancholy,' said Shirin. 'You either sit in the driver's seat and step on the gas while Mr Depression screams his head off at the back. Or you let him do the driving, and he frightens you instead.'

'What difference does it make?' asked Peri. 'If you're going to run smack into a tree anyway.'

'Yeah, but you get to drive, sister, not that sad old Mr Depression. Isn't that something?'

Sensing that she could not win this argument, Peri tried to change the subject in the only way she could think of. 'By the way, that professor you mentioned, Azur, I looked up his seminar.'

'You did?' A shade of pink crept up Shirin's cheeks. 'Isn't he charming?'

'I haven't met him, only read the description in the options list.'

'Oh! Well, what do you think?'

'It looks interesting.'

Shirin strode towards the door. 'May I offer some friendly advice? From an Iranian woman to a Turkish sister, chalk it up to the camaraderie of the doomed. If you manage to get into Azur's seminar, don't ever use the word "interesting". He loathes it. He says there is nothing remotely interesting in the word "interesting".'

With that Shirin walked out and closed the door behind her, leaving Peri alone with her nightmares.

The Music Box

Istanbul, 2016

The desserts arrived, served on crystal plates: hazelnut-mousse cake with a chocolate-custard centre and an oven-baked quince with buffalo cream on top. The guests broke into a chorus, half of compliments, half of concern.

'Ah, I must have put on two pounds tonight,' said the PR woman, patting her belly.

'Don't worry, you'll burn it off by the time you get home,' reassured the businessman's wife.

'Just keep arguing about politics,' said the journalist. 'That's how we burn calories in this country.'

When the maid appeared beside her, Peri murmured, 'No, thank you.'

'Certainly, madam,' said the maid, dropping her voice, a willing accomplice.

But the hostess, having heard the exchange, intervened from her end of the table: 'No, darling! I wasn't cross when you opposed our views, but I'd not be best pleased if you don't try my cake.'

Peri conceded, as she had to. She would eat both the quince and the cake. It never ceased to puzzle her why women were so keen on fattening each other up. Something to do with the 'law of comparative aesthetics' – when many were on the chubby side, no one actually was. But perhaps she was being cynical. The long-lost voice of Shirin sounded in her head. 'Believe me, Mouse, not cynical enough.'

As soon as the hostess, now satisfied, turned her attention to the next guest, Peri grabbed her wine glass. She had been drinking more than usual this evening, though nobody seemed to notice, least of all herself. A crack had appeared in the dam she had erected over the years to block the flow of unwanted emotions into her heart. Now through that tiny slit a trickle of melancholy was seeping in. Meanwhile another part of her, conscious of the danger and destruction that this might cause, was on high alert, frantically trying to seal the opening so that everything could return to normal.

'I thought we had a psychic coming today,' said the journalist's girlfriend in a husky smoker's voice. Everyone knew she was wrought up over the rumours – recently posted on a media website – that the journalist had been spotted having a romantic dinner with his ex-wife and the couple might be getting back together.

'He was supposed to be here an hour ago,' said the businessman. 'Apparently the poor fellow got stuck in traffic.'

'Huh, even psychics don't know which roads to take in Istanbul,' quipped the American hedge-fund manager.

'You'll see, my friend, this guy is the best,' said the businessman half in English, half in Turkish. 'They say he foresaw the financial crisis.'

'Maybe we should all consult psychics, since political experts are worthless and financial experts are even worse,' said the PR woman.

On an impulse, Peri excused herself from the table.

'Oh, no, did we bore you again?' said the architect over his drink, his eyes glazed. A man of petty grudges, he had not forgiven her for challenging him.

Peri looked at him. 'Just going to make a call to check on the kids.'

'Of course,' said the businessman. 'Why don't you go upstairs to my office? There you'll have some peace and quiet.'

Borrowing her husband's mobile, Peri made her way up to the first floor, listening all the while to the voices from the dinner table.

The businessman's office boasted full-length windows that provided a spectacular view of the Bosphorus. With leather-panelled walls, a wooden coffered ceiling, a massive mahogany-and-marble desk, high armchairs the colour of egg yolk, antique objects d'art and fine paintings, the room resembled less a work space than the private lounge of an extravagant mafia boss.

One corner was decorated with framed photos of the businessman – with politicians, celebrities and oligarchs. Among them Peri noticed the porcelain smile of a Middle Eastern dictator, no longer in power, shaking hands with her host in front of what looked like an elaborate Bedouin tent. Behind it, in another photo, glared the cast-iron face of a late Central Asian autocrat notorious for garlanding his home town with his own image, even naming a month after himself and another after his mother. Peri inhaled deeply, holding an imaginary cloud of smoke in her lungs, unable to breathe out. What was she doing here in this mansion, built with money that flowed in through secrets and shadows? In that moment, she felt like a pebble in a river, tossed about endlessly in the current. If Professor Azur were here, he might have smiled and quoted from his book *The Guide to Remaining Perplexed*: *There's no wisdom without love. No love without freedom. And no freedom unless we dare to walk away from what we have become.*

Quickly, as if fleeing her own mind, she dialled her home number. Leaning her forehead against the window, she examined the view outside as she waited for her mother, who was minding the children, to pick up the phone. Behind the glass, under a crescent moon too luminous to be real, the city spread outwards – houses tilting to one side as if murmuring secrets to one another; streets with sharp bends winding up steep hills; the last of the tea houses closing their doors and the last of the customers departing . . . She wondered what the children who stole her handbag were doing. Were they sleeping, and, if so, had they gone to bed hungry? It occurred to Peri that they might be dreaming now and that she could be somewhere in their dreams, a crazy woman holding her high-heeled shoes in her hands, chasing them through the streets.

Selma answered the phone on the fourth ring. 'Is the dinner over?'

'Not yet,' said Peri. 'We're still here. Are the boys okay?'

'Of course, why wouldn't they be okay? They had a great time with Grandma. Now they're sleeping.'

'Have they eaten?'

'You think I'd let them go hungry? I made manti,* they wolfed it down. Poor things, they looked like they had missed it.'

Peri, who had not inherited Selma's culinary talents, heard the reprimand in her mother's voice. She said, 'Thanks, I'm sure they loved it.'

'You're welcome. See you in the morning. I might be asleep by the time you come back.'

'Wait!' Peri paused. 'Mum, can you do me a favour?'

There was a shuffling sound and Peri knew her mother had moved the telephone to her left ear so she could hear better. She had visibly aged since her husband passed away. Oddly enough, after all those years of hostility, Selma's world had fallen apart the day Mensur died, as though it had been the fight she put up against her husband that kept her fully alive.

'In the bedroom, in the second drawer, there must be a notebook,' said Peri. 'Turquoise. Leather.'

'The one your father gave you.' A bitter tone crept into her voice – even after all these years, Selma resented the bond between her husband and her daughter. Mensur's death had not altered her feelings. This Peri knew from experience: it was possible to envy the dead and the hold they had over the living.

'Yes, Mother,' said Peri. 'It's locked but there's a key in the bottom drawer. Under the towels. On the back page there's a phone number. It says "Shirin". Can you give it to me?'

'Can't it wait till morning?' Selma asked. 'You know my eyes are not as sharp as they used to be.'

'Please, I need to make a call,' Peri pleaded. 'Tonight.'

'All right, wait a bit,' Selma said with a sigh. 'Let me see what I can do.'

'Oh, Mother . . .'

'Yes?'

'Afterwards, could you please lock up the notebook again?'

'Step by step,' Selma said wearily. 'Don't confuse me.'

* *manti*: 'homemade dumplings filled with meat'.

Peri heard a clunk as her mother put the receiver aside. The sound of retreating footsteps, heavy and hurried. She waited, chewing her bottom lip. Far in the distance, under the lights from the Second Bridge, the sea was greenish-blue, the colour of anticipation. She studied her reflection in the window, noting with disapproval her flabby midriff. Still, she had yet to begin to age quickly, as she had feared she might. There were different ways of growing old, perhaps. Some withered first in body, others in mind, yet others in soul.

There was a box inside the part of the brain that stored memory – a music box, its enamel paint chipped, its notes that of a haunting melody. Stashed away in it were all the things that the mind neither wanted to forget nor dared to remember. At moments of stress or trauma, or perhaps for no apparent reason, the box snapped open and all its contents scattered about. This was what she felt was happening to her tonight.

'I couldn't find it,' Selma said, breathing hard from the exertion.

'Will you please try again? Let me know when you find it.'

'I was watching TV,' Selma objected, then adopted a more conciliatory tone. 'Fine, I'll do my best.'

Things had improved between them for the very reason that had previously kept them apart: Mensur. Divisive in life, his absence had brought them closer together.

'One more thing,' Peri rushed to add, 'my phone's been stolen. Text Adnan, but don't say anything about this. Just write "Call home", and I'll give you a ring.'

'What's going on?' asked Selma. A fleeting pause of suspicion. 'Isn't Shirin that dreadful girl back in England?'

Peri felt her heart give a lurch.

'Why do you want to speak to her?' Selma pressed. 'She was no friend of yours.'

She was my best friend, Peri thought to herself but refrained from saying it. *She and Mona and I. The three of us: the Sinner, the Believer, the Confused.*

Instead she said, 'It's been a long time, Mother, we're all grown-ups now. Nothing for you to worry about. I'm sure Shirin has left it all behind.'

Even as she uttered these words, and forced herself to believe them, Peri knew none of it was likely to be true. Shirin could never leave the past behind. No more than Peri had been able to.

Mona – the believer
Peri – the confused
Shirin – the sinner

The Maidenhood Belt

Oxford, Istanbul, 2000

One afternoon on the cusp of winter, the wind tasting of sea salt and sulphur, Peri arrived in Istanbul for her brother's wedding. She had missed her city of birth dearly – however lonely she might have felt when she lived here, she had been lonelier while she was away. As if to prevent herself from harbouring melancholy thoughts, from the moment she put her suitcase down she was inundated by a list of obligations – relatives to visit, gifts to buy, chores to complete.

It didn't take Peri long to sense that in her absence a pyramid of tension had been erected in the Nalbantoğlu household, making the air heavy, difficult to breathe. Some of the ill feeling was old – the usual bitter and short-tempered exchanges between her parents. A large part of it, however, was recent, precipitated by the wedding preparations. The bride's family had insisted on a lavish ceremony, one *worthy of their daughter*. The salon that had been rented was replaced at the last minute by a bigger venue, which meant inviting more people, ordering more food and, ultimately, spending more money. Still, no one was satisfied. While the two families kept exchanging pleasantries and compliments, underneath the veneer of graciousness, a tide of resentment flowed both ways.

The morning of the wedding, Peri woke up to succulent smells drifting through the house. When she went into the kitchen, she found her mother wearing an apron with yellow daisies printed all over it, baking three different kinds of börek – spinach, white cheese, minced meat. Scrubbing, waxing, dusting, washing, Selma had been labouring at a superhuman pace and seemed unable to slow down.

'Tell that woman, she's going to work herself to death,' said Mensur to his daughter, sitting at the kitchen table, without lifting his eyes from his newspaper – a centre-left daily he had subscribed to for as long as Peri could remember.

'Tell that man, *his* son is getting married. It happens once in a lifetime,' riposted Selma.

Peri sighed. 'You two are like kids – why aren't you speaking to each other?'

At this her father turned the page; her mother rolled out another lump of dough. Sitting on a chair between them, as if to create a buffer zone, Peri asked, 'So how was the henna night?'

Selma bit her lower lip, her stare like splintered glass. 'You missed it. You should have been here.'

'Mum, I told you I wouldn't be able to make it. I had classes.'

'Well, just so you know, everyone asked about you. Behind my back, they have been gossiping. The son is not here, the daughter is not here . . . What a family!'

'Umut is not coming?' asked Peri.

'He said he was. He promised. I made his favourite dishes. I told everyone he was coming. But at the last minute he calls and says, "Mum, I have important things to do." What important things? He thinks I'm a fool? I don't understand that boy.'

But Peri did. Since he had been released from prison, Umut preferred a quiet life in a southern town, making knick-knacks for tourists in a cabin he called home, his smile no less brittle than the seashells that now provided his livelihood. They had visited him a few times in the past. He was always polite and reserved, as though talking to strangers. The woman he lived with – a divorcee with two children – said he was fine, but sometimes his mood darkened unexpectedly: he became peevish, irritable, unable to get out of bed, unable to wash his face; she said sometimes he *snapped* so badly she had to keep an eye on him day and night, not because she feared he might hurt her or her children, but because he might hurt himself; she kept the razors out of sight, as those cuts, they did not heal easily; neither did she dwell on this, nor did the Nalbantoğlus probe further for fear it was too much for them to handle.

'Look, I'm sorry, I'd have come earlier if I could,' said Peri. She had no intention of quarrelling with her mother. 'How was it, tell me.'

'Oh, the usual thing, nothing fancy,' Selma said. 'In return, they expect us to shower them in diamonds.'

Like a meticulous accountant, Selma had been keeping a record of how much money the Nalbantoğlus had forked out versus the other family; how many people the groom would be inviting versus the bride's guest list; and so on. It was as though a grocer's scale had materialized in the midst of their lives: whatever weight one family placed in one pan had to be counterbalanced by the other side. If this were a tug-of-war of sorts, it was done with the utmost propriety. Peri was amazed to observe how one minute her mother would compare and complain, and the next minute merrily chatter with the bride's mother on the phone, joking and giggling like a schoolgirl.

Regardless of the expenditure, there were qualities about the bride that pleased Selma endlessly – her family being quite religious, for one.

'In fairness, they brought a brilliant hodja to henna night,' Selma said. 'Voice like a nightingale! Everyone wept. The bride's family are more pious than our seven-generation ancestry. They descend from hajis and sheikhs.' She enunciated the last words with emphasis, making sure they reached her husband's unenlightened ears.

'Splendid!' Mensur retorted from his corner. 'That means there are just as many heretics in their bloodline. Peri, explain to your mother. There's a basic concept in dialectics. The negation of the negation. Every doctrine creates its opposition. Where there are many saints, there are bound to be many sinners!'

Selma's brow furrowed. 'Peri, tell him he's talking nonsense.'

'Dad, Mum, enough . . .' Peri said. 'We're lucky that my brother found a partner who makes him happy. That's all that matters.'

She had met the bride a couple of times. A young woman with dimpled cheeks, hazel eyes that widened at the slightest surprise and a fondness for golden bangles; she appeared rather shy. She wore a headscarf, tying it in a style that Peri learned was called the *Dubai way*. The *Istanbul way* suited round faces, the *Dubai way* oval faces and the *Gulf way* square faces. Peri was astonished to discover a whole line of Islamic fashion that was either newly emerging or had hitherto escaped her attention. With 'haute couture hijab', 'burqini swimwear' and 'halal trousers', this was a fashion trend – and a huge industry.

Unlike many secularists she knew, including her father, Peri was not in a state of constant opposition to covered women – hence her easy friendship with Mona. She preferred to consider not what was on top of people's heads but what was inside of them. And that is where her quandary lay. Despite her acceptance of the bride's outlook, deep within Peri looked down on her. She had never revealed this to her parents, and found it almost as hard to admit to herself. The girl was not well read; the last time she picked up a book was probably in school. They could not maintain a conversation unless it involved subjects that Peri had no interest in – popular TV series, low-carb diets. To be fair, the bride was no more uninformed than her husband-to-be, whom Peri also secretly belittled. She couldn't remember ever having had a proper conversation with Hakan.

This intellectual snobbery of hers was limited only to youth. She was not at all troubled by the unlettered elderly, who had never had access to knowledge. But anyone of her own age who sounded as if they treated books as decorative objects to match their furniture, Peri held in mild contempt.

If I ever fall in love, she promised herself, *it'll be with someone's brain. I won't care about his looks or status or age, only his intellect.*

The venue hired for the wedding was the Grand Salon of a five-star hotel with a magnificent view of the Bosphorus. Satin table runners, cascades of silk flowers, sashed chairs with golden bows, an eight-tier cake with arches and hand-crafted sugar leaves, and a colour-changing crystal tree as centrepiece. Peri was aware that the evening had swallowed a great chunk of her parents' savings. Her expenses at Oxford had already added a burden to the family budget. Watching the extravaganza around her now, she resolved to find a part-time job as soon as she returned to England.

Shortly the guests began to arrive. Relatives, neighbours and friends on both sides took their seats at the garlanded tables lined up across the vast ballroom space. Meanwhile the newlyweds looked nervous, he waving at everyone, she gazing downwards; he too loud, she far too quiet. The bride wore a lace-and-taffeta long-sleeved ivory dress, embroidered in silver and studded with rhinestones – a dress defined as 'classy and chic hijabi' in the sales brochure. It was pretty, if a little thick, and under the spotlights she was already perspiring. The groom, rigged out in a black tuxedo suit, seemed more at ease and took his jacket off when he grew hot. One by one, the guests approached them to offer their congratulations and pin their offerings: gold coins and cold hard cash (lira and dollars). The bride's gown was adorned with so many banknotes and ribboned coins that when she stood up to pose for a photograph she might have been a contemporary sculpture, delicately poised between the avant-garde and the lunatic.

In the background an amateur rock band played a range of melodies, from Anatolian folk songs to the best of the Beatles, and every now and then threw in an air of their own, however disharmonious. Despite the objections of the bride's family, alcohol was available in one corner of the room. Mensur had dug in his heels and threatened not to attend the happiest day of his son's life if raqi, his lifelong companion, was banned. Most of the guests opted for soft drinks but enough seemed to have located the unholy bar. Among the pioneers in this forbidden territory was, surprisingly, the uncle of the bride. Given the speed with which he downed the drinks, it didn't take him long to become soused – a detail Mensur observed with delight.

Playing the part of the host, Peri – in an aquamarine knee-length dress and her hair coiffured into a bun so large that it shifted her head's centre of gravity – had to talk with many guests and smile often. As she cooed at children, kissed the hands of the elderly, listened to the tittle-tattle of her peers, she noticed a young man staring at her, intently. This wasn't the kind of male gaze that conveyed attraction and stopped at that fine line, but one that pushed, insisted, claimed. He seemed not to understand that only a Lilliputian step separated assertiveness from aggression. When their eyes locked, Peri scowled, hoping to make it clear that she was not interested in him. He gave a smirk in return, leaving her signal suspended in mid-air, undelivered.

Half an hour later, when she headed to the ladies' room, the young man blocked her way. Putting his hand on the wall so that she couldn't pass, he said, 'You look like a fairy. Obviously, your parents gave you the right name.'

'Excuse me. Don't you have better things to do?'

'Don't blame me, you shouldn't be so pretty,' he said, leering at her.

Peri felt her blood boil, the words stumbling out of her mouth. 'Leave me alone! No one gave you the right to bother me.'

Taken aback, he blinked. With exaggerated effort he lowered his arm. His face, which until a few seconds ago had held a confident smile, now showed unmistakable hostility. 'They said you were uppity. I should've listened. Just because you go to Oxford, you think you're better than us!'

'This,' she said evenly, 'has nothing to do with Oxford.'

'Arrogant bitch,' he said under his breath, loud enough for her to hear.

Peri's face turned white as she watched him stalk away. How easy it was to switch from liking to loathing. In the kingdom of the East, the male heart, like the orb at the end of a pendulum, swung from one extreme to the other. Oscillating between overplayed adoration to overplayed contempt, dangling over the emotional detritus that just the day before had been passion, men loved too much, raged too much, hated too much, always too much.

Upon returning to the salon, Peri found the bride and the groom engaged in the dance everyone had been waiting for. Dozens of eyes pressed against them from all sides. Their backs ramrod straight, their hands rigid, they held their poses without touching and swayed in tandem – two sleepwalkers trapped in the same dream.

Peri felt sad. The chasm between the person she carried inside and the one she was expected to be felt wider than ever. She sensed the distance, unbridgeable as it was, between the environment she came from and the one she wished to head towards. She would not be such a bride. She would not live the life of her mother. She would not be inhibited, limited and reduced to something she was not.

A thought crossed her mind with lightning speed: *I should never marry a man from this part of the world.* It jarred with everything she had been taught, was so deliciously wrong, so unspeakably blasphemous, she had to look down, lest others could see it in her eyes. Her husband she would choose from a culture as distant and different from hers as possible. An Eskimo perhaps. Someone named Aqbalibaaqtuq.

She broke into a grin as she imagined how her father would invite his Inuit son-in-law to knock back a few drinks together, with fish-head soup, raw whale meat and fermented seal flippers his new mezes. Meanwhile her mother would insist that he convert to Islam, circumcision and all. Aqbalibaaqtuq would become Abdullah. Then her brother Hakan would take him out for a crash course in Turkish masculinity. Aqbalibaaqtuq would fill many idle hours in the tea house playing cards and smoking nargileh. Before long, if he spent enough time in bad company, he would be inducted into the ways of the country's male archetype, demanding the privileges accorded to his sex. Their arctic love would swiftly melt in the heat of patriarchal customs.

Past midnight the celebration came to an end. One by one the remaining guests said their farewells and the band members packed up and cleared out, leaving only close family members behind. The next morning the newlyweds would embark on their one-week honeymoon. Their destination was an exclusive resort hotel on Turkey's Mediterranean coast, which had made a name for itself, and caused some controversy, through its creation of halal restaurants, halal pools and halal discos, all with gender-specific sections. They had even divided the beach, and parted the sea, into a women's section and a men's section.

But tonight, on Selma's insistence and for the sake of convenience, the newlyweds would spend the night at the Nalbantoğlus' home close to the airport. The bride's parents – who lived on the other side of the town – were also invited. Thus they all squeezed into the mini-van, carrying bags and baskets, and a silk bouquet, after so many hours its woven petals creased and frayed.

It was unseasonably cold for this time of year, the wind lashing against the windows with a vengeance, like a wronged spirit.

As the mini-van sped through rain-slicked streets, Peri saw the bride's mother pull out a bright red sash – 'the Maidenhood Belt' – from her handbag and tie it around her daughter's waist. The sash puzzled her, even though she knew in many parts of the country it was common practice. Not giving it any further thought, she tried to chat to Hakan, who was sitting next to her. Her brother looked tired and distracted, and she noticed a thin film of perspiration on his forehead; soon Peri, too, succumbed to the silence.

The Hospital

Istanbul, 2000

On arriving home, the newlyweds were given the master bedroom, while the bride's parents were placed in Peri's. Selma and Mensur had no choice but to take their son's room and share the same bed. As for Peri, she would have to make do with the sofa in the sitting room.

As soon as her head hit the pillow, Peri felt a wave of exhaustion sweep over her. Between wakefulness and sleep she heard a distant murmur, words floating in the air just before the last light was turned off. Someone was saying prayers. She tried to guess who it was, but the voice seemed devoid of age and gender. Perhaps she was already dreaming. Lulled by the ticking of the clock in the hallway, too drowsy even to brush her teeth, her chest rising and falling with each breath, she drifted off.

Deep in the night, an hour later or more, Peri woke with a start. She thought she had heard a sound but could not be sure. She propped herself up on her elbow, rigid and still. As she strained her ears, waiting, she wondered whether it was she listening to the dark or the other way round. Holding her breath, she counted heartbeats: three, four, five . . . there came the sound again. Someone was crying. Between sobs, a steady, insistent rustle was heard like wind through a grove of trees before a storm. A door opened and slammed shut, if not by accident then by a furious hand.

Although she sensed in her gut that something was wrong, Peri lay back, hoping that whatever it was would fade away on its own. But the sounds multiplied. Whispers rose into shouts, footsteps echoed down the corridor, and, in the background, not a sob any more but a moan, the call of a soul in pain.

'What's going on?' Peri said aloud, as she stood up, her voice travelling ahead of her into the depths of the house.

She reached the room where her parents should have been asleep. Her mother was up and awake, her face ashen. Her father was pacing left and right, his hands clasped, his hair in disarray. Next to them was her brother Hakan, a cigarette smouldering between his fingers; he inhaled with a gesture of exaggerated despair. Looking at them, she had the odd sensation that she didn't know any of these people – strangers impersonating her loved ones.

'Why is everyone awake?' Peri asked.

Her brother glared at her, his eyes as narrow as the edge of a blade. 'Go to your room!'

'But –'

'I said, go!'

Peri took a step back. She had never seen Hakan like that – even though he was always prone to fits of temper and swearing, this time his anger was so out of control and fierce it felt like a wild creature in the room.

Instead of returning to the sitting room, Peri veered towards the master bedroom, only to find the door ajar, the bride perched on the edge of the bed in a nightgown, her dark hair tumbling down over her shoulders. Her parents were sitting on either side of her, their mouths drawn into thin lines.

'I swear it's not true,' the bride said.

'Then why does he say such a thing?' her mother rasped.

'You believe him or your own daughter?'

The mother was quiet for a moment. 'I'll believe what the doctor says.'

Slowly, as though in a trance, Peri understood the reason behind the sounds she had heard earlier: her brother had stormed out of the bedroom, convinced that his new wife was no virgin.

'What doctor?' the bride asked; her eyes, red-rimmed and frightened, stared out of the window into the city. The sky, coal-black with the moon hidden behind a cloud, bled a hue of purple on the horizon, the harbinger of dawn.

'That's the only way to get to the bottom of this,' said the woman as she rose to her feet, grabbed her daughter by the hand and pulled her from the bed.

'Mum, please don't,' the bride whispered, her voice smaller than a pearl.

But the woman was not listening. 'Go and get our coats,' she said to her husband, at which he nodded, out of habit if not agreement.

Blood rushing to her face, Peri hurried back to her parents' side. 'Baba, stop them. They're going to the hospital!'

Mensur, in his cotton pyjamas, had the wretched look of someone who'd been thrust into a play in which he didn't know his lines. He glanced at his daughter, then at the bride and her mother, who were now passing in front of them, heading for the door. It was the same helplessness he had displayed years ago, the night the police had raided their home.

'Let us all calm down,' said Mensur. 'No need to involve strangers. We're a family now.'

The bride's mother deflected these words with a wave of her hand. 'If my daughter is at fault, I'll punish her myself. But if your son is lying, as Allah is my witness, I'll make him regret this.'

Mensur said, 'Please, we must not act with anger –'

'Let them do whatever they want,' interjected Hakan, cigarette smoke curling from his nostrils. 'I want to learn the truth too. I've a right to know what kind of a woman I married.'

Peri gaped at her brother. 'How can you say such a thing?'

'Shut up!' Hakan said in a voice so flat it didn't quite match the harshness of the message. 'I told you to stay out of this.'

In less than half an hour they were all sitting on a bench in the nearest hospital. All save for the bride.

Of that night, which would replay in her memory for years to come, several details would remain with Peri: the cracks on the ceiling that resembled the map of a forgotten continent; the nurse's shoes that click-clacked against the concrete floor; the odour of disinfectant mixed with the smells of blood and infection; the moss-green paint daubed on the walls; the sign EMERGENCY SECTIO with the missing letter; and the disturbing thought, drilling into her brain, that no matter how surreal she found everything that was happening, it could easily have been her subjected to the same examination, had her parents married her off to a family that cared about these things. Yes, Peri understood it with a sinking heart.

She had heard about wedding-night crises but she always assumed such things happened to other people – peasants in godforsaken villages, provincials who knew no better. Hers was not a family to get entangled in a virginity test at a ramshackle hospital. Since her childhood she had been treated as an equal to her brothers, if not more favourably. She was treasured, spoiled and loved by both parents. All the same, growing up in a tight neighbourhood where there were eyes behind every lace curtain, watching and judging, she was mindful of the boundaries not to cross, what not to wear, how to sit in public, when to return home from an evening out . . . that is, most of the time. In the last year of school, the whirlpool of dissent and defiance that had caught most of her classmates in its current and carried them far and wide had at first left her untouched, moored on the high moral ground. While her peers had broken taboos and each other's hearts with equal fervour, Peri had led a tranquil life. But then she had fallen in love, and love, though as brief as it was bold, smashed her well-preserved boundaries. Unknown to her parents, she had gone all the way with her leftist boyfriend. She could now see the fragility of her position as the 'beloved daughter'. She felt like a hypocrite. Here she was, waiting for the result of another young woman's virginity test when she was not a virgin herself.

'Why is it taking so long? Is there a problem?' said the bride's father, jumping to his feet, only to sit back down again.

'Of course not,' his wife lashed out at him. The woman was so agitated that the nurse on duty had twice come to tell her to lower her voice.

An hour – or what felt like it – passed. Finally, the doctor appeared, her hair tied up, her grey eyes blazing behind her glasses. She scanned them with undisguised contempt. It was obvious she loathed what she had done and she loathed them more for asking her to do it.

'Since you are keen to know, she's a virgin,' the doctor announced. 'Some girls are born without a hymen, and some hymens can be torn during sex or a simple physical activity but never bleed.'

She seemed to be doing it deliberately, using medical facts to humiliate them – an act of revenge for the embarrassment they had caused the bride.

'You've destroyed this young woman's sanity. I advise you to take her to a therapist, if you care for her, that is. I want you all to leave now. We have patients with real problems. You people waste our time.'

Without another word, the doctor turned her back and left. For one full minute no one spoke. It was the bride's mother who shattered the silence.

'Allah is great,' she cried out. 'They tried to smear my daughter. But God, my God, smacked them across the face and said, "How dare you sully a virgin? How dare you tarnish a rosebud?"'

In the periphery of her vision, Peri saw her father lower his head, his stare fixed on the concrete floor as though he wanted it to swallow him up.

'It's your son who couldn't do it, hear me! If he's not man enough, how can you blame my daughter? Instead you should've taken your son to you-know-where!'

'Wife, calm down,' murmured her husband, looking uneasy and uncertain that this was the right approach.

His intervention only served to further incense the woman. 'Why should I? Why should I spare them the shame?'

A door down the corridor opened and the bride emerged. She moved towards them, her steps measured and unhurried. In a flash, her mother bolted forward, beating her thighs with her fists as though in mourning. 'My rosebud, what have they done to you? May they sink into the mud they tried to drag us into!'

Ignoring her mother, the bride strode towards the exit. As she passed the Nalbantoğlus, and her husband, whose leg shook so violently that the bench was vibrating, she kept her chin up, refusing to make eye contact with anyone. Peri noticed her hands, manicured and hennaed, and her palms, studded with red crescents. It was this detail that affected her more than anything she witnessed during this miserable night. The marks a young woman digs with her fingernails during a virginity examination.

'Feride . . . wait . . .'

It was the first time Peri pronounced her name. To this day she had always been 'her' or 'you' or simply 'the bride'.

Though she slowed down, Feride neither stopped nor turned around. Walking straight ahead, through the automatic doors, she disappeared with her parents in tow.

Peri felt a seething rage inside – at her brother, whose selfishness and insecurity had brought this misery; at her parents, who hadn't tried harder to stop the offence; at the ages-old tradition that determined a human being's worth was between her legs; but mostly at herself. She could have done something to help Feride and yet she hadn't. It was always like this. In moments of stress, just when she had to take action and demonstrate resolve, she tumbled into lethargy, as if pushed down by an invisible hand, from where she observed the world around her fade and flatten into a blur, and her feelings grow dim, like light bulbs turned down, one by one.

On the way back home, in the mini-van they had rented for the wedding, the Nalbantoğlus were alone. While Hakan drove and Mensur sat in the back, staring out of the window, Peri took the seat next to her mother.

'What will happen now?' Peri asked.

'Nothing, inshallah,' said Selma. 'We'll buy chocolates, silks, jewellery . . . and apologize. We'll do everything we can to make it up to them, even though it was their idea to go to the hospital, not ours.'

Peri considered for a moment. 'How can a marriage survive after such an awful start?'

Her mother smiled askew, the light from a street lamp splitting her face into two: half flame, half shadow. 'Believe me, Pericim, many a marriage has survived worse than this. It'll be fine, inshallah.'

Peri stared, perhaps for the first time seeing, really seeing her mother. It occurred to her that her parents' marriage might not be all that it appeared to be, and her darling father not always the gentleman she believed he was.

Her thoughts flitted to the wedding portrait of her parents that they kept in the cabinet, framed but not on display. Mensur and Selma, both young and thin, stood stiff and unsmiling, as if they had just been hit by the gravity of what they had done. Behind them was an absurd background of wild orchids and flying geese. Around her yet uncovered head, Selma wore a chaplet of plaited daisies – their plastic beauty no less fake than their happiness.

Peri held her mother's hand, more by instinct than intention, and squeezed it gently. It occurred to her that the mother she had always seen as frail and tearful might have an inner resilience of her own. Selma dealt with emotional crises the way she did her household chores. Diligently, she picked up the pieces, just as she tidied up the knick-knacks scattered around the house.

As though she had sensed her daughter's thoughts, Selma said, 'I have faith, that helps. There must be a reason why we went through this. We don't know it yet, but Allah does.'

Peri could see from the flush in her cheeks and the glint in her eyes that her mother was sincere. Faith, whichever way Selma understood it, infused her with a sense of surrender that could have been a cause of weakness had it not made her stronger. Was religion an empowering force for women who otherwise had limited power in a society designed for and by men, or was it yet another tool for facilitating their submission?

The next day Peri flew back to England, her mind ablaze with questions – and unable to say whether it was best to search for the answers or to leave them undisturbed.

The Scavenger

Istanbul, 2016

Once she hung up the phone with her mother, Peri made her way down the main staircase adorned with faux-Grecian urns, across the polished marble floor and back to the dinner table. A part of her was disappointed not to have got Shirin's number. Another part was relieved. She had no idea what she would have said and, even if she'd found the right words, whether Shirin would have listened. She had called her a few times in the past, soon after she had left Oxford, but Shirin had been too angry to talk, the wound too raw. Although years had passed since, there was no guarantee that it would be any different now.

The guests' laughter grating in her ears, Peri entered the dining room, only to find the PR woman standing by the drinks cabinet, waiting for her.

'Hey, I called my brother while you were away,' the woman said with a smile that did not quite extend to her eyes. 'He was delighted to hear you were at Oxford around the same time that he was. I'm sure you two knew people in common.'

Peri returned her stare with equal intensity. 'Maybe, but Oxford is a big university.'

'I told him you had a photo of the scandal professor. He was very surprised.'

Peri clenched her jaw as she braced herself for what was coming.

'What was he called? My brother mentioned it but I forgot.'

'Azur,' Peri said, his name burning her tongue like a drop of fire.

'Exactly, I knew it was weird!' The PR woman snapped her fingers to punctuate her point. 'Uhm, my brother was curious . . . he wanted me to ask you, were you his student?'

'No, I didn't know the professor that well,' Peri said without missing a beat. 'The girls in the photo were his students. I was just a friend. Lost touch with all of them anyhow.'

'Oh,' said the PR woman, disappointment darkening her expression but not yet ready to let go. 'Try Facebook. I've reconnected with all my college friends – even ones from primary school. We have pilaff and beans days –'

Peri nodded, eager to get rid of this woman who, like a hostile army that invaded her land, was pillaging her privacy, her past. She would never tell her how many times she had googled Azur's name – his achievements, his books, his photos – and pored over the hundreds of entries about him; and then googled the scandal, after which he had stopped teaching but continued to give interviews and talks.

'My brother said he remembers hearing rumours that there was a Turkish girl taking this professor's course. He said it was the talk of the town.'

Tension filled the space between them like a filthy puddle. 'What are you trying to say?' Peri asked, amazed at the coldness in her voice.

'Nothing, I was just curious.'

The image of the tramp flashed before Peri's eyes. His gaunt frame, his penetrating eyes, his eczema-patched hands. This woman, though privileged and moneyed, was no less of an addict than he was. Peri imagined her holding a plastic bag full of other people's misfortunes and dark secrets, into which she poked her nose and inhaled as a respite from her own life.

'I wish I had something more interesting to tell you,' Peri said, the word interesting making her pause for a split second. Her remark, though intended for the busybody, seemed addressed to no one but herself. 'I was a quiet student, not the type to be involved in a scandal.'

The PR woman smiled as though in sympathy.

'Next time you talk to your brother, tell him it must have been someone else.'

'Oh, sure.'

For the rest of the dinner, Peri avoided making eye contact with the PR woman. She didn't feel bad about lying. She was not going to reveal her past to a stranger, especially to a scavenger-type-of-a-stranger hunting for bits of gossip to feed on. Besides, it wasn't exactly a lie, come to think of it. After all, it had been a different girl, a different Peri from the woman she was today, who had once been Professor Azur's favourite student and, later on, the cause of his ruin.

The Dusk Run

Oxford, 2000

Back at college Peri burrowed herself into her studies. In the mornings when she picked up her coffee – so unlike the sweet and strong Turkish coffee – she would observe the undergraduates and the dons with absorbed expressions on their faces, books and notes clutched to their chests as they hurried from one building to another; she would wonder how many of them had had a taste of life elsewhere. How easy it was to assume that Oxford – or anywhere, for that matter – was the centre of the world.

On Wednesday, she left the library at dusk. She had been reading for almost three hours and her brain was saturated with ideas. She imagined her mind as a rambling house with many rooms in which she stored all the things she read, heard and saw, and where they were inspected, processed and registered by a little clerk, a homunculus entirely at her unconscious service. Yet it was possible, she believed, that one's thoughts could be hidden even from oneself.

She decided to go for a run. After a quick stop by her staircase to drop off the books she had borrowed and change into her running clothes, she set off down Holywell Street, slowly finding her rhythm. The cold wind on her face was like a balm.

Cyclists passed silently by, their reflectors winking conspiratorially in the dark. People rode everywhere – to shops, restaurants, seminars – and one of her favourite sights was seeing the senior dons on their bikes, their gowns billowing gently in the wind. She herself was not a good cyclist. It was one of those things she had to work at – like happiness.

Having veered off her usual course, she dashed through streets and alleys that felt deserted. She inhaled the smell of anonymous winter plants, turned a corner and stopped, panting hard. She found herself face to face with a poster on a wall.

The Oxford University
Museum of Natural History presents
THE GOD DEBATE
Professor Robert Fowler, Professor John Peter
&
Professor A. Z. Azur
Come and join a spectacular debate
among the brightest minds of our times

Peri's eyes widened. She checked the time and location printed on the poster. It was the same day. 5 p.m. Museum of Natural History.

It had already started. The place was at least two miles away, and she had no ticket and no money on her even if tickets were still available. She had no idea how she would get in, and yet, on the spot, she turned in the direction of the museum, took a deep breath and began to run.

The Third Path

Oxford, 2000

By the time Peri, her hair dishevelled and rivulets of sweat running down her neck, reached her destination, the sun had already set in a low amber sky. She approached the neo-Gothic edifice that had been designed as 'a cathedral to science'. Architecture in Oxford fell into two categories: the kind that remembered and the kind that dreamed. The Museum of Natural History was both. The gravel crunching beneath her feet, Peri thought that the building – independent of the collections inside – demanded of its visitors awe and respect.

There were two attendants, a girl and a boy, at the main entrance – students by the look of them – wearing the same bright blue shirts and bored expressions. One of them nodded in her direction.

'I came for the debate,' Peri said, trying to catch her breath.

'Do you have a ticket?' asked the boy – a gangling youth with a protruding lower lip and a narrow forehead that was crowned by bushy, ginger hair.

'Uhm . . . no,' Peri said anxiously. 'And I don't have my wallet with me.'

'It'd have made no difference.' He shook his head. 'Sold out weeks ago.'

Words, of their own volition, spilled out of Peri's mouth. 'Oh, but I ran all the way here!'

At Peri's response, so loud and spontaneous, the girl smiled with sympathy. 'It's about to end anyway, you're late.'

Clinging to a thread of hope Peri asked, 'Can I at least take a peek?'

The girl shrugged. She had no objections. But the boy was of a different mind. 'We can't allow that,' he said, with the tone of someone who, having unexpectedly found himself in a position of authority, was determined to make the most of it.

'The debate's being recorded. There'll be a free screening later on,' the girl suggested.

Peri was not satisfied. Even so, she nodded. 'Okay, thanks.'

She turned back. Sulking in the faint glow of dusk, she had the look of a disappointed child. If anyone had asked her why she was so keen to go inside, the only answer she could have come up with was *instinct*. Something told her that many of the questions that had been tugging at the recesses of her mind were being addressed in there. It was this conviction that prompted her to do what she did next.

Instead of heading towards the main road, Peri wandered around in search of a side door. There was no need. Another opportunity to get in arose when she noticed, gazing back over her shoulder towards the entrance, that the girl was no longer there. The other attendant waited for a few seconds, and then disappeared into the building.

On impulse, Peri took advantage of the unguarded doorway and entered the museum. Once inside, she moved cautiously, her senses alert as she half expected the ginger-haired boy to pounce from behind a corner and throw her out. But he was nowhere to be seen. Following the signs that said GOD DEBATE, she soon found herself in a large, crowded hall.

In tight rows, an audience of students and academics sat with rapt attention, their gazes fixed on the four figures on stage. One of them was a prominent BBC journalist moderating the discussion; he seemed to be wrapping up the event. Peri studied the three professors, wondering which one was Azur.

The first professor – a tall, gaunt man with slanting, intelligent eyes – had a bald head and a spreading, salt-and-pepper beard, which he fiddled with nervously whenever he heard something not quite to his taste. A grey suit, pink check shirt, red braces with metal clasps and a hint of belligerence that slipped now and then from under his elaborate smile. He stared at his hands most of the time, as though they held a mystery he was hopeful to solve.

The second professor, the oldest of the three, had a broad face, ruddy complexion, thinning grey hair and a paunch he forgot to hide when he became excited. He wore a russet jacket that he found either constricting or uncomfortable in some other way, for he seemed ill at ease, hunched in his chair, his gaze unfocused. To Peri he seemed a gentle type, the sort of man who'd rather spend time with his students or his grandchildren than debating God on a podium.

The third speaker, sitting apart from the others to the left of the moderator, had brown-blond hair falling in elegant waves over his collar, and a prominent nose that was finely poised between the hideous and the magnificent. His eyes shone like specks of obsidian behind his classic black-and-tortoiseshell frame spectacles as he stared out at the audience with a world-weary smile. Peri could not decide whether his placidity was the sign of a soul at peace with itself or the reflection of a well-polished hubris. It was equally hard to guess how old he was. There was a taut litheness in his posture that suggested he was younger than the others, and his demeanour projected a spiritedness that might or might not have been due to his relative youth. Peri was certain he was the professor Shirin had been raving about.

'I believe I'm speaking for everyone present when I say we've had a fascinating discussion, some provocative ideas to chew on,' enthused the moderator. He seemed rather exhausted and relieved that the event was coming to an end. Peri wondered what had transpired before she arrived, sensing a groundswell of tension under the veneer of academic courtesy.

'Now it's time to open the floor to the audience. Some basic rules: keep your questions brief and to the point. Please wait for the roving mic and don't forget to introduce yourselves before you speak.'

A ripple of excitement travelled across the hall, like a breeze over a field of wheat. Immediately, a few hands went up, the brave and the bold.

A male student was the first to go. Briefly introducing himself, he unleashed a tirade about the dichotomy of good and evil, beginning with Ancient Greece and Rome up to the Middle Ages. By the time he had reached the Renaissance, the audience was getting restless, and the journalist interrupted, 'Okay, sir . . . did you have a question in mind or are you planning to give a secular sermon?'

Laughter rose. The student blushed and when he finally parted with the microphone – still having not asked a question – it was with visible reluctance.

The next person to stand up was a cleric in a black cassock, an Anglican pastor perhaps: Peri could not tell the difference. He said he had enjoyed the panel debate but was astonished to hear the first speaker claim that religion brooked no free discussion. The history of the Christian Church was replete with counter examples. The seeds of many universities across Europe, including their very own, had been sown through theology. Atheists were entitled to their opinions so long as they did not distort the facts, he concluded.

A brief exchange followed between the cleric and the bearded professor, whom Peri understood was the 'atheist' in question. The professor said that religion, far from being an ally of free discussion, was its age-old nemesis. When Spinoza questioned the teachings of the rabbis, he was not commended for his intellect; instead he was expelled from the synagogue. The same troubling pattern could be seen in the history of Christianity and Islam alike. As a man devoted to science and clarity he could not be placed under the sway of dogma.

The next audience member to reach for the microphone was an elegant middle-aged woman. Science and religion could never be bedfellows, she said, citing examples of philosophers and scientists – East and West – who had been persecuted by religious authorities throughout history. She railed at the second professor, who, Peri realized – besides being a famous scholar – was a man of considerable piety.

This second professor, though not as eloquent as his atheist peer, spoke mildly in a rich Irish brogue, enunciating each word slowly, like a delicacy to be savoured. He said from his point of view there was no conflict between religion and science. The two could go hand in hand, if we only stopped thinking of them as oil and water. He personally knew of several scientists, experts in their fields, who were devout Christians. As Darwin – who had never considered himself an atheist – argued, it was absurd to doubt that a man could be both an ardent theist and an evolutionist. Many scientists hailed as 'staunch atheists' today were, in fact, theists in heart.

Meanwhile, Peri, not having found an empty seat, leaned against the wall. She scrutinized Azur, who was listening to the exchange, his hair drifting across his forehead, his face lit with an enigmatic gleam and his chin resting in his palm. He wouldn't be able to stay in this position for long. The next question was directed at him.

A young woman in the front row rose to her feet. Shoulders squared off, her black pony-tail catching the light from the ceiling, she stood firmly upright. Even when her back was turned, Peri could see it was Shirin.

'Professor Azur, as a free spirit, I have a problem with the religion I was born into. I can't stand the arrogance of so-called "experts" or "thinkers" or the self-serving platitudes of imams and priests and rabbis. Excuse my French, it's a total fucking charade. When I read you I find a voice that addresses my anger. On sensitive matters you speak with conviction. And you show me how to empathize with others. When you sit down to write, do you have a specific reader in mind?'

Azur tilted his head to one side with a gentle smile of understanding and complicity – a nuance of expression that escaped Peri's notice. At the edge of her vision, a blue patterned shirt had distracted her. It was the male attendant she had met outside! Fearing he was looking for her, she shrank back against the wall. But the young man, his face glowering with unmistakable hostility, was staring at the stage, his jaw clenched, his eyes glued on one speaker in particular: Azur.

As soon as Shirin sat down, the same boy lurched forward, zigzagging through the audience. He stopped next to Shirin, closely leaning in as he asked for the mic. Peri had no clue about what was passing between them, but she could see Shirin's back stiffen. Grabbing the mic nonetheless, the boy turned towards the panelists, his booming voice almost a shout. 'I've a question for Professor Azur!'

Azur's face darkened. His nod, slow and deliberate, suggested he knew the young man. 'I'm listening, Troy,' he said.

'Professor, you wrote in one of your earlier books – I believe it was *Smash the Duality* – that you'd not engage in debates with atheists or with theists, but here you are doing exactly that, unless I'm addressing a clone. What has changed? Were you wrong back then or are you making a mistake now?'

Azur gave him a smile – different from the one he had offered Shirin – that exuded cold confidence.

'You are entitled to criticize my words so long as you quote them truthfully. I did not say I'd never debate with atheists and theists. What I said was . . .' He arched an eyebrow. 'Does anyone have a copy? I need to see what I said.'

Laughter broke out.

The moderator handed him a book. Promptly, Azur found the page he was looking for. 'Here it is!'

Clearing his throat – rather theatrically, Peri thought – he began to read: 'The prevailing question whether God exists elicits one of the most tedious, unproductive and ill-advised disputations in which otherwise intelligent people have been engaged. We have seen, all too often, that neither theists nor atheists are ready to abandon the Hegemony of Certainty. Their seeming disagreement is a circle of refrains. It is not even accurate to call this battle of words a "debate", since the participants, irrespective of their points of view, are known to be intransigent in their positions. Where there is no possibility of change, there is no ground for a real dialogue.'

Azur craned his head and scanned the audience before he closed the book. 'You see, participating in an open debate is a bit like falling in love.' His voice was serene; his gestures emphatic, smooth, plentiful. 'You are a different person by the time it comes to an end. Therefore, my friends, if you are unwilling to change, do not enter into philosophical arguments. That's what I said in the past and that's what I'm saying right now.'

Pockets of applause rose from the audience.

'I'm afraid we are running out of time. One final question from our listeners,' announced the moderator.

An old man stood up. 'May I ask the distinguished scholars if they have a favourite poem on God – whether they believe in Him or not?'

The audience stirred in their seats with anticipation.

The first professor said: 'My favourite poems tend to change as time passes . . . but at the moment I'm thinking of a few verses from Lord Byron's "Prometheus".'

Titan! to whose immortal eyes
The sufferings of mortality,
Seen in their sad reality,
Were not as things that gods despise;
What was thy pity's recompense?
A silent suffering, and intense;
The rock, the vulture, and the chain . . .

'I'm not at all good at memorizing poems,' the second professor said. 'I'll try T. S. Eliot.'

Many desire to see their names in print,
Many read nothing but the race reports.
Much is your reading, but not the Word of GOD,
Much is your building, but not the House of GOD.

Though it was his turn, Azur remained quiet for what seemed like a second too long. Into the expectant silence he said, 'Mine will be from the great Persian – Hafez. I might change the words somewhat, since, as you know, every act of translation is a lover's betrayal.'

He spoke so softly that Peri had to lean forward in order to hear him. She noticed several in the audience doing the same thing.

I have learned so much from God
that I can no longer call myself
A Christian, a Hindu, a Muslim, a Buddhist, a Jew
The Truth has shared so much of itself with me
that I can no longer call myself
a man, a woman, an angel or even a pure soul

As he uttered these verses, Azur lifted his eyes and stared straight ahead over the audience. Although he was looking at no one in particular, and seemed at equal distance from his admirers and critics, in that instant Peri could not help but feel that his words were aimed at her.

The moderator stole a glance at his watch. 'We have time for one last remark from each speaker,' he announced. 'Gentlemen, how would you summarize your views in one sentence?'

The atheist professor said, 'I'll repeat a well-known quote and leave it at that: *Religion is a fairy tale for those who are afraid of the dark.*'

'In that case, atheism is a fairy tale for those who are afraid of the light,' countered the pious professor in his soft Irish burr.

All heads turned to Azur. 'Actually, I quite like fairy tales,' he said, full of mischief. 'My colleagues here are equally misguided. One wishes to deny faith, the other doubt. They seem not to understand that I, as a simple human being, need both faith and doubt. Uncertainty, gentlemen, is a blessing. We do not crush it. We celebrate it. That's the way of the Third Path.'

'On that note I'd like to thank our distinguished guests and bring our discussion to a close,' the moderator jumped in, worried that Azur's remarks might spark a fresh outburst. He commented that today's event was a perfect example of a sincere, uncensored and open debate in the best British and Oxford tradition.

'Let's have a warm round of applause for all our speakers! And don't forget, they'll now be signing their books.'

The audience broke into a prolonged applause. Then, those keen on wanting signed copies rushed towards a stall piled high with the professors' books, while others made their way towards the stage, hoping for a personal word with one of the speakers; some stayed seated, whispering among themselves. The rest of the audience shuffled steadily towards the exit.

In the meantime, the three speakers moved to the table set aside for them. A yellow rose had been placed in front of each by the organizers of the event.

Peri inched forward with the crowd, eavesdropping on conversations to her left and right. Just before she was swept out of the hall, she stopped and turned back as though she wished to gather every detail within the reach of her gaze. She watched the moderator thrust his notes into his briefcase. She watched the two older professors chat with their readers. And she watched an untidy queue of admirers form in front of Azur – until he disappeared little by little amidst the stream of bodies.

The Optimizer

Istanbul, Oxford, 2001

The first term ended in a blur. Peri, home for the Christmas holidays, persuaded herself that her father's health had not worsened and that her mother's preoccupation with hygiene had not turned into an obsession. The entire house smelled of bleaching powder and lemon cologne. Draped over every radiator were drying clothes, washed so often that their patterns and colours had all but faded, tiny pools of water gathering underneath like tears shed for things gone by.

On New Year's Eve they were in front of the TV, father and daughter, munching roasted chestnuts as they watched a belly dancer – Mensur's traditional way of celebrating the arrival of a new year. Selma, as always, had gone to her room early, not to sleep but to pray. With both Umut and Hakan gone, it was only the two of them, father and daughter – just like in the past. They did not speak much, as if between them silence had a language of its own. It was the rituals, *their* rituals, Peri had missed most – taking long walks by the sea, cooking menemen, playing backgammon on the card table next to the cactus in the window.

A week later Peri returned to Oxford. Two consecutive trips to Istanbul having drained her budget, she was determined to get a part-time job. There was also one more thing on her mind: to find out more about Professor Azur.

The spring term began with fresh hopes and fresh decisions. Peri made an appointment to see her tutor for academic advice. A man with wire-rimmed glasses and a permanently distracted air, as if he were trying to solve a quadratic equation in his head, Dr Raymond was short in stature and firm-jawed. He encouraged every student he worked with to find *the perfect schedule to optimize his or her intellectual resources.* In return, the undergraduates had a nickname for him: Sir Optimizer.

Dr Raymond and Peri spoke at length about which courses she should take in her second year. Not that there was much flexibility. The programme was more or less fixed, with only a few minor adjustments allowed.

'There's a seminar I was hoping to take. Everyone says it's great,' Peri said briskly. 'Well, not exactly everyone, but a friend of mine does.'

'And which seminar might that be?' Dr Raymond asked, taking off his glasses.

Over the years he had seen, time and again, students misdirect one another. What worked for one person brought misery to someone else. Besides, young people had a tendency to change their minds as often as they changed their top-five songs. The course they went into raptures about at the beginning of the term they lambasted at the end. In his twenty-three years as a fellow of the college, he had arrived at the conclusion that it was best not to give students too many options. Choice and confusion were conjoined twins.

Unaware of the thoughts crossing her tutor's mind, Peri carried on, 'A series of seminars on God. The professor's name is Azur. Do you know him?'

Dr Raymond's mouth, fixed in an amiable smile, twisted downwards almost imperceptibly. Only the slightest twitch of an eyebrow gave away his discomfort. 'Oh, I know *of* him – who doesn't?'

Peri's mind raced as she attempted to deconstruct the intonation of this apparently simple remark. She had come to learn that the English had an indirect way of expressing their opinions. Unlike the Turks, they did not communicate resentment through resentment or anger through double anger. No, there were layers to their conversation; the deepest discomfort could be conveyed with a reticent smile. They complimented when, in truth, they wished to denounce; they clothed their criticisms in cryptic praise. *If I gave a bad performance on stage,* Peri thought to herself, *in Turkey, they'd pelt me with twigs of prickly holly; in England, I imagine it'd be with roses – confident that I'd get the message from the thorns. Totally different styles.*

In the meantime, Dr Raymond paused, mulling over how best to approach a delicate issue. When he spoke again he articulated each word carefully – like a parent explaining an unwelcome fact of life to a sullen child. 'I'm not entirely convinced that this would be the right choice for you.'

'But you said I could choose a subject of interest as long as it was on the options list and this one is. I checked it.'

'Perhaps you could tell me why you want to take this seminar?'

'The subject is . . . important to me for family reasons.'

'Family reasons?'

'God was always a contentious issue in our house. Or religion, I should say. My mother and father have conflicting views. I'd like to study it, properly.'

Dr Raymond cleared his throat. 'We are lucky to have one of the world's greatest collection of books; you can read on God as much as you want.'

'Wouldn't it be better to do that under the guidance of a professor?'

It was a question Dr Raymond preferred not to answer and he didn't. 'Azur is very knowledgeable, that's for sure, but I must warn you, his teaching method is, how shall I put it, unorthodox. It doesn't work well with everyone. This seminar divides students – some enjoy it, others become profoundly unhappy. They come to me to complain.'

Peri sat still. Oddly, her adviser's lack of enthusiasm had whetted her curiosity; she was now even more eager to take the seminar.

'Bear in mind it's a small class. Azur accepts few students and he expects them to attend every week and to do all the reading and assignments. It's a lot of work.'

'I don't shy away from hard work,' said Peri.

Dr Raymond heaved an audible sigh. 'Well, by all means go and talk to Azur, ask him to show you the syllabus.' He couldn't help adding, 'If he has one, that is.'

'What do you mean, sir?'

Dr Raymond paused, disquiet passing across his usually genial features. Then he did something he had never done in his long years as an Oxford don: to speak negatively to a student about a colleague behind his back. 'Look, Azur is seen as a bit of an oddball around here. He believes he is a genius and geniuses think they're not bound by the rules of common people.'

'Oh,' Peri gasped. 'But is it true?'

'Is what true?'

'Is he a genius?'

Dr Raymond realized that his cynicism had backfired, and whatever he said next might drive him further into a corner. His solemn expression changed to one of light-heartedness. 'It was meant in jest.'

'A joke? I see . . .'

'Don't rush, take it easy,' Dr Raymond said, putting his spectacles back on, signalling the end of the conversation. 'See how you feel about it first. If in doubt, come back and talk to me, we'll easily find you another option. A more suitable one.'

Peri jumped to her feet, having heard only what she wanted to hear. 'Great, thank you, sir!'

After Peri left, her adviser's lips turned downward in contemplation. His jaw set even more tautly, his nostrils flaring and his fingers laced together under his chin, he sat in his armchair for a while, motionless. Finally, he shrugged, deciding he had done what he could. If that silly girl was going to bite off more than she could chew, she would have only herself to blame.

The Youth

Istanbul, 2016

Deniz, standing behind Peri's chair, leaned down, gave her a cursory peck on the cheek and whispered into her mother's ear: 'Mum, I want to leave.'

Her face caught the light from the Murano chandelier. Her friend was by her side, twirling a strand of hair around a finger. The two teenagers looked bored. Much as they craved inclusion in the grown-up world, it was obvious they found it dull and perhaps predictable.

'Selim is going to take us home,' Deniz added.

She wasn't asking her mother for permission, only informing her. The other girl, the daughter of the bank CEO, was also coming – a last-minute sleepover. They had made their plans. Probably they would stay up late, listening to music, texting their friends, nibbling midnight snacks, laughing at people's Instagram photos and YouTube videos; nonetheless Deniz would be complaining, a barrage of grievances having accumulated in her breast, as if it were a detention centre she lived in and not the house of her loving parents.

'Okay, sweetheart,' Peri said. She trusted her husband's driver, Selim, who had been with the family for long years. 'You can leave early; Dad and I won't be late.'

The guests smiled. A few rolled their eyes. It was a familiar conversation to anyone with teenage children.

'Ciao, girls!' The CEO waved from his corner.

'Let me walk you girls out,' Peri said, as she pushed her chair back.

Adnan rose to his feet. 'No, you stay, darling. I'll do it.'

His eyes lit up as their gazes met. He did not seem upset about the Polaroid any more. He had dropped the subject. He was good at that, knowing when to let things go – unlike Peri. Effortlessly he smiled at her, the smile that meant he was assuming responsibility and putting things in order. Level-headed and sensible, Adnan enjoyed solving problems; and if he couldn't solve them, he knew how to manage them. So different from Peri. For her, problems were like insect bites: she'd scratch and scratch away at them. She could neither allow them to heal nor leave them alone. Whereas he liked to repair broken things – and broken people. *How else to explain his attraction to instability,* Peri thought. *How else to explain his attraction to me.*

As her husband and daughter passed by, Peri stood up. She kissed Adnan on the lips, even though she knew some guests would regard it as poor etiquette and others as indecent behaviour. 'Thank you, darling.'

Sometimes when she thanked him for the small things in life, she sensed, in truth, she was thanking him for those larger things that were better left unexpressed. Yes, she was grateful to him, grateful to the Fate that had brought him to her. But, then again, she knew gratitude was not love.

Listen to me, Mouse, there are two kinds of men: the breakers and the fixers. We fall in love with the first, but we marry the second. She hated to think that life, her life, had vindicated Shirin's theory.

Her eyes brimming with affection, Peri smiled at her daughter. She was about to give Deniz a hug but something in the girl's expression said *Mum, please don't, not in front of this group.*

'I love you,' Peri said quietly.

Deniz paused for a second. 'Love you too. How's your hand?'

Peri turned over the bandage, dried blood on the edges. 'It's fine. It'll be as good as new tomorrow.'

'Just don't do it again,' whispered Deniz, as if she were the concerned mother and Peri the wayward daughter. Then cheerily she said to the guests, 'Good night, everyone. Don't smoke. Remember, it's bad for you.'

'Good night,' came a chorus of voices.

'Oh, youth!' said the businessman's wife as soon as the teenagers left the room. 'How I wish I could rewind time. Sixty is the new forty? It's all lies.'

'Speak for yourself,' said the businessman to his wife. 'I'm as young as a freshly minted coin. Watch out, I might divorce you and get myself a younger model.'

The journalist gave a false cough. 'It's an Eastern phenomenon, though, I mean, early ageing. Look at Westerners. All wrinkles and grey hair, still touristing abroad. It's embarrassing to see American oldies mobbing our Hagia Sophia and hopping over the stones at Ephesus. What do they call themselves – grey panthers? I've yet to see a seventy-year-old Middle Easterner travelling the world. Turks, Arabs, Iranians, Pakistanis . . . We have big ideas about the world – but we never see it!'

The architect who had displayed his nationalistic sensitivities throughout the evening glowered at him.

The businessman's wife, suddenly busy texting on her mobile phone, lifted her head, her face glowing. 'Good news, everyone! The psychic is ten minutes away, I just got his message.'

'Lovely,' said the PR woman as she leaned back in her chair. 'We've so much to ask him. The kids have left, our drinks are refreshed – now we can start talking naughty. I'd love to dig out a few secrets tonight.'

So saying, the woman winked at Peri. A gesture she left unreturned.

The Colourful Stranger

Oxford, 2001

Having never had a job before, Peri was baffled as to where to begin looking for one. Yet she was bent on finding some kind of employment, despite the demands of her timetable, not to mention her student visa, which only allowed her a limited number of hours of work a week. So she went straight to her exuberant friend who had an opinion on everything – even on matters she knew nothing about.

'You must have a CV,' Shirin opined, 'that shows your work experience.'

'But I have none.'

'Duh, make it up! Who is going to check whether you waitressed at some pizzeria in Istanbul?'

'You want me to lie?'

Shirin rolled her eyes. 'Oh, the power of semantics! Sounds awful when you put it that way. Use your imagination, is all I'm saying. It's a bit like applying makeup to your biography. Don't tell me you're against makeup!'

For a fleeting moment the two women stood staring at each other's faces: one, painted; one, free of all cosmetics. It was Shirin who broke the silence. 'I think I'd better give you a hand.'

Early next morning Peri found an envelope pushed under her door. Apparently, Shirin had already prepared a CV for her.

A minute later, Peri was at her friend's door, knocking. The second she heard a faint mumble coming from inside, she dashed in, waving a sheet of paper. 'What is this? I haven't done any of these things!'

From Shirin, still in bed with her head buried under a pillow, came a muffled, 'Urgh. I knew it, kindness never pays off.'

'I appreciate your help,' said Peri. 'But this says I was a bartender in a trendy underground bar in Istanbul until it burned down. An arson attack! And that I worked in the library of Ottoman manuscripts, specializing in palace jesters and eunuchs! Oh, one more: that in the summers I took care of an octopus at a private aquarium!'

Shirin, sitting up in salmon-pink satin pyjamas, pushed up the blindfold from her eyes and giggled. 'I might have got carried away with that last bit.'

'Only with the last bit? How do you think this nonsense is going to help me to find a part-time job?'

'It won't. But it'll make you a foreign curiosity. Trust me, educated Brits get a thrill out of multiculturalism. Not too much, though, just enough. People like you and me are allowed to be a bit . . . *eccentric*. It makes us fun to be around. So you might as well play it up, take advantage of it. If foreigners aren't going to bring excitement – and good food – who wants them in England!'

Peri was silent.

'Listen, what do you think the average Brit knows about your country? They assume everyone over there is either swimming with dolphins and eating calamari or wearing burqas and chanting Islamist slogans.'

Peri blinked as a surfeit of images filled her head.

'What I'm saying is they either have a sunny impression – sandy beaches and Eastern hospitality, that kind of shit. Or a gloomy one – Islamic fundamentalists, police brutality and *Midnight Express*. When they want to be nice to you, they throw in the first; when they want to challenge you, it's the second. Even the most educated are not immune to clichés.' Shirin stood up to wash her face in the sink by the wall. 'Like it or not, sister, what you hear from my mouth is the cold hard truth. You must stand up against stereotypes.'

'And this is the way to do that, through falsification?' Peri asked, glancing at the CV in her hand.

'That's one fucking way,' said Shirin, running her fingers through her hair, droplets of water clinging to her chin.

Guiltily motivated, Peri took to the streets with her CV. At first, she searched for signs posted in shop windows that said, 'Help Needed'. There were none. Mustering her courage she entered a cake shop and spoke with the manager. She was politely rejected. Next she tried her luck at the pub she had been to with her parents. Same outcome. The third place she called on was her favourite bookshop – Two Kinds of Intelligence. The owners were not surprised to hear Peri's inquiry. Students were always stopping in looking for a part-time job.

'Have you worked anywhere before, dear?' said the husband.

Peri hesitated. 'I'm afraid I haven't. But you know I love books.'

The wife smiled. 'This is your lucky day! We've been looking for someone to help us out over the next few weeks. We can't promise to keep you on after that. Maybe every now and again when things get busy. What do you think?'

'Sounds perfect!' Peri said, hardly believing what she'd just heard.

As she was leaving the shop, she spotted, there on a shelf, the *Rubáiyát of Omar Khayyám* – her father's beloved poet. With an introduction by the translator Edward FitzGerald and filled with illustrations, the beautiful old edition was irresistible. Luckily, they offered her a nice discount.

Outside, it started to drizzle. Thin, lukewarm drops that brightened her mood. She smiled, put her CV inside the book and checked her watch. Still an hour before her next tutorial. It occurred to her she had enough time to go and find Azur, to get the syllabus for his seminar on God. From all that Shirin had said about him – not to mention her own mixed feelings as she had watched him on the panel – she slightly dreaded meeting him in person.

Still thinking of the professor, she opened at random the book of poems, which were Khayyám's breath and soul:

Ah, Love! could thou and I with Fate conspire
To grasp this sorry Scheme of Things entire

She read the lines carefully, slowly. Was there an omen here of things to come? If so, what could it be? Had her father seen her searching for a sign in the words of a poet who had lived almost a thousand years before, he would not be pleased.

But Peri did not think she defied her father's golden rule by consulting Khayyám. 'That's why I love poetry so,' she murmured to herself. 'I can touch, see, hear, smell and taste poems. All my senses are at work, trust me, Baba!'

It was time, therefore, that she finally came face to face with the professor.

PART THREE

The Siskin

Oxford, 2001

Not knowing where to find Professor Azur, Peri hazarded a guess that she would be able to track him down at the Divinity School. If he taught God, surely that was where he should be.

Grand and modest, this medieval building was the oldest structure in Oxford built for lecturing and teaching. From a distance, with its compound arches, carved wooden doors and flying buttresses, it resembled less the feat of architecture that it was than a delicate water-colour by a dreamy artist. A drowsy expectation hung in the air, as though the ancient stones, having tired of decades of tranquillity, were awaiting something – or so it seemed to Peri as she approached it on that particular day.

Something drew her inside, something soaring and spiritual in the sublime lines of the fifteenth-century vaulted ceiling. No one stopped her going in, and there seemed no one in the long room illuminated by Perpendicular-style windows – except for a student sitting cross-legged on the floor, immersed in a book. At Peri's footsteps he glanced up. Under the light slanting through a high window, his features were blurred for a second, and then became visible – the narrow forehead, the ginger hair, the freckled cheeks. It was the attendant who had stopped Peri at the entrance to the God Debate; the attendant who had taken a swipe at Professor Azur in front of everyone. She remembered his name – only because it was the same as the ancient Turkish city of Troy.

'Hello,' Peri said cautiously.

'Hi there.' The smile on his face was one of recognition.

'You were at the museum the other day. Do you work there?' Peri asked.

'Nope, only volunteering. I'm a lowly undergraduate – just like you.'

Peri half expected him to reprimand her for sneaking into the debate, but either he had not spotted her, or he simply preferred not to bring the subject up. Instead he chatted nonchalantly, asking her where she came from and what she studied. Now that he was stripped of any vestige of authority, he was approachable, even affable.

'I'm looking for Professor Azur,' said Peri, when the conversation hit a lull. 'Do you know where his office might be?'

Troy's face remained motionless for a moment. His voice, when he spoke again, sounded hollow, like a balloon that had fizzled out. 'You won't find him here. These are university offices nowadays. Why are you looking for him anyway?'

Not expecting to be questioned, Peri's voice faltered. 'Uhm . . . I'm interested in his seminar.'

'Don't tell me you are planning to take "God"?'

'Why not?' Peri asked. 'What's wrong with it?'

'Everything,' Troy said. 'The guy's a wolf in professor's clothing!'

'You don't like him?'

'He kicked me out of his class. I'm suing him, by the way. Going to take him down in court.'

'Wow, didn't know students could do that,' said Peri. 'I mean . . . Sorry to hear you had a problem.'

'Problem?' Troy echoed the word with disdain. 'Azur is the devil himself. Mephistopheles. Do you know who that is?'

'Sure, from *Faust*.'

Troy looked pleasantly surprised that a Turkish girl would know about Faust. 'Look, you seem nice, but you're a foreigner, you won't be able to tell just how insane this man is. You have to listen to me. Stay away from Azur!'

'Well, thanks for the warning,' Peri said, whatever sympathy that had formed between them ebbing away. 'But I'll decide for myself.'

Troy shrugged. 'Okay, it's your choice. He has rooms at his college. The entrance is on Merton Street. In the front quad, find the third staircase on the left. At the open entrance you'll see a list of names painted white on black.'

Peri thanked him, though deep within she thought it was rather odd that he was so eager to guide her towards a man he regarded as the devil.

Professor Azur's college was down an ancient cobbled lane just off the High Street that you entered through a honey-toned Gothic arch and a stone courtyard.

Peri easily found the staircase. Chalked on either side of the outside wall were the results of the latest college boat race, surmounted with a pair of crossed oars. Inside the porch she read the names inserted in slats on a board: Prof. T. J. Patterson. G. L. Spencer. Prof. M. Litzinger . . . and Prof. A. Z. Azur, on the first floor. She made her way down the dark, narrow, flagstoned corridor. There, on the right, was an entrance, its lintel angled with the weight of antiquity; the door slightly ajar, a sheet of paper pinned to it.

Professor A. Z. AZUR
Available: Tuesdays 10 a.m.–12 p.m./Fridays 2–4 p.m.

Theory: You have a question, visit during office hours
Counter-theory: You have an urgent question outside office hours, drop in & see what happens
Choose carefully whether it is theory or counter-theory that applies to your case

Since it was neither a Tuesday nor a Friday, Peri knew she should leave and come back another time. Yet she was emboldened by the ambiguity in the note. She knocked on the door – an empty gesture since, given the silence reigning inside, she sensed there was no one to answer. She tapped again, just to be sure. From the depths of the room, she heard a sound too dulcet to be human, evocative, perhaps, of a beetle trilling for a mate or a butterfly breaking free from its chrysalis. Peri listened intently, her body taut. Once again, the silence was absolute.

A rush of curiosity came over her, that gnawing hunger for things out of reach. In a flash, she decided that she would peek inside and then leave as quietly as she had come. She pushed the door open, ever so gently. It creaked.

Nothing had prepared Peri for the sight that awaited her. Under a saffron light spilling through the tall half-open sash window that looked on to an exquisite English garden, were towers of books, handwritten notes, manuscripts and engravings. The walls were lined with bookcases, packed floor to ceiling. Criss-crossing the room, between facing shelves, various colourful strings – like the laundry lines of Istanbul's impoverished neighbourhoods – were stretched, on which notes and maps had been hung with pegs. Across from the door stood a claw-footed, cherry-coloured, antique desk, every inch covered with more books. Red slips of paper poked out from between their pages, like miniature tongues sticking out in mock surprise. The armchair, the sofa and the coffee table, even the handwoven scarlet rug, were covered with volumes and volumes. If ever there was a shrine dedicated to the printed word, this was it.

But it was neither the abundance of books nor the disarray in the room that had stopped Peri in her tracks. There was a bird, a siskin with yellow-green feathers and a forked tail, trapped inside. It must have flown in through the window and was flapping around, searching frantically for the freedom it must have just lost. Peri took a few tentative steps and held her breath. Cupping her hands, she tried to catch the delicate creature as gingerly as she could, but the bird, terrified by her presence, was now in a crazed state. In circles of panic, it darted from one corner to the other and at times came tantalizingly close to the open window, yet failed to discover the way out.

Moving deftly, Peri put the copy of the *Rubáiyát* down on top of a pile of books and tried to push the old, heavy window up further. But the sash must have been jammed from above, for it could not be forced any wider. She wiggled it with all her strength. The bird, scared witless by the noise, darted by her and threw itself against the glass, beyond which, so close yet so distant, was the infinite sky. Trembling from the impact, it landed on a shelf close enough for Peri to be able to see its bead-like eyes, gleaming with terror. She looked towards the dainty creature with compassion, its distress in the alien surroundings all too familiar to her.

Peri searched around for a tool that might help her to release the window sash. As her eyes scanned left and right, she detected a smell she could not quite identify. Mingling with the musty scent of books was the sweet-sour fragrance of decaying grapefruits in a bamboo bowl, their pastel brightness in contrast with the earthy hues dominating the room. Beyond that there was another scent. It didn't take her long to discern the source. There, on a ledge, an incense stick burned in a bronze holder in which a finger of ash had formed.

She found a metal letter-opener, its sharp end perfect for unscrewing the clasps that she could see were holding the window. Once she unfastened the frame on each end, she gave one last push. The window slid upwards halfway, more easily than she had thought. Now all she needed to do was to direct the bird towards what had become a bigger possibility for escape. Taking her sweater off, she began to wave it in the air.

'Is this a new dance or something?' a voice inquired from behind.

Peri was so startled that she let out a gasp. When she turned around, she saw Professor Azur standing in the doorway, one arm resting on the doorframe, watching her, his lips twisted in amusement. Up close his long brown hair had golden overtones, like gilded threads woven into a dark tapestry. He was not wearing glasses today.

'Oh, oh, I'm terribly sorry,' she blurted out, taking a step towards him and immediately taking a step back. 'I really didn't mean to barge in without permission.'

'Then why did you?' he asked, sounding genuinely keen to know.

'Uhm, I saw this bird.'

'What bird?'

Peri pointed to her left, where the creature had been a moment ago, but now there was only empty space. She glanced around nervously. The siskin had disappeared without a trace. 'It must have left through the window while we were talking.'

For one full minute he stood silent, eyes focused and emanating a strange familiarity, as though she were yet another book he had read in times past that he was now trying to recall. Finally, he said, 'That was amber, by the way.'

'Excuse me?'

'The incense you were looking at,' he said. 'Thursdays are amber. I burn different kinds on different days. Do you like amber?'

Peri's heart skipped a beat. Yes, she knew about the power of amber.

'Roman women carried balls of amber. Some say for the fragrance; others, for protection against witches.'

Peri's eyes widened. She couldn't tell whether it was the effect of Troy's warning or something in Azur's presence, but she felt flustered.

'Don't tell me you're afraid?' he asked, sensing her discomfort.

'Of amber?'

'Of witches!'

'Of course not,' Peri said quickly. A voice inside told her that if he had seen her examining the incense, he must have been here long enough to see the bird. 'Again, Professor, I'm very sorry for having entered your room.'

'How often do you apologize?' Azur asked. 'Twice in three minutes. If that's your average, it's a bit too much, don't you think?'

Peri blushed. He had a point. She apologized excessively – for being a few minutes late to an appointment; for letting go of a door she was holding for the next person a second too soon; for passing someone on the pavement; for barely touching a shopper with her trolley in the supermarket . . . She said 'sorry' all the time.

'Here's a hypothesis,' said Azur, flipping his hair out of his eyes. 'People who apologize unnecessarily are also inclined to thank unnecessarily.'

Peri swallowed hard. 'Maybe they're just anxious souls trying to get by. They do what they can to keep up with others but they know there's always a gap.'

'What sort of a gap?' asked Azur.

'Like we don't really belong,' said Peri, and immediately regretted what she said. Why was she revealing her feelings to this man, who was not only a stranger but also a professor, twice removed from her world?

Azur walked past Peri, sat behind his desk, scribbled a note on a piece of paper and pinned it on the laundry line above his head. 'So you're worried that the other students might think you're not one of them? An impostor pretending to be like everyone else? You think you're . . . different? Possessed? Weird? Crazy?'

'I didn't say that,' Peri objected. Every muscle in her body felt tense, waiting for the next blow.

Oblivious to her reaction, he said, 'Tell me, what makes you think you don't deserve to be at Oxford?'

'I didn't say that either!' Her stare fell on the scarlet rug that reminded her of the carpets back home. 'People here are so smart,' she said to her feet.

'You're not?'

'I am but I need to work hard. The other students, they adapt easily to university life. Whereas for me it's more complicated,' said Peri, only now remembering why she had come here. 'Actually, I'd like to see the details of your seminar on God. Dr Raymond suggested that I should ask you directly.'

'Ah, Dr Raymond?'

Azur sounded as if he didn't think much of her 'moral tutor' – her academic adviser – but he did not dwell on it. Instead he pulled out a note from a leatherbound book, scanned it with a grimace, screwed it into a ball, threw it deftly into a waste-paper basket and announced, 'You're considering it for the Michaelmas term, I suppose. The seminar is full and there's a waiting list.'

This Peri wasn't expecting. Now that she had been told the seminar was beyond her reach, she was itching to get in.

'However,' said Azur, seeing her disappointment, 'there's one student who will have to drop out. So we might have an opening at some point.'

Peri's face lit up. Underneath her eagerness, she felt a tad uneasy as it occurred to her that the student to whom he referred was probably Troy.

'There was a boy –'

'Yes . . . he's angry and aggressive,' Azur said. 'The angry and the aggressive cannot study God.'

Silence extended between them, unfolding like a scroll. From behind his desk, Azur fixed his eyes on Peri. 'Now tell me, why do *you* want to attend this seminar?'

'In my family, faith is a divisive subject. My father is –'

'Your parents aren't here. I'm asking *you*.'

'Well, I've always felt ambivalent about matters of faith – and also curious. I need to clarify my thoughts.'

'Curiosity is sacred. Uncertainty is a blessing,' Azur said, repeating the views he had expressed at the panel. 'As for clarifying your thoughts, I'm the last person in Oxford you should come to for that.'

Outside a bird chirruped and Peri wondered if it might be the siskin, back in the nature that, though full of danger and savagery, was nevertheless home. In her distraction she didn't notice the professor leaning forward and reaching for the book of poems she had laid down.

'Aha! What have we here? I say, an old edition of the *Rubáiyát*!' Azur said. Before she could react he had already opened it and found the CV inside.

'Oh, that's just a . . .' Peri stumbled.

With a mixture of delight and disbelief, Professor Azur scanned the page that Shirin had prepared. 'Well, well. You have taken care of an octopus?'

Peri froze.

'Mysterious creature, extremely intelligent,' he said. 'About two-thirds of its neurons reside in its tentacles, as I'm sure you know.'

Having no other option, Peri agreed.

'Do you think the arms of an octopus have minds of their own?' asked Azur. To Peri's relief, he didn't seem to expect an answer. 'For decades people thought the larger an animal's brain, the cleverer it was. They associated intelligence with brain size. How sexist! Men have more brain tissue than women. Then comes the magnificent octopus, debunking myths with its six arms – not eight, by the way, people mistakenly count the legs. What if, instead of a big clunky centralized brain, a complex network of multiple brains was the next step in evolution?'

A subtle thrill of excitement spread through Peri, almost against her will. She enjoyed listening to him, she realized.

'Since it gets smarter with age, if it only lived longer, the octopus would be the most brilliant species on earth. But Aristotle, that greatest of philosophers, thought octopuses were dumb. Now what does that say about Aristotle?'

Peri had the strangest feeling that wherever this conversation was heading, it was not about a philosopher and a mollusc any more, but about Azur and herself. She said, 'That Aristotle was wrong, maybe biased. He thought there was nothing interesting about the octopus; he already knew what there was to know. So he failed to see it was full of wonders.'

The professor smiled. 'That's right . . . Peri,' he said, glancing at her name on the resumé. 'Just like Aristotle's octopus, God is an enigma that calls for exploration.'

'But it's different. We don't need to *believe* in an octopus; we know it exists. Whereas with God, we can't even agree on whether there is one or not.'

Azur frowned. 'My seminar has nothing to do with belief. We're seeking knowledge.'

A firmness in his voice. Brooding and impatient. Peri suspected that when he talked to himself, while working late into the night or walking on dew-soaked mornings, this was the tone he used.

'The seminar on God is a meeting of curious minds. We come from all sorts of backgrounds but we have one thing in common. The spirit of inquiry! It is a programme that requires a lot of reading and research. I don't care whether you're a believer or not. Amongst my students, there is only one sin: laziness.'

Peri asked, cautiously, 'And the syllabus –'

'Oh, the holy syllabus!' Azur thundered. 'Academia abhors improvisation. Undergraduates must be told what they'll be reading every week, one must give them a month's notice. Otherwise, they'll panic!'

Thus saying, he opened a drawer, took out a sheet, put it inside the *Rubáiyát* and handed it to her. 'Here it is, if you must,' he said. The CV he kept for himself.

'Thank you,' Peri said, even though she suspected the document she held was no more representative of the truth than the CV Shirin had prepared for her.

'Before you go,' Azur said, 'you said you were confused and curious, and you seem to make things complicated for yourself: these are the three C's essential to an honest study of the *possibility* of God.'

'You mean confusion and curiosity –'

'And complicatedness! Some call it chaos!' Azur added. 'Anyone who has the necessary C's is in a good position to study God.'

Not sure whether that meant she would be admitted to the seminar, but feeling the need to thank him nonetheless, Peri smiled and gently closed the door on Azur. As she crossed the quadrangle, she glanced back towards the building, trying to find the window that had trapped the siskin. Her eyes travelled across the weathered façade and fixed on one glazed sash, behind which the professor's shadow glided past, like a fleeting thought. But perhaps it was only her imagination.

The Holy Syllabus

Entering the Mind of God/God of the Mind
(Honour School of Philosophy and Theology)
Thursdays 2 p.m.–4.30 p.m.
Lecture Room, 10 Merton Street

Seminar Description

In this course of weekly classes we shall address questions of growing relevance to a large number of people around the world today. Our aim is to equip ourselves with the necessary intellectual tools for better understanding and to encourage a free debate devoid of all manner of bigotry and dogmatism. Students are expected to read, research, ruminate on and respect opinions that they might not personally share.

This seminar does NOT promote any particular religion or adhere to any particular view. Whether you are Jewish, Hindu, Zoroastrian, Buddhist, Taoist, Christian, Muslim, Tibetan Buddhist, Mormon, Bahai, agnostic, atheist, New Age practitioner or about to initiate your own cult, you will have an equal say. In the lecture room we hold our discussions sitting in a circle so that everyone is equidistant from the centre.

Seminar Objectives

1. *To promote empathy, knowledge, understanding and wisdom, sophos, in matters pertaining to the notion of God;*
2. *To provide students with a wide array of answers to the most demanding questions of our times;*

3. *To encourage students to think critically and carefully about a topic that is important not only in theology or philosophy, but also in psychology, sociology, politics and international relations;*
4. *To approach universal dilemmas without mechanical repetition, lack of information, fanaticism and fear of offending others;*
5. *In short, to confuse and to be confused . . .*

Seminar Materials

The reading lists will be tailored individually according to your determination, diligence and academic performance. Be prepared to be assigned materials that may be at odds with your own beliefs and to comment on them (e.g. atheist students might be given books by pious authors; theist students will study works by atheist scholars, etc.).

What to Expect from This Seminar

Since God is our main subject, this seminar is open-ended, with no beginning and probably no conclusion. It is up to the student to decide how much to take from the experience and how far to journey.

a. *The Cranes. Those who, dissatisfied with flying at average altitudes, aim to rise above everyone else, including their tutor. They will ask for additional readings, question the questions, demand intellectual challenges, soar over the mountain passes.*
b. *The Owls. Not as ambitious as the cranes, the owls are nonetheless great thinkers. Instead of devouring hundreds of pages, they prefer to dig into the material at hand, aiming for depth. They will doubt the seminar, doubt the readings, doubt the instructor, even doubt themselves. Their contribution to the group will be immense and unique.*
c. *The Alpine Swifts. Perhaps not as motivated as the cranes or as intense as the owls, the swifts will nevertheless fly the longest*

distances. They will continue reading on the subject long after the seminar has come to an end, even long after they have graduated.

d. *The Robins. Content with the minimum, concerned more about the grade they will receive at the end than about the intellectual challenges along the way, timid and reluctant to go beyond surface-level thinking, the robins will in all likelihood derive the least from the seminar.*

Rules of This Seminar

All ideas, provided they are supported by research, a skilful presentation and an openness of mind, are welcome. Eating during class does not constitute a problem. In truth, food (within reason, don't go overboard) and beverages (non-alcoholic, we need our brains sober) are encouraged – not only because they lift the mood and help the intellect to focus, but also because it is hard to feel hostile towards someone you share bread with. Ergo, share your food with fellow classmates, especially with those who oppose your views.

*Bullying, tyranny, hate speech or malicious conduct against other students will not be tolerated (nor will it be allowed against your tutor, needless to say). Taking offence will not be permitted either. By agreeing to join this seminar, you are entering a tacit agreement to give primacy to freedom of speech over your personal sensitivities. If you cannot stand hearing objectionable ideas, we cannot have a free debate. When you feel offended, which is human, remember the counsel of a wise man: 'If you are irritated by every rub, how will your mirror be polished?'**

If you think you already know all you need to know about God and are not interested in filling your mind with new information, kindly stay away and 'stand out of my light'.† Time is precious – mine and yours. This seminar

* Rumi.

† Diogenes.

is for the Seekers. Those who are 'willing to be a beginner every single morning'. If all this seems like too much drudgery, bear in mind: 'The highest activity a human being can attain is learning for understanding, because to understand is to be free.'†*

* Meister Eckhart.

† Spinoza, of course.

The Marketing Strategy

Istanbul, 2016

Two maids – wearing starched black uniforms, crisp white aprons and identical expressions – bustled in bearing crystal plates of chocolate truffles.

'Everyone, try them! They're my babies,' said the businessman's wife.

This, too, had been in the newspapers. The businessman had taken over a chocolate factory that had gone bankrupt. As an anniversary gift to his wife, he had put her in charge of production and marketing. She had changed the name of the factory to *Atelier* and called the brand *Les Bonbons du harem*. Turkish customers could not pronounce the name in full, but its Frenchness, Europeanness, otherness was enough to make the product desirable, sophisticated, à la mode.

Now the hostess enthused, 'Just taste one, I reckon *you'll eat your fingers too*.'

The guests leaned forward to examine the delicacies, neatly arranged on lacy paper doilies.

'We've named them after world cities. See the one with raspberries, that's Amsterdam. This with marzipan, Madrid. Berlin is with beer and ginger. London, with aged whisky. When it comes to ingredients, we spare no expense.'

'You can say that again!' chimed in the businessman. 'She insisted on using eighteen-year-old single malt! It will ruin me.'

The guests laughed.

Ignoring the interruption, the hostess said, 'I'm no longer called the businessman's wife. From now on I am a businesswoman in my own right.'

The guests cheered.

Emboldened, the businesswoman carried on, 'Venice, with cherry liquor. Milano, we've made with Amaretto. Zurich, cognac and passion fruit. And Paris, with champagne!'

'Tell them about your marketing strategy,' said the businessman.

'We have two selections: for the toper and the teetotal,' the businesswoman explained. 'Same box, different products. To Europe and Russia, we export truffles with alcohol. To the Middle East, the ones without. Smart, don't you think?'

'Do the halal chocolates also have names?' asked the journalist.

'Sure, darling.' The businesswoman pointed at the next crystal plate. 'Medina, with dates. Dubai, coconut cream. Amman, caramel and hazelnuts. That pink one with rosewater, Isfahan.'

'How about Istanbul?' asked Peri

'A-ha, how can we forget!' said the businesswoman. 'Istanbul had to be based on contrasts: vanilla custard meets cracked black pepper!'

As they kept chattering and devouring the truffles, the maids began to serve hot drinks. Most of the women opted for chamomile or black tea, while most of the men asked for coffee – espresso, Americano. No one at the table requested Turkish coffee, except for the American hedge-fund manager, who was determined to adhere to the maxim 'When in Rome . . .' although in this case the Romans themselves behaved as though they were not in Rome.

Eager to do things the local way, the American asked, 'Can someone read my cup afterwards?'

'Don't worry,' the businesswoman replied in English. 'You don't have to save coffee grounds. The psychic will be here any minute now!'

'I can't wait for him to arrive,' said the journalist's girlfriend. 'I need some time with him.'

Peri looked around. These were God-fearing, husband-fearing, divorce-fearing, poverty-fearing, terrorism-fearing, crowd-fearing, disgrace-fearing, madness-fearing women, whose houses were immaculately clean, whose minds were clear about what they expected from the future. Early on in their lives they had exchanged 'the art of coaxing the father' for 'the art of coaxing the husband'. Those who had been married long enough had become bolder and louder in their opinions, yet they knew when not to cross the line.

Peri, for her part, did not share their concerns; she had never feared her father, never feared her husband, and, as for God, though not always on the best of terms, she was determined not to fear Him either. The true source of her uneasiness was of a different nature. It was she herself, her own darkness, that filled her with trepidation.

'Hey, we're not going to let that psychic have private sessions with all the pretty women!' said the businessman. Under his breath he added a tasteless joke, to which the male guests responded with guffaws and the female guests with feigned deafness.

Peri recalled how easily Shirin used to swear in public, waving her hands as if swatting a fly that kept irritating her. She remembered that she, too, swore when she was in Oxford, though only once, giving a mouthful to Professor Azur when she was upset with him. How easy it was to hate a loved one.

Here in this land, there were two kinds of women: those who used profanity with abandon and did not give a damn about the stigma of indecency (a tiny minority) and those who at no time would do so (the majority). The middle-to-upper-class ladies at the dinner belonged to the second group. They never cursed, except when they spoke English or French or German. It was somehow all right to swear in a foreign language. An obscenity they would not dream of uttering in their mother tongue, they sang out in a European language without a trace of guilt. It was easier – and somehow less offensive – to say the unsayable in someone else's language, like a masquerade party-goer dropping her guard behind a costume and a mask.

Men, on the other hand, were free to use expletives and did so generously and not always out of anger. Swearing cut across the class spectrum. It bound the male species together.

'By the way, there're a couple of truffles we haven't named yet,' said the businesswoman. 'One is with sherry and lemon zest. Tonight, Pericim, you gave me an idea. Let's call it Oxford!'

Having said that, the businesswoman stood up, searching the plates.

'Ah, there it is!' With her little finger curled daintily, she picked up the chocolate ball and offered it to Peri. 'Try it.'

Under everyone's gaze, Peri popped it into her mouth, the flavours dissolving on her tongue. Beneath the initial sweetness a sharp citrusy tang hit her palate, both tempting and deceiving in a single bite – like the seminars of Professor Azur.

The Deadly Kiss

Oxford, 2001

Peri did not go home over the Easter holiday. She still had to get used to the way the academic year was divided into three terms in England. The long breaks always threw her off. Not only because she couldn't travel back home as frequently as the rest of the students. Not only because she was neither an extrovert nor an explorer and therefore disinclined to investigate her surroundings. But also because she felt the gulf between herself and the others more acutely during these times. When everyone was writing essays, attending lectures, she could easily go with the flow; but she didn't know what to do with herself when she was expected to relax and have some fun.

Nonetheless, that same week she received an unexpected invitation. Mona, who had also stayed around after the term, running from one social activity to another, as was her habit, had two cousins visiting from America. Together they were planning to travel to the Welsh countryside, where they had rented a cottage.

'Why don't you come with us?' said Mona. 'You'll enjoy it. Lots of fresh air.'

Filling her suitcase with more books – including two by Professor Azur – than she could possibly read in a week, Peri agreed to join them. She guessed Mona would be mostly preoccupied with her relatives. She would be in company and alone at once. It sounded tolerable.

She was taken aback the first time she saw road signs in Welsh and English. Until then it had never occurred to her that you could have more than one official language inside the same country. In Turkey she had never come across a public notice in Turkish and Kurdish. Such was her surprise that every time she spotted one she had to stop to photograph it.

'You are crazy,' said Mona, laughing. 'The landscape is stunning and you're photographing road signs?'

The views were glorious indeed. Sheep with their newborn lambs grazing in fields that were rife with colour; carpets of green dotted with purple heathers, bluebells and cuckoo flowers. Their holiday rental turned out to be a tiny, timber-framed, whitewashed cottage high up on the west side of a valley. In the mornings it was bathed in a splendid sun; in the afternoons, a deep shade of tranquillity. In the distance the River Wye ran like a sinuous silver thread, winding its way between the hillsides.

Peri loved the cottage: the cast-iron stove, the low ceilings, the logs piled outside, flagstone ground floors, even the smell of the sheets that always felt ice cold when you first got into bed. She shared the room with Mona, and the cousins took the next room. Although the nearest village was a mile away, there was so much to do during the day, she had little time to read. She, who had always been a city girl, observed nature with a curious delight, the wonders in little things, and it felt like this was all that mattered – those little things. Always jumping to negative thoughts, she imagined a catastrophe had happened – a nuclear bomb – and they were the only survivors, away from civilization. She knew her mother would be shocked if she saw her daughter staying here, four girls in the middle of nowhere.

One night from her bed, she watched Mona praying in a corner, her face turned towards Mecca. They had not talked about religion at all, both of them avoiding the topic. Had Shirin been with them, she would surely have brought it up.

When Mona switched off the light, a sudden silence descended upon the room. Peri tossed and turned. 'When I was a child, I was stung by a bee on my lip,' she muttered slowly, as if she were dusting off the memory. 'My mouth became so swollen it looked like a water balloon. My father said the bee was madly in love . . . with me. It wanted to kiss me. I always wondered, did it know it would die as soon as it used its stinger? Weird, isn't it, if it knows it and does it anyway. Self-destruction.'

Mona rolled on her side. In the moonlight from the window her silhouette resembled a sculpture. 'Only humans have consciousness. It's the divine order. That's why Allah holds us humans responsible for our behaviour.'

'But you see, animals don't want to die. They have a survival instinct. Then they go and sting. They must know they're taking their own lives. I mean, you look at nature and you think, wow, how lovely and sweet. In fact, it's awfully cruel.'

Mona sighed. 'You're not running the world, remember. He is in charge of everything, not you. Have faith.'

How could Peri possibly trust a system in which bees were destined to die no sooner than they fell in love? And if this were the divine order that people raved about, how could they call it just and holy? She pulled up the quilt to her chin, feeling cold.

Peri screamed out in her sleep that night and murmured words in Turkish that sounded like the hum of a thousand bees trying to break free.

The cousins, awakened by the noise, giggled from the next room. Mona, sat up in her bed, astounded. She prayed that whatever demons were harassing her friend would be dispelled far and wide. The next morning they all returned to Oxford. Whenever Mona and Peri talked about their trip to Wales, it would be with a buoyant smile – even though each had sensed, in her own way, that beneath the special moments lay something darker.

The Empty Page

Istanbul, Summer 2001

Her first year at Oxford finally over, Peri spent the holidays in Istanbul. Every now and then, her mother mentioned this or that young man in passing, using the same set of descriptors. For Selma, Peri's education was less an intellectual awakening or the precursor to a promising career than a brief interlude before her wedding. She had gone to seven shrines just this past month: lighting candles, tying strips of silk and uttering wishes for a forthcoming good marriage for her daughter.

'New neighbours moved in while you were away. Decent family,' said Selma, as she podded a pile of broad beans that she was preparing for dinner. 'They have a son. Such a clever boy, handsome, honourable . . .'

'You mean you've found me a suitable husband,' murmured Peri. She twirled a tuft of hair around her finger, pulling awkwardly. She noticed it was much shorter than the rest and had a sudden creepy suspicion that her mother had cut a lock of her hair while she was sleeping. The idea that her hair was now in one of those shrines, buried among Selma's offerings, made her slightly ill.

'Leave the girl alone, woman,' said Mensur from his chair. 'You're confusing her. She's got classes to focus on. We're after a diploma, not a husband.'

'This boy has a diploma,' protested Selma. 'He went to university. They can get engaged now and marry after she graduates. What does she have to lose?'

'Only my freedom and my youth and my mind,' said Peri.

'You talk just like your father,' Selma said, and went back to her beans, as if she'd proved her point.

The subject was closed – but not for long.

End of summer, on a balmy day in Istanbul, Peri went out shopping. A raincoat, a new pair of running shoes, a backpack . . . she had to purchase them before she left for Oxford. When she got off the bus, near Taksim Square, she spotted a crowd of people. They were standing on the pavement, in front of a tea house frequented by students, staring through the open windows at the TV blaring away inside. Shadows danced on their contours, brushed by an apricot light where the sun caught their profiles.

A broad-shouldered man had placed his hands on his forehead, his brows drawn together. A girl with a pony-tail looked startled, her body rigid. Their expressions irked Peri. She inched her way through the group, curiously.

That was when she saw what was on TV: a plane slamming into a skyscraper against a blue so bright it almost hurt her eyes. The scene was being played over and over, as if in slow motion, though each time it seemed less real. Billows of smoke rose from the building. Sheets of paper drifted aimlessly in the wind. As though catapulted from a sling, an object hurtled downward, then another . . . Peri gasped, only now realizing these were no mere objects, but humans plunging to their deaths.

'Americans . . .' the man beside her muttered. 'That's what you get when you meddle in other people's affairs.'

'Well, they thought they ruled the world, didn't they?' said a woman, and shook her head, sending her hoop earrings swaying. 'Now they know they are mortal – like the rest of us.'

Peri's eyes met the pony-tailed girl's. For a second it seemed only the two of them were feeling the sorrow, the shock, the terror. But the girl quickly averted her gaze, offering little camaraderie. Disturbed by the talk around her, Peri strode away, her head bursting with questions. Wherever she turned, she found people looking for conspiracy theories to feed on, like foraging bees buzzing about for nectar.

I must call Shirin, she thought to herself. In need of hearing her friend's confident voice, she rang her from a pay phone. Thankfully, she answered immediately.

'Hey, Peri. Fucked-up world, eh! May we live in interesting times.'

'It's just horrible,' said Peri. 'I don't know what to make of this.'

'Innocents slaughtered,' cut in Shirin almost shouting. 'Why, because some depraved bastards believe they'll go to paradise if they kill in the name of God. It'll get worse, you'll see. Now all Muslims will be vilified. More innocents will have to suffer from all sides.'

Peri noticed a wad of chewing gum had been stuck under the phone box – a small act of malice, but malice nonetheless. 'Awful! Atrocious. And so scary. How could this happen?'

'Well, I'm sure that's what everyone will be arguing about. For months, years even. Journalists, experts, academics. But really there's nothing to discuss. Religion fuels intolerance and that leads to hatred and that leads to violence. End of story.'

'But isn't that unfair?' Peri said. 'There are many religious people who would never hurt anyone. It wasn't religion that did this. It was pure evil.'

'You know what, Mouse, I'm not going to argue with you. This time, I'm as confused as you are. I need to talk to Azur or I'll go mad.'

Peri felt a jolt inside of her. 'You're going to see him? But the term hasn't started yet.'

'Who cares? I'm going up to Oxford tomorrow. I know he's there. Change your ticket, come with me.'

'I'll try,' said Peri. She didn't feel the need to point out that even if she could get a last-minute ticket, she couldn't afford it.

At home, Peri found her mother and her father as bewildered as she was, watching the same scenes on TV that were being run repeatedly.

'Fanatics are taking control of the world,' said Mensur.

He had started drinking earlier than usual, and by the look of him he had already downed quite a few. For the first time he seemed hesitant about his daughter going to Oxford. 'Maybe we shouldn't have sent you abroad; nowhere is safe any more. I never thought I would say this, but maybe the West has now become more dangerous than the East.'

'East, West, what difference does it make? No one can escape their *kismet* . . .' said Selma. 'If Allah has written it on your forehead with His invisible ink, it doesn't matter whether you are here or in China. Death will come and find you.'

At this Mensur grabbed the ballpoint pen he used for crossword puzzles and wrote in a squiggly line on his forehead the number 100.

'What are you doing?' asked Selma.

'Changing my Fate! I'm going to live 100 years.'

Peri did not stay around to hear what her mother said in return. She had no patience for her parents' quarrels. Seized by an acute sense of loneliness, she went to her room and took out her God-diary. As much as she tried to compose something sensible, she could not write. Not today. She had so many questions about religion and faith and God – the kind of God that allowed atrocities to happen and still expected obedience. She stared at the page, swallowed by its emptiness. She wondered what Azur would tell Shirin when the two of them met in his office. How she wished she could secretly sneak into that room, like the siskin, and eavesdrop. She, too, had things to ask the professor. Perhaps Shirin was right to insist; Peri needed a seminar on God – not so much to discover new truths about a supreme being as to make sense of the simmering uncertainties within herself.

Then she did something she would never tell anyone: She prayed for all the people killed in the Twin Towers. She prayed for their families and loved ones. And before she concluded her prayer, she added a small request to God to be admitted into Azur's seminar, so that she could learn more about Him and hopefully make some sense of the chaos both inside and outside her mind.

The Circle

Oxford, 2001

The first week of the new term, early one afternoon, the sky placid as a village pond, Peri got ready for the first session of 'Entering the Mind of God/God of the Mind'. Only a few days earlier she had discovered an envelope in her pigeonhole at the Porter's Lodge from no other than Professor Azur. The note inside ran across the card in a slightly declining diagonal, evidently written in haste:

Dear Ms Nalbantoğlu,

If you are still interested in my seminar, it begins next Thursday at 2 p.m. sharp! Bring amber if you need it – but not apologies.
The octopus awaits.

A. Z. Azur

Since getting the note, between tutorials and her part-time job at the bookshop, she'd had no chance to reflect on what she might be in for. Now, as she headed towards the seminar room with a notebook held tight to her chest, she was surprised at how anxious she felt.

On walking into the room, Peri mentally counted ten students: five boys, five girls. Among them to her amazement was Mona, who greeted her with equal surprise.

Peri scanned the other students, taking in their awkward smiles, and the way they sat at polite distances from one another, relieved to see she wasn't the only one who looked nervous. Some of the students were immersed in their thoughts, while others were chatting in hushed voices or reading the seminar description – probably for the umpteenth time; and one boy, his head resting on his writing pad, seemed asleep.

Peri perched herself on a chair by the window and gazed out at a spreading oak tree, its decaying leaves shimmering ruby and gold. She wondered if there was time to visit the ladies' but the dread of returning after the seminar had started kept her rooted to her seat. Outside the day had turned overcast, and even though it was still early in the afternoon, it felt like dusk.

Exactly on the hour the door opened and Professor Azur strode in, carrying a stack of files, a large box of crayons and what looked like an hourglass. He was wearing a navy corduroy jacket with leather elbow patches. Although his crisp white shirt was immaculately ironed, his tie was undone, as if he had been too bored to knot it, and his hair was a ruffled mess. He either had been trudging into a stiff wind or had repeatedly run his fingers through it.

Quick as a whip, he dropped everything on to the desk and placed the hourglass on a lectern, instantly turning it over – particles of sand trickled from the upper bulb into the lower one, like tiny pilgrims on a holy journey. He stood in front of the white board, tall and slender, and said, with a briskness that upended the lethargy in the classroom:

'Hello, everyone! Shalom Aleichem! Salamun Alaykum! Peace be with you! Namaste! Jai Jinendra! Sat Nam! Sat Sri Akaal! I utter my greetings in no particular order of preference or precedence, in case you were wondering.'

'Aloha,' someone called back.

Others chipped in with myriad greetings, a jumble of voices and laughter.

'Great!' Azur said, rubbing his hands together. 'I see you're full of brash confidence. Always a promising sign – or a recipe for disaster. We'll see which.'

Behind his black-and-tortoiseshell spectacles, his eyes shone like beads of burnished sea-glass. His tone surged in waves of enthusiasm, like an explorer back from far-off lands now sharing his adventures among friends. He congratulated everyone for having the curiosity and chutzpah to enrol in the seminar and added, with a wink, that he also expected them to have the stamina to go all the way to the end. From the ease and speed with which he spoke it was hard, if not impossible, to fathom when he was joking and when he was serious.

'As you may have already noticed, there are eleven of you – ten would have been too perfect, and perfection is boring,' Azur said. He looked around and clucked his tongue. 'I can see we have work to do . . . You've spread out your chairs as if you're afraid of catching pneumonia. So if I may trouble you, ladies and gentlemen, could you please stand up?'

Surprised, amused, the students did as they were told.

'How obedient! The highest virtue in the eyes of the Lord, they say. Now could you rearrange your chairs to make a circle – that being the most suitable shape for talking about God.'

Different subjects required different sitting arrangements, Azur explained. For politics, scattered and amorphous; for sociology, a neat triangle; for statistics, a rectangle; and for international relations, a parallelogram. But God had to be discussed in a circle, everyone on the circumference equidistant from the centre, looking at one another's eyes.

'From now on, when I walk in each week, I'll expect to find you sitting in a ring.'

It took them a few minutes, and a bit of chair scraping and shuffling around, to accomplish the task. When they finished, the shape they'd formed resembled more of a squeezed lemon than a proper circle. Professor Azur, though not fully pleased, thanked them for their efforts. Next, he asked them to introduce themselves in a few sentences, mentioning their backgrounds and, in particular, why they were interested in God, 'when there are surely more entertaining things for young people out there'.

The first to speak was Mona. She said after the tragedy of 9/11, she was extremely worried about the perception of Islam in the West. Careful with her words, she said she was proud to be a young Muslim woman, loved her faith with all her heart, but was frustrated by the amount of prejudice she had to deal with almost every day. 'People who don't know anything about Islam make gross generalizations about my religion, my Prophet, my faith.' She added quickly, 'And my headscarf.' She said she was here to engage in honest discussions about the nature of the Almighty, since they were all created by Him and created differently for a reason. 'I respect diversity, but I also expect to be respected in return.'

The young man beside Mona, when it was his turn to speak, straightened his back and cleared his throat. His name was Ed. Coming from a scientific background, he said he approached God 'with objective caution and intellectual neutrality'. He believed that science and faith could marry, as likely as not, but one had to filter out the irrational parts of religion, of which there were many. 'My dad is Jewish, my mum is Protestant, both non-observant,' he added. 'I suppose, like Mona, but in a different way, I'm interested in identity and faith in the modern age – although God has never been an issue for me, frankly.'

'Then why are you here?' asked a muscular and slightly pockmarked, sandy-haired boy, spinning a pencil between his fingers. 'I thought everyone in this class had an issue with God!'

Peri noticed Ed glance up at Professor Azur, who gave him an almost imperceptible nod. Something passed between them – a message she could not decode.

Azur turned to the sandy-haired boy. 'Normally, I expect and encourage students to comment on each other's words, but not at this early stage. We are baby chicks hatching. Let's first poke our heads out of the egg.'

The next to speak was Róisín, a pretty girl with a noticeable Irish accent. She had large brown eyes and dark sleek hair, a strand of which momentarily caught on her lip as she began to speak. She said she was raised Catholic and attended Mass every week. She was fortunate to be surrounded by wonderful people at the Oxford Catholic Society, but she wished to broaden her perspective. 'I thought it'd be interesting to take this seminar. Just to see how God is being discussed outside my comfort zone. So . . .' She left the sentence unfinished, as if she trusted others to finish it for her.

'I guess I'm next,' kicked in the sandy-haired boy, spinning the pencil faster now. 'I'm Kevin – a Rhodes Scholar from Fresno, California.'

His broad face contorting, Kevin argued that Ernest Hemingway, who was right about everything, had nailed it when he said all thinking people were atheists. He himself was a devoted atheist for one. 'I don't believe in any of this bullshit and that's why I'm here. I want to engage in constructive debates on science, evolution and what you guys keep calling God. I'm sure I'll soon piss everyone off.'

Someone sniffed, either with derision or pity, impossible to tell.

'Hello, everyone. My name is Avi. I'm a member of the Oxford Chabad Society. I also work part time at the Samson Judaica Library, which is the largest Judaica library around. Some of you might not know that Oxford has a rich Jewish heritage.'

Avi argued there was enough hatred in the world to catapult humanity into World War Three. The ghost of history haunted the present moment. He said human beings were capable of horrible atrocities, as seen in the Holocaust and in the destruction of the Twin Towers. The need to foster a true dialogue across religions was urgent. Fear of God was the strongest deterrent against the violent streak in *Homo sapiens*. In the modern age, God was needed more than ever before.

Avi seemed willing to say more but the dark-haired girl next to him interjected, brisk and restless. Her name was Sujatha. She talked about the differences between Eastern philosophy and its Western counterpart – 'or Middle Eastern, I should say, since Abrahamic religions all come from the same region. It takes an outsider to notice how similar they are.'

Sujatha said, as a Brit of Indian origin, her motto in life was: 'Your idea of you creates your reality.' In her eyes, God had no attributes. She didn't mean to offend anyone but she found the Abrahamic God too stern, judgemental, aloof. 'I say: everything is God. Whereas you say: everything is God's. That little apostrophe makes a huge difference.'

At once compliant and defiant, Sujatha concluded by saying how much she was looking forward to discussing these philosophical disparities at length.

With every person that spoke, Peri slid further down in her chair, visibly shrinking herself. She wished she could disappear altogether. She began to have a gnawing suspicion that Professor Azur had cherry-picked the students, not so much on the merits of their academic credentials as on their personal stories and ambitions. No two students came from the same background and there were obvious differences of opinion among them that could easily escalate into a clash. Perhaps that was what Azur wanted: a conflict – or many. Perhaps he was experimenting on his students without their being aware, as though they were a litter of mice, scurrying and scrapping inside the walls of his mental laboratory. If so, what could he possibly be testing – a new idea of God?

There was something else that troubled Peri. If every person around her had been selected so as to assemble a miniature Babel, why had she been chosen? What could Azur know about her when she had told him so little? The more she racked her brain, the more insecure she felt. Dr Raymond's words echoed in her ears: *His teaching method is unorthodox. It doesn't sit well with everyone. It's a seminar that divides students. Some enjoy it; others become profoundly unhappy.*

'Hi, I'm Kimber,' said a girl with hair so curly that whenever she moved her head a few ringlets bounced up and down. 'I have a long answer and a short answer.'

'Start with the long one,' said Professor Azur.

Kimber explained that her father was a priest in the Church of Jesus Christ of Latter-Day Saints. They were Mormons. All her family and friends were Mormons. She said she was interested in this seminar because God gave meaning to her life and she intended to expand her understanding of Him. She added that young people today were solely interested in dating or studying for exams or finding a job with more money than anyone could ever use. But she believed there had to be more to life. 'We each have a distinct purpose on earth. I'm still searching for mine.'

'And the short answer?' Azur demanded.

Kimber giggled. 'I made a bet with my friend. She said you're the meanest tutor when it comes to marking essays. I'm a straight-A student. Never failed in any class since kindergarten. So I took the challenge.'

A serene smile crossed Azur's lips. '"Truth is so rare a thing; it is delightful to tell it."'

Peri, her mouth half covered by her hand, could not help murmuring to herself, 'Emily Dickinson.'

'Let's move on. Next!' instructed the professor.

Adam. Rounded nose, cleft chin and high eyebrows that made him look as though the world were a constant surprise to him. He said culturally he was an Anglican but not a churchgoer. It was not necessary to go to church, he added, since he believed God was about Love and God loved him the way he was. 'I believe in the universal principle of "Live, Love, Learn". All with a capital *L*. That's all.'

'Is it my turn?' asked the girl beside him. 'My name is Elizabeth. Born and bred in Oxfordshire, haven't travelled far from home. My family comes from a proud Quaker heritage. I don't have an issue with God but I do have a problem with a He-God.'

Elizabeth explained that human beings had lost touch with nature and the Earth as Goddess. Throughout history, femininity had been suppressed. The price was paid in wars, bloodshed and violence. She said she was into old religions, Shamanism, Wicca, Tibetan Buddhism. 'Anything that helps us to reconnect with the Mother Earth.' She urged everyone to stop thinking of God as a He, and to start practising saying She.

Now it was only Peri and the boy beside her who were yet to talk. Peri gestured with her hand that he should go first and he gestured for her to go instead. She yielded.

'Okay, my name is Peri . . .'

'And that quote was from Emily Dickinson, well done,' Azur cut in.

Peri knew she was blushing. She had no idea the professor had heard her. 'I come from Istanbul and . . .' She lost her train of thought and stammered, feeling foolish for mentioning the city she was born in instead of saying something more substantive like the others had. 'Uhm . . . I'm not . . . I'm not . . . sure why I'm here.'

'Then quit,' said Kevin cheekily. 'That'll make us ten again. I want the perfect number!'

A ripple of laughter spread through the circle. Peri lowered her gaze. How had she managed to stumble over a simple introduction when all the others, despite their apparent differences, had sailed through theirs seamlessly?

The last to speak was a boy called Bruno. He said he was not a Marxist or anything, but on the issue of religion being the poison of the people, he agreed with Marx – and the former Albanian leader Enver Hoxha, whose views he had read once and found remarkable in their clarity on the subject of religion.

'That's fine, young man,' Azur said, 'but when we quote others, particularly philosophers and poets for whom words are important, we must do so with precision. What Marx actually said was: "Religion is the sigh of the oppressed creature, the heart of a heartless world, and the soul of soulless conditions. It is the opium of the people."'

'Right. Same thing,' Bruno rejoined, barely disguising his irritation at being interrupted on a topic he felt passionate about. His chin jutting out as if preparing for a blow, he said Mona had asked for honest discussions and he was going to be honest to the point of being blunt. He was aware that some people might not like to hear what he had to say, but he believed this was a seminar that valued free debate. He had a problem with Islam. To be fair, he added, he would have an issue with all monotheistic religions, but Christianity and Judaism were reformed, whereas Islam was not.

Bruno argued that Islam's treatment of women was unacceptable and had he been born a woman into this faith he would have abandoned it at the speed of light. He said that Islam would have to be thoroughly altered to be suitable for today's world, but under the circumstances that was inconceivable, because both the Holy Book and the hadiths were seen as absolute, unequivocal.

'If change is forbidden, how can we improve this religion?'

From her corner Mona gave him an icy look and a piece of her mind. 'Who says I need *you* to improve my religion?'

'Brilliant, everyone; great start!' interjected Azur. 'Thank you for sharing your thoughts so eloquently. After listening to you harangue each other about religion, instead of God, which is our main subject, I need to explain, in no uncertain terms, what this seminar will be about.'

Walking in a circle inside the ring of students, the professor moved with assurance and spoke with ardour. 'We're not here to confer about Islam or Christianity or Judaism or Hinduism. We might touch upon these traditions, but only insofar as our central topic requires it. Ours is a scientific inquiry into the nature of God. You can't let your personal beliefs get in the way. When you become emotional about a subject, any subject, just remember, as Russell noted, "The degree of one's emotions varies inversely with one's knowledge of the facts." '

The light in the room faded as the sun passed behind a large cloud. Azur's eyes glinted. 'Are we all clear on that?'

'Yes,' the students answered in an effervescent chorus.

Then, a few seconds later, softly: 'No.' It was Peri.

Azur stopped. 'What was that you said?'

'Sorry . . . it's . . . I just don't think there's anything wrong about responding to emotions.' Peri gesticulated with both hands. 'We're human beings. That means we are driven more by emotions than by reason. So why belittle emotions?' She glanced up at the professor, dreading the expression she might find on his face.

He was calm, supportive, even slightly impressed by her objection. 'That's good, Istanbul girl, keep challenging.'

Azur said that if, at the end of their years at Oxford, they still spoke, thought and wrote in the same way as they did when they had started university, they would have wasted their time and their families' money. They might as well go back home now. 'Be prepared to change, all of you. Only stone boulders do not change – actually, they do too.'

Here they were, at the oldest university in the English-speaking world, Azur said. Oxford had not only been a centre for academic study and scientific research throughout centuries, but also a hub of theological debate and religious dispute.

'You're lucky! You're in the right place to talk God!'

As Professor Azur kept lecturing, his entire demeanour changed.

His face, hitherto settled, now became distinctly animated. His tone, no longer careful and contained, had an edge, a blade of steel that he normally kept in the shadows, but that he now made no attempt to conceal. He reminded Peri of a street cat in Istanbul, not the timid and bruised kind that gave humans a wide berth, but one of those independent felines that crept along the highest of walls, full of strutting aplomb, surveying the neighbourhood as if it were its secret kingdom.

'All right, here's a question. If someone from the Bronze Age appeared and asked you to describe God, what would you say?'

'He's merciful,' Mona said.

'Self-sufficient,' Avi added.

'Not He, but She,' said Elizabeth.

'Neither He nor She,' said Kevin. 'It's all lies.'

Professor Azur frowned. 'Bravo, you stupendously failed the test.'

'Why's that?' Bruno objected.

'Because you do not share the same language, remember, you and your hairy ancestor.' He produced a stack of papers and a box of crayons, which he asked Róisín to hand out. 'Forget words. Explain through images!'

'What?' Bruno exclaimed. 'You want us to draw? Are we little kids?'

'I wish you were,' Azur said. 'You'd have a greater imagination and a better grasp of complexity.'

Mona put up her hand. 'Sir, Islam forbids idols. We don't depict God. We believe He is beyond our perception.'

'Fair enough. Draw what you just told me.'

For the next ten minutes they shifted and shuffled, sighed and complained but, by and by, began producing an array of work. A picture of the universe – stars and galaxies and meteors. A cluster of white clouds pierced by a bolt of lightning. An image of Jesus Christ with his arms wide open. A mosque with golden domes under the sun. Lord Ganesha with his elephant head. A goddess with plump breasts. A candle in the dark. A page deliberately left blank . . . Everyone visualized God in their own way. As for Peri, after a brief hesitation, she made a dot, which she then turned into a question mark.

'Time's up,' said Professor Azur. He distributed another batch of paper. 'Having sketched what God is, I'd like you to illustrate what God is not.'

'What?'

Azur arched his eyebrows. 'Stop reacting, Bruno, and get to work.'

A demon with snake-yellow eyes. An iron mask of horror. A foetid swamp. A smoking gun. A knife caked in blood. Fire. Destruction. A fragment from hell . . . Oddly, imagining what God was not proved harder than imagining what He was. Only Elizabeth seemed to find the task easy. She simply drew a man.

'Thank you for your cooperation,' said Professor Azur. 'Could you lift the two drawings and hold them side by side? Show them to everyone in the circle.'

This they did, inspecting one another's works.

'Now turn the images towards yourselves. Okay? Great! We're about to examine a question raised by philosophers, scholars and mystics throughout history: what is the relationship between the two pictures?'

'Huh?' This time Bruno was not alone.

'Does the first drawing – of what God is – embody or exclude the second drawing – of what God is not?' Azur started pacing. 'For instance, if God is omnipotent and omnipresent, all-powerful and all-benevolent, does that mean that He – or She – embodies evil too, or does it mean that evil is external to Him – or Her – an outside force that He/She needs to fight? What exactly is the relation between what-God-is and what-God-is-not?'

Azur continued. 'You have drawn two pictures. Tell me how they are connected. Write an essay. It can be in any style so long as it is brave, bold, honest and supported by academic research!'

No one said a word. When they were sketching, they had taken the exercise lightly, not much believing in it. Had they known they would be asked to write an essay on the connection between the two images they would have been more thoughtful. But it was too late.

'Go back to philosophers, mystics, scholars of the past. Stay away from today. Stay away from your own mind.'

'Stay away from our own mind?' Kevin repeated.

'This, then, is your assignment for next week. Do your best, impress me!' Azur announced as he grabbed his files, the crayons, the hourglass, in which the last grain of sand had just slid into the bulb below. 'But I warn you, I'm not easy to impress!'

The Shadow Play

Oxford, 2001

On Friday evening, when most students went to pubs and clubs for some well-earned downtime, Peri stayed in the college library, reading. As the last remaining students left, the silence inside the building thickened, uninterrupted by coughs or whispers, the flicker of pages. To replace studying with pleasure was akin to replacing dieting with banqueting and she lamented, not for the first time, her social inadequacy. But she enjoyed being around books, which gave her a sense of freedom as nothing else could. She tried not to muse about the fact that most of her readings these days related to Professor Azur. Several times over the past weeks she had caught herself daydreaming about how she would say something unexpected in the seminar, something brilliant and bold that would stop him in his tracks and make him see her in a new light.

Next to her on the table was the folding Polaroid camera she had recently bought. On her runs she sometimes encountered the most astonishing skies – coral-pink sunrises, thunderous sunsets, frost-encrusted meadows – which she wanted to capture on film. It had cost her, but it was worth the money. She had also spent too much on books and planned to get a new personal computer. *What the hell,* she thought. *I'll just have to work harder.*

She stood up, stretched her legs. She was alone in this section – it felt as if she were alone in the entire building. As she walked among the stacks, she sensed a sudden movement, as quiet as a shadow. Swiftly, she turned around. It was Troy.

'Hi, didn't mean to scare you.'

'You're not following me, right?' Peri asked.

'No – well, yes. Don't worry, I won't bite.' Troy grinned and nodded at the book in her hand. 'What's that you're reading?... *Atheism in Ancient Greece*. Is that for Azur?'

'It is,' Peri said, feeling slightly uncomfortable.

'Told you that man was the devil, but you didn't take me seriously.'

'Why do you hate him so much?'

'Because he doesn't know his limits. I know that may sound like a good thing to you, but it's not. A don should behave like a don. Period.'

'And you don't think he does?'

Troy heaved a sigh. 'Are you kidding? That guy doesn't teach God. He believes he is God.'

'Wow, that's harsh.'

'Wait and see,' said Troy, and instantly took a step back, as if he had revealed more than he had intended. 'Anyway, need to go. Friends are waiting at the Bear; would you like to join us?'

'Thank you, but I've got work to do,' Peri said, surprised that he asked.

'All right. Have a good weekend. Think about what I said.'

By the time Peri left the library, the sky had turned deep blue-black, except for the ghostly reflection of the street lights, and it seemed so close she could have reached up and pulled it over her shoulders like an indigo shawl. She kept her head up as she walked, glancing at the gargoyles and grotesques leaning down towards her from the battlements of the quadrangle, as if guarding the secrets of the centuries. In that moment she was struck by the ancient theological disputes of the town, its aching scholastic bones, still stalking its rooms. She zipped her jacket all the way up to her chin; soon she would have to buy a winter coat. She was saving money.

When she turned a corner, she was surprised to see people holding candles in the dark. A vigil. She approached, her gaze scanning rows of photos and flowers laid on the pavement. One poster said REMEMBER SREBRENICA.

Peri combed the faces of the dead – boys, fathers, husbands; one of them resembled her brother Umut around the time he had been arrested.

Among the group holding the vigil Peri spotted Mona, wearing a magenta headscarf she had draped around her head and shoulders. She, too, had seen Peri and stepped forward to talk to her, a candle in her hand.

Peri pointed at the faces in the photos. 'It's so sad.'

'It's more than sad,' said Mona. 'It's genocide. We must never forget.' She paused, looking at Peri with a new interest. 'Why don't you join us?'

'Uhm, sure,' Peri said. She grabbed a candle and the photo of the boy who looked like her brother, and took her place on the pavement. The night closed around her like a swollen river.

'Are only Muslim students doing this?' asked Peri.

'Well, the Muslim Student Council organized it, but others have come to show their support. There are people from Azur's seminar. Look, Ed's here.'

So he was. Peri went to talk to him when Mona, busy with her fellow organizers, left her alone.

'Hi, Ed.'

'Peri, hi. Looks like I'm the only Jew here. Or half-Jew.'

As if the mention of his religion were a logical segue, Peri said, 'Do you mind if I ask you why you're taking the seminar on God?'

'It's because of Azur. The man changed my life.'

'Really?' Peri recalled the glance between Ed and the professor.

'Last year he helped me a lot. I was going to break up with my girlfriend.'

'And he told you not to?'

'Not exactly. He told me to try to understand her first,' said Ed. 'She and I had been together since secondary school. But she changed. She turned religious – just like that. I couldn't recognize her any more.' With her decision to strictly observe the Torah and his commitment to science, the gulf between her priorities and his priorities had become unbridgeable. 'I went to Azur, don't know why. I could have gone to a rabbi or something, but Azur felt like the right person.'

'What did he tell you?'

'It was weird. He said for forty days, listen to everything she says. One month and ten days. Not that hard, if you love someone. He said do Shabbat together. Whatever she wants to show me, just let her take me into her world. Don't object, don't comment.'

'Did you do it?'

'I did. It was ridiculously hard! When I hear gibberish – I'm sorry, but that's what it is – all that religious talk, my mind rebels. Azur said leave judging to judges. Philosophers do not judge. They understand.' Ed chuckled. 'But that's not all.'

'What else?'

'After forty days, Azur calls me and says, well done, now it's your girlfriend's turn. For forty days you'll talk, she'll listen. She'll go through a religion detox.'

'Did she do it?'

'Of course not.' Ed shook his head. 'We broke up. But I understood what Azur was trying to do. I liked him for that.'

His enthusiasm irked her, that unbridled trust of a disciple for his master. She said, 'But we're not philosophers. We're undergraduates.'

'That's the thing. All the dons give us space – except Azur. He pushes us hard. He believes that, whatever our call in life, we must all be philosophers.'

'Isn't that too much to expect from ordinary students?'

Ed looked at her. 'You're not ordinary. No one is.'

Peri pressed her lips together.

'What's the matter? You don't like him?' Ed asked.

'I do, it's just . . .' Peri swallowed. 'I wonder if he's experimenting with us, and I feel uncomfortable with that.'

'Perhaps he is, but who cares?' Ed said. 'He changed my life. For the better.'

It began to rain – a slight drizzle that could at any moment have turned into a downpour. The vigil had to be postponed. They put away the posters, candles and photos. Mona was running left and right, taking care of things.

Peri extended a hand to Ed. Ignoring her gesture, he pulled her towards him and gave her a warm hug. 'You take care. And trust Azur, he's a great guy.'

Alone in the dark, Peri walked back to her quad, the air rich with the mingled smells of rain and earth. She didn't mind getting wet. She surveyed the buildings that had witnessed centuries of heated debates; neighbours turned into foes, books destroyed, ideas silenced, thinkers persecuted . . . all in the name of God.

Who was right, Troy or Ed? In one night she had heard two opposing views of the professor; and the trouble was, she had a feeling they could both be right. As in an old Ottoman shadow play, a curtain separated her from the reality, and she found herself grasping at images instead. Azur was the puppeteer behind the screen – present and in control at all times, yet still unknown, always out of reach.

The Oppressed

Istanbul, 2016

The last of *Les Bonbons du harem* had hardly disappeared from the table when a dog trotted in through the open door, wagging its tail with a vigour that belied its slight frame. A Pomeranian with a shrunken head, soulful eyes and a bushy fur coat the colour of faded autumn leaves.

'Pom-Pom, darling, did you miss me?' said the businesswoman.

Sweeping the creature off the floor, she placed it on her lap. From there the animal watched the guests, blinking, its fox-like features set in a passive expression that could at any moment turn into snarling hostility.

'You know when it dawned on me this country had changed?' the businesswoman asked no one in particular. 'When I took Pom-Pom to the vet last month.'

Normally the vet would come on a regular basis, she explained, but a few weeks ago the man had injured his leg and, though he continued to work as before, he'd been unable to make house calls. With Pom-Pom tucked under her arm, she'd headed to the clinic. In the past, dog owners had been an almost identical lot – modern, urban, secularist, Westernized. Since conservative Muslims regarded dogs as makrooh, detestable, they were not keen to share their living space with canines.

'I've never understood what those people have against dogs. All that nonsense about angels refusing to enter a house with a dog,' the businesswoman said. 'Or a house with paintings.'

'It's a hadith by al-Bukhari,' said a newspaper tycoon who had only recently joined the circle. His collarless, crisp white shirt emphasized his dark hair, which had been cut to the same length all over. He wore no moustache, no beard, cleanly shaven. Unlike everyone else at the dinner, he was from the newly emerging, Islamic-bourgeoisie. Despite his eagerness to socialize with the country's Westernized elite, he wouldn't dream of bringing his wife, who wore a headscarf, to such dinners. *She'd be uncomfortable among them,* he reasoned to himself. In reality, it was he who was uncomfortable with her around. Sure, he was pleased with her as a wife – Allah knew what a giving mother she was to their five kids – but outside the house, especially outside their circle, he found her unrefined, unbecoming even; he watched her every move and listened to her every comment with an arched eyebrow. Better if she stayed at home.

Now he sat back and said, 'The hadith does not say, by the way, just any picture. It warns against portraits to prevent idolatry.'

'Well, then, we're screwed,' said the businessman. With a complacent laugh he opened both arms and gestured towards the artwork on the walls. 'We have a dog and plenty of portraits. Even nudes. Maybe tonight stones will rain on our heads!'

Despite the jovial tone, his words visibly disturbed some of the guests, who smiled in discomfort. Sensing the tension, Pom-Pom snarled, his fangs dripping bright with saliva.

'Hushhh, Mama's here,' said the businesswoman to the miniature creature, and to her husband in a less affectionate tone, 'Don't tempt destiny, something bad might happen.' She downed her water, as if irritation had dehydrated her. 'Now where was I? So when I visited the vet, I was surprised to see headscarved women in the waiting room with dogs by their feet! Chihuahuas, shih-tzus, poodles. They were more into canines than you and me! Obviously religious Muslims are changing.'

'I wouldn't say they are *changing,*' said the newspaper tycoon. 'Look, we religious sorts never had the freedoms you enjoyed. We've been oppressed for decades by a modernist elite like yourselves – no offence.'

'Even if that were true, those days are gone. Now you're the ones in full power,' muttered Peri, her voice wavering, as if she were reluctant to speak her mind but, once again, couldn't help it.

The newspaper tycoon objected. 'I disagree. Once oppressed, always oppressed. You don't know what it feels like to be oppressed. We have to cling to power, otherwise you might snatch it back from us.'

'Oh, give me a break!' cried the journalist's girlfriend, who had a notoriously low threshold for alcohol. She pointed her finger at the tycoon. 'You're not oppressed! Your wife is not oppressed! I am oppressed!' She tapped her chest. 'Me with my blonde hair and my mini-skirt and my makeup and my womanhood and my glass of wine . . . I'm the one who's trapped in this despotic culture.'

The journalist's eyes widened in alarm. Worried that his girlfriend might draw the ire of the tycoon, and cost him his job, he tried to kick her under the table, his foot swinging through the air in vain.

'Well, we're all oppressed,' said the hostess in a lame attempt to reduce the tension.

'It's simple,' said the plastic surgeon. 'As people make more money, they crave a better lifestyle. I've many patients who are wearing headscarves. When it comes to sagging breasts and turkey necks, religious Muslim women are not that different from the rest.'

The businessman nodded heartily. 'That only proves my theory: capitalism is the only cure to our problems. The antidote to those jihadi freaks is the free market. If only capitalism could run its course without intervention, it'd win over even the most resolute minds.'

With that he opened a polished burr-walnut humidor, an image of Fidel Castro inlaid on its lid, and passed it to the journalist with a wink. 'Limited edition from the Beirut Duty Free. Take one. Take two.'

The male guests, glancing sheepishly at their hostess, each fumbled in the box and took a cigar.

'Don't worry about my wife,' said the businessman. 'There's freedom in this house. Laissez-faire!'

Everyone laughed. Pom-Pom, disturbed by the noise, yapped angrily.

Seizing the opportunity, Peri lit a cigarette. She noticed that the maid she had seen at the entrance was now tiptoeing around and setting down ashtrays. She wondered what this woman thought about them all. It was probably better not to know.

'Our darling Peri is very thoughtful tonight,' said the businesswoman.

'It was a long day,' Peri said, deflecting the comment.

Her husband leaned forward as if to share a secret. It was his habit to drink his coffee black and strong, and with a piece of sugar in his mouth. Now, as the sugar cube dissolved on his tongue, Adnan said, 'Sometimes I've a feeling Peri likes people in fiction more than those in real life. Instead of tweeting her friends, she'd rather pin up her favourite poems on strings suspended across our bedroom.'

Peri smiled. It was yet another ritual she had learned from Professor Azur.

'I envy you,' said the interior designer. 'I can never find the time to read.'

'Oh, I love poetry,' said the PR woman. 'I feel like abandoning everything and moving to a fishing village. Istanbul corrupts our souls!'

'Come to Miami, we bought a house by the ocean,' said the businessman.

His wife arched her brows. 'The nerve of this man! No artistic sensibility. We say poetry, he says Miami.'

'What did I do this time?' protested the businessman.

No one criticized him. He was too rich to be criticized to his face.

Just then the doorbell rang, once, twice, thrice – a mixture of frustration, apology and impatience.

'Oh, finally.' The businesswoman leaped to her feet. 'The psychic is here!'

'Hooray!' came a collective cry.

Pom-Pom ran towards the door, yapping and barking furiously.

In the commotion that followed, Peri picked up a beeping sound nearby. She reached for her husband's phone, checked the screen. There was a detailed message from her mother, even though she had told her only to write 'call me'. 'Found the number, missed my TV show.' Underneath was the requested information: 'Shirin: 01865 . . .' The digits danced in front of Peri's eyes, a combination of numbers to open a safe that had been locked for too long.

The Dream Interpreter

Oxford, 2001

Professor Azur arrived in the classroom, his arms full of books. He was followed by someone else – a porter, it turned out – pushing a wheelbarrow heaped with a pottery stove, rolls of black paper, a CD player and several pillows, such as those found on airplanes. The two men walked to the middle of the room and unloaded everything.

Like a play, Peri thought to herself. *He's an actor on stage; we, the audience.*

'Thank you for your trouble, Jim, I owe you one,' Azur said to the porter.

'No trouble, sir.'

'Don't forget to come back at the end of class.'

The man gave a perfunctory nod and took his leave.

Azur scanned the young expectant faces forming a ring around him. In the raw light his eyes looked tired, a darker shade of green – a forest creek stirred by whorls of current. 'How's everyone this morning?'

The answers came in a lively chorus.

'Well, if you need to catch up on sleep, which is scientifically proven to be impossible, here's a chance. Could you please pass around these pillows?'

Each student took one. Meanwhile, the professor busied himself with the stove.

'Sir, are we going to burn down the college?' piped up Kevin.

'How did you guess my evil plans? No, we won't be burning anything.'

In a few seconds, the electric stove glowed a bright red.

'All right, boys and girls. You are, let's pretend, in your warm, cosy rooms; it's freezing cold outside. What can you do, but fall asleep!'

The students glanced at one another.

'Rest your heads on your pillows!' Azur ordered.

They did as told. Everyone except Peri, who sat ramrod straight, eyes wide open with suspicion.

'That's the spirit, Peri. Be cautious. You never know, I might've filled the pillows with angry cats.'

She blushed, this time obeying.

Next Azur took the black paper and produced a roll of sticky tape from his pocket. He began to cover the windows. Cut off from the outside light, the room sank into semi-darkness. He turned on the CD player: the sound of a crackling fire drifted over them.

'What're we doing, sir?' It was Kevin again.

'We're going to a place René Descartes visited often. A place of dreams!'

Someone suppressed a laugh but the rest of the group seemed interested.

'He was about your age, the great philosopher. Have any of you done anything meaningful yet?'

Nobody answered.

'Descartes had big ambitions. Yours are bigger, I'm sure. But his were based on methodological and philosophical inquiry.'

'So are ours!' said Bruno.

Azur rolled his eyes. 'We'll visit Descartes's visions. In the first, the young philosopher is trudging up a hill. He fears he's going to fall down. He knows he must try harder to reach his goals, but he thinks he cannot achieve anything without the help of a supreme power – God.'

Her head on her pillow, her eyes half closed, Peri listened.

'Far in the distance he sees a chapel – the House of God. The wind lifts him up and carries him with such force that he is flung against its walls.'

'Told you God was no good,' said Kevin.

'He gets up and brushes himself off. He enters a courtyard where he sees a man who tries to give him a melon – a fruit from a foreign land.'

'That's weird,' murmured Ed, sitting beside Peri. He had brought along a tin of homemade biscuits, which he now opened and offered left and right.

Azur carried on, 'Descartes wakes up in pain, sweating. He's worried that the dream was caused by the devil. Where do evil thoughts come from – outside or within? He prays to God for protection. But what is God – an external source or a product of our mind? It is this question that leads him to the second dream when he manages to fall asleep again.'

Azur skipped to the next recording on the CD. The sound of thunder filled the room. 'A tempest is raging around the philosopher. A storm is coming. Why do bad things occur in life, he asks. How can God let them happen if He is who He is? Descartes is confused. Alone. Resentful. This dream is dark, depressing.'

Peri thought of her brother Umut, not as the man he was today, hunched over a table where he made wind-chimes out of seashells for tourists he would never get to know, but as the young idealist who once wanted to change the world and correct every wrong. She remembered the conversations she had with her father, trying to make sense of why God had forsaken them. Her throat ached. The sadness that descended on her was so sharp her eyes welled with tears. She didn't know what she believed in. Maybe God was a game only those with happy childhoods could play.

To defuse the flow of negative feelings, she rushed to ask, 'What about the third dream, sir?'

Azur gave her a curious look. 'Well, that's the most important one. Descartes sees a book on a table, a dictionary. Then he sees another book, a book of poems. He opens the latter at random, reads a poem by Ausonius.'

'Who?' said Bruno, confounded.

'Decimus Magnus Ausonius. Roman poet, grammarian, rhetorician.' Azur pointed his finger at Peri. 'Did you know he visited your city – Constantinople?'

Peri shook her head.

'The poem's first line is: *What road shall I pursue in life?*' Azur said. 'A man appears and asks Descartes what he thinks about it. But the philosopher can't answer. Disappointed, the man disappears. Descartes feels embarrassed. He's full of doubt – like all intelligent people. Now who'd like to interpret this dream?'

'Well, that melon sounded naughty,' said Bruno. 'Maybe Descartes was in the closet. He had a crush on that Mr N. – whoever he is.'

'Maybe.' Azur sighed. 'Or else, the dictionary represented science and knowledge. Poetry symbolized philosophy, love, wisdom. He thought God was telling him to bring them all together by means of reason and create a "marvellous science". Here's a question: can you create a marvellous science of your own to study God?'

'How do we do that?' said Mona.

'Be polymaths,' Azur replied. 'Knit together different disciplines, synthesize, don't just focus on "religion". In fact, stay away from religion, it only divides and muddles. Go to mathematics, physics, music, painting, poetry, art, architecture . . . Approach God through unlikely channels.'

Peri felt a swell of excitement. Could she create her own marvellous science? How wonderful would that be! Could she throw into the mixture her love of books, her passion for science and learning and poetry, her unfailing melancholy, and also add in her elder brother's broken spirit and lacerated flesh, her father's blasphemies and drinking habits, her mother's prayers and bleeding hands, her other brother's seething anger, and blend them all into something solid, reliable, whole? Was it possible to make something delicious out of poor ingredients?

Azur said, 'The third dream makes me wonder if the philosopher was afraid of being judged by others. To us, he's the great René Descartes! But he thought of himself as small, insignificant. If any of you ever feel like you are not special enough, remember, even Descartes felt that way sometimes.'

Peri lowered her eyes. She understood what Azur was doing and she both hated and loved him for that. He was telling her, and her alone, to have more confidence in herself. He hadn't forgotten the talk they had in his room.

When he finished the lecture, Azur played the last tune on his CD.

'Beethoven, *Missa solemnis*,' he said. 'Immerse yourselves in it. Go back to sleep!'

Heads on their pillows, they savoured the music. No one spoke.

'Lecture over,' announced the professor and pressed the stop button.

Simultaneously, there was a light tap on the door. Azur called out in its direction, 'Jim, come on in. On time as always.'

The porter entered, heading straight for the stove to take it away.

'All right, everyone,' Azur said. 'In light of our discussion today, write an essay about Descartes's Quest for Certitude and God. Before you put pen to paper, make sure you do your research. Speculation without knowledge is self-indulgent twaddle. Understood?'

'Yes, sir,' the students replied in chorus.

When Peri walked outside, her head was pounding. The wind and the force of things beyond control; the duality of good and evil; the need to make sense of chaos; the codes embedded in dreams and the dreamlike quality of life; the loneliness of a young philosopher seeking truth; the first line of an old poem still relevant today: *What road shall I pursue in life?* Something inside her had shifted as she listened to Azur – a change so subtle as to be almost imperceptible, and also irreversible, leaving a void into which she was scared to peer for fear of what she might find. Beneath the surface of her usually reticent self, a fissure had opened, exposing her galloping heart. She wished he would carry on talking for days on end, to her and to her alone.

When Azur spoke of God and life and faith and science, his words clung together like tiny grains of steamed rice, ready to feed hungry minds. In his company, Peri felt consummate, undivided, as if there were, after all, another way of looking at things – different from her father's approach as well as her mother's. In Azur's words she found a passage out of the tiresome duality she had grown up with in the Nalbantoğlu household. Next to Azur she could embrace the many facets of who she was and still be welcomed. She did not have to suppress, control or hide any side of her. Azur's universe was outside the rigid dichotomies of good and evil, God and Sheitan, light and dark, superstition and reason, theism and atheism. He himself was above all the quarrels that Mensur and Selma had had over the years, and, somehow, passed on to their daughter. Peri sensed deep in her soul, though she would deny it for as long as possible, that she was infatuated with her professor. There was something frighteningly dangerous in the expectation that someone had the answer to most of our questions, and that through that person was a shortcut to all that was left unsolved henceforth.

The Mantle

Oxford, 2001

'Find new narratives, always plural. We often try to reduce our understanding of God to a single answer – a formula. Wrong!'

Professor Azur was walking rapidly from side to side, hands in his pockets.

Up until a few decades ago, he said, even the brightest scholars were certain that by the twenty-first century religion would have vanished from the face of the earth. Instead religion made a spectacular comeback in the late 1970s, like a diva returning to the stage, and ever since it has been here to stay, its voice louder with each passing year. 'Today's heated arguments revolve around matters of faith.'

This century was bound to be more religious than the preceding one – at least, demographically, since the pious tended to have more children than the secular. But in our fixation with religious, political and cultural conflicts, we let slip a crucial riddle: God. Whereas in former times, philosophers – and their pupils – grappled more with the idea of God than with religion, now it was the other way round. Even the theist–atheist debates, which had become quite popular in intellectual circles on both sides of the Atlantic, were more about politics and religion and the state of the world than the possibility of God. By weakening our cognitive ability to put forth existential and epistemological questions about God and by severing our link with philosophers of times past, we were losing the divinity of imagination.

Peri saw that most of the students were taking notes, bent on capturing every word. She was content just to listen.

'Too many suffer from M.O.C.,' said Azur. 'Anybody know what that is?'

Kevin ventured. 'Modern Obesity Curse?'

'Machismo of the Crazed?' Elizabeth joined in.

Azur smiled as if he were expecting these answers and said, 'The Malady of Certainty.'

Certainty was to curiosity what the sun was to the wings of Icarus. Where one shone forcefully, the other couldn't survive. With certainty came arrogance; with arrogance, blindness; with blindness, darkness; and with darkness, more certainty. This he called, *the converse nature of convictions*. During these lectures they were not going to be sure of anything, not even the seminar syllabus, which was, like everything else, subject to change. They were fishermen casting wide nets into the ocean of knowledge. Ultimately, they might catch a swordfish; or they might return empty-handed.

They were travellers too, companions of the road, having yet to arrive at any particular destination and perhaps never to do so. They were only striving, searching. For in a world of elusive complexity, only this was clear: diligence was better than idleness, spiritedness preferable to apathy. Questions mattered more than answers; curiosity was superior to certitude. They were, in short, 'The Learners'.

The Malady of Certainty, though impossible to shed once and for all, could be imagined as a cloak that could be taken off. 'A metaphor, I agree, but don't treat metaphors lightly – they alter the speaker. The word comes, after all, from the Greek *metaphorá*, "to transfer".'

From now on, Azur said, before they entered the classroom he would like everyone to strip themselves of this mantle. This included himself, as he too was inclined to wear one. 'Think of it as an old coat, hang it on a peg. I've actually put one up right outside the door. You're welcome to go and check.'

It took the students a minute to realize he was serious. Sujatha was the first on her feet. She strode across the classroom, opened the door and stepped into the hall. Her face brightened when she saw there really was a peg. Pretending she had a cloak on her shoulders, she peeled it off, hung it up and walked back in, triumphant. One by one the other students followed suit. Lastly, Professor Azur stepped out. Judging by the way he flailed his arms in the air, his cloak seemed to be rather heavy. After he freed himself of it, he returned to the classroom and clapped his hands. 'Brilliant! Now that we've rid ourselves of our Egos, at least symbolically, let's get started.'

'Why did we do that?' Bruno said, shaking his head.

'Rituals are important, don't underestimate them,' said Azur. 'Religions understand this well. But rituals don't need to be religious. We'll have our own shared practices in this seminar.'

He picked up a marker and scribbled on the board: GOD AS WORD.

'Civilization as we define it today is about 6,000 years old. But human beings have been around for much longer – with skulls dating back 290 million years. What we know about ourselves is trivial compared with what we are yet to discover. Archaeological evidence makes it plain that for thousands of years, human beings thought of a god or gods in varying forms – a tree, an animal, a force of nature or a person. Then, somewhere along the flow of history, a leap of imagination occurred. From God as a tangible thing, humans switched to God as word. From that time hence nothing has been the same.'

Azur looked around, noticing Peri was the only one not taking notes. 'Are you with me, Istanbul girl?'

Trying not to blush again under his scrutiny, Peri sat straight up in her chair. 'Yes, sir.'

His gaze, open and trusting, lingered on her a few more seconds, as if he had expected her to say something different, and, in not doing so, she had disappointed him. He addressed his next remark to everyone, 'If I were to inform you that behind this door God awaits, you can't see Him – or Her – but you can hear His voice, what would you want Him to tell you? Not you as a generic representative of humankind, but you in person – one and only.'

'I'd like to hear that he loves me,' said Adam.

'Yeah, he loves me and is happy to know that I love Him,' said Kimber.

'Love . . .' several others repeated in their own words.

'That He agrees with me – all this talk about Him is tripe,' said Kevin.

'Wait a minute, God can't tell you that unless He exists,' said Avi. 'You're contradicting yourself.'

Kevin frowned. 'I'm just playing along with this silly game.'

Now it was Mona's turn. 'I'd like to hear from Allah that heaven is real . . . and that good people will be there and love and peace will prosper, inshallah.'

Azur turned to Peri – so swiftly she didn't have time to avert her gaze and found it impossible to tear her eyes away from his.

'What about you? What would you like God to tell you – Peri?'

'I'd like Him to apologize,' she said. She had no idea where that had come from, but made no attempt to hold back her words.

'Apologize . . .' Azur said. 'For what?'

'For all the injustice,' replied Peri.

'You mean the injustice done to you or to the world?'

'Both,' Peri said, more quietly than she'd intended.

Outside, a solitary leaf from the old oak tree twisted in the wind one last time and fell to the ground. Inside, the students were so attentive the silence was almost palpable.

Into the stillness, Azur said, 'Justice! What a fancy word. Justice according to what or whom? The greatest bigots in history committed the gravest injustices in the name of justice.'

Azur's tone hardened. 'As you can see, two approaches to God have emerged from our discussion – we thank Kevin for playing along. The first associates God with love. In looking for God we are looking for love. Then we have Peri's approach, looking for justice.'

Peri swallowed hard. She had opened up her heart and now Azur had taken a scalpel, cutting into it in front of everyone. If he had no tolerance for her views, why had he encouraged her to speak up in the first place? Besides, how could she be accused of potential fanaticism? She, her father's daughter, the last thing she could be was a bigot!

Azur heard none of these silent protests. He pointed a finger at Peri. 'You'd better be careful with that mighty "justice"! It's quite possible that people with your ideas are making this world worse. All fanatics have one thing in common: they live in the past. As you do!'

The lecture ended soon after. Peri didn't hear the last few minutes. Her mind was elsewhere, her head was pounding. She could not move or look at anyone for fear that her hurt would show. After everyone had left, including Azur, she found herself alone with Mona.

'Hey, Peri,' Mona said, putting a hand on Peri's shoulder. 'I know he was rude to you. Ignore him, honestly.'

Peri lowered her face, feeling tears well up. 'I don't understand. I had thought he was amazing. Shirin always said he was. But he is so . . .'

'Patronizing,' Mona offered helpfully.

They walked outside together. 'You can drop the seminar, you know,' Mona said. 'If he gets on your nerves, I mean.'

'Yes,' Peri said, sniffing. 'I probably will. I hate him!'

That night Peri did not sleep well. Her mind, burdened all these years with so many anxieties and fears, was fixated on one thought and one thought only. Much as she tried, she could not stop thinking about Azur. Had she glimpsed an awful side to his character, which he concealed, waiting for a moment to strike, or was all this his way of showing her that he cared for her and her intellectual advancement?

In the morning, she saw Mona and Bruno in a café, sitting at opposite ends of a table, their expressions tense with something akin to mutual animosity. Azur had asked them to collaborate on the next assignment and to spend a night in the library working on it together. *Share food, share ideas*. He was doing it deliberately: forcing Bruno, who had never hidden his aversion to Muslims, to team up with Mona, who was always sensitive about her faith. What Azur didn't seem to realize was that his plan to have a rapport develop between them, noble as it might seem, was not working. Both students were distressed.

By now, Peri had no doubt that there was nothing accidental about Azur's seminars. Everything had been meticulously planned and orchestrated. Each student was a piece on the mental board in a game he played against no one but himself. Her cheeks burned at the mere suspicion that she, too, was only a pawn. She loathed him for that.

A day later, Peri found another note in her pigeonhole.

To Peri,

The girl who reads Emily Dickinson and Omar Khayyám and takes everything so seriously; the girl who cannot leave her country behind and carries it with her everywhere; the girl who quarrels, not so much with others as with herself; the girl who is her own most ruthless critic; the girl who expects an apology from God while needlessly apologizing to fellow humans –

You probably think I'm a dreadful person and you're considering dropping the seminar. But if you give up now, you'll never know whether your suspicions are true. Isn't the search for Truth enough of an incentive to keep going?

Peri, don't quit. Remember, daring to 'know thyself' means daring to 'destroy thyself'. First, we must pull ourselves apart. Then, with the same pieces, we will assemble a new Self.

What matters is that you believe in what we're doing.

The note tucked in her pocket, Peri put on her trainers and went out for a run. Breathing deeply, she zipped her sweatshirt to her chin and set off. Her muscles ached; her joints, stiff and sore, cried out. As she moved in the morning air, which carried smells of damp earth and autumn leaves, she unleashed a curse. What an arrogant bastard, who the hell did he think he was! Fuck him!

Yes, for the first time in her life, Peri swore a mouthful, every word a grain of salt on her tongue in the cold, cold wind. Why had she never done this before? Swearing and running was a great combination. Delicious. Empowering.

The Prophecy

Istanbul, 2016

An electrified silence canopied the table while the guests waited for the psychic to appear. Through the open door they could hear their hostess welcome him, her voice tinkling like glass chimes.

'Where have you been?'

'The traffic! It's a nightmare,' a male voice, high-pitched and nasal, burst out.

'Don't we know,' the businesswoman said. 'Come, darling, there are people inside who're dying to meet you.'

Seconds later, the psychic emerged, clad in dark trousers, white shirt and an aqua-gold paisley brocade waistcoat from another era. He had patchy, light stubble that might well have grown on the way to the party. Small and close-set eyes, an angular face punctuated by a narrow and pointed nose, and an afterthought of a chin, all of which gave him the look of a prowling fox.

'So many guests!' he exclaimed as he strolled in. 'I'll have to camp here if all of you want your future read.'

'Please do,' the businesswoman said.

'Only the ladies,' said the businessman from his corner. As far as he was concerned, nothing could be quite as tedious as listening to other people's fortunes. He liked to make his own fortune. He wanted to have a private conversation with the bank CEO while his wife had her stuff and nonsense. 'Why don't you ladies move over to the sofas; it'll be more comfortable,' he proposed.

Obediently, the businesswoman ushered the psychic and the women towards the leather sofas. She signalled to a maid, 'Bring our new guest a –'

'Hot tea will do,' said the psychic.

'What? Nonsense! You must have a drink. I insist.'

'When I've finished my work,' the psychic said. 'Right now, my glass must be clear, like my mind.'

Peri, who had overheard this exchange, thought to herself: *Tea is not exactly clear. Nor is this man.* Meanwhile, the male guests had huddled under an art installation – a wall sculpture of a giant prehistoric fish with rouged lips and a tasselled Ottoman fez. Finally freed from polite company, they could swear to their hearts' content and not have to worry about which way to blow their cigar smoke. The businessman signalled to the same maid, 'Evladim,* bring us cognac and almonds.'

Having left the table with everyone else, Peri lingered in the middle of the salon. She felt torn as she always did in such situations. She disliked the gender segregation common in Istanbul social gatherings. In conservative households, such was the extent of the separation that men and women could spend the entire night without exchanging words, clustered in separate parts of the house. Couples would split up on arrival and meet again at the end of the evening before heading out of the door.

Even liberal circles did not exclude the practice. After dinner, women would congregate together as if they needed one another for warmth, for comfort, for assurance. They would chat about an assortment of topics, their moods changing in tandem: vitamins, supplements and gluten-free recipes; children and schools; Pilates, yoga and fitness; public scandals and private gossips ... They would discuss celebrities as though they were their friends and their friends as though they were celebrities.

As for Peri, she mostly preferred male conversation over female, despite the fact that the subjects in the former tended to be darker. In the past she would automatically go to join the men and engage in whatever they bantered about: the economy, politics, football ... They wouldn't mind her presence, half seeing her as one of them, although they would never talk about sex with her around. Her behaviour would attract the attention, if not the ire, of other women. She had noticed, to

* *Evladim:* 'My child'.

her bewilderment, some wives felt uncomfortable with her sitting next to their husbands. Gradually, she abandoned her small rebellion – yet another sacrifice on the altar of convention.

Right now she wanted neither female nor male company, just to be alone. Gingerly, she slipped out on to the terrace. A chill wind, sweeping up from the sea, made her shudder. She smelled the scent of low tide. Across the Bosphorus, over on the Asian side of the city, the sky had turned the darkest shade of blue. A wispy fog curled off the water, reminiscent of shreds of muslin. Far off, a fishing boat was getting ready to set sail. She thought about the fishermen, austere and taciturn, their voices muffled so as not to scare the fish, their gaze fixed on the waters that gave them their daily bread. A part of her longed to be there, on that boat, in that hopeful stillness.

Just then, as if mocking her wishes, police sirens pierced the air somewhere on the European side of the city. While she stood absorbing the landscape, someone was being beaten, someone shot, someone raped . . . and, yes – at this moment – someone was falling in love in Istanbul.

In her left palm was her husband's phone. Tightening her grasp around its metal frame, Peri made up her mind. It had been years since she had spoken to Shirin. Her number might have changed for all she knew. Even if the number were correct, there was no guarantee that Shirin would want to talk to her. But the urge to try, no matter what, was too strong not to yield to it. Now that she had allowed the past to infiltrate the present, she was overwhelmed by feelings of regret.

As she fiddled with the phone, Peri scrolled up and down the contact list. Her thumb paused at a familiar entry: Mensur. Next to it, 'Baba'. The rituals of marriage – your spouse's parents automatically became your parents, as if someone else's past, all those years of love, misunderstanding and frustration, could, in one day and with one signature, be transferred. Her husband had not erased Mensur's name after his sudden death. Maybe that was the first sign of getting old – allowing dead friends and relatives to continue a virtual existence by not deleting them from your address book. Because one day you, too, would become one such name and one such number.

Peri tapped in the number she had obtained from her mother. She waited, the silence coming from the phone expanding; that second of suspense, when you don't know whether you're going to be connected or get an engaged tone; the fleeting doubt preceding all international calls.

'Peri, are you coming?'

She turned back, the mobile still pressed to her ear. Adnan had popped his head out, leaning over the doorsill, a glass of water in his hand. Even though for most of her marriage Peri had been relieved to see he was not and would never become a drinker, there were times when she wished he would lose control – every now and then, make mistakes he would regret the next day.

'People are wondering where you are,' Adnan said.

In that second the phone began to ring, lands and seas away, in England, in a house, she imagined, so different from this one.

'I'll be with you in a minute,' Peri said.

Adnan nodded, a shadow crossing his face. 'Okay, dear. Don't be long.'

She watched him turn around and walk towards the crowd, which sounded louder and merrier since she'd left them. She counted: one, two, three . . . A click. Her heart skipped a beat as she braced herself to hear Shirin's voice. It was her voice indeed, but a cold, mechanized version of it. Her voicemail message.

'Hello, you've reached Shirin's phone. Sorry, I'm not here right now. If you have nice things to say, please leave your message, name and number after the tone. Otherwise, speak before the tone and don't call again!'

Instantly, Peri hung up. She hated leaving messages, their fake friendliness. Straight away, she dialled the number again. This time, she left a message.

'Hi, Shirin . . . it's me, Peri.' She heard the feebleness in her voice. 'You might not want to talk to me, I don't blame you. It's been years . . .' She swallowed, her mouth as dry as chalk. 'I need to talk to Azur. I must hear from him, if he's forgiven me –'

A beep. The screen went blank. Peri stood still, processing the implications of the words that had flowed, almost of their own volition, out of her mouth. Strangely, she felt unburdened. Her mind was no longer an orchestra of anxieties and what-ifs and secrets and suppressed desires. She had done it. She had called Shirin. Whatever the outcome, she was ready to face it. She felt the night, not as an external force, but as an internal one – growing inside her chest, burning in her lungs, pushing forth through her veins, raring to manifest itself. *There is no feeling of lightness,* she thought, *like the one that comes after conquering a long-held fear.*

The Limousine

Oxford, 2001

In the heart of winter, Shirin walked into Peri's room, pulling a pink suitcase on wheels. She was going home to see her family for the Christmas holiday. Everyone was going home: students, academics, college staff. Everyone except Peri, who, having run well over her budget for the term, had left it too late to buy a cheap air flight and resigned herself to staying in Oxford for the break.

'You sure you don't want to come with me to London?' Shirin asked for what felt like the tenth time.

'Sure. I'll be fine here,' Peri said.

In truth, she wasn't exactly going to be 'here'. At Oxford, students were expected to empty their rooms during the holiday so that the college facilities could be used for conference attendees or tourists. For those who needed to stay, like herself, the college provided alternative places, temporary and smaller.

Shirin took a step closer to Peri, looking intently into her eyes. 'Look, Mouse, I'm serious. If you change your mind, give me a call. Mum would love to meet you. She's thrilled when my friends come to stay – she can complain about me for hours. It's a fucked-up family. We tear each other apart, but we're kind to outsiders. We'll be nice to you.'

'I promise I'll call if I get too lonely,' said Peri.

'Okey dokey. Don't forget, when I come back, we're moving out. Time to get our own house.'

Peri had half hoped Shirin had forgotten the idea, but she clearly hadn't. Countless students in Oxford had made the same journey: starting off in the intimate embrace of college life, where everything was relatively easy with its scouts, dining hall, library and common rooms; gradually finding it suffocating; putting together a small group of potential flatmates and moving out in their second year. Many had to do so anyway because their colleges couldn't provide enough accommodation for all their students.

Until now, each time Shirin had brought up the subject, Peri had declined, politely and firmly. But Shirin, as always, was relentless, her passion almost contagious. Sharing photographs of the houses an estate agent had shown her, she assured Peri that, for her, it made no difference to pay a bit more every month. In return, Shirin would gain her private space and peace of mind. Since she hated loneliness and could never have taken a flat by herself, if Peri accepted her proposal, Shirin would be indebted to her, not the other way round.

'I'll think about it,' Peri said uneasily.

'There's nothing to think about. College life is for freshers. The only ones who stay here are those who are too timid to make the move . . . and the nerds.'

'Or those who lack the money.'

'Money?' Shirin said with the kind of disdain she reserved for obnoxious people or unavoidable nuisances, such as burst sewers and uncollected rubbish. 'That should be the least of your concerns. Leave that to me.'

From time to time Shirin had intimated, though never openly said, that her family was well off. Certainly her life had had its share of hardships, but shortage of money was not among them. Peri assumed that the leaky, dilapidated house in London that she went on about was nothing of the sort. Shirin was willing to cover the entire rent. All Peri needed to do was put her books and clothes into a few boxes and follow her on this new adventure.

'Okay, darling, need to go.' Shirin kissed Peri on both cheeks, engulfing her in a cloud of scent. 'Happy New Year! Can't wait for 2002! I've a feeling this will be the best time of our lives.'

Peri grabbed the bottle of water on her desk and walked her friend to the front lodge.

The head porter stood to attention by the entrance. An ex-army officer, he seemed to know all the students by name. 'You have a great holiday, Shirin, see you next year,' he said cheerily. 'And you, Peri.'

Peri thought she detected an extra note of warmth in his voice as he greeted her. He felt badly for her, probably. The only student not going home.

There was a black limousine with a driver waiting outside. As she watched Shirin walk away on her high heels, tottering slightly with her suitcase in tow, Peri felt rent by opposing emotions. To share the same house with Shirin risked exacerbating the intimidation she felt from her friend's forceful personality. Besides, did she really want to be in Shirin's – anyone's – debt? And yet, wouldn't it be fantastic to have their own place?

As the car pulled away, Peri tossed the water into its wake, following an old Turkish tradition, *Go like water, come back like water, my friend.*

The Snowflake

Oxford, 2001

The festive season approached in a frenzy. Peri, who was accustomed to more sedate New Year celebrations in Istanbul, was first astonished, then amused to observe the elaborate preparations – streets adorned with arched, glittering displays of light, shops cascading with consumer goods, carol singers carrying lanterns that gleamed like fireflies in the dark.

Oxford without students seemed to lose its soul; to be a lone student at Christmas was doubly alienating, even for Peri, who was normally quite happy on her own. Every day she ate by herself at a Chinese restaurant with just three tables. The food was good, but oddly inconsistent. Maybe the cook was bipolar, she mused, with his mood swings reflected in the dishes. Some days she felt sick afterwards.

She went back to her part-time job at Two Kinds of Intelligence. The owners said that for years they had tried various window-display ideas to attract clientele for the holiday season – a snowman propped up in an armchair reading a book, strings of alphabets dangling from the ceiling. This time they wanted something different.

'How about a Christmas Tree of Forbidden Books?' Peri said. Similar to the Tree of Knowledge that had borne forbidden fruit, their tree would carry books banned somewhere in the world.

They liked it well enough to hand over the task to her. Absorbed, Peri set up a silvery tree in the centre of the shop window. On its branches she hung *Alice in Wonderland, 1984, Catch-22, Brave New World, Lady Chatterley's Lover, Lolita, The Naked Lunch, Animal Farm* . . . The list of banned titles from Turkey alone was so long that several boughs had to be devoted to them and it was still not enough. Kafka, Bertolt Brecht, Stefan Zweig and Jack London met Omar Khayyám, Nazim Hikmet and Fatima Mernissi. All over the branches she scattered the phosphorescent cards she had prepared: 'Banned', 'Censured', 'Burned'.

As she continued, her mind wandered, back to another Christmas time – she must have been ten or eleven – when Mensur had brought home a plastic Christmas tree. No other house in the neighbourhood had such a tree, though many shops and supermarkets displayed their own.

As it was carried from the doorstep to its chosen corner, the tree shed plastic needles, like the child in the fairy tale leaving breadcrumbs to find its way back home. Regardless, Peri and Mensur decorated it in earnest – silver, gold, blue tinsel. When they had no more trinkets left, they made some of their own: painted walnuts, sprayed pinecones, bottle caps and cork animals. Everything about their tree was cheap and mismatched; yet they adored it.

When Selma returned from running errands, her face fell. 'Why the need for this thing?'

'A new year is coming,' said Mensur, in the unlikely event that his wife was unaware.

'It's a Christian custom,' Selma said.

'Are we not entitled to a drop of pleasure?' Mensur rolled his eyes. 'You think He wouldn't love me were I to have a bit of fun?'

'Why should Allah love you when you do nothing to endear yourself to Him?' Selma said.

Aware that her father had purchased this controversial conifer to make her happy, Peri felt responsible for the tension in the air. She had to find a way to make things right. That night she waited until everyone had gone to sleep and put her plan into action, staying up till the small hours.

The next morning, when the Nalbantoğlus walked into their living room, they found a curiously dressed evergreen. Selma's beloved prayer beads, porcelain cats and silk headscarves, these last shredded into ribbons, adorned its branches. On top of the tree was a tiny brass mosque, and next to it a Book of Hadiths, carefully balanced.

'You see, it's not Christian any more,' said Peri, beaming.

The world seemed to come to a standstill as she waited for her mother's reaction. Selma's jaw dropped in horrified incredulity, seemingly on the verge of saying something. But, before she could speak, Mensur, standing behind them, began to giggle, his shoulders convulsing. At the sound of her husband's amusement, Selma's expression darkened. She walked out.

Still to this day Peri did not know what her mother would have said and what she had really made of her Islamic Christmas Tree.

The day before New Year's Eve, Peri was again at the bookshop. Other than an elderly woman, there more for warmth than for literature, there were no customers. The owners were away, visiting a friend, and the rest of the staff had taken the day off.

Peri dusted the shelves, brewed coffee, swept the floors, rearranged the bean bags, checked the stock; at ease in a place she'd grown to love. Her tasks done, she took down a book by A. Z. Azur and curled up in an armchair, packing cushions around her. She had dug out his entire backlist in the shop: nine publications with seductive titles and geometric dust covers. The sales figures showed they sold well. It was one of his early works she was reading now: *The Guide to Remaining Perplexed*.

The old woman shuffled over to the chair opposite and sat down, her eyelids drooping, head bowed. Soon she was asleep. Peri fetched a blanket from under the till and gently laid it over her. Time stretched and slowed down, a gluey mystery like the pine resin from the conifers of Anatolia. A sense that the universe was full of possibilities coursed through her mind, like an intoxicating drug. Surrounded by books, all of which she wanted to read, and accompanied by Azur's writing – half provoking, half soothing – she felt more peaceful than she had in years. True, she was still angry at him, but she could not remain angry at his books. And she had not stopped thinking about his seminar. She had not been able to.

Barely had she finished a chapter when the shop door opened with the tinkling of a brass bell. A chilly gust of air swept in along with none other than Professor Azur in a long, dark coat and a saffron scarf, bound to draw the envy of any Buddhist monk. A velvet fedora, barely taming his rebellious locks, completed his natty appearance.

'May we come in?' he said, addressing no one in particular.

As she stood up and darted towards the door, catching her toe on a crack in the floorboard, Peri saw what he meant by 'we'. Next to him, thick-coated, sharp-snouted, with a sable, mahogany and white coat, was a long-haired collie.

Azur's eyebrows arched. 'Hi, Peri. What a surprise. What are you doing here?'

'I work in the bookshop, part time.'

'Splendid! So what shall I do with Spinoza?'

'Excuse me?'

'My dog,' he said. 'It's too cold outside.'

'Oh, that's fine, you can bring him in,' Peri said, and then, remembering the owners' aversion to dogs in the shop, had second thoughts. 'Perhaps it . . . Spinoza . . . can wait for you by the entrance?'

But Professor Azur was already well inside, his dog in tow, both of them holding their heads up, their eyes straight ahead, like two Egyptian hieroglyphs.

'I haven't been here in a while,' said Azur, scanning the room. 'This place has changed. It looks bigger – and brighter.'

'We rearranged a few things and got rid of the clunky furniture,' Peri said. She watched as Spinoza sniffed around, then settled himself on the softest bean bag, his fur fanning out over the floor.

If Professor Azur noticed her discomfort, he didn't show it. His voice undulating in its distinctive way, he had already moved on to another subject. 'Love the Forbidden Tree in the window, by the way. Great idea.'

Peri felt a glow of pride. She wanted to tell him it was her creation, but she did not want him to think she was bragging. Instead, she said the first thing that came to mind. 'Were you looking for a particular book?'

'Not now,' Azur said. 'My publicist asked me to pop in and sign a few copies. I promised her I would.' His eyes fell on the armchair in which Peri had been sitting. 'That looks familiar. Are you reading it?'

Peri shuffled her feet. 'Yes, just started.'

He waited for her to fill the silence. She waited too, as if they had yet to discover the language in which they could really communicate. In the end she said, gesturing towards the table, 'Why don't you have a seat please? I'll find your books.'

There were so many. Seven titles were in stock; the other two had been reordered. With ten to fifteen copies of each, there were enough books to build a small tower. Professor Azur pulled up a chair, threw off his coat, produced a fountain pen and diligently began to sign. She brought him coffee and busied herself in a corner from where she could watch him.

Halfway through the stack, Azur stopped and fixed her with a quizzical look over his spectacles. 'Why aren't you celebrating the New Year with your family?'

'I wasn't able to travel,' Peri said, gesturing casually with her hand, as if Istanbul were waiting outside the door. 'But it's okay, Christmas is no big deal for us.'

A long, penetrating look. 'Are you telling me you're not sad that you couldn't spend the holidays with your family?'

'That's not what I meant.' She had known him for months, but she was still under the impression that his misunderstanding of her was deliberate. 'It's just this season is more important for Christian students.' She paused. Had she said anything wrong? She was always careful with her words, as if she were treading on ice, stopping to check, every now and then, that the surface beneath her feet had not cracked – yet.

He studied her, a strange gleam in his eyes that seemed to look right through her. 'Your parents are Muslims, practising?'

'My mother and one brother are,' Peri said. 'But not my father and my other brother.'

'Ah, what a split,' said Azur, with the triumph of someone who had found the missing jigsaw piece that had been in front of his eyes the whole time. 'Let me guess. You are close to your father and your elder brother.'

She swallowed hard. 'Uhm, yes, that's true.'

Nodding, he went back to the books.

'What about you?' Peri asked tentatively. 'I mean, are you celebrating with your family?'

He appeared not to hear, just kept on signing his name, and she dared not repeat herself. For a few minutes, or so it felt, the only sounds in the bookstore were the collie snoozing, the elderly customer snoring, the ticking of a longcase clock and the scratch of his fountain pen. She saw him set his jaw, his eyes lose focus momentarily. Everything about him seemed transitory, evanescent, in motion. No past, no future, only this present moment, already fleeting and gone.

He took a sip of coffee. 'Spinoza is my family now.'

Now. The way he pronounced the word made Peri feel as if she had prised open a lid she had no right to touch and glimpsed the sadness inside. 'I'm sorry,' she said.

The pen stopped moving. 'Let's make a deal, you and I,' Azur said. 'You've already said sorry to me so many times that from now on, even if you do something horrible, I don't want to hear your apologies. Promise?'

She could feel the pounding of her heart in her ribcage, though quite why she didn't know; it felt like a vaguely illicit pact. Even so, she did not hesitate. 'I promise.'

'Good!' Having signed the pile of books, he rose to his feet. 'Thanks for the coffee.'

'I'll put stickers on the books,' she said. 'Signed copies.'

'Thank you.' He smiled towards Peri.

They strode towards the door, the long-haired professor and the long-haired collie, their bodies in a harmony perfected by years of friendship. As he reached for the doorknob, Azur paused, turned and glanced at her. 'Tell you what, we're having an informal dinner, some old friends, a few colleagues, assistants, one of them just about your age, could be nice, could be boring. But you should not be alone on New Year's Eve.

England has a peculiar way of making foreigners feel exhilaratingly free and depressingly alone. Would you like to join us?'

Before she could think of an answer, he had taken out his notepad, torn out a page, and written out the address and the time.

'Here, think about it, no pressure. If you feel like coming, drop in. Don't bring anything. No flowers, no wine, no Turkish Delight, just yourself.'

He opened the door and stepped outside. It had begun to snow. The flakes twirled aimlessly in the wind, directionless, as if they had spiralled up from the ground instead of falling from the sky. Oxford resembled a town in a snow globe.

'Fabulous,' said Azur, to his dog, to himself or to Peri.

'Beautiful,' she said quietly, from the doorway.

Then she did something quite unexpected. Even though it was late and cold, and he was leaving and she was shivering in her jumper with her arms folded, she began to talk about his book, unable to stop herself, her breath coming out in clouds of condensation: 'You say our life is only one of many possible lives we could have led. And deep inside I think we all know this. Even in happy marriages and successful careers there's an element of doubt. We can't help wondering what our lives could have been like had we chosen another path . . . or paths, always plural! And you tell us that our idea of God is only one of many. So what is the point of being dogmatic about God – whether we are theists or atheists?'

'That's right,' Azur said, his gaze sweeping across her face, surprised and pleased to hear such an outburst from her.

'But you have to know there are many in this world, like my mother,' Peri continued, 'whose sense of security comes from their faith. They're convinced that there is only one interpretation of God: their own. These people already have enough to deal with, and you want to take away their only protection: their certainty. My mother . . . I mean sometimes I look at her and I see so much sorrow, I can sense she would've gone crazy without her faith to hold on to.'

Silence opened up between them as delicately as a silk fan.

'I understand. But absolutism of all kinds is a weakness,' Azur said. 'Absolute atheism or absolute theism. To my mind, Peri, they are equally problematic. My task is to inject the faithless with a dose of faith and the believers with a dose of scepticism.'

'But why?'

Azur's eyes cut into her. 'Because I am not a purist. It inhibits intellectual progress.' A snowflake came to rest on his hat, another in his hair. 'You see, some scholars are inclined to divide and categorize; others, to blend and unite. The splitters and the lumpers. Whereas I want all my senses awake – like your prodigious octopus. Let's not depend on one centralized brain. Let's bring poetry into philosophy and philosophy straight into our daily lives. The problem today is that the world values answers over questions. But questions should matter so much more! I guess I want to bring the devil into God and God into the devil.'

'I – we . . . how do we do that?'

'Wherever we see a duality, we'll smash it into tiny little pieces. We'll make plurality out of singularity and complexity out of simplicity.'

'What does that mean?'

'It means we'll mess things up, we'll blur the lines. We'll bring irreconcilable ideas and unlikely people together. Imagine, an Islamophobe develops a crush on a Muslim woman . . . or an anti-Semite becomes best friends with a Jew . . . on and on, until we grasp categories for what they really are: figments of our imagination. The faces we see in the mirrors are not really ours. Just reflections. We can find our true selves only in the faces of the Other. The absolutists, they venerate purity, we hybridity. They wish to reduce everyone down to a single identity. We strive for the opposite: to multiply everyone into a hundred belongings, a thousand beating hearts. If I am a human, I should be big enough to feel for people everywhere. Look at history. Observe life. It evolves from simplicity to complexity. Not vice versa, that would be devolution.'

'But is that not too much?' said Peri. 'People need simplification.'

'Nonsense, my dear. Our brains are wired for twists and turns!'

Then there was nothing else to say. He raised his hand in farewell and she nodded. So they went into the darkness extending before them, man and dog. Peri's stomach felt weak, her breathing uneven; she was both elated and terrified at the same time, on the verge of something unknown. She watched them until they turned the corner. This, for her, was no ordinary moment. One always knew the moment one fell in love.

The Psychic

Istanbul, 2016

Aromas of coffee, cognac and cigars blending uneasily with the expensive perfumes in the air hit Peri as soon as she came back into the room. She was still thinking about the message she had left on Shirin's answering machine when she noticed the psychic a few feet away. With a complacent smile spreading across his features, the man sat on a chaise-longue, surrounded by kneeling and fawning women, like a sultan in a grotesque Orientalist fantasy. The American hedge-fund manager was also there, waiting patiently for his coffee cup to be read.

Peri walked towards the men's circle, oblivious to the rules of social conduct. She sat herself down in the middle of the group, beside her husband, under clouds of blue-grey smoke from multiple cigars.

Adnan placed his hand on her shoulder and squeezed gently. Once, twice. A code between them signifying, 'Are you bored?' She took his hand, squeezed back, only once. 'I'm fine.'

'Mark my words, the Middle Eastern map will be redrawn,' the architect was saying to those around him. 'It's clear the Western powers have a major plan.'

'That's for sure. They'll never allow us Muslims to prosper,' concurred the Islamist newspaper tycoon. 'The Crusades have never ended!'

'Yes, but Turkey is not the same Turkey,' said the nationalist architect. 'We are no meek lamb. Not the sick man of Europe any more. Europe's now scared of us – and will do anything to stir up unrest.'

The tycoon agreed. 'They certainly know how to foment chaos. An invisible hand pushes a button and it all flares up again, bloodshed and violence. We must be on the alert.'

The rest of the men were listening intently – some nodding, others quiet.

Through the cigar smoke Peri looked at them. 'To me what you're saying sounds like sheer paranoia,' she said softly. 'Europeans ... Westerners ... Russians ... Arabs ... If you were to get to know them, not as a category, but individually, then you would see how we are all, more or less, flesh and mind, the same.' She paused. 'We can only recognize ourselves in the faces of ... the Other.'

The architect and the tycoon gaped at her in astonishment. Adnan gave her a wink. 'Well said, darling.'

Smiling at her husband, Peri excused herself and stood up. She crossed to the opposite side of the room and approached the women's circle.

Seeing her, the PR woman leaned over and whispered something into the psychic's ear. The man listened, his eyebrows raised. He looked up and stared at Peri. He smiled. She didn't. His smile grew wider. Like all those accustomed to being flattered and fawned upon, he was most intrigued by the one person who tried to avoid him.

'Why doesn't your guest join us?' the psychic asked the hostess, who was sitting across from him with Pom-Pom nestled on her lap.

Adamant, the businesswoman jumped to her feet. One hand under Pom-Pom's belly, she cupped the other around Peri's elbow, gently but firmly steering her towards the guest of honour.

'Did you meet our friend Peri?' she said to the psychic. 'She was late, just like you. She had an accident on the way here.'

'Sounds like you had a tough day,' the man said, eyeing Peri's bandaged hand and damaged dress.

'Nothing important ...' Peri said.

'You deserve a gift. Would you like me to read your future?' He rose to his feet and added with a smile. 'For free.'

The girlfriend of the journalist and the PR woman sitting on either side of him, waiting for their turns, were not pleased.

Peri shook her head. 'You have enough to do.'

'Don't worry, I'm here for everyone.' A slow smile crept over his face, as if he had intended to say something else but decided to keep it to himself.

'I think I'll skip it this time.'

He chuckled, though his eyes had acquired a steely gleam. 'I've been doing this for twenty-five years, and I've yet to meet a woman who doesn't want to know her future.'

The PR woman saw an opportunity. 'How about her past?'

'But no . . . It's just not her *thing*,' the man said, holding his gaze on Peri and offering his hand to her. 'It was nice to meet you, though.'

Peri extended her left hand, almost reflexively. Instead of shaking it, he grabbed her wrist, not letting go. Something passed from him to her, a tingling sensation, a flash of warmth.

Still holding her hand, he said, 'Distrust charlatans, but not a real psychic.'

'Oh, he's the best, nothing like the others,' confirmed the businesswoman.

'Maybe another day,' said Peri, pulling back.

No sooner had she taken a step than the psychic's voice caught up with her. 'You miss someone.'

Peri glanced over her shoulder at him. 'What did you say?'

He came closer. 'Someone you loved. You lost him.'

Peri quickly composed herself. 'You could say the same thing to half the women – and men – in the world.'

He laughed, a false brightness in his voice. 'This is different.'

Involuntarily, she folded her arms over her chest, determined not to have any further contact.

'I can see the first letter of his name,' he said with a confidential tone that was still loud enough for all the women to hear. 'It's an *A*.'

'Most male names start with *A*,' Peri said without thinking. 'My husband's, for instance.'

'You know what, I won't embarrass you in front of everyone. I'll put it on a napkin.'

'*Kizim*,' yelled the businesswoman in a twitter. 'Bring us a pen, hurry up!'

The PR woman said mischievously, 'If it's an old story, why not share it?'

'Who said it was old?' added the psychic. 'It's alive, breathing.'

Peri managed to remain calm while a tempest brewed inside. She just wanted him to leave her alone. Not only him, but all these women and all these men, and this city with its endless chaos.

The waitress appeared with the requested item, so fast it was almost as if she had been waiting for this moment. The psychic made a show of writing so the others couldn't see, folding the napkin – each move painfully slow and ceremonious.

'It's my gift for you,' he said as he gave it to Peri.

'Right, thanks.'

She walked away from the women, passed by the men, stepped out on to the terrace. The fishing boat was gone, the water stretched out ahead, darker than the deepest regrets. A car tore down the street with its engine roaring and loud music – a romantic song in English – blasting from its open windows. Peri squinted her eyes, trying to imagine the man – always a man – who would play such music at these decibels and at this hour.

Gingerly, she unclenched her left fist – the hand she used for writing, the hand that was her strongest. There, on the surface of a crumpled napkin, the psychic had drawn three female figures – like the three wise monkeys. *The three of them.*

Under the first one was written: 'She Saw Evil.' Under the second: 'She Heard Evil.' And under the third were these words: 'She Did Evil.'

PART FOUR

The Seed

Oxford, 2001

On New Year's Eve, Peri was too excited to do even half the things she wanted to do. In the morning she went out running, but could not keep up her rhythm and the cramp in her calf was so bad that she had to finish early. When she sat down at her desk to read, she found herself unable to concentrate, the words crawling like hungry ants across the white paper. She felt just as famished. With a tendency to episodes of 'comfort eating,' she feared that in her agitated state, if she had one bite, she might not be able to stop. So she nibbled apples instead. And she listened to the radio. That helped, the steady sound soothing her nerves. She tuned in to the world news, the local news, political debates and a BBC documentary on the Aztec Empire. But a documentary – even one on the mighty Aztecs – could only last so long. No matter how hard she tried to put the evening out of her mind, it loomed large in her thoughts. In the end it came as a relief when it was time to get ready. No dinner with Professor Azur could be worse than its anticipation.

Peri applied mascara, black eyeliner and lip gloss, and left it at that. She examined her face in the mirror, finding the nose she had inherited from her mother too plump. If there was a way, with the right cosmetics, to make it look thinner, she hadn't a clue. Had Shirin been here, Peri might have asked her advice. Then again, had Shirin been here, Peri would probably not be going to Azur's. *You should not be alone on New Year's Eve*, the professor had said. He hadn't invited her out of pity, she hoped.

What to wear was a challenge. Not that she was lost for choice. But with the few pieces she had, she put together multiple combinations, all of which she tried on, one by one. The denim black skirt with the loose blouse, the blouse with the jeans, the jeans with the green jacket . . . She didn't want to look like a student, or, worse, to look as if she didn't want to look like a student. At last, with a pile of clothes on the bed, she settled on a velvet skirt and a cerulean-blue jumper – its softness giving the impression of cashmere. She finished the outfit with a deep-blue necklace of evil-eye beads.

Though he had been clear about not bringing anything, she had learned from her mother never to go anywhere empty-handed. She bought eight small tarts from a delicatessen in Little Clarendon Street, which was silly of her as they cost more than a whole cake.

She walked to the bus stop and waited. In less than five minutes the bus arrived. She stood and watched as the bus doors opened and closed again. Then she watched the bus depart without her as she walked back to her place to change the skirt and the jumper. A long black dress and heavy boots. Better.

Azur lived just outside town, up the Woodstock Road, about twenty minutes by bus, in the village of Godstow. In spring it would be enfolded in the lush greenery of the English countryside, with clean views across Port Meadow to the dreaming spires of Oxford, though now darkness had fallen. By the time she got off the bus, it had begun to snow again – big fluffy flakes on her hair, on her coat. There were no other houses within direct sight, which didn't surprise Peri. She had more than once suspected her tutor of being a secret misanthrope.

It was an imposing stone-clad, double-fronted house, though it was hard to tell its age, not unlike its owner. It looked like a place with a past – a house with stories. She walked towards it slowly, careful not to slip, on a winding path with leafless oaks on both sides. The wind cut through her coat. She shivered, as much from nerves as from the cold. She glanced back at the bus stop, as though worried that it might not still be there later that night. How would she get home? There had to be people at the party who lived in Oxford and one of them was bound to be able to give her a lift. It was typical of her to get overwrought about the end of an evening before it had even started.

Lights spilled from the ground-floor windows, warm and golden like honey. Clutching the box of pastries against her chest, Peri stood by the door, listening to the noise coming from inside – merry chatter, peals of laughter and, in the background, waves of music. The kind of music that none of her friends listened to, nor did she. The music, just like the light, was at once inviting and intimidating.

As Peri took a step forward she heard a hiss, like the swish of a distant car. But there was nothing on the road. No bus, no motorcycle, and surely no bikes in this weather. In the meantime, a different part of her brain, slower and wiser, warned her that the sound was much closer. She peered around. Her gaze fell on the high hedge to her right. She froze, her heart accelerating. Nothing moved, not even the wind, and yet she was now certain that something or someone was watching her.

Instinctively she called out, 'Who's there?'

In the murky blackness Peri thought she spotted a silhouette flitting behind the bushes. She took a step forward. 'Troy! Is that you?'

The boy emerged, looking pale and embarrassed.

'My God, you scared me,' Peri said. 'Are you following me?'

'Not you, silly,' Troy said, and nodded towards the house. 'It's the devil I'm after.' He paused. 'What are you doing here?'

Peri refused to answer. 'You're spying on the professor!'

'Told you, I'm suing him. Need evidence in court.'

You are obsessed with him, Peri thought. Strange it was that among the many kinds of obsession, hatred and love were only shades apart, like adjacent hues on an artist's palate.

A wave of laughter rose from the house. Troy darted back behind the hedgerow. 'Please don't tell them I'm here.'

Peri frowned. 'You have no right to do this. I'll go in and wait for ten minutes. Then I'll come out and check. If you haven't left by then, I'm telling Azur. If he doesn't call the police, I will!'

'Wow, calm down,' said Troy, hands in the air. 'Don't shoot.'

She left him and turned towards the front door, which had a panel of stained glass: amber, olive and crimson. She quickly rang the bell. A birdlike tone pierced the air. Not a sweet canary or a nightingale, but more like a squawking parrot, laughing at the hapless visitor. The sounds from inside ceased for a moment and just as quickly resumed. On the other side of the coloured glass a shadow appeared. She could hear approaching footsteps. She had not renewed her lip gloss, but it was too late.

The door opened.

A woman stood blocking the entrance. A tall blonde, toned, lithe and good-looking. She examined Peri up and down, her mouth fixed in a smile that could have been friendly were it not for its imperiousness. She knew she was sexy; the midnight-blue strapless dress that clung to her body revealed an hourglass figure. *Definitely not a professor*, thought Peri. She was glad she had changed her jumper. She wanted nothing in common with this woman. Not even a shade of blue.

Azur had said that his dog, Spinoza, was his family now, but that didn't mean he didn't have a girlfriend. Or even a wife. He didn't wear a wedding ring, but not every husband felt bound to display one. Why had it not occurred to her that he had someone in his life? Of course he did. At his age everyone did.

'Hello there, pretty young face,' said the woman, as she grabbed the box from Peri's hand. 'You must be the Turkish girl.'

Just then, to the sound of hasty footsteps, Azur appeared, holding an unopened bottle of wine directed towards them like a miniature ship's cannon. He wore a gun-metal grey turtleneck sweater and a burgundy wool-and-cashmere jacket.

'Peri, you came!' the professor exclaimed, his forehead glistening in the light. 'Don't stand there in the cold. Come in, come in!'

She followed him – them – into the drawing room. Along the corridor the walls were covered in framed photographs. Portraits of people from different parts of the world stared at her, aloof and self-absorbed, as though they already knew something she was yet to discover.

'Fascinating photographs. Who took them?' asked Peri.

Azur answered with a wink. 'I did.'

'Oh, really? You must have travelled a lot.'

'Just a bit. You know I've been to Turkey.'

'To Istanbul?'

He shook his head. Not Istanbul, where everybody went or felt like they had to someday. No, Azur had been to other places – Mount Nemrut, with its giant statues of ancient deities; the Byzantine Monastery of Sumela, nestled upon a steep cliff; and Mount Ararat, where Noah's Ark had come to rest. Peri swallowed, worried that he might ask her about these sites, none of which she had visited.

In the living room, there were full-height bookcases lining two opposite walls. Between them stood an elegant group of people, chatting heartily, holding champagne flutes and wine glasses.

Turning towards the assembled guests, Azur called out to a young man, 'Darren, come over here. I want you to meet one of my best students,' and as soon as he saw him coming, he disappeared.

Darren turned out to be a graduate student in Physics. He brought a glass of champagne to Peri, his manners polite and polished. He complimented her on her 'exotic' accent, an accolade it seemed she had earned. He asked her about her background, but was more eager to talk about himself, speaking as if he were racing against the clock. Yes, he was intelligent, ambitious – and desperate for affection. He tried to make her laugh, cracking jokes, one after another, having probably read somewhere that women fell for men with a great sense of humour. He rolled his eyes each time, as if even he didn't find his delivery funny. Nice guy, though. *The kind of man who would love and respect his girlfriend, not compete with her*, Peri thought.

But she knew there would never be more than a flitting spark between them. Why did it have to be this way? Why did she not feel attracted to this boy, who was kind and personable, close to her in age and probably good for her? Instead it was the professor for whom she secretly yearned – a man not only old, unknown and unavailable, but also wrong. It puzzled her endlessly that she was not, and had never really been, interested in happiness – that magic word that was the subject of so many books, workshops and TV shows. She did not want to be unhappy.

Of course, she didn't. It just did not occur to her to seek happiness as a worthwhile goal in life. How otherwise could she allow herself to carry a torch for a man like Azur?

She breathed in. A boldness she never thought would come her way began to engulf her, like a heady perfume. Could other people, too, sense she was changing inside? Beyond all the gracious words and forced smiles of social life was a frontier that separated responsible individuals from misfits seeking confrontation and buccaneers seeking adventures. A borderline as thin as a whisper, which kept modest Turkish girls away from all kinds of trouble and sin. What would it be like to inch close to that divide, drawing so close as to feel the end of the hard earth under her feet and the beginning of the void beyond, and, suddenly, letting herself fall, light and listless?

Though she was neither brave nor eccentric, a seed of unorthodoxy had been sown in her heart somewhere along the journey of her youth, germinating unnoticed, waiting to burst through the topsoil. Nazperi Nalbantoğlu, always proper and careful and balanced, yearned to transgress, yearned to err.

'Dinner time,' said Azur, with an enticing grin from across the room, brandishing a large serving fork as if it were a spear intended for an unsuspecting guest.

The Night

Oxford, 2001/2

Peri followed everyone over to a large oak refectory dining table that might have been a prop in a medieval play. She could see it, in her mind's eye, surrounded by lords and knights, laden with spit-roasted meats, stuffed peacocks and gleaming jellies. Except this one had no silver platters and golden goblets, only plain crockery.

Behind the table was a fireplace with majolica tiles running up both sides of the mantelpiece and a framed black-and-white photograph hanging above it. Peri approached the blazing fire, drawn to the dancing flames. Each of the tiles seemed to depict a different character – mostly men, but also a few women; their clothes from another era, their expressions grave. They were images of prophets, messengers and saints. On some of the tiles their names were inscribed: King Solomon, St Francis, Abraham, Buddha, St Teresa, Ramananda . . . The figures were carrying water, writing on parchment, talking to their disciples or walking alone in a desert landscape. They seemed to be arranged in no particular order. Seeing them all side by side, as if they were attending a banquet of their own, felt awkward. It was easier to imagine these sacred figures separately. Peri's gaze searched for the Prophet Mohammed, wondering if he, too, had been included. There he was, ascending on a steed up to heaven, his face veiled, his head surrounded by flames, as in the Persian and Turkish miniatures in days past. There too was the Virgin Mary with the Christ Child, her skin pale as the snow outside, escorted by winged angels. She saw Moses pointing at a rod on the ground, half of which had been turned into a snake.

Why on earth had Azur placed these images around his fireplace? If it wasn't a matter of aesthetics, was it a manifestation of his belief system – and, if so, what exactly did he believe? She had read several of his books by now, but he still remained an enigma. Unable to answer the questions plaguing her mind, she focused instead on the photograph above the fireplace.

It was a shot of the house, clearly taken some years earlier. The oak tree she had seen, walking from the bus stop, was there, as well as the winding path. In the photo too was a thickly planted flower garden and dense, heavy white clouds so close they seemed to be touching the roof. The house looked different, smaller; perhaps there had been additions over the years. While the picture showed spring and nature at its best, to Peri it felt like a lost Arcadia, a time of light-hearted joy never to be regained.

By now all the guests had circled the table, glasses in their hands, waiting patiently to be guided to their seats.

'Azur, how would you like us to sit?' asked a thin, lantern-jawed man, who, Peri later learned, was an eminent professor in quantum physics.

'As if he'd be so prescriptive! Seating is a matter of personal choice in this house,' said another man of some considerable girth. A professor in the Faculty of Theology and Religion, he was an old friend of Azur and one of the people who knew him best. To emphasize his point, he pulled out a chair and sat down.

Taking their cue from him, the other guests, one by one, placed themselves around the table. As soon as Peri found a seat, Darren took the place beside her. The beautiful blonde sat on the opposite side, next to Azur.

The theology professor leaned back, taking in the music still playing in the background. After a moment, he raised his glass. 'I'd like us to toast our generous host. We thank him for bringing us together – we forsaken and forlorn souls in Oxford, consumed by the frosty night.'

Looking over an iron candelabrum with three lit candles, which threw overlapping shadows on the walls, Azur returned the compliment with a smile.

Peri glanced around at her dinner companions – a mixed bunch of scholars and students from various disciplines. When she first walked in, she had assumed that all these people, despite their differences, shared the same forte: intelligence. They must be special to be in Azur's inner circle, she had decided, more knowledgeable and more sensitive than the average. How presumptuous she had been. What they all had in common was that each of them, for one reason or another, was about to celebrate the New Year alone – before Azur had intervened and collected them, like scattered shells on a remote beach.

'There's another reason why I should like us to toast our host,' continued the elderly professor. 'For playing Bach on repeat. If everyone listened to Bach for ten minutes every day, I can assure you there'd be an increase in the number of believers.'

Azur shook his head. 'Be careful, John. As you know better than I do, Bach is a theological minefield. It's true, his music is seen as the sublime instrument of the voice of God. But the more you listen, the less God appears necessary to its creation. You'll come to understand his works as simply the highest expression of the human spirit. Bach could make you a believer – or a true sceptic.'

Several people laughed.

'Please help yourselves,' said Azur, opening his hands.

All at once the guests turned their attention to the food. Three large serving plates stood in the middle of the table. On the first was a pile of steamed beans; on the second, black rice; and on the third, a large turkey roasted golden. And a decanter of ruby-red wine. That was it. There were no dressings or condiments. It was all simple, almost affectedly so. Peri smiled to herself as she thought of her mother. Selma would rather die than invite people to such a modest table. She had told her daughter that the secret of a successful dinner party was 'making sure you provide two special dishes per person. For four guests, you must have eight; for five, you must have ten.' Tonight there were twelve people and three dishes. Her mother would have been appalled.

The guests began to serve themselves from each platter, before passing it to the next person. When it was her turn, Peri took generous portions, suddenly aware that she had not eaten all day long.

The nameless blonde leaned into Azur. 'Did you make all of this yourself?'

Peri perked up. If she had to ask him that, she couldn't possibly be his wife.

'Yes, my dear, let's see how you'll enjoy it,' said Azur, and then, addressing everyone, he added, 'Bon appétit.'

In the dancing candlelight, his eyes were forest-green; the tips of his eyelashes seemed to glow and his lips, which Peri had never dared to examine before, appeared nearly as vivid a colour as the wine he was drinking.

Azur angled his head and looked sideways at Peri through lowered lids, his expression one of mild surprise. She blushed, horrified at the realization that she had been staring at him too long. Immediately, she turned to Darren, grateful for his presence.

Dessert was Christmas plum pudding. Azur poured a splash of brandy over the still warm pudding and lit it with a match. Blue flames burst out all over the surface; they swirled and made merry, before exuding the last sigh of their brief, innocent lives. With a practised hand, Azur sliced the pudding and served everyone a generous piece with custard sauce. The guests, who had fallen silent as they watched the performance, having savoured their first bite, complimented their host on his culinary skills.

'You should write a cookbook,' the physics professor suggested. 'This is delicious. How did you make it?'

'Well, one learns,' Azur murmured.

For Peri, those words offered a clue to his private life. He must be single, she deduced. She hoped someone would probe the matter but no one did. Instead, they plunged into a conversation about the invasion of Afghanistan. The energy around the table changed as some of the guests aired discontent with Tony Blair, praising the backbench rebellion in the Labour Party. Just the same, there was a sense of calmness in their tone that Peri found hard to associate with politics. In Turkey, all the political exchanges she had ever witnessed, from those of her father's friends to her own, were besieged with the three capital

R's: Resentment, Rage and Resignedness. When subjects were heavy, emotions were high and the prospect of things improving slim, style was the first thing to be sacrificed in a conversation. Whereas here they spoke in such a way as to prioritize style over content. So suffused was her mind with cultural comparisons that she lost track of the talk at the table and when she saw everyone looking at her, she didn't immediately grasp why.

The elderly professor came to her aid. 'We were just saying, you've an interesting country.'

Remembering Shirin's warning against the word 'interesting', Peri glanced at her professor. But Azur, observing her over the rim of his glass, looked curious to hear what she was going to say.

'What do you think? Will Turkey ever get the chance to be admitted into the EU?' asked a woman with short white hair spiked into feathery wisps. She was the elderly professor's wife.

'Well, I hope so,' Peri said.

'Don't you think it's culturally . . . different?' butted in the blonde.

'I don't know what you mean by *different*,' Peri said, a battleground opening up in her soul. On the one hand, she wished to speak critically, there being so many things about her country that frustrated her. On the other hand, she wanted these people to like her motherland. A defensiveness descended on her. A sense of responsibility. Never before had she felt as if she were representing a collective entity.

'So you don't see religion as an obstacle?' asked the physics professor. 'Do you ever worry that Turkey could become like Iran?'

Peri said, 'There's that danger. But Iran is a society of memory and tradition. We Turks are good at amnesia.'

'Which do you think is preferable?' asked Darren beside her. 'Remembering or forgetting?'

'They both have their drawbacks,' Peri replied without hesitation. 'But I'd rather forget. The past is a burden. What's the use of remembering when we can't change anything?'

'Only the young have the luxury to forget,' said the elderly professor.

Peri bowed her head. She had not wanted to sound young. If anything, she had wanted to sound clever and wise. Much to her surprise, however, she noticed Azur nod in agreement. 'If I had to make a choice, I might have opted out of having a memory too. I can't wait to get Alzheimer's.'

The beautiful woman placed her hand on Azur's. 'Darling, you don't mean that.'

Peri averted her eyes. She didn't know these people; their pasts, their connections, were all beyond her. She could only sense but not catch on to the things left unsaid, the subjects they gently tiptoed around.

Shortly before midnight, as tea and coffee were being served, she excused herself to go to the lavatory. The face she saw in the mirror while washing her hands was that of a young woman who, time and again, failed to be confident and light-hearted. She had always blamed herself for not knowing how to be joyful. Surely she must have done something wrong so as to spawn unbidden unhappiness. But perhaps people who could not pass the Happiness Test were not at fault. Sadness was not a manifestation of laziness or self-pity. Perhaps such people were simply born this way. Struggling to be happier was as futile as struggling to be taller.

On the way out, in the hall, amidst portraits of all kinds, Peri saw a photo that made her stop.

The woman in the picture – high cheekbones, wide-apart eyes, full lips – was naked save for a crimson scarf tied loosely around the waist. Her hair was pulled back into a careless bun, her shoulders pale and shiny, like ornaments made of polished ivory. Her breasts were large and round, the nipples erect in the midst of dark circles; her navel was slightly prominent, and with one hand she held the cloth that covered her legs, ready to let go of it at any moment. The smile on her lips hinted at her pleasure in being photographed. It also said she knew the photographer.

In a daze, Peri swayed forward as if she had trespassed on a forbidden zone. She stood motionless, paralysed in the moment. Somewhere in the bowels of the house a clock ticked away. A presentiment, both familiar and impossible to get used to. With a surge of trepidation she sensed the presence of the baby in the mist, alarmingly close. There it was, the same round face, trusting eyes, purple stain covering half his face. He was trying to tell her something – about the woman in the picture. Sadness. There was so much of it around here – intense, untouched. Peri could not tell whether she had stumbled upon an old sorrow or whether she herself had brought it along.

'Go away!' Peri whispered in horror. She had no patience for him. Not now. Not here.

The baby in the mist pouted.

'What are you trying to tell me? You can't come here, this place –'

A voice cut her off. 'Who are you talking to, Peri?'

She turned around to find Azur standing behind her. His eyes glimmering with golden sparks gave nothing way.

'I was just talking to myself . . . and looking at her,' Peri said, pointing at the wall. Sneaking a sideways glance, she was relieved to see the baby in the mist had started to dissolve, a coil of steam in the air.

'My wife,' Azur said.

'Your wife?'

'She died four years ago.'

'Oh, I'm so sorry.'

'Again?' he asked, his gaze jumping from the woman in the photograph to the one in front of him. 'You really must stop . . .'

'Her features are Middle Eastern,' Peri quickly added to deflect his criticism.

'Yes, her father was Algerian. Berbers, like St Augustine.'

'St Augustine was a Berber? But he was a Christian.'

Azur looked at her, taking in her youth. 'History is vast. Berbers were Jewish, Christian, even pagan once. And Muslims. The past is full of encounters that may seem bizarre to us today but made perfect sense back then.'

The words, though they had nothing to do with her, opened up a vacuum inside Peri, an unexplored space. In her experience, not only the past but the present, too, was full of encounters that defied reason.

'You look pale,' he said.

That was when she opened up to him. As they stood there listening to the sounds of the guests close by, Peri told her professor that ever since she was a child, for a reason she could not fathom, she had had 'surreal experiences'. She had shared this with her father, who had dismissed it as 'superstition' and with her mother, who had feared she was possessed by a jinni. Since then she had shared it with no one, lest they judge her too.

Azur listened, a look of wonder spreading across his face. 'I can't comment on your *surreal* experience. But I can tell you one thing with conviction: don't be afraid of being different. You are very special.'

A burst of excited voices from the drawing room interrupted them.

'It must be midnight!' said Azur, raking his fingers through his hair. 'Let's continue this later. We must! Come to my rooms.'

He moved towards her and kissed her on both cheeks. 'Happy New Year!'

Then off he went to kiss the others.

'Happy New Year, Professor!' Peri murmured to his back, his warmth lingering on her skin.

Come to my rooms. Surely this was no ordinary remark. Unbidden excitement rushed through her. He had said she was special – very special. He could see through her like no one else could. As she stood there, unmoving, contemplating, it all became steadily clearer, the final drop before all her expectations, all her hopes, crystallized. By the time she returned to the celebration, she had convinced herself that her professor, too, had feelings for her.

Shortly after midnight the guests began to leave. Only when she stepped into the cold did Peri remember Troy. She threw a nervous glance at the high hedge – there was nothing there save the night.

Everyone seemed to have a car, except for Peri and Darren. The beautiful blonde – a proud teetotaller, in her own words – offered to give them a ride.

It was a short drive back to Oxford, oddly silent after the hubbub of the evening. BBC Radio 4 was broadcasting a programme about the love-letters of Gustave Flaubert. Sensual words filled the car, infusing the listeners with a sense of solitude, a longing for a romance yet to come. Sitting next to the driver, Peri wondered if in the past people had a better understanding of love. She rested her head against the half-frosted window and kept her gaze on the road ahead, patches of which were illuminated under the car's headlights before being swallowed up by the night. She thought of Azur and the woman in the photograph. What had their sex life been like? She thought about how he smiled when he saw his guests refill their plates; how he cradled his coffee mug in both hands and held it up, enjoying the steam as it caressed his face; how he helped the women with their coats, including her, as he saw everyone off at the end of the night and how different he was from the way he was in the classroom, unintimidating, tender, surprisingly fragile.

Back in Oxford, Peri and Darren got out of the car together. The cutting cold of early evening had been replaced by a crispness in the air. They walked, talking non-stop, until they reached Peri's temporary lodging. They kissed under a street light. They kissed again in the dark. Feeling tipsy, less from the wine than the intensity of the evening, Peri closed her eyes, excited more by his excitement than her own.

'May I come upstairs?' he asked.

She saw the boy he had once been – clutching his mother's hand as they crossed the street, learning how to treat women with respect. If she said no, she knew he wouldn't insist. He would go his way, perhaps disappointed but without being rude. The next day if they ran into each other he would be kind to her and she to him.

'Yes,' she said, acting on an impulse she didn't want to question.

She was aware that in the morning she would wake up with a harrowing feeling. Guilt for sleeping with someone who, in truth, she cared little about; guilt for letting down her father and making her mother's worst fears come true. Even though they would never learn any of this, she would have a bad conscience the next time she talked to them and probably for a long while afterwards. But there was something that bothered her even more. As she returned Darren's touches and kisses, she was thinking about someone else. Overriding all her emotions was the knowledge that it was her professor she desired.

They said, what one did in the first hours of the New Year would determine what one did the rest of the year. If only that weren't true. For she had entered the first day of January with complicated emotions pressing on her heart. She hoped that 2002 would not be the year of guilt.

The Lie

Oxford, 2002

Before the holiday ended, Peri took the train down to London, having decided to accept Shirin's invitation. She watched students and families with small children file onto the coaches. In her compartment – she'd bought a first-class ticket by mistake – were three smartly dressed middle-aged men indistinguishable from each other and a woman of uncertain age, her auburn hair in a perfect coiffure. They eyed Peri coldly, as if to say: *You don't look like you belong in this carriage*. Finding her seat number, she buried herself in *The Complete Mystical Works of Meister Eckhart*.

She had taken her God-diary with her, into which she now wrote: *The eye through which I see God is the same eye through which God sees me, Eckhart says. If I approach God with rigidity, God approaches me with rigidity. If I see God through Love, God sees me through Love. My eye and God's eye are One.*

The train thrust forward, its steady rhythm pounding in her consciousness. In a little while a steward approached, clattering into the compartment with a trolley from which he distributed plastic trays with breakfast and a variety of drinks. Coming to Peri, he informed her that she had two choices. Menu one: ham & cheese croissant. Menu two: scrambled eggs with pork sausage.

Peri shook her head. 'Do you have anything else?'

'Vegetarian?' asked the steward.

'No, it's the pork,' Peri said.

The man's eyes, dark and sunken in his thinly bearded face, studied her for a brief moment. Peri's gaze slid to his nametag: Mohammed.

'I'll see what I can do,' he said and disappeared.

A minute later Mohammed appeared with a chicken sandwich. He gave it to Peri, smiling. Only when the man had moved on did it occur to Peri that he might have given her his own food. His lunch, probably. Invisible strands of solidarity threaded among strangers who, upon finding out they shared the same religion or nationality, developed an instant affinity. A camaraderie that manifested itself in the smallest details – a smile, a nod, a sandwich. She felt like an impostor, though. The man seemed to have taken her for a good Muslim, but was she really?

Culturally she was a Muslim, no doubt. Yet the number of prayers she had learned by heart would not exceed the fingers of her hand. She neither practised her religion nor acknowledged, as Shirin did, being a lapsed Muslim. There was something about the word 'lapsed' that brought to mind eggs past their sell-by date or butter gone rancid. Her relationship with Islam, whether practising or not, had not *expired*. Her confusion was a continuing affair. Alive. Perpetual. If she stood anywhere at all, it was with the bewildered. But if she told this to Mohammed, would he want his sandwich back?

When Peri was little, quarrels would erupt in their house every Eid al-Adha. Mensur was against the ritual of sacrificing animals. He believed that money spent on a lamb would be better given to those in need. That way the hungry could fill their stomachs while the sated could pat themselves on the back; and no animals would have to die in the process.

Selma disagreed. There was a reason why God had wanted things to be this way, she said. 'If only you cared to read the Holy Book, you'd understand.'

'I read it,' Mensur said. 'I mean, that part. It makes no sense.'

'What makes no sense?' Selma said irritably.

'In the Quran, God never instructed Abraham to go and sacrifice his son – the man got it all wrong.'

'The man!'

'But listen, wife, Abraham didn't actually hear God order him to kill his son. He had a dream, right? What if he misinterpreted? I think God in His mercy saw how wrong Abraham got it all and in order to save His son, He sent the lamb.'

Selma sighed. 'You are like a big, sulky boy. I've raised my children, thank God. I have no desire for another child in the house.'

Determined to buy her own sheep, Selma would put aside money. The animal would be kept in the garden, hennaed and fed, until it was sent to slaughter. Its meat would then be distributed among seven neighbours and the poor.

One such year – Peri must have been thirteen years old – the same neighbours decided to pool their liras to buy a bull. They had expected a majestic creature that radiated power, trailed by its dark shadow. The bull that arrived, though huge, looked nervous, almost crazed with fear. He was neither a meek sacrificial lamb nor a glorious offering. He was a disappointment.

They put the animal in the garage where, over the next two days, its distress escalated. At nights they could hear it struggling, trying to escape, roars that sounded like they came from deep down in his soul. Perhaps it had sensed its fate. On the third day, as soon as they took it out into the sun, the bull broke free. Galloping at full speed, it charged at the first man, a hapless passer-by in its path, dragging him to the ground. He managed to disentangle himself and hide behind a rubbish bin. Laughter rose from the spectators who had gathered in the meantime. Someone patted the survivor on the back. Children ran to find out what the hullabaloo was about. Climbing up on the garden wall, Peri could see the bull's horns swinging, the lonely beast scattering the crowd, its terror now almost absolute.

Unlike lambs before slaughter, the bull was a fighter and what a fight he had put up – against twenty men chasing him from all sides. He charged on to the highway, a battleground of tarmac where he would be surrounded by an army of metallic monsters. It took the men three hours to get the animal under control, and then only after they had shot it with a tranquillizer gun before killing it. Later, a few people cautioned that its meat was not halal since the tranquillizers had made it dizzy. But by then no one cared an iota about their opinion.

'What kind of barbarism is this?' Mensur complained to his wife back home. 'Islam says do not hurt anyone, animals included. That poor creature died in fear. They tortured him. I'm not eating this meat.'

Selma said nothing for a moment. 'Don't eat it, fine. Maybe I won't either. But don't say anything bad. Have respect, husband.'

Peri, who had expected a row, was surprised to see her parents agree for once. The meat that was their share was distributed to families in need.

That evening at the dinner table, Peri noticed her father refilled his glass rather too often. 'What a day, eh?' he said distractedly. 'Chasing people chasing a bull. I haven't felt this tired since you kids were born and kept us awake half the night.' His words were slurred.

Peri, who was filling her glass with water from a jug, almost spilled it. 'What do you mean, "you kids"?'

Mensur drew a hand across his forehead. His was the face of a man who just realized he had made a careless slip. For a moment he seemed to be debating whether to keep on talking. 'Well, I'm sure you must remember.'

'Remember what?'

'There was a boy, your twin. He didn't survive.'

Something was forming at the edge of her consciousness. 'Why?'

'Oh, bumblebee, don't ask. It was so long ago,' Mensur said, but then, overwhelmed by curiosity, added, 'You really have no idea?'

'I don't know what you are talking about, Baba.'

'I see, that's odd . . . I always thought you might recall – things.'

It would take Peri years to discover what he meant by that.

The train pulled into Paddington Station. Shirin was waiting by the ticket machines, wearing a silver-grey fur coat reaching to her knees. In the heart of the city, she looked like a creature from the steppes.

'How many animals have been killed for that thing?' Peri asked.

'Don't worry, it's not real,' said Shirin, as she kissed her on the cheeks.

Peri studied her friend's face. 'You're lying, right?'

'Huh!' Shirin huffed. 'It's the first time you caught me out. Congratulations, I'm so happy for you, Mouse. Your eyes are opening.'

Peri knew she was teasing her. Much as she laughed, she felt a stab of unease as she detected a small truth in her friend's words: Shirin had lied to her before, probably more than once, but about what or why Peri had yet to discover.

The Belly Dancer

Oxford, 2002

Peri opened the window, enjoying the touch of cold air. She was happy to be back in her room, though she longed for a bigger space. She sat on the bed with a book in her hand and pulled her legs towards herself. In one of his earlier classes Azur had asked the students to read an article on the idea of God in Kantian philosophy. She found Kant more puzzling on the second reading than the first. She could see why theologians were drawn to the German philosopher. But, then again, notorious thinkers in the opposite camp, e.g. Nietzsche or Darwin, could also be traced back to him. Peri concluded that Immanuel Kant, like Istanbul, had many facets to his nature.

No wonder Azur liked him so. He, too, was multifarious. There were Azurs, a whole cast of them. The self-confident debater in the panel discussion; the actor in daily life who loved and craved attention; the intimidating professor in the classroom; the demanding Inquisitor in his office; the gentle host in the privacy of his house – how many more faces did he have? Her thoughts flicked back to the New Year's Eve dinner and its aftermath. Since then she had been avoiding Darren, although he had called numerous times and left messages that sounded increasingly concerned, if not hurt. She would have gladly locked herself in her room until she could clear her mind, had it not been for classes and the part-time job in the bookshop – and for Shirin, who always found a fresh excuse to knock on her door.

Her attraction to Azur had rendered daily life painfully intense. Whenever she visited him in his rooms to talk about the baby in the mist, his every gesture, every word, she read and misread, unable to see him with any degree of equanimity. Like a necromancer who found divine signs everywhere, she searched for hidden messages within the most mundane. She worked harder than ever, however, determined to make an impression on Azur with her intelligence and brilliance. But that opportunity to impress him, the revelatory moment that she waited and waited for, never came. She remained withdrawn next to him, most of the time, her stomach in knots. Every now and then she swung the other way. Armed with a burst of courage or desperation, she objected and debated, challenged and questioned, and then sank back into silence again.

This would never happen to her, she had thought. She was not one of those girls who developed an obsession with older men; girls who, in her opinion, were looking for the father figure absent in their lives. Why she was drawn to Azur, she didn't think she could explain to anyone, least of all to herself. Not that she wished to share what she felt for him. Like the God-diary she had kept since childhood, like the baby in the mist, Azur had become a carefully guarded secret. Nevertheless, she developed the habit of holding one of his books in her hands before going to sleep, tracing the letters of his name with her fingers in the dark, some schmaltzy music on in the background. During the day she hung around near his college, furtively glancing round a corner in case he might be around. Whenever she didn't have a lecture or a tutorial, she went out of her way to buy a morning coffee from the café that he frequented, although the few times when she saw him coming, she hid in the lavatory. As she kept doing all these ridiculous things, another part of her, distant and judgemental, watched disapprovingly, hoping it was all a season of madness and would someday soon come to an end.

Now, unable to stand either her own thoughts or Kant's, Peri put on her trainers and went out for a run. Despite the cold, the promise of joy lingered in the evening air like crystals of dew. The lack of noise that had struck her when she first moved to this town from Istanbul did not surprise her any more.

At the corner of Longwall Street, she saw a phone box. Given the two hours' time difference, her father would be drinking at home – alone or with friends.

Mensur picked up the phone. 'Hello?'

'Baba . . . I'm sorry, did I call at a bad time?'

'Peri, my dear,' he exclaimed. 'What do you mean "bad time", you can always call. I wish you did more often.'

Her breath caught in her throat at the tenderness in his voice.

'You all right?'

'I'm fine,' she said. 'How is Mother?'

'In her room. Do you want me to call her?'

'No, I'll talk to her another time.' She added, gently, 'I miss you so much.'

'Oh, you are going to make me cry, bumblebee.'

'I feel terrible for not being able to come home for New Year's Eve.'

'Ah, who cares about New Year's Eve?' Mensur said. 'Your mum overcooked the turkey and burned the pilaff. So we ate bone-dry meat and black rice. We played Tombala. Your mum won. She claims she didn't cheat but can we believe her? Oh, and we watched a belly dancer on TV – I mean, I did. That was all.'

There were things he hadn't mentioned but Peri heard them nonetheless: Mensur's persistent drinking and the scantily clad dancer shaking her hips, both of which would have enraged Selma; the quarrel her parents had had, yet again.

As though he had read her thoughts, Mensur said, 'I had a few, yes. What better occasion? You know what they say, the way you spend the first hours of the New Year will be how you spend all the other days of the year.'

Peri's heart fell.

'It's all right that you couldn't come,' Mensur said. 'We'll have many more years to celebrate. School is the most important thing.'

School . . . Not university or college, but school. That basic word that had an almost sacred quality for countless parents who, though not fully educated themselves, believed in education and invested all they could in their children's future.

'How is my brother?' Peri inquired. She didn't feel the need to specify which one. It had to be Hakan, since they rarely talked about Umut, and, when they did, it was always in a different tone.

'Good, good. They're expecting a baby.'

'Really?'

'Yes,' Mensur said, his voice soaring with pride. 'A boy.'

It had been more than a year since that terrible night at the hospital, but the memory of it was still fresh in her mind. The smell of disinfectants, the moss-green paint, the red crescents on the bride's palms – and now Feride was having his baby. Her mother's words echoed in her head: *Many a marriage has been built on shakier foundations.*

'I don't think I could ever do that.'

'Do what?'

'Marry someone who treats me badly.'

Mensur huffed – half sigh, half laugh. 'Your mother and I love you,' he said and paused, unused to mentioning the two of them in the same breath. 'Whatever makes you happy, we'll support.'

Tears welled in her eyes. She always felt more vulnerable when people treated her with compassion than with animosity.

'What's wrong, my soul? Are you crying?'

She ignored the question. 'But, Baba . . . what if one day I shame you? Would you reject me?'

'I'll never reject my own daughter no matter what,' Mensur said. 'As long as you don't bring home a bearded imam for a son-in-law. Now that'd kill me! And you probably shouldn't date one of those musicians with tattooed biceps either, what are they called? Metal-heads. I wouldn't mind but that'd drive your mum mad. So other than an imam or a metalhead, there are plenty of options.'

Peri laughed. She remembered their rituals in front of the TV, the times he had taught her how to whistle, how to blow a bubble with chewing gum, how to eat salted sunflower seeds, deftly breaking the shells between her teeth.

'Seriously, who is this lucky boy?' Mensur asked.

That last word, 'boy', was sobering. From her father's perspective she could only love a boy, someone her own age.

'Oh, just a student, it's nothing serious. I'm too young for anything serious.'

'Yes, Pericim.' He sounded relieved. 'It'll pass. Focus on your lessons.'

'I will, Baba.'

'Oh, don't mention this to your mother. There's no need to worry her.'

'Of course not.'

After she hung up, she ran for a good hour. Her feet slipped on the icy paving stones but she persevered. By the time she returned to the quad, she had pushed herself so hard her calves throbbed with pain and her throat felt sore every time she swallowed, the first signs of a nasty flu. She fell asleep immediately, still running in her dreams, clutching a note Shirin had written and left on her bed.

Peri, I've found the perfect home for us! Get ready, we're moving out!

The List

Istanbul, 2016

'Did you hear what just happened? Awful, awful!'

It was the PR woman, addressing her question to the room at large. She had stepped out to visit the lavatory, but returned immediately, her face flushed.

'What is it *this time?*' someone said.

There are two kinds of cities in the world: those that reassure their residents that tomorrow and the day after, and the day after that, will be much the same; and those that do the opposite, insidiously reminding their inhabitants of life's uncertainty. Istanbul is of the second kind. There is no room for introspection, no time to wait for the clocks to catch up with the pace of events. Istanbulites dart from one breaking news story to the next, moving fast, consuming faster, until something else happens that demands their full attention.

'I saw it on my Twitter feed, an explosion,' said the PR woman.

'In Istanbul?' asked the businessman. 'When?'

The three fundamental questions, always in this order: What? Where? When? What: a terrible explosion had been reported. Where: in one of the most densely populated neighbourhoods in the historic quarter of the city. When: no more than four minutes ago. Such was the magnitude of the blast, it had demolished the façade of the building where it happened and shattered the windows all the way down to the next street, injuring passers-by, setting off car alarms and altering, for a fleeting moment, the colour of the night sky to a rusty brown.

Most of the guests, led by the businesswoman, rushed upstairs to watch the news on TV. Peri followed them, if slowly, into a bright, comfortable room. She stood at the back of the group, from where she could get a glimpse of the large flat screen. An agitated reporter – a young woman with hair so long she could have used it as a cloak – spoke fast, holding the microphone with both hands. 'We still don't know how many have been killed, how many injured, but it's not looking good. Not good. All we know is that it was a powerful bomb.'

A bomb. The word, like a toxic fume out of nowhere, hung in the middle of the room. Until that point, the guests had secretly hoped it might have been a gas leak or a faulty generator that caused the mayhem. Not that it would have diminished the gravity of what had occurred. But a bomb was different. A bomb meant not only a tragic incident, but also an intent to kill. Disasters were scary, all right. Evil combined with disasters was terrifying.

Even so, they had learned to live with bombs – or the possibility of them. Random and erratic though they were, terrorists were believed to follow certain patterns. They did not strike at night. They almost always chose daylight hours, when they could target the greatest number of people in the briefest amount of time and make it into the next day's headlines. The night, dangerous though in other ways, was safe from such violence. Or so they had thought.

Hence, the businesswoman asked, 'A bomb? At this odd hour?'

'Probably the terrorists got stuck in traffic too,' quipped the businessman. 'Nothing runs on time in Istanbul any more, not even Azrael.'

They laughed – a brief, mirthless chuckle. Jokes in the face of calamity made one feel dirty, guilty; they also dissolved the fear and lessened the weight of uncertainty, of which there was too much to bear.

Meanwhile on the TV screen, in the background, a crowd of children and men had gathered, hanging on the reporter's every word, hoping to be the one chosen to be interviewed. A boy, no older than twelve, waved his hand, excited to see the lens pointed at his face.

Now the screen switched to a helicopter view, showing the neighbourhood from above. Houses built on top of one another, clustered so densely that they resembled an uninterrupted block of concrete. Upon closer inspection the differences, however, were discernible. One building, in particular, looked as if it had been through years of civil war. Blasted-out windows, burned-down walls, broken glass on the pavement outside.

'We were at home, the whole family, in front of the TV, we heard this sound, the ground shook. I thought it was an earthquake,' said an eyewitness – a short, stocky man in pyjamas. In his voice there was an excitement he could barely contain – dumbfounded that he was now on the same network he had been watching only minutes ago, being viewed by millions. As he went on to describe 'how he felt', at the reporter's request, a red banner ran along the bottom of the screen announcing the death toll.

In the seaside mansion, the guests returned to the salon, one by one, to bring the rest of the group up to date. 'Five dead, fifteen injured.'

'That number might increase. Some of the injured are in critical condition,' said the journalist, who had stayed put to call his office.

With the ease with which they passed on plates of meze at the dinner table, they now exchanged morsels of gory detail. Redundancy did not matter, much less repetition. The more they shared, the less real it all felt. Tragedy was a commodity like any other. It was meant to be consumed – individually and collectively.

The journalist's girlfriend took in a lungful of air before she said, 'So they were making a bomb in their flat. Imagine. They put the pieces together, like some sort of demonic Lego. It detonated. Good news: the terrorists died on the spot. Bad news: the neighbour upstairs also lost his life. He was a retired teacher.'

'Probably taught geography, poor chap,' the businessman said, slightly slurring. 'What a fate . . . must have been a decent citizen, marking student papers, wearing threadbare suits. After years of hard work, he retires. Enough of wrestling with ignorant little brats. Bunch of terrorists move in downstairs . . . the hell with them, they start cooking bombs . . . Boom! End of the teacher. Taught his students about oxbow lakes and capital cities, when all around them is the fucking geography of terror!'

It was a moment before anyone spoke again. 'Do we know who the bombers were?' asked the PR woman. 'Was it Marxists? Kurdish separatists? Islamists?'

The architect chuckled. 'What a rich menu!'

Peri heard her husband clear his throat, softly. 'It's not only terrorism or the horror of it,' Adnan said. 'It's how easily we get used to such news. Tomorrow this time few people will be talking about the teacher. In a week, he'll be forgotten.'

Peri looked down, the sadness in his words reaching her heart and staying there, like the heat that languishes in the dying embers of a logfire.

The Face of the Other

Oxford, 2002

Outside the front gate a cab was waiting for them. They rode in silence for a while, until Peri punctuated the calm with a sneeze.

'Bless you, Mouse!'

'Well, thank you . . . I still can't believe I'm moving in with you!' Peri groaned as she watched the streets sliding by through the window.

Oblivious to Peri's resistance, Shirin had kept searching for a place. She had managed to persuade the college authorities that they could move out in the middle of the academic year. With her irrepressible zeal it hadn't taken her long to find the house. As diligent as a bumblebee buzzing from flower to flower, she had paid the deposit and the first month's rent, and arranged for the car that would carry their modest belongings. She had organized everything so seamlessly and with such ruthlessness that when the day arrived, Peri had only to grab her coat and accompany her friend out of the door.

'Relax, we're going to have fun,' Shirin enthused. 'The three of us!'

Peri caught her breath. 'Who else is coming?'

Shirin fished a powder compact out of her bag and looked at herself in the mirror, as if she had to check her expression before she could answer. 'Mona's joining us.'

'What? And you're telling me this now?'

'Well, when it comes to sharing a house, three is better than two.' Shirin grinned, even she didn't seem to believe her words.

Peri shook her head. 'You should have asked me.'

'Sorry, I forgot. There's been too much on my mind.' Shirin's voice softened. 'What's the matter? I thought you liked Mona.'

'Yes I do, but you two don't get along!'

'Precisely,' said Shirin. 'I need the challenge.'

'What do you mean?'

If Shirin had an explanation, it would have to wait. They had arrived at the address. A Victorian terraced house in Jericho with ground-floor bay windows, high ceilings and a small rear garden.

Mona was standing on the steps by the front door, bags and boxes by her side. She waved at them and came down, her face betraying her nervousness. One glance and Peri knew that Mona had been roped in by Shirin – just as she herself had.

'Hi, Mona,' Shirin called out once she had paid the cab fare and jumped out.

Awkwardly the three of them stood on the pavement, exchanging greetings. Their differences contrasted with the architectural harmony of the street: Mona with her long umber coat and beige headscarf; Shirin with her full makeup, short black dress and high-heeled boots; Peri in her jeans and blue trenchcoat.

'We'll have a couple of copies made,' announced Shirin, jangling the keys in her hand. 'This is going to be exciting.'

And with those words she unlocked the door and dashed into the house. Next entered Mona, right foot first, her lips moving in a prayer. 'Bismillah ir-rahman ir-rahim.'

Last in, Peri, sneezing and coughing. Even though she had seen photos of the house earlier and even though it was furnished, it seemed half empty. Being under the same roof with other people, interacting with them at unpredictable hours, day in day out, felt intimidating – such compulsory closeness among people who, though not lovers, shared a certain intimacy. She tried to dismiss her worries. It didn't help. Fate was a gambler who loved raising the stakes. At the end of this experience, Peri sensed, they were either going to be great friends, sisters for life, or the whole thing was going to dissolve in fights and tears.

If houses had attitudes, this one would be that of a grumbling teenager. It never ceased to complain. The staircase squeaked, the floorboards creaked, the door hinges whinged, the kitchen cupboards squawked, the fridge rasped, and the coffee machine groaned, resenting every drop it gave up. Still, it belonged to them – as long as they paid the rent. They even had their own little garden, where they planned to have a barbecue when the weather picked up.

Of the three bedrooms upstairs, two were more or less the same size, whereas the one at the back was smaller and darker. Peri insisted on taking this one. Given her meagre contribution it seemed only fair. She suspected Shirin and Mona had, without consulting her, agreed to share the expenses. Most of the money would come from Shirin, true to her word. Mona would contribute to the bills, which would probably not exceed what she used to pay for her college room. As for Peri, she was expected to chip in only for grocery shopping. Under these circumstances she would never agree to one of the larger rooms.

'Nonsense!' Mona objected. 'We must draw straws. The one who gets the shortest will have the third room.'

'So you're going to leave it to fate?' Shirin said, shaking her head in wonder.

'What's your suggestion?' asked Mona.

'I've a better idea,' Shirin said. 'Let's take turns. Every month we'll pack up and move to the next room, like nomadic tribes. We'll be the Huns, more peaceful. That way everyone will be equal.'

'Well, thank you very much, both of you. But I'm having none of it,' Peri jumped in. 'I either get the small room or I leave.'

Shirin and Mona exchanged amused glances. They had never heard her talk like this before.

'Fine!' Shirin yielded. 'But you must stop getting riled up about money. Life is too short. I mean, who knows how much I'll owe you by the end? Maybe you'll teach me some priceless lesson, huh?'

Over the next few hours, they retreated to their respective rooms, busying themselves with unpacking. Despite its size and sparse furnishings, her space, with a window that looked out on to the garden, instantly charmed Peri. But its biggest surprise was the heavy wooden four-poster bed enveloped by drapes. A relic from another era, she felt as if she were in a horse-drawn carriage when she lay down inside and pulled the curtains. There was also a snug alcove by the window. She placed a chair there, declaring it 'the reading corner'.

At supper time she knocked on Mona's door, which was opposite hers. The two of them went downstairs to the kitchen, eager to prepare their first meal together. They were surprised to find Shirin already at the table, arranging a bottle of wine, a carton of apple juice, a plate of olives and three glasses.

'We must celebrate,' Shirin said. 'Three young Muslim women in Oxford! The Sinner, the Believer and the Confused.'

There was a brief silence while Mona and Peri worked out which epithet was meant for whom. Peri took her wine glass and raised it in the air, 'To our friendship!'

'To our collective existential crisis!' said Shirin.

'Speak for yourself,' said Mona, sipping her apple juice.

'Well, you're in denial,' said Shirin. 'Right now we Muslims are going through an identity crisis. Especially the women. And women like us even more so!'

'Meaning?'

'Meaning, those who are exposed to more than one culture! We're asking big questions. Eat your heart out, Jean-Paul Sartre! Get a load of this! We have an existential crisis like you've never seen!'

'I don't like this kind of talk,' said Mona as she took a seat. 'What makes you think we're so different from others? You speak as if we're from another planet!'

Shirin took a rapid gulp of her wine. 'Hello-o, wake up, sister! There are crazies out there doing really sick stuff in the name of religion, *our* religion. Maybe not mine, but definitely yours. Doesn't that bother you?'

'What's that got to do with me?' Mona said, sticking her chin out. 'Do you ask every Christian you meet to apologize for the horrors of the Inquisition?'

'If we were living in the Middle Ages, then yes, I might well have done.'

'Oh, so today's Christians and Jews are all wingless angels?' Mona said. 'Have you ever been through a checkpoint in Gaza? I don't think you have! What about the genocide in Rwanda? Srebrenica? You don't hold all the Christians in the world responsible for those horrific killings, and you certainly should not! But why, then, blame all Muslims for the actions of a bunch of maniacs?'

'Uhm, can you two please stop fighting?' Peri said in between coughs. She felt a fever coming on.

Shirin persisted. 'Sure, there are plenty of freaks among Christians and Jews as well and we have to condemn every sort of bigotry, no matter where it comes from. But you can't deny that right now, there is more fanaticism in the Middle East than anywhere else. Can you walk around alone in Egypt without being sexually assaulted? Forget about streets after dark! I personally know women who were harassed on their way to pilgrimage. In sacred places! In plain daylight! In front of the Saudi police! Women keep quiet about these things because they're embarrassed. And why are we embarrassed and not the molesters? There's a helluva lot we need to question.'

'I *am* questioning,' Mona said. 'I question history. Politics. Global poverty. Capitalism. Income gap. Brain drain. War industry. Don't forget the appalling legacy of colonialism. Centuries of plunder and exploitation. That's why the West is so rich! Let's leave Islam in peace and start talking about hardcore issues!'

'Typical,' Shirin said, throwing her hands up in despair. 'Blaming others for *our* problems.'

'Uhm . . . shall we have dinner?' Peri attempted one more time, not that she expected a response. It was a situation she knew only too well – like living with her parents all over again. Angry accusations flying back and forth; a ping-pong of misunderstandings. Even so, she found it easier to be a witness this time. The tension in the air did not affect her the way it did back home. Shirin and Mona were not her mother and her father at each other's throats. She felt no need to mediate. Without any emotional responsibility to weigh her down, her mind was free to analyse. So she listened, secretly envying them. Despite their glaring polarity, they were equally passionate. Mona had her faith; Shirin had her fury. What did she have to hold on to?

'All I'm saying is,' carried on Shirin, 'the challenges a young Muslim faces today are deeper than the challenges facing a Buddhist monk or a Mormon minister. Let's accept that.'

'I'm not accepting anything,' said Mona. 'So long as you're biased against your own religion, we can't have a proper conversation.'

'Here we go again,' said Shirin, her voice rising. 'The moment I open my mouth and speak my mind, you're offended. Can somebody tell me why young Muslims are so easily offended?'

'Maybe because we're under attack?' said Mona. 'Every day I have to defend myself when I've done nothing wrong. I'm expected to *prove* that I'm not a potential suicide bomber. I feel under scrutiny all the time – do you know how lonely that is?'

As though in response, the rainclouds that had been accumulating all day long broke over the town, pelting against the window. Peri thought about the River Thames nearby, swelling, trying to break free from its course.

'You, lonely? Give me a break!' said Shirin. 'You have millions standing with you. Governments. Conventional religion. Mainstream media. Popular culture. You also assume you have God on your side, which must be something. How much more company can you want? You know who are the real loners in our region? Atheists. Yazidis. Gays. Drag queens. Environmentalists. Conscientious objectors. Those are the outcasts. Unless you fall into one of these categories, don't complain about loneliness.'

'You know nothing,' said Mona. 'I've been bullied, called names, pushed off a bus, treated as if I were dumb – all because of my headscarf. You've no idea how horribly I've been treated! It's just a small piece of cloth.'

'Then why do you wear it?'

'It's my choice, my identity! I'm not bothered by your ways, why are you bothered by mine? Who is the liberal here, think!'

'Bloody ignorant,' said Shirin. 'First, it's just one, then it's ten, then millions. Before you know it it's a republic of headscarves. That's why my parents left Iran: your *small piece of cloth* sent us into exile!'

With every word uttered, Peri's expression hardened. She stared down at the wooden table, chipped at one corner. She had always been drawn to scars and the imperfections beneath a smooth surface.

'What do you think, Peri?' Shirin suddenly asked.

'Yes, tell us, which one of us is right?' Mona said.

Peri fidgeted under their gaze. She glanced from one expectant face to the other, fumbling for words. In some respects Shirin was right, she said, in other respects, Mona. For instance, she agreed that life could be systematically unfair for a member of a minority – be it cultural or religious or sexual – in a closed Muslim culture, though she was also aware of the hardships facing a headscarved woman in a Western society. For her, it always depended on the context. Whoever was the disempowered, the disadvantaged side in a given place and time, she wanted to support them. Hence she was not categorically for anyone, save the weaker party.

'That's too abstract,' said Shirin, drumming her fingers impatiently on the table. Judging by Mona's expression, for once they seemed to agree. Peri's answer, balanced though it was, had satisfied no one.

'Let me make one thing clear,' Mona said, once again turning to Shirin. 'I don't have anything against atheists. Or gays. Or drag queens. It's their life. But I do mind Islamophobes. If you're going to sound like a warmongering neo-con, I'd better move out of this house.'

'Me, a neo-con?' Shirin put down her glass with such force that wine slopped on to the table. 'You want to leave? Fine! But that'd be taking the easy way out. We must try to latch on to what the other is saying.'

Latch on to. I must remember this phrase, Peri thought to herself.

'I agree,' said Mona.

'Great,' said Shirin. 'We'll write a Muslim Women's Manifesto. It'd make a lovely logo, MWM. We'll put everything that frustrates us into it. Fanaticism. Sexism.'

'Islamophobia,' said Mona.

'I really think we should start preparing supper now,' said Peri.

They all laughed. For a moment it was almost as though the storm had passed. It felt calm. Outside the rain had eased up; the early evening seeped into nightfall; the moon was a pearlescent talisman in the bosom of the sky. Across Port Meadow the Thames ran strong in deep swirling eddies, winding its silvery way through the darkness.

'You know what,' said Mona with a resigned sigh, as if she were revealing something it had taken her a while to understand. 'You were born into a remarkable religion, you were given a wonderful Prophet as your guide, but, instead of counting your blessings and trying to be a better human being, all you do is complain.'

Shirin said, 'Speaking of the Prophet, there are things I find –'

'Don't even think about it,' Mona interjected, her voice quivering for the first time. 'You can have a go at me. That's all right. But I can't have people rail against my Prophet when they know next to nothing about him. Criticize the Muslim world, okay, but leave him out of it.'

Shirin huffed with frustration. 'Why should we spare anyone from critical thinking? Especially when we're at university!'

'Because what you call critical thinking is self-serving nonsense!' said Mona. 'Because I know what you're going to say and I also know your gaze is impure, your knowledge tainted. You can't judge the seventh century through the lens of the twenty-first!'

'Yes, I can, if the seventh century is trying to rule over the twenty-first!'

'I wish you could be proud of who you are,' said Mona. 'You know what you are – a self-hating Muslim.'

'Ouch,' Shirin said in mock pain. 'I've never understood people who're proud to be American, Arab or Russian . . . Christian, Jewish or Muslim. Why should I feel satisfaction with something I had no role in choosing? It's like saying I'm proud of being five foot nine. Or congratulating myself on my hooked nose. Genetic lottery!'

'But you are quite pleased with your atheism,' said Mona.

'Well, I used to be a militant atheist . . . I'm no more, thanks to Professor Azur,' Shirin said with a theatrical flair. 'But I really worked hard for my scepticism. I put my mind and heart and courage into it. I separated myself from crowds and congregations! I didn't find it dropped into my lap. Yeah, I'm proud of my journey.'

'So it's true, you despise your culture. You despise . . . me. For you, I'm either backward or brainwashed. Oppressed. Ignorant. But I've studied the Quran, unlike you. I thought it was profoundly eloquent, wise, poetic. I've studied the Prophet's life. The more I read about him, the more I admired his personality. I find peace in my faith. Do you care? I don't even know why I agreed to move in with you!'

Next, Mona was stomping upstairs to her room. The floorboards protested under the weight of her emotions.

Shirin raised her empty glass and flung it with all her might against the wall. Tiny fragments rained on the floor, like sad confetti. Peri flinched but instantly rose to her feet to go and clean.

'Don't move,' Shirin said to Peri. 'It's my mess. I'll get it.'

'Okay,' Peri said. She knew Shirin would pick up only the bigger pieces, but the splinters would stay, stuck between floorboards, waiting to cut them someday. 'I'm going to my room.'

Shirin let out a sigh. 'Goodnight, Mouse.'

Peri took a few steps, but then lingered, her eyes fixed on Shirin, whose face had suddenly lost its bravado.

'He warned me it wouldn't be easy,' Shirin muttered to herself when she thought she was alone.

'Who warned you?' Peri asked.

Shirin lifted her head, her eyelids fluttering in disarray. 'Nothing,' she said. There was an edge to her tone that hadn't been there before. 'Look, we'll talk later, okay? I need a bath now. It's been a long day.'

Unable to sleep, alone in the kitchen, Peri poured herself another glass of wine, her mind whirling. Had she accidentally stumbled on a secret? Shirin's inadvertent remark niggled at her. Whether by intuition or by reason, she suspected that behind Shirin's eagerness to move in together, there was a master manipulator: Azur.

She recalled a passage in one of his earlier books where he explored the peculiar idea that people in bitter disagreement and mutual recrimination should be left alone together in a closed space and made to look each other in the eye. A white supremacist prisoner should be put in the same cell with a black prisoner; a jade miner in a room with an environmentalist; a trophy hunter with an endangered-animal conservationist. At the time she had read those lines, she had not given them much thought, but now it all fell into place. She was inside a game, unwittingly playing her part, controlled by some faraway brain.

In dismay, she slipped upstairs. Mona's bedroom door was closed. From the bathroom at the end of the corridor came the sound of running water. Inside Shirin was humming a tune that sounded faintly familiar, the melody almost haunting.

Peri tiptoed into Shirin's bedroom. There were cardboard boxes everywhere. Clearly Shirin hadn't done much to unpack. On one of the larger cartons was written in capital letters: BOOKS. It was open and Peri could see some of the volumes had been placed on the shelf. By the look of things Shirin had tired of the chore, leaving the rest of the box untouched.

Peri rummaged through the contents. It didn't take her long to find what she was looking for. Title by title, she fished out all of Professor Azur's backlist. Grabbing the first one, she turned to the title page. It was signed, just as she had expected.

To Sweet Shirin,
Perpetual émigrée, fearless mutineer, philosophical outcast,
The girl who knows how to ask questions and is not afraid of pursuing the answers . . .

A. Z. Azur

Peri snapped the book shut with a pang of jealousy. Not that she didn't know Shirin visited the professor regularly, at least twice a week, and that the two of them were close, but it tortured her to see Shirin's value in his eyes. She checked the other titles only to find out that they, too, were inscribed. The last one she grabbed, Azur's latest publication, had a longer inscription.

To Shirin, who is unlike her name,
sweet and sharp, like the pomegranates of Persia,
the land of the lion and the sun . . .
But must come to know, if not to love, what she regards with contempt;

for only in the mirror of the Other,
can one glimpse the face of God.
Love, my dear,
Love thy stepsister . . .

A. Z. Azur

What stepsister? Peri knew Shirin did not have one – unless, it was a metaphor for 'the other woman'.

Peri took a breath as the enormity of the set-up dawned on her. Shirin despised religion and religious people. While she laid into all denominations, it was the faith she was brought up in that she criticized most. She was particularly allergic to young Muslim women who covered their heads out of personal choice. 'The mullahs and the morality police silence us on the outside. But those girls who sincerely believe they must cover themselves so as not to seduce men, they silence us from inside,' she had once said. The more Peri mulled it over, the more convinced she was that Professor Azur had placed Shirin in a social laboratory as a way of forcing her to interact with her 'Other': Mona.

Shaken though she was by the discovery, there was something that troubled Peri even more. Maybe it wasn't just Mona. She swallowed hard, seeing herself, for the first time, through Shirin's eyes. Her lack of certainty, her hesitancy, her timidity, her passivity . . . Qualities someone like Shirin would abhor. *Three Muslim women in Oxford: the Sinner, the Believer and the Confused.* It wasn't only Mona who had been selected for this bizarre social experiment. She now understood: the second stepsister was Peri herself.

She put back the book, closed the box, left the room. How she regretted leaving the peace and quiet of her college room and ending up in this house, where their every move would be reported to Professor Azur. She felt like a fly inside a glass jar; warm and safe at first glance, trapped nonetheless.

The Chakras

Istanbul, 2016

'The retired teacher will be forgotten,' Adnan said one more time. 'Nothing shocks us any more. We've become desensitized.'

'But, darling, aren't you being a bit harsh, what else can we do?' asked the businesswoman. 'Otherwise, we'd go mad!'

At these words, the psychic joined in with an impatient toss of his head, 'Nations have a zodiac sign, like individuals. This country was born on the 29th of October. Scorpio, ruled by Mars and Pluto. Who is Mars? The God of War. Who is Pluto? The God of the Underworld. The planets say it all.'

'Astrological mumbo-jumbo,' said the religious newspaper tycoon. 'What do you mean by "gods" when we all believe in one Allah?'

The psychic straightened his back, looking offended.

'The entire Middle East has its chakras blocked,' said the journalist.

'No wonder,' the businessman interjected. 'The only energy they know is oil. Talk about spiritual energy!'

'So which chakras in your professional opinion need to be opened?' asked the businesswoman, ignoring her husband's remark.

'The fifth,' came the answer. 'It is the throat chakra. Stifled thoughts, unexpressed desires. It starts here at the back of the mouth and puts pressure on the oesophagus and stomach.'

A few guests touched their necks.

'Speaking of which, my throat is dry, I need to open up my chakra,' said the businessman. 'Kizim, bring us more whisky.'

The psychic went on, 'There's a technique that can be used to unblock a nation's chakras . . .'

'Is it called democracy?' Peri suggested.

The plastic surgeon checked his watch. 'Oh, gosh, it's late. I'd better get going. I've got an early flight.' Although he had settled in Stockholm many moons ago, he often returned to Istanbul, where he had business interests and, according to rumours, a lover young enough to be his daughter.

'Fine, you'll disappear and we'll deal with the mess,' the PR woman said.

Those who went away in search of better lives in foreign lands were at once envied and belittled. It wasn't about New York, London or Rome. To those who stayed behind it was the very *idea* of life elsewhere. They, too, longed for new skies to walk under. Over breakfasts and brunches they made elaborate plans to move abroad – almost always meaning the West. But their plans, like sand castles, slowly eroded with the rising tide of familiarity. Relatives, friends and shared memories anchored them. Little by little, they forgot their yearnings for another place – until the day they ran into someone who had actually done what they had once wished to do. That's when resentment kicked in.

The plastic surgeon sensed the mood against him. He said, 'Sweden isn't paradise either.'

A feeble line of reasoning that convinced no one. Come tomorrow he would travel back to Europe and leave them alone with their problems. He would eat cinnamon buns while they would be dealing with regional instability, political turbulence and bombs.

Peri smiled at him in sympathy. 'Not easy to stay, not easy to leave.'

She wanted to explain that those who stayed behind, despite the hardships, enjoyed lasting friendships and wider social networks, while the ones who migrated for good remained incomplete, jigsaw puzzles missing a critical piece.

'Well, how tragic he has to live in the Alps!' said the journalist's girlfriend, who, despite her boyfriend's nudges, was still drinking.

'The Alps are in Switzerland, not Sweden,' someone tried to correct her but the journalist's girlfriend ignored the comment. With her tummy tucked into her tight mini-skirt, she jumped to her feet and pointed a painted, half-chewed fingernail at the plastic surgeon. 'You lot are deserters! You go and live abroad in comfort . . . we're the ones who deal with the extremism and fundamentalism and sexism and . . .' She turned around as if looking for another -ism nearby. 'It's *my* freedoms that're in danger . . .'

'Speaking of danger . . .' The hostess turned to the psychic. 'Darling, I must show you the house. Only you can tell me why we've had so many freak accidents. First, there was the flood, then the lightning. And did you hear about the ship? Sailed straight into the mansion, like an action movie!' She glanced at her husband to check if she had forgotten something.

'The tree,' said the businessman helpfully.

'Oh, yes, a tree fell on our roof! Do you think it's the evil eye?'

'Sounds like it. Never underestimate the power of envy,' said the psychic. 'Did you have the maids' rooms checked? One of them might have put a curse on you.'

'You think they would dare? I'll throw them out in a heartbeat if we find anything suspicious.' The businesswoman felt her throat as if she couldn't breathe. 'Where would you like to start?'

'The basement. If you are looking for a jinx, always check the darkest corners.'

As the psychic and the hostess brushed past, Peri picked up a vibration. Another second passed before she recognized it was her husband's phone. She paled – Shirin was calling back.

The House in Jericho

Oxford, 2002

Soon it became clear that they each had a different part of the house as their favourite spot. For Shirin it was the bathroom – more precisely, the freestanding claw-footed bathtub. With candles, bath salts, creams and oils, she turned it into a shrine to self-indulgence. Her evening ritual was to fill the tub to the brim with hot water, into which she added a dizzying mixture of scents. Soaking up to an hour, she would read magazines, listen to music, file her nails, daydream.

Mona's preferred place was the kitchen. She woke up early, never missing her morning prayer. She performed her ablutions, spread out her silk prayer mat – a gift from her grandmother – and prayed for herself and others, including Shirin, who, Mona believed, was in need of a divine nudge. What the force of that nudge might be, she left to Allah, for He knew best. Afterwards she went downstairs to the kitchen and prepared breakfast for everyone – pancakes, ful mudammas, omelettes.

As for Peri, her special spot was the four-poster bed in her room. Shirin had given her an extra set of Egyptian-cotton bedlinen, as soft as rabbit's fur, which made Peri even more attached to this item of furniture. She studied here. At nights when she lay on her bed, she would listen to the rustling of the wind in the upper branches of the alder tree outside or the distant coursing of the river. On the opposite wall shadows would sway to a silent rhythm. She saw shapes that reminded her of country maps, imaginary and real; territories for which people had been killed in scores of thousands, blood upon blood. Exhausted by the pace of her imaginings she would fall asleep, soothed with the knowledge that when she woke up the next day the world would still be there, just as it was.

In the mornings while Shirin, a late sleeper, was still in bed, and Mona, an early riser, was praying, Peri would go out for a run. As she urged her body along she would think about Azur. What had he expected when he urged Shirin to bring the three of them together – what was in this for him? The harder she tried to solve this mystery, the stronger was her resentment, rising up from inside, like bile.

Most of the acrimony revolved around the kitchen table, often to the smell of baking bread. Once Shirin stormed out, screaming, she was done with it, but then she returned for dinner. Another time it was Mona who followed the same pattern. Their arguments focused on God, religion, faith, identity and, a few times, sex. Mona believed in remaining a virgin until marriage – a devotion she expected of both herself and her future husband – while Shirin poked fun at the whole idea. As for Peri, who was neither devoted to the notion of virginity nor as comfortable with sexuality as she would have liked, she listened, feeling somewhere in between, as she often did.

Thursday afternoon, when Peri returned to the house in Jericho, she found Mona and Shirin mutely watching a scene of chaos on TV. The camera was jerking around to the sound of wailing sirens, shattered glass, blood on the ground. A synagogue in Tunisia had been attacked by terrorists. A lorry loaded with natural gas and explosives had detonated in front of the building, killing nineteen people.

Biting at the inside of her mouth, Mona said: 'God, please may it not be a Muslim who did this.'

'God won't hear you,' Shirin said.

Mona gave her an icy stare. When she spoke again the softness had drained from her voice. 'You . . . are mocking me!'

'I'm mocking the futility of your prayer,' Shirin replied. 'Do you really think you can change the facts if you plead hard enough? What's happened has happened.'

The mutual aggravation between Mona and Shirin was growing by the minute. The fight they had that evening was the worst ever.

Peri retreated to her room without dinner, threw herself on to her bed and cupped her hands over her ears as their shouting continued downstairs.

Tomorrow morning, she thought, and hoped, *they'll be ashamed of the things they've said to each other.*

In all likelihood, however, they would leave it behind – until the next quarrel. Of the three, only Peri would commit to memory their every word, every gesture, every hurt. Since childhood she was a dedicated archivist, a recorder of painful reminiscences. Her memory she treated as a duty, a responsibility that had to be honoured to the very end – even though she sensed that a burden so large could only pull her down someday.

When Peri was little she could understand the language of the wind, read the signs sculpted in half-reaped fields or in the snow falling from acacias, sing with the water flowing from a tap. She even thought that she could one day see God with her own eyes, if only she tried. Once, while walking with her mother, she encountered a hedgehog that had been run over by a car. She insisted on praying for its soul – which appalled Selma. Heaven was a small, confined space reserved for the select few. Animals were not accepted, her mother explained.

'Who else can't go to heaven?' Peri asked.

'The sinners, the evildoers, those who abandon our religion and swerve from the right path . . . and those who commit suicide. They won't even be given a funeral prayer.'

And hedgehogs, apparently. The roadkill was thrown into their rubbish bin. That night Peri slipped out of the house and took the dead creature from the smelly receptacle. She had not been able to find any gloves and when she touched its lifeless body she shivered, as if something had passed from the animal's corpse into her. She dug a hole with her hands, buried the hedgehog and marked the place with a headstone she'd made out of a wooden ruler. Then she prayed. Gradually, it became a favourite game of hers, choreographing funerals. She organized burials for dead bees and withered petals, broken-winged butterflies and toys damaged beyond repair. Those unwelcome in Cennet.

As she grew up, she learned to suppress her oddities, one by one. All her anomalies were pulverized by family, school and society into a dull powder of ordinariness. Save for the baby in the mist. But she always knew that she was *different*. A strangeness she must do her best to hide; a scar that would remain forever etched on her skin. She put so much effort into being normal that often she had no energy left to be anything else, leaving her with feelings of worthlessness. At some point unbeknownst to her, solitude had stopped being a choice and become a curse instead. An emptiness inside her chest, so profound and so permanent that she imagined it could be compared only with the absence of God. Yes, perhaps that was it. She carried the absence of God within. No wonder it felt so heavy.

The Pawn

Oxford, 2002

Peri wheeled her bicycle across Radcliffe Square with a shoulder bag of books and a bunch of grapes left over from lunch. In front of the Radcliffe Camera, she spotted Troy sitting on a bench with a group of friends, talking animatedly. When he saw Peri, he broke from the group and walked towards her.

'Hi, Peri. Still reading for Azur?'

'And you . . . still spying on him?'

The curling of his lip was affirmation enough. 'That man shouldn't be allowed to teach at a respectable institution. You know he doesn't give a toss about his students? It's all about his ego.'

'The students like him.'

'Yeah, sure. Especially female ones . . . Your friend, for instance. Shirin.' His head jerked oddly as he pronounced her name.

Peri dug the heel of her shoe into the gravel. 'What about her?'

'Come on, as if you don't know.' He stared at her. 'Do I have to spell it out?'

'Spell what out?'

Troy's eyes glittered. 'That Azur is having an affair with Shirin.'

A troubled silence fell between them, though not for too long. 'But she's an old student of his . . .' Peri said, her words trailing away.

'She was sleeping with him while she took his seminar. I bet they marked her essays in bed together.'

Peri looked away. In that moment she saw what she had failed to see all this time: whatever hatred Troy harboured for Azur was compounded by his jealousy. This boy was in love with Shirin.

'Sometimes she goes to his college rooms. They lock the door. It takes them twenty minutes to half an hour, depending on the day. I've timed it, I've waited outside.'

'Stop it.' Peri's face grew hot.

'I know you visit him too. I've seen you.'

'To discuss my . . .' Peri paused before adding, 'My work.'

'Liar, you don't have a seminar with him this term!'

'I . . . I had something important to tell him,' said Peri.

There was no way she could explain that she had been there a few times to talk about the baby in the mist. Azur had asked her dozens of detailed questions about how it began and how differently her parents had reacted. The fear of the jinn, the visit to the exorcist, the things she scribbled in her God-diary . . . She had told him everything, turning her childhood memories into a bridge that she hoped in the end would enable her to reach his heart. When Azur had had enough, however, he pulled down the bridge and put a stop to the invitations to come to his rooms.

'Don't you see?' Troy said. 'The man is an egomaniacal predator. He's looking for young minds and young bodies to feed on.'

'I need to go,' Peri said, her voice a whisper.

Overcome by a terrible migraine, she stopped by a chemist's on the way home. Since she arrived in Oxford she had tried all the over-the-counter painkillers. Now she walked the familiar aisles, slowing down by the shelves full of contraceptives in varieties she'd never seen in Istanbul. Glittering packets, voluptuous colours, grotesque designs, sizzling words. It crossed her mind that if only her father and mother had used one of these products she would never have been born. Nor would *he*. It would have been a delicious nothingness. No suffering, no guilt, no nothing.

It had taken her many years to discover the truth that her parents had carefully hidden from her while she was growing up. True, Selma had had a surprise pregnancy at a late age, but she had given birth to two, not one. A girl and a boy. Peri and Poyraz – for the girl, the name of a fairy spun with golden thread, and for the boy, the name of the wildest north-east wind.

When they were four years old, one hot and drowsy afternoon, Selma briefly left the toddlers alone on the sofa to go to the kitchen. She was making plum jam – one of her specialities. They had bought the fruit in abundance from the local bazaar, and now some were in a bowl on the coffee table, the rest on the kitchen worktop waiting to be boiled, sweetened and preserved. The world was washed in purple.

Soon, bored, Peri managed to crawl down from the sofa on to the carpet. She reached for the plums in the bowl, grabbed one, inspected it curiously, bit into it. Too sour. She changed her mind. She gave it to her brother, who accepted the gift with glee. It took only a few seconds, no more. By the time Selma returned from the kitchen, her baby son had stopped fighting for breath, his face akin to the colour of the fruit that had blocked his airway. Peri had witnessed it all, uncomprehending, unmoving.

'Why didn't you call me?' Selma shouted at her daughter in front of relatives and neighbours who had gathered at the house after the funeral. 'What got into you? You watched your brother die and did not make a sound. Evil child!'

The distance between them would never be overcome. Peri knew, deep inside, her mother would always blame her for her twin brother's death. *How difficult can it be for a four-year-old to shout for help? If she had called me, I could have saved him.*

Numbness. That was what Peri sought most of all. If only she could manage not to feel or remember anything. But no matter how hard she tried, the past kept coming back, and, alongside it, the pain. The memory of that afternoon accompanied her through the attendant ghost of her twin brother. And so did the guilt and the shame and the self-hatred, which lodged inside her chest, as though it were not a feeling but a hard, physical substance.

That same evening Peri found Shirin alone in the kitchen, slicing tomatoes for a salad. Shirin was watching her weight, which fluctuated like her mood. Mona had gone out to dinner with relatives visiting from out of town, and would be coming home late.

'I need to ask you something,' said Peri.

'Sure, shoot.'

'Was this Azur's plan? Our sharing the same house, I mean. Our friendship, right from the beginning – was it his idea?'

Shirin arched an eyebrow. 'What makes you think that?'

'Please don't lie . . . any more,' said Peri. 'This is an experiment for him, right? Azur's social laboratory.'

'Wow, what a conspiracy.' Shirin tossed the tomatoes into a bowl of lettuce and added some olives. 'What's your problem with the professor?'

'He seems to enjoy interfering in his students' lives.'

'Huh,' said Shirin. 'How else can he teach? How do you think scholars trained their pupils throughout history? Masters and apprentices. Philosophers and their protégés. Years of hard work and discipline. But we've forgotten all that. Universities are now so dependent on money, those students who can afford tuition are treated like bloody royalty.'

'He's not our master and we're not his apprentices.'

'Well, I am,' said Shirin, as she grabbed a set of tongs and began to mix her salad. 'I count myself his devoted disciple.'

Peri fell quiet, unsure how to respond.

'Our respect for Azur is the only thing Mona and I have in common. What's wrong with you? I thought you liked the professor.'

Peri felt her cheeks redden; she hated herself for being so transparent. 'I fear he expects too much from us and we won't be able to meet his demands.'

'Oh, so you're worried about disappointing him,' Shirin said with a knowing smile as she grabbed the bowl and headed to her room. 'Then, don't!'

'Wait,' said Peri.

Her mouth felt dry. She feared the consequences if she revealed the question that had been gnawing at her, and yet she had to ask. 'Are you having an affair with him?'

Shirin, halfway up the stairs, stopped. Placing one hand on the balustrade, she stared down at her friend, her eyes balls of fire.

'If you're asking because you're paranoid, it's your problem, not mine. If you're asking because you're jealous, again, it's your problem, not mine.'

'I'm neither paranoid nor jealous,' Peri said, unable to keep her voice down.

'Really?' Shirin laughed. 'In Iran there's a proverb Mamani taught me. *She who makes a mouse of herself will be eaten by cats.*'

'What are you trying to say?'

'I say, stay out of my business, Mouse, or I'll eat you alive.'

At that Shirin stomped up to her room, leaving Peri in the kitchen, feeling small and insignificant.

How she loathed Azur. His arrogance. His recklessness. His indifference towards her while he flirted with Shirin and God knows who else. She felt giddy as a wheel of hatred whirled inside her soul, spinning uncontrollably. She'd had such high expectations of him. He who with his knowledge and vision would show her the way out of the quandary that had tormented her since childhood. He had done nothing of the sort.

But, mostly, she detested herself: her tormented mind, which produced not happy thoughts but anxieties and nightmares; her unbecoming body, which she endured as a daily burden, unable to delight in its pleasures; her mawkish features, which she had wished, so many times, to swap with someone else – her twin brother, for instance. And why had he died and she survived? Was it another of God's terrible mistakes?

She was sure she could be like neither Shirin – bold, confident – nor Mona – faithful, resilient. She was tired of herself, hurt by the past, scared of the future. Dark in spirit, confused by nature, timid like a newborn tiger, yet incapable of honouring the wildness she carried inside . . . No one could know how exhausting it was to be Peri. If only she could sleep and wake up as someone else. Or, better yet, not wake up at all.

That night the baby in the mist came again. The purple stain on his face seemed to have grown. He cried purple tears on her bedsheets. A dark, rich colour spread all around, reminiscent of ripened plums. The baby kept talking in his garbled language, urging her to do something long overdue. This time she understood what he was telling her and she agreed. Perhaps she would meet that ill-fated hedgehog again. What had become of the animal, its body, its soul? She would learn, first-hand, what happened to those who were refused entry to God's paradise.

The Passage

Istanbul, 2016

When Peri stepped on to the terrace to phone back Shirin, she noticed there were two figures huddled in the corner, half in shadow, though impossible not to recognize – the businessman and the bank CEO. Shoulders hunched, heads bowed, eyes fixed on the ground, they seemed to be discussing a matter of some gravity.

'So what are you gonna do?' asked the CEO.

'Haven't decided,' said the businessman, spitting out a plume of cigar smoke. 'But I swear to God, I'm gonna make those sons-of-bitches pay. They'll find out who they're fucking around with.'

'Make sure you have nothing in writing,' said the CEO.

The two men hadn't seen Peri standing by the door. Discreetly, she slipped away, her head dizzy with what she had just heard. The framed photos she had seen in the office that exhibited his ties with corrupt leaders and Third World dictators; the rumours about his embezzlement of public funds; his ties with mafia bosses – it was all of a piece. Their host's business deals were dubious, and she suspected several guests at the dinner – including perhaps her husband – knew it. But they were not going to let a shady reputation get in the way of a good evening with a rich and powerful man. At what point did one become an accomplice to a crime – when one actively took part in its workings or when one passively feigned ignorance?

There was a small passage between the kitchen and the drawing room, with a mirror running along one wall. Here Peri stood, in this narrow place, clutching the phone as if worried someone might snatch it away. Each time a maid went in or out through the swinging door, she peeked into the kitchen – the chef was chopping garlic, the knife in his hand tapping out a fandango on a wooden board. The man looked tired, irritated. After all the food he had prepared, he had just been asked to cook a tripe soup – as a cure for the after-effects of drinking, in the best Istanbul tradition.

Peri saw the chef mutter something under his breath to his assistant, who threw back his head in laughter. They had eavesdropped on everything uttered at the table, she was almost certain, making fun of them all. The door closed, separating her from the vivid world in the kitchen. Now alone in the passageway, a familiar feeling of dread crept over her. Daring to do something that had been postponed for far too long was like diving into a freezing cold sea. If you hesitated a single second, you would lose your nerve. Quickly, she dialled Shirin's number. It was answered on the first ring.

'Hi. Shirin . . . It's Peri.'

A sharp intake of breath. 'Yes, I know.'

Her voice had not changed a bit – the same brisk, resonant, assured tone.

'It's been a while,' said Peri.

'I couldn't believe it when I heard your message,' said Shirin. Then, more subdued, 'Funny, I had rehearsed this moment. Planned what I was going to say if you ever called again but now . . .'

'What was it you were going to say?' Peri asked, moving the phone from one ear to the other.

'Trust me, you wouldn't want to know,' Shirin said. 'Why haven't you called before?'

'I was worried you'd still be angry.'

'I was,' Shirin said. 'I still don't get it, I don't get *you*. Crazy what you did to yourself . . . and to him. You didn't even tell him you were sorry.'

'We had a deal,' Peri said. The words, like every other inch of her, felt brittle, breaking. 'He made me promise never to apologize to him, no matter what.'

'Bullshit.'

Peri swallowed a sigh. 'I was young.'

'You were jealous!'

Peri nodded to herself. 'Yes . . . I was.'

The kitchen door opened; a maid bustled out with a large tray full of steaming bowls. A strong odour of garlic and vinegar hit Peri's nostrils.

'Where are you?' asked Shirin.

'At a party in a seaside mansion. Fish tanks, designer bags, fat cigars, truffles . . . You would hate it.'

Shirin laughed.

'I've had such a weird day,' said Peri. Now that she had started talking, the words flowed effortlessly. 'I got mugged. I could have killed the thug.' She did not mention he had attempted to rape her. Had Shirin experienced something similar, she would have shared it, unashamed. How different they had been; how different they still were. 'He found a photo of us I keep in my wallet.'

'You carry around a photo of us?' Shirin asked. 'Which one?'

'Remember, in front of the Bod, wintertime?' Peri didn't wait for Shirin to comment. 'You, Mona and me . . . Professor Azur. All these years I convinced myself I had left Oxford behind, but I've been fooling myself.'

'I never understood how you lost interest in academia. You were such a stellar student.'

'One changes,' said Peri. 'I'm a mother, a wife . . .' She paused. 'A housewife, a charity trustee! I throw parties for my husband's boss – exactly the kind of woman I always dreaded becoming. A modern version of my mother. And you know what? I like it – most of the time.'

Shirin asked, 'Have you been drinking?'

'More than I should.'

A quiet laugh like the faint rustling of leaves. If Shirin said something else, Peri didn't catch it, for just then the psychic marched past her arm in arm with the hostess, having looked over the entire house in the hunt for the evil eye. He turned aside and glanced at Peri with a slight a twitch of his lips, as if he knew who she was talking to.

'How are your twins?' asked Shirin.

'How do you know I have twins?'

'Heard it.' Her source wasn't hard for Peri to guess; each had separately been in touch with Mona throughout the years.

'They're growing up. My daughter's waged a Cold War against me. So far, she's winning.'

Shirin gave a sigh of sympathy. She was being nice – far nicer than Peri expected.

'How are things at home?' Peri asked. She, too, had heard things. She knew Shirin and her long-term partner – a human rights lawyer – had lost count of how many times they had broken up and got back together.

'Fine . . . actually, I'm pregnant. I'm due in May.'

So that was it. The hormones. Shirin was about to become a mother. She was in a phase when forgiveness came more naturally than rancour. It was hard to hold old grudges when you were preparing to welcome a new life.

'Congratulations, that's wonderful news,' Peri said. 'I'm so happy for you. Boy or girl?'

'Boy.'

'Do you have a name in mind?' Peri asked and immediately sensed the answer.

'I think you already know what I'll call him,' Shirin said. The briefest silence. A trace of enmity crept into the silence, like smoke from an old samovar. 'I've hated you for so long, I've run out of hatred.'

'What about Azur? How does he feel about me?'

It had been almost fourteen years since she had last talked to him. At times Peri could not be sure whether the professor's presence in her life had been as strong as she recalled, so completely had he faded into the past.

'Find out for yourself. He should be at home right now. Do you have a pen?'

Taken aback, Peri glanced around. 'Just a sec.'

She pushed open the kitchen door, phone held to her ear, and made a writing gesture with her bandaged hand. The chef gave her a fountain pen from his breast pocket and a page from a notepad stuck on the fridge.

'Thank you,' Peri mouthed at him.

Shirin repeated the number, less because she needed to than because it gave her something to say. She added, 'Call him.'

Just then the sound of the downstairs doorbell echoed through the seaside mansion. A maid dashed out of the kitchen to find out who it was. She seemed to be concealing some food in her hand. Peri wondered if the staff had been able to taste any of the fabulous dishes they had served; if they had had any dinner at all.

A sudden bang was heard – an open door slammed back against a wall, followed by a succession of noises: a shriek, muffled; footsteps, hurried and heavy.

'I miss you,' Peri heard herself say.

'Mouse, I miss you too.'

From the passageway Peri saw, on the opposite side of the drawing room, two men burst in, their faces covered with black scarves, shotguns in their hands. One of them shouted at the top of his voice. 'Everybody stand up!'

'What's going on?' yelled the businesswoman.

'Shut up! Do as we say, now!'

'You can't talk to me like that . . .!' A muffled, choking sound came from the businesswoman. Her husband was presumably still on the terrace.

'One more stupid word, I swear to God, and you'll regret it!'

The metallic click of a trigger. It was the second time in her life Peri was seeing a gun at such close quarters. Unlike the one her brother Umut had been caught with, the raiders' guns were big and dark green.

'Mouse, are you there?' Shirin asked.

Peri could not answer. Not a word. Slowly, as silent as the fog creeping in from the Bosphorus, she hung up.

The Glass of Sherry

Oxford, 2002

The President's Lodgings occupied an entire side of a fifteenth-century front quadrangle. Azur strode up to the polished black front door and rang the bell. A few seconds later a senior scout appeared and ushered him into the expansive entrance hall.

'This way, Professor, please,' the man said, as he led Azur up an Elizabethan oak staircase, through a panelled long gallery to the President's study.

Inside, the President busied himself organizing his papers – top-priority in the ivory tray, important-but-less-urgent in the brown tray, and all the rest in the yellow one – as he always did when faced with an appointment he would rather not have. It was going to be a difficult talk and he needed to order his thoughts. In the meantime, he turned to tidying his desk. The sticky notes, the stapler, the mother-of-pearl letter opener with the silver handle ... He put the pencils – each sharpened to perfection – in a cylindrical leather box. It was a gift from his daughter.

A sharp knock on the door jolted him out of his reverie. 'Do come in.'

Azur entered, sporting a velvet jacket, richly coloured, just the right tint of purple. Underneath, he wore a turtleneck of a lighter shade. His hair, as always, was a studied mess.

'Good morning, Leo. It's been a while.'

'Azur, how wonderful to see you,' said the President, his voice polite and affectionate but strained. 'A while indeed. I was thinking of tea; would you care to join me – or, what time is it ... a glass of sherry, perhaps?'

Azur had never adopted the late-morning sherry habit among dons, but this morning he thought that he, or the President, might need a drink. 'Sure, why not.'

In a few seconds, an even older scout appeared – his countenance chiselled to stony reticence, his back hunched by years of service. Like the portraits on the walls, the Gothic oak chairs by the window, one could hardly imagine a time when he wasn't a part of the college.

For a while the two men watched the scout, an arm locked behind his back and his hand trembling, pour the sherry with an agonizing slowness. Silver decanter, crystal glasses, salted almonds.

'Read your recent interview in *The Times*, good stuff,' said the President when they were alone again.

'Thanks, Leo.'

An awkward silence ensued.

'You know how much I admire you,' said the President. 'We're fortunate to have you as a fellow. And I was very fond of Anissa.'

'Thank you, but you haven't invited me here to talk about my late wife,' said Azur. 'I've known you long enough to know when you're upset. What is it, tell me.'

The President took out his sticky notepads. Earlier he had colour-coordinated them – the oranges, the greens, the pinks. Without glancing up at Azur, he muttered, 'There are complaints about you.'

Azur examined the President – his hair greying at the temples, his creased forehead, the nervous twitch of his mouth; every inch the former Treasury mandarin he once was. He said, 'You don't need to mince words with me.'

'No, of course not. Wouldn't dream of it. Each time you were under attack, and God knows there have been a few occasions . . . either because of your views or your teaching style . . . I mean, you are popular, but not with everyone, surely you must know that . . . I've supported you, all this time.'

'I know,' Azur said calmly.

The President built a tiny tower with the sticky notepads. 'I stood by your side because I believed in your intellectual integrity. I respected your commitment to knowledge and objectivity.' A sigh. 'Why, pray, have you upset so many?'

Undergrads in tears, spoken and written charges about Azur and his teaching techniques, accusing him of pushing his students too far, exposing their weaknesses, humiliating them in front of their friends, being ostentatiously controversial and offensive. 'Offensive,' said the President out loud.

'They need to learn not to be offended,' said Azur. 'This is not a nursery. It's a university. Time to grow up. They can't be pampered and coddled forever. Our students must learn how to deal with things. Stuff happens.'

'Yes, but that's not exactly in your job description.'

'I believe it is.'

'Your job is to teach them philosophy.'

'Precisely!'

'Philosophy as in textbooks.'

'Philosophy as in *life*.'

Another sigh. 'They can't go around feeling offended and pushed to the limit. Too many students complain.' The President knocked down the tower of sticky pads. 'But there's something else . . . important.'

'What is it?'

'A female student.'

The words hung in the air, refusing to dissolve.

'They're saying you're having affairs with some of the students,' said the President.

'It's nobody's business, is it? So long as I'm not taking advantage of anyone . . . or I'm not being taken advantage of.'

The President shook his head. 'The morality of that position is debatable.'

'Is this about Shirin? She's not my student, you must know. Not any more.'

'Uhm . . . No, that's not her name.'

Azur gave a quizzical frown. 'Who are you talking about?'

'A Turkish student. She's in your class.' The President lifted his tired eyes. 'She tried to commit suicide last night.'

Azur paled. 'Peri? My God! Is she all right?'

'Yes, fine . . . youth,' said the President. 'Paracetamol overdose. She has a resilient liver.'

'I can't believe it.' Azur slouched in his seat, his face drained of all its vigour.

'The story is that you had an affair with her and you . . . abandoned her.'

Azur inhaled sharply as if he had been punched. 'She said that?'

'Well, not exactly. The girl is in no state to talk right now,' the President said. 'It's that boy who sued you, Troy . . . He's threatened to talk to the press. He seemed quite agitated. I have his written statement here.'

'May I see it?'

'I'm afraid not. It needs to go to the Ethics Committee.'

'I can assure you nothing happened between me and Peri. All you need to do is ask her; I'm confident she'll tell you the truth.'

'Look, you're a very fine teacher but, first and foremost, a fellow of this college. We can't let the college's good name be compromised. Surely you must know you've made many enemies over the years.' The President took a sip of sherry. 'You can imagine the media . . . they'll feast on this story, they're carnivores.'

'What are you suggesting?'

'Well . . . you may like to consider taking a brief hiatus. Stop teaching for a while. Let this die down and the committee finish their investigation. Once this girl testifies it will be fine. Until then we need to close down this . . . *thing*.'

Azur stared at him, searching. Then he stood up. 'Leo, you've known me for a long time, I have never behaved unethically.'

The President also rose to his feet. 'Listen –'

'Troy's testimony is flawed, I can assure you. What did Anaïs Nin say? *We don't see things as they are. We see them as we are*.'

'For goodness' sake, Anaïs Nin is the last person you should be quoting under the circumstances.'

'I'll wait for Peri to tell the truth,' said Azur. He shook his head. 'Poor girl, what did she do to herself?'

Then he was gone. As a fellow of the college, they surely could not get rid of him if he didn't want to go. Yet, while even now he didn't really care what others thought of him, deep within he knew that he had become an embarrassment to the faculty. His head was thumping as if something long trapped within was trying to break its way out. With swift, swinging strides, he marched out of the building and into the rain, which had been falling unceasingly all morning.

The Sound of God's Absence

Oxford, 2002

When Peri came to her senses in a room inside the John Radcliffe Hospital, she could not tell immediately where she was. The colours were too bright, aggressive – the whites of the bedsheets too immaculate, the blues of the bedcovers too cheerful. The grey of the sky outside the window reminded her of the lumps of lead her mother melted against the evil eye. She heard murmurs inside her head, futile prayers. Uneasy, she tried to close her eyes again, wishing the sound away, but the patient beside her – a woman of sixty or so – seemed eager to talk.

'Good heavens, girl, you're awake! I thought you'd sleep forever.'

Speaking with a breezy abandon, the woman said she had been married for forty years and hospitalized so many times she knew the entire staff by name. Her voice filled the room like a swelling balloon, raising the pressure inside Peri's ears.

'What about you, girl? A first timer or a repeater?'

Peri cleared her throat as an awful chemical taste rose in her mouth. She searched for her voice and shook her head, unable to talk. Shrinking into the sheets, she turned her face towards the window. Fragments of the day before began to flock into her mind. What had she done?

A tear ran down her cheek as her father came to mind and she recalled his words: *You are my clever daughter. Only you among my children can do this. Education will save you and you will save our broken family. Youth like you will rescue this country from its backwardness.* The dream child sent to Oxford to bring pride to the Nalbantoğlus had brought humiliation and failure instead. Without realizing it, Peri began to sob so hard and so loudly that the other patient, fearing for her state of mind, pressed the emergency button and called the nurse. In a few minutes, Peri was given a peach-coloured liquid, which smelled horrible but strangely had no flavour. She buried her head into her pillow, her eyelids weighed down by exhaustion.

In her state of semi-delirium the only face that she kept seeing was that of the baby in the mist. Where was he now when she needed him? Did he have an existence and a will outside of her or was he simply a trick of a mind riddled with guilt?

The next morning Peri met her psychiatrist for the first time. A young doctor with a kind, generous smile. You are not alone, he said. They would work as a team. He would give her the tools with which she could build a new Peri; she would be the architect of her soul. The author of herself. He had the habit of pausing too often and ending every statement with the same question, 'How does that sound?' The treatment would not make self-destructive thoughts disappear, he explained, but rather teach her how to cope with them in case they returned. He made suicidal tendencies sound like the weather, like a spell of heavy rain. You could not avoid it, but if you knew how to stay dry, you would be less affected by it.

'There's one more thing,' he said. 'When you're ready, no pressure, you might be asked a question or two about a certain professor. We understand there are accusations of bullying students, including you, in front of everyone. The university is investigating the claims – for your own benefit and for the benefit of other students. Whenever you're ready, no rush. How does that sound?'

Peri felt a chill down her spine. So they thought it was Azur who had triggered her suicide attempt. Astounded though she was to hear this, still she said nothing.

The Dawn Redwood

Oxford, 2002

The morning she was expected to appear before the committee, Peri sat alone in the Botanic Garden, just off Magdalen Bridge. Each time she came here she felt as if she were strolling in a favourite childhood place, at ease with her surroundings. A sixty-foot dawn redwood – how she loved the name! – towered above the bench where she was seated. The tree, previously known only from fossils, had been found growing in a remote Chinese valley. She relished that magical story of botanical discovery.

The sun on her back, she pulled her legs towards herself, her knees up against her chin, finding a strange calm amidst rare plants and trees. In her hand she held a coffee cup, which she pressed against her cheek, the warmth as comforting as the touch of a lover.

The voice of Shirin rang in her ears. *Why do you always make yourself so fucking miserable, Mouse? Why the sad, worn face? You seem like a ninety-year-old swallowed you whole. When will you learn to have a bit of fun?*

Azur, however, said the best way to approach 'the question of God' was neither through religiosity nor scepticism but through solitude. There was a reason why all those ascetics and hermits had withdrawn into the desert to fulfil their spiritual quest. In the company of others, one was more likely to commune with the devil than with God, Azur argued. A joke, of course – though with Azur you never knew.

Yes, she would go to testify on his behalf. She owed him that. He had contributed to her misery, for sure – an unrequited love was the last thing she needed in life – but he could not be held responsible for her suicide attempt. Besides, she was thankful to him. He had opened up another dimension in her consciousness that, unknown to her, had been lying inert. He expected, no, he *demanded* his students see their cultural and personal prejudices and, ultimately, to cast them off. He was an extraordinary teacher, a scholar of integrity. He had managed to shake her, motivate her, challenge her. She had worked harder in his seminar than in any other class. He had shown her the poetry in wisdom and the wisdom in poetry. In his seminars all were welcome and treated equally, regardless of their backgrounds or their views. If there was anything Azur held sacred, surely it was knowledge.

She adored the way the last rays of sun tinted his hair gold and the way his eyes sparkled when his mind flew as he spoke about a favourite book or a beloved philosopher. She adored his love of teaching, which at times felt even stronger than his will. So many tutors taught the syllabus, year in year out, while he improvised in every class. In his universe there were no routines, only risks worth taking. She remembered him quoting Chesterton: *Life looks just a little more mathematical and regular than it is; its exactitude is obvious, but its inexactitude is hidden; its wildness lies in wait.*

But then, as infatuated as she was with him, she abhorred his air of superiority, his bloated pride, the hubris that infused his whole being. He dismissed the worries of others, indoctrinating students with his own perspective, exercising a form of power over them, often at the expense of hurting their feelings.

She imagined his hand running through Shirin's hair and down her neck . . . it was more than she could bear. The thought of the two of them together – talking, laughing, making love. These were the scenes that played non-stop in her mind when her head hit the pillow at night. How close Azur had been to Shirin, while he had remained aloof and inaccessible to her. Only when he had learned about the otherworldly episodes she had with the baby in the mist did he pay more attention to her. For him she had been yet another scientific experiment, another source of curiosity. He had quickly lost interest in her, like a spoiled child with a new toy. She loathed the avarice he conflated with a spirit of inquiry, the vanity he hid behind academic research. She could not tell which upset her more: that he had been secretly sleeping with Shirin or that he had refused to love her in the same way. He had burst into her life and left destruction in its wake. Yes, she would testify against him.

Shirin and Mona had been deeply shocked when they heard about Peri's suicide attempt. As soon as they were allowed to visit, they had come, bringing nothing but their concern, etched on their faces. They were bent on finding out why she had done it – a question Peri didn't know how to answer. Shirin had also begged her to give evidence in Azur's defence. She had asked her to save her darling professor. Was it because Shirin trusted her and saw her as a dear friend, Peri wondered; or did she simply think that she – Mouse – was easy to manipulate?

Be objective, she told herself. *Separate your feelings from facts, that at least you owe to Azur. Make sure you aren't driven by emotion. He taught you how to do that.* Regarding his affair with Shirin, well, they were two consenting adults, neither exploiting the other. As for Troy's motives in seeking to bring him down, were they entirely selfless?

On a bench in the Botanic Garden, each question piercing her mind led to a more complicated one. The psychiatrist had told her it was best to put off making serious decisions until she was feeling better, stronger. But how could she do that under the circumstances? Peri felt lost; the thin rope mooring her snapped and she drifted in unknown waters, not sure which way to swim. Soon she would appear before the committee members. What would she tell them? What kind of things might they ask her in return? Her feelings swirled in circles, with such speed that she was not sure she could put them into words, least of all in front of strangers and in a language other than her own.

She checked her watch. Her heart pounding so hard it could have burst through her chest, she stood up and began to walk towards the building where Professor Azur's reputation would be on trial.

Swathed in the tranquillity of his college rooms, Azur sat at his desk, staring out of the window. He tried not to let his mind dwell on the outcome of the committee meeting. It weighed heavily on his conscience that people who loved him might get hurt at the end. He knew Shirin would be grilled with questions about their affair. She would try to disguise the truth to protect him. Fruitless, he reasoned, since he had already decided to tell everything straight out. He had nothing to hide. He had done nothing wrong.

Troy, too, would be summoned. He would unload the pack of lies he called truth. He had never liked that boy. Sneaky. Good thing he had kicked him out of the class. Over the years he had heard many stories of students and professors clashing over political definitions, historical views and so on. For his part, he had rarely been bothered by differences of opinion. Every year one received a few difficult cases, students who wanted to show how clever, how special, how far-above-their-peers they were. And that was fine. It was Troy's attitude in the classroom that had put him off. Bossing other students about, ridiculing anyone he didn't agree with, calling people names, following them after hours and bullying them with his opinions on God. At first he had thought Troy's presence would provoke everyone into thinking more clearly, but it had quickly become clear that most students felt intimidated by him. So he had thrown him out of the class, leaving the boy excluded, hostile, dangerously vindictive.

Azur was aware that his critics, who were plentiful, were rubbing their hands, thrilled to anticipate a scandal unfolding with him at the centre. Some openly wished him to be sacked. There was a certain type of person who rejoiced in another's miseries, as pointless as a man who expected to fill his stomach with someone else's hunger.

And Peri . . . beautiful, timid, fragile, self-reproaching Peri. What would she say about him? He was not worried about her. After all, the accusations regarding Peri were baseless, and he felt sure she would be objective, honest. She would testify, if not for him, for truth, which would amount to the same thing.

In his hands Azur held an imaginary set of scales, the pros and cons of his case resting on each palm. Against him: pressuring students with assignments that some might deem objectionable, even offensive; causing some of them to break down in class and to collapse psychologically; and, of course, having an affair with the irresistible Shirin. In his defence: his long years of teaching, research and work; his contribution to intellectual and academic life; his productivity in turning out books and articles; and the fact that Shirin – the only 'moral' aspect of his file – was not his student at the time their affair began.

Despite the best attempts of Troy and his allies, the case against him was weak.

He had always reasoned that if you didn't know how to take a punch, you wouldn't know how to win a fight. Even so, he could see how vain he had been. He had wanted to develop God into a language that was, if not spoken, at least understood and shared by many. God, not as a transcendental being or a vengeful judge or a tribal totem, but as a unifying idea, a common quest. Could the search for God, when stripped of all labels and dogmas, be turned into a neutral space where everyone, including atheists and non-monotheists, could find a discussion of value? Could God unite people, simply as an object of study? It was a mental experiment: if each soul on earth completed God, as Hafez claimed, what would happen when unlikely individuals were put in the same room, made to look each other in the eye and encouraged to complete one another's *understanding* of God? He admitted being demanding, and controlling, at times. True, he had used his classroom as a laboratory. But it was all for a good reason.

The students . . . disadvantaged in knowledge, advantaged in age, quick to judge and self-centred to the core. It never occurred to them that their teachers, too, had a story, a secret, a life elsewhere. Azur had created a Tower of Babel with them. He had pushed them as far as he could. He had failed.

One great mistake had been to become involved with Peri. It had piqued his interest that a girl this quiet and withdrawn had a hidden side, in touch with what she called 'the mystical'. Peri, more than any other student in his seminar, had a personal dispute with God and he had been attracted to that. Yes, he had spent extra time with her, even though he saw – for how could he not? – the girl had feelings for him. She was too young. Too naive. Too bottled-up. He should have been more careful, but when was the last time he was?

Azur himself had not been raised in a religious household. His father was a wealthy English entrepreneur, whose happiness was inversely proportional to his success; his mother a talented but frustrated Chilean pianist who was filled with resentment at not having received the recognition in her lifetime that she thought she deserved. His family had a business in Havana, Cuba, where Azur was born. His father told tales of shark fishing with Ernest Hemingway – though little evidence of that remarkable friendship remained, save for a few photographs and handwritten notes. Azur had chosen Philosophy as his calling in defiance of family duties and expectations. However, to make his parents happy, he had agreed to major in Economics, which he did, at Harvard.

In his last year at university, his life changed when he began to take classes with a specialist in Middle Eastern Studies. Professor Naseem had challenged young Azur like no one had done before. From an Algerian Berber family, he had exposed Azur to different cultures and shifting perspectives and uneasy questions. He had also introduced him to the works of mystics – Ibn Arabi, Meister Eckhart, Rumi, Isaac Luria, Fariduddin Attar and his *Conference of the Birds*, and his favourite, Hafez.

One afternoon Azur visited Professor Naseem at his house in Brookline. It was there that he met Naseem's younger daughter, Anissa. Big hazel eyes, dark curly hair and a vivacity that touched and kindled everyone around her. They talked endlessly – about books, music, politics. She dreamed of moving out to her own flat. 'But wherever I live, I must see the water,' she said.

The same evening Azur was invited to stay for dinner. Of course the food was good, unlike anything he had tasted before, but it was the easy laughter and the Arabic melodies that mesmerized him. Anissa's eyes darted over his face in the candlelight. In that moment Azur wished that this were his family. How different was their spontaneity, their unforced effervescence, from the measured politeness he knew from home. To this day, Azur was unsure whether he had fallen in love with Anissa or with her family.

Less than seven weeks later they were married.

Before long the young couple discovered how incompatible they were. Anissa lived mostly in her own mind. She was fiercely possessive and extremely jealous, and prone to emotional breakdowns, sometimes for the stupidest reasons. She had been on medication since she was a teenager.

Anissa had an older half-sister – Nour – from Professor Naseem's first marriage. Considerate, thoughtful, kind, every time the family would get together, she would sit at the table next to them, listening to the conversation between Azur and her father, asking probing questions. Slowly, Azur began to see her in a different light. The sweetness of her smile, the brightness of her gaze, the delicacy of her fingers, the sharpness of her mind. She respected his views. He respected hers. Never before had Azur thought that such respect in itself could be a source of attraction.

The same year, at the end of the summer, Azur and Nour crossed a threshold. The family soon found it out. Professor Nassim, that fine old man, summoned Azur and shouted in his face; the veins on his neck were bulging blue creeks. He accused his young prodigy of acting like Sheitan, sneaking into his home with the sole intention of destroying his peace and hard-earned reputation.

Azur and Anissa moved out and managed to make up. They decided to get away from Boston. Start afresh in Europe. *It won't follow us, your shame*, Anissa said. *Shame can't swim oceans*. She never stopped talking about it, though, not openly but through insinuations and sarcastic remarks, convinced that no amount of remorse on Azur's part could mend what he had so badly broken. In some incidental way, she seemed to savour her husband's sin, which gave her a moral advantage in their marriage, a sense of righteousness sweeter than ripe berries.

They arrived in Oxford, with a view over the water, where Anissa seemed to adapt easily and Azur quickly found his feet. He thrived here. His wife was welcomed by the Oxford community. What no one who met her could see was the depth of the darkness gnawing at her soul. When happy, she was euphoric. When sad, she was crushed. In joy or in sorrow, it was always extremes with Anissa.

She was four months pregnant when she disappeared. Early in the morning, the mist hanging close to the ground, she went walking down the river and never returned. Her body was found twenty-six days later, even though the police divers had repeatedly searched the river. There was an article about it in the *Oxford Mail* carrying a photograph of her in her wedding dress with a spring-blossom wreath. How they had got hold of that photo Azur had never worked out. Her death was being treated as *unexplained*, the police spokesman said. Foul play was not suspected. The coroner gave an open verdict, but Azur became obsessed with that one remark: the unexplained.

Professor Naseem blamed Azur and his affair with Nour for Anissa's mood swings and sudden disappearance. The family never forgave him, nor deep within did Azur forgive himself. It made him hypersensitive to apologies, though. He hated it when people asked for pardon for trivial things when there were bigger apologies in life that could never be expressed. Between the freethinking of his upbringing and the justice-orientated faith of Professor Naseem, he tore open a space for himself. He would teach the unexplained. He would teach God.

As the morning wind mellowed into a breeze, Peri approached the committee hearing in a dreamlike state. Her legs felt heavy and stiff. The sun hid behind a cloud, a swift soared overhead and it felt like another season – as though the world had changed since she had left the Botanic Garden and the dawn redwood that had shaded her.

Troy was pacing back and forth at the entrance. Shirin was sitting at the stairs, her arms folded across her chest, her eyes swollen from crying. Each was keenly waiting for Peri to arrive so that they could pull her over to their side. Somewhere inside that building were people with impenetrable expressions and impertinent questions.

Where was Azur, she wondered, and what was going through his mind. How she wished he were next to her now, so they could shelter inside one of the many fantasies she had about him. They could walk past these people, oblivious to their judging stares, unaffected by this calamity that had struck them out of nowhere. She wished it were night-time and that he would talk to her about poetry and philosophy and the paradox of God, words that flew in the wind like sparks from the embers of open fires; only the two of them under a sky that could have been anywhere, a dreaming university town or a teeming city, her head resting in the crook of his neck. She wished for all the differences in their ages, status and cultures to evaporate into the air. She wished for him to lean over and touch her face, kiss her lips and speak her name like an incantation. She wished for her mind and her heart to fuse into a blade that would destroy the spirit of Shirin that resided within him. It was so long since she had desired anything this fervently.

Peri pulled her coat tight, feeling the cold penetrating her skin. If she testified on his behalf, as she felt morally bound to do, maybe he would understand how much she cared for him and he would love her – at least a little. Maybe ... Yet in her heart she knew none of these things was likely to happen. His name would be cleared and he would celebrate it with Shirin – who always got whatever she wanted.

From a distance, Peri thought all these things. Then, slowly, as if she had run out of energy, she stopped. Was she not the girl who had watched her twin brother choke to death and not cried for help? Always in-between, afraid of drawing attention to herself, unwilling to choose sides, so focused on not upsetting anyone that in the end everyone was left disappointed. Despite all her attempts to change herself, she wasn't strong enough to overcome the emotional paralysis ingrained in her soul. She, Peri, Nazperi, Rosa, Mouse, would not testify. Neither now, nor later. She was not an actor but a mere spectator. This was *their* problem. Their stupid game. She turned back and walked away as though it were a stranger's good name at stake and not the future of the man she had loved, dreamed of and desired with all her being.

Years had to pass before she came to the realization that her passivity actively contributed to the ruination of the man she loved. When she betrayed Azur, she betrayed the truth.

The Wardrobe

Istanbul, 2016

A third man, his face half covered with a bandana, had joined the two intruders. From the way he spoke, he seemed to be their leader. He must have waited outside in the garden while the other two had barged into the mansion, clearing the way for him.

'Do as we say and nobody gets hurt,' he roared. Yet he sounded neither angry nor agitated; just cold, detached. 'Your choice.'

Peri realized she was shaking. Her heart thumped inside her ribcage. Should she run or hide? Who were these men – organized mafia, ordinary robbers or terrorists – all of whom populated Istanbul in great numbers? Or was this about money? How many people had the businessman pissed off as he accumulated money and envy in equal measure? She recalled his troubled expression on the terrace. But there was no time to contemplate. Eyeing the kitchen door from the passage where she found herself crouching, she paused. She couldn't run in there without being seen from the drawing room. She took a step backwards. Her hands felt the surface of the mirror behind her. It moved slightly – the door of a built-in wardrobe.

She pushed it open. Inside there were coats, boxes, shoes, umbrellas. Without thinking, she jumped in and pulled the magnetic catch closed. Her back pressed against the wooden plank, she hunched up into a tight ball in the dark. Once again in her life she became a terrified hedgehog.

A minute later, maybe less, somebody stomped up and down the corridor, shouting. 'Get out of the kitchen! All of you. Now!'

They were rounding up the staff. The chef, the assistant, the maids hired for the night. Hurried footsteps. The heavy tread of boots. Frightened whispers.

Inside the wardrobe, Peri clicked the mute button on the mobile and typed a message to her mother. *Call the police, urgent. You know where I am.*

'Damn!' she said, realizing Selma had probably gone to bed and might not see her text until the next morning. She felt immensely relieved that Deniz had left, and was safe. But Adnan was here ... *there.* Her husband, her confidant, her best friend. Her breath came out in a sharp whimper.

She heard a thud. A woman screamed. Peri picked out a cry, which devolved into hysterical laughter. It sounded like the girlfriend of the famous journalist. 'You didn't see them coming? You call yourself a psychic – psychic my arse!'

Clutching her knees, Peri froze. Was all this about the businessman getting his just deserts? Or was it merely a coincidence – another chance occurrence that one tried in vain to make sense of? She remembered the security cameras and barbed wire she had seen at the entrance – all to no avail. The world was full of danger. Chaos and disorder lurked around every corner. Was evil some sort of divine retribution for our actions, or the fickle workings of an arbitrary fate? If randomness ruled, what point was there in trying to be a better person? How did one atone for past sins if not by changing one's ways? She had been good – except to the man she had loved years ago, and, in some untouched corner of her heart, still did. Professor Azur had taught her that uncertainty was precious. But what if confusion was all there was to it?

Sick to her stomach, she dialled the police. An officer picked up and instantly began bombarding her with questions, treating her less as a witness than a criminal. Peri cut him off in the most muted tone she could manage, 'There are armed men ...'

'Can't hear you. Speak louder,' the officer reprimanded.

Peri gave him the address.

'Why are you in that house?' said the officer.

'I am a guest,' she hissed in frustration. 'They've got guns.'

'Where are you in the house?' asked the officer but did not wait for an answer. He wanted to know her name, what she did, where she lived. Useless questions. She had been an exemplary citizen all this time, but in the database of the state she was a digital creation, a number without a story.

Finally, the man said, 'O-kay, we'll send out a team.'

Afterwards, she checked the battery. It would last for another fifteen minutes or probably less. She wondered what would happen in the interim: would she be discovered and taken hostage along with the rest or would the police arrive and launch an operation, during which they could all be rescued or killed? Perhaps by the time the battery died, this Last Supper of the Turkish Bourgeoisie would be over for good or bad. Life often felt unjust, but death was the bigger injustice. Which was harder to accept: that there was a hidden purpose in this madness, if one only knew where to look; or that there was no logic at all, and therefore no justice?

Her hand was throbbing again, as if it had a mind of its own, the arm of an octopus. In the phosphorescent light from the mobile's screen, squeezed in among the racks of coats and shoes while outside her husband and friends were hostages, she held up the number Shirin had given her.

She called Azur.

The Disgrace

Oxford, 2016

Every day at dusk Azur went out for a walk. He hiked for a good five to seven miles, following historic pathways, passing through ancient woodlands and over rolling farmland. A clarity of mind descended on a person in the open air, he thought, purposeful and measured but with no particular destination in mind. If there was one firm belief he had come to hold about human beings, it was that they were mental chameleons, capable of adapting even to shame and disgrace. He knew this not from speculation but from personal experience. He had been shamed. He had been disgraced. If someone had told his younger self as he climbed his way up both in academia and in society, ambitious and ever-confident, that he would one day fall to earth as if he'd flown too close to the sun, he would have found it too depressing to believe. In truth, the principled, younger Azur would have probably said it was better to die than to live with that kind of dishonour. Yet here he was, more than a decade after the scandal, still around, still alive and still deeply bruised inside.

Fourteen years ago he had been forced to leave his teaching position. Since then he had retained a loose tie with the college that was once his academic home, like an umbilical cord that no longer provided sustenance but could not be severed. He had not been asked to come back and teach, and he had not tried, lest his name brought embarrassment on his colleagues or department. Over the years he had read a number of articles about himself, but one was like no other. It accused him of being a megalomaniac with delusions of authority, a Foucaultian amalgam of power and knowledge that blighted young, insecure minds like a canker. Drawing a perfect whole of evil, the writer had connected Peri's suicide attempt with Anissa's disappearance. 'Here is a man who clearly brought tragedy to every young woman he seduced intellectually.' Passionately written and fearsomely well researched, the article had destabilized Azur, pushing him into a depression so intense it was impossible for him to recall a time when his world wasn't suffused with melancholy. Nevertheless, he had kept on working, as though he knew that if he stopped writing he would have no reason to look forward to another day. Work was a survival instinct.

He could have gone to America or Australia and started all over again. But he had chosen to stay. Without administrative and teaching responsibilities he had found plenty of time to read, research and write. This, combined with a new fire that had seized his soul, had motivated him to publish one book after another. Each of the titles he completed in all these years propelled him forward into fame and recognition, so that today he was at a point he would have never reached had he not lost his post. Perhaps Plutarch was right, after all. Fate did lead those who were willing to be led, and those who resisted the idea, like himself, were dragged forcefully instead.

He still lived in the same house with the bay windows looking into the woods. In the garden he grew culinary herbs and vegetables; socialized with a handful of old friends, no more. He cooked. Life was quiet, ordered, and this was how he wanted it. He still had lovers, several, and it no longer mattered whether the women he shared his bed with were affiliated with the university. There was something paradoxical about public disgrace that, insofar as it robbed one of social roles and respectability, was liberating. Yes, he was as free as a bird and almost as unconcerned. But he knew, of course, that birds were creatures of habit, therefore not exactly free, and had plenty of things to worry about.

Every now and then he received a call or email from a journalist set on interviewing him or a student writing a thesis on his books. He accepted some, refused others, acting purely on impulse. In the beginning, he had adamantly rejected every attempt to intrude on his private space. He was aware that the first question they would ask him would be about the scandal, despite the amount of time that had gone by. Even if they did not bring it up in the interview, there would always be a mention in their piece, which could be worse. So he had refused for as long as he could. But inaccessibility had only rendered him more alluring in the eyes of his readers. He had a loyal audience who knew, read and shared everything he produced. As one journalist had put it, among the most dishonoured thinkers of the times, he was the most revered.

After Spinoza passed away, he had refused to take care of another dog. The decision had not lasted long. A two-month-old Romanian shepherd puppy had appeared at his door with a golden bow attached to his collar – a birthday gift from Shirin. Thick, white fluffy hair with pale grey patches all over. Calm and clever, an animal made for the mountains. It seemed apposite to name him after the Romanian philosopher famous for his saturnine views on God and everything else. Besides, it suited Azur's mood. Henceforth it was Cioran who accompanied him on his walks.

This afternoon, Shirin had knocked at his door, her belly huge, her cheeks aflame. Pregnancy made some women more beatific in appearance, and she was one of them. If ever there was a sinner saint, it would have been her.

'You're going to come, right? Please don't say no. I'll raise hell,' she said, tapping her bright green manicured fingernails on his table.

Shirin had become a fine academic; after the scandal she had gone to Princeton, from where she wrote him almost every day without fail. Upon her return she had found a teaching position at her old college. Since then they had remained good friends, despite the age difference and their discordant lifestyles. That neither of them had tried to revive their past affair was commendable and the right thing to do, but also sad, Azur had thought. He knew he was getting old.

'Look, this man is awful. Racist. Homophobe. Islamophobe, poor Mona would have had a heart attack. He has no shame. He says God speaks through his mouth.'

Azur smiled. 'There are many of them; get used to it.'

'I won't,' Shirin said. 'Please come.'

'What do you want from me, darling? You think my presence means anything to anyone, least of all to him? I'm a walking disgrace in their eyes. Besides, I stopped debating God. Don't do it any more.'

'I don't believe that for a second. Just come, please.'

After she left, he made himself tea and sat at the kitchen table. A ray of sunlight slanting through the foliage of the sycamore tree outside formed a mottled patchwork on his face, accentuating his chiselled features. A local newspaper was folded beside him. There was an article about the Dutch scholar known for his contentious views on Islam, refugees, gay marriage and the state of the world. He claimed direct access to God – a privileged club membership. For near on two centuries the Oxford Union had invited eminent outside speakers, ranging from conventional to controversial. But no one could remember such a hue and cry as there had been for this one-man address.

Azur lifted the teacup, leaving a stain on the newspaper that circled the speaker's head – now the man looked holy indeed. He stared at the image for a moment, transfixed. Then, on impulse, he grabbed his jacket and his car keys.

Twenty minutes later, as Azur approached the building, silhouetted against the overcast sky, he noticed a group of students waiting outside with placards protesting against the speaker, demanding that he should be turned off university soil.

A young man stopped him. A fresher by the look of him. He would not know Azur.

'We launched a petition to stop this monster, will you sign?' His English was accented but easy on the ears.

'Isn't it a bit late?' Azur said. 'The man will be speaking in ten minutes.'

'Doesn't matter. If we collect enough signatures the Union will have to think twice before inviting someone like him next time. Besides, we are planning to go in and interrupt the talk.' He thrust a ballpoint pen and a pad in front of Azur.

'Sorry to disappoint you,' Azur said, 'but I won't sign.'

A look of contempt crossed the young man's face. 'So you agree with him? A fascist?'

'I didn't say I shared his worldview.'

But the student, having already lost interest, turned back and walked away, a fast shuffle. Azur felt torn between letting him go and catching up with him.

'Wait!' He hurried after him.

The student stopped, surprised.

'You're Muslim, right?'

A cautious nod.

'You've read Rumi, I presume. Remember the line? If you are irritated by every rub, how will your mirror be polished?'

'What?'

'Let this guy speak. Ideas must be challenged with ideas. Books with better books. However stupid they might be, you can't shut down people's voices. Banning speakers is no way to go.'

'Keep your high-flown philosophy to yourself,' he said. 'No one has the right to insult my religion and what's sacred to me.'

'But imagine how free you'll feel if you can rise above this man's hatred? We must answer insult with wisdom.'

'Is that your Rumi again?'

'Actually it's Shams, his companion and –'

'Just leave me alone,' the young man said before he strode towards his friends, and whispered something to them. They all stared up at Azur.

Why couldn't he ever hold his tongue? This tongue that had caused him enough trouble in life already. Running his fingers through his thinning, grey-flecked hair, he entered the Oxford Union. There was a poster at the entrance with the title of the talk: 'Save Europe for Europeans.'

A tense excitement buzzed among the crowd that had gathered in the hall. Some had arrived here with feelings of anger, disdain and disbelief towards the speaker, who had made a career out of being insulting and derisive; some with a smug satisfaction that someone was finally saying aloud what they had been thinking.

As Azur inched his way through the audience, a few colleagues from way back waved at him, while others pretended not to have noticed him. Shame was a cloak of invisibility. He wore it in public. It did not hurt him, not as much as before, observing just how readily people judged and distanced themselves. At times like this, he thought about Peri, wondering what she was doing in Istanbul, what kind of a life she had built for herself. If he had been condemned to lifelong disgrace, she must have been condemned to lifelong remorse. Who could possibly tell which was harder on the soul?

Seeing him coming, Shirin stood up, waving, one hand on her belly. Her excitement was so touching Azur felt sad. It wasn't his cowardly accusers or opportunistic rivals who had made him feel vulnerable. It was those who, no matter what, loved and respected and supported him regardless. They had waited for him to clear his name. This he had refused to do. He had always thought that the more you protested your innocence in front of others, the more you would be incriminated in their eyes. Besides, opening up old files would have hurt Peri too.

'Thank you for coming,' Shirin said. 'I knew you would.'

'I'm going to leave early. Don't think I could stand him till the end.'

She agreed.

In a little while the speaker walked on stage, tieless in an electric-blue cashmere suit. He spoke for thirty minutes about the dangers awaiting Western civilization. His voice undulated in a calculated rhythm, dropping now and then to a hoarse whisper, rising upon words that he knew would induce fear. He was not a racist, he said. Certainly not a xenophobe. His favourite bakery was run by an Arab couple, his private doctor was of Pakistani origin and he had spent the best holiday of his life years before in Beirut, where a cab driver had recovered his lost wallet. But the doors of Europe had to be securely bolted. It was the only logical consequence of an entire omnishambles created by others. Europe was home. Muslims were strangers. Even a five-year-old knew one did not invite strangers into one's house. Everyone in the world envied the wealth of the West and it had to be protected both from the outsiders and the Judases within, who did not see that diluting a culture, adulterating a race, defiling a heritage was wrong. Wrong!

Wrong! Interracial and interfaith marriages, they all endangered the integrity of Western society. We should not be ashamed to talk about purity. Racial, cultural, social and religious purity. He was eloquent, well mannered and – like all good demagogues – knew when to crack a joke.

Europe's problem was that it had abandoned God. People were finally waking up to this historical mistake. It was time to bring God the Saviour back – back into academia, back into the family, back into the public space. Freedoms should never be confused with Godlessness. Europe had been wasting its time debating foolish subjects – like same-sex marriage – while the barbarian hordes were massing at our gates. If people chose to be gay, fine, but they had to bear the consequences. They could not lay claim to marriage – clearly stated as a covenant with God between a man and a woman. The present turmoil – terrorism, refugee crisis, Islamic extremism on European soil – was God's way of teaching Europeans a lesson. Testing, correcting, honing, perfecting. In the past the Lord had rained down fire and brimstone on sinful cities; today He rained refugees and terrorists upon us. Every age brought its own punishment.

'My friends, God is here with us today. They tried to banish Him from universities. They have offended Him for so long. But He is present in all His glory. I'm nothing but His vessel, His humble mouthpiece.'

From his seat in the audience Azur scoffed, loud and bold, piercing a moment of silence in the hall. All eyes turned to him, including the speaker.

'Whom do I see before us? We are honoured by the presence of Professor Azur, if I'm not mistaken,' the speaker said, 'though not a professor any more.'

Whispers rippled across the hall as colleagues and students craned their heads to get a better view of the unruly listener. Azur stood up. Beside him Shirin sat still, her face as white as a ghost's.

'You are right. I don't teach any more.'

His mouth turned down, the speaker said, 'Yes, I heard. It even reached our quiet little corner in Amsterdam.' A fake smile of sympathy spread across his face. 'But I'm pleased to see with my own eyes how God has brought you back to the light.'

'Who said I'd been in the dark?' Azur said.

'Well, it's obvious . . .'

Azur nodded. 'Then I must give you hope. I've been all things unholy. If God can work through me, He can work miracles through anyone – maybe even open up a closed mind like yours.'

'How splendid of you to quote St Francis. For your own purposes, I presume. It's what people do. Someday we must have a debate. It'll be fun.'

And with that the preacher moved on, leaving Azur still standing up, itching to engage in a debate that would not be granted anytime soon.

When he returned from his evening walk, still reliving the moment at the Oxford Union, the house felt chilly. The photographs on the walls, the tiles by the fireplace. As he was heating a lasagne from the day before, his phone began to ring. An unfamiliar number, it looked international. Not in the mood to talk to anyone, he decided not to answer it. It stopped halfway, a moment of dead silence. Cioran by his feet gave a little whimper. Then it started ringing again.

This time something inside nudged him to pick up the phone. And he did. On the other end of the line, from a seaside mansion in Istanbul, was Peri, trying to find her voice.

The Three Passions

Istanbul, 2016

Breathe in. Breathe out. For a moment, time seemed to have melted away and she became the girl she once was, catapulted from a bad dream or thrust into yet another – the wardrobe she had climbed into was like her brother's prison cell. Meanwhile, outside, the guests and the staff had been taken upstairs to the gilded office. Peri had heard their footsteps as they were herded together, but now an ominous silence had descended on the household. She tightened her grip on her husband's phone as she waited for the ring. A sudden lump formed in her throat as she heard Azur's voice at the end of the line.

'Hello?'

The familiar timbre brought tears to her eyes. Her mouth felt as though it were full of tiny particles, fine grains of remorse. It was frightening the speed with which the shared past, like liquid pain, flowed into the silences of the present.

'Hello? Who is this?'

She almost hung up, so sharply did the words abandon her. Yet she was tired of running away from herself and the impulse to confront her fears propelled her forward. 'Azur . . . it's me, Peri.'

'Pe-ri . . .' he repeated and paused, as if the very invocation of her name embraced the totality of things, the good and the bad and everything in between.

Her mind was racing. Her pulse was racing. Yet when she spoke again her voice sounded calm. 'I should have called you before. I acted like a coward.'

Azur remained silent. He had known this moment would come, but he had never planned for it.

'What a surprise,' he said at last. He seemed about to say something else but changed his mind. 'You all right?'

'Not really,' she replied without dwelling on it. She did not tell him there were armed men in the house. Nor did she say that this conversation could be cut off abruptly, as her battery was running low. She heard a dog bark in the background. 'Spinoza?'

'Spinoza is dead, my dear. I'm hoping he's in a better world.'

She began to cry, silently. 'I owe you an apology, Azur. I should have spoken in front of the committee.'

'Don't blame yourself,' he said gently. 'You were in no state to make a sound judgement. You were too young.'

'I was old enough.'

'Well . . . I should have been more careful.'

That took her by surprise. So he had not hated her all this time, as she'd feared. Instead he had taken it on himself.

I read your latest book, she wanted to say. *I have read every single title you have published since . . . You have changed. You sound more cynical . . . dispassionate. And I wonder if that means you've lost your restlessness, the playful spirit that could charm your students and mesmerize entire audiences. I hope not.*

From upstairs she heard the distant drum of footsteps. A brief commotion. Someone yelled. A gunshot pierced the air. A thud.

Peri's whole frame went rigid, her breath coming in rasps.

'What was that?' asked Azur.

'Nothing,' she said.

'Where are you?'

Inside a wardrobe in a posh villa in Istanbul that has just been taken over by thugs, in my mouth the taste of fear and a truffle named Oxford. No, she couldn't tell him that.

'Does it matter?' she said, keeping her voice impossibly low.

He said, 'When I met you, Peri, I thought, this girl doesn't know it but she carries the three passions of Bertrand Russell: the longing for love, the search for knowledge and the unbearable compassion for the suffering of mankind.'

Her face clouded over.

'You had all three of them,' he said. 'So deep was your need for love. Your thirst for learning. Your sensitivity towards others . . . to the point of self-effacement. I felt for you. But I also felt *angry* at you. You reminded me of a woman I had known.'

'Your wife?' she asked cautiously.

'No, my dear. This was someone called Nour. I became anxious that I could hurt you just like I had hurt her. The truth is, I know I've ended up harming every woman who's reached out to me.'

'Except Shirin.'

'True, she was invincible. She seemed so. She was younger, but she was strong, stubborn. A natural-born warrior. Next to her there was nothing to worry about. Nothing bad would ever happen to her.'

'You wanted a love devoid of guilt.'

'Maybe,' Azur said. 'You see, you're not the only one apologizing to God.'

On the screen the battery turned from black to red. 'Would you do something for me?'

'Go ahead.'

'I'd like to have one more seminar. Now.'

He laughed. 'What do you mean? On what?'

'On forgiveness and love,' she said. 'And knowledge. I'll be the professor this time, deal?'

A wary pause. 'I'm listening, dear.'

'Well,' she said. 'Today's lecture is on Ibn Arabi and Ibn Rushd – Averroës. Ibn Rushd was an eminent philosopher, Ibn Arabi a young and hopeful student when the two of them met for the first time. They immediately felt a rapport, as they were both devoted to books and learning and neither embraced the orthodoxy. But they were also very different.'

'How?'

'You see, it's the same question East and West, isn't it? How do you increase your knowledge of yourself and of the world? Ibn Rushd had a clear answer: through reflective thinking. Reasoning. Studying.'

'And Ibn Arabi?'

'He wanted both reason and *mystical insights*. He believed it was our duty as human beings to expand our wisdom. But he also recognized there were things beyond the limits of the mind. Before they went their separate ways, Ibn Rushd asked Ibn Arabi, one last time, *Is it through rational consideration that we unveil the Truth?*'

'And what did Ibn Arabi say?'

'He said yes, and he said no. "Between the yes and the no," he said, "spirits fly from their matter and minds from their bodies." He thought no one was more ignorant than those who seek God and yet only those who pursue a truth bigger than themselves have a chance to attain it.'

'Tell me, Peri, why were *you* interested in this story?'

'Because I was always in that limbo between yes and no. No stranger to faith, no stranger to doubt. Undecided. Vacillating. Never self-confident. Maybe it made me who I am, all that uncertainty. It also became my worst enemy. I saw no way out of it.' She paused. 'I told you about the baby in the mist. If not a hallucination, it was a type of experience you had never heard of before. Another scholar would have scoffed at it, sure, but you didn't. You were always open to the new. I admired you for that.'

'You think you were the only one confused. But many of us are.'

Us. A sigh of a word. So tiny, so huge. We the confused.

Peri shook her head. 'I admired you too much. Now I can see it clearly. When we fall in love we turn the other person into our god – how dangerous is that? And when he doesn't love us back, we respond with anger, resentment, hatred . . .'

She said, 'There's something about love that resembles faith. It's a kind of blind trust, isn't it? The sweetest euphoria. The magic of connecting with a being beyond our limited, familiar selves. But if we get carried away by love – or by faith – it turns into a dogma, a fixation. The sweetness becomes sour. We suffer in the hands of the gods that we ourselves created.'

'I must be one of the last persons on earth to be considered a god,' Azur said.

'It wasn't you,' Peri said. 'It was the Azur I had created for myself. The one I needed in order to make sense of my own fragmented past. That's the professor I was infatuated with. The Azur in my mind.'

So she continued. Her voice building in strength, her eyes now fully adjusted to the dark, a mobile flickering in her injured hand, she gave a lecture to a man in a house outside Oxford while his dog waited patiently by his side. It could easily have been the other way round: he in danger, she in safety. Today she was the tutor; he, the pupil. Roles shifted, words never stayed still. The shape of life was a circle, and every point on that circle was at an equal distance from the centre – whether one called that God or something else altogether.

She heard the sound of sirens closing in on the seaside mansion. In a few minutes, no more, everything was going to change – a new beginning or an end too soon. As the phone gave one last beep before it died completely, she opened the door of the wardrobe and stepped out.

Acknowledgements

My motherland, Turkey, is a river country, neither solid nor settled. During the course of writing this novel that river changed so many times, flowing with a dizzying speed.

My heartfelt thanks to two people who are very dear to me: my agent Jonny Geller and my editor Venetia Butterfield. I am indebted to both for their encouragement, support and faith; for taking care of my anxieties and panic attacks and for being on this journey together. Special thanks to Daisy Meyrick, Mairi Friesen-Escandell, Catherine Cho, Anna Ridley, Emma Brown, Isabel Wall and Keith Taylor: the wonderful teams at Curtis Brown and Penguin, it is a true joy to work with you.

I owe a 'thank you' the size of Istanbul's traffic to Stephen Barber, who has read and reread this book, offering me most precious advice. I am grateful to Lorna Owen for her valuable insights and contribution. It is a blessing for an author to work with the brilliant Donna Poppy. Thank you to Nigel Newton for his enthusiasm and camaraderie.

Thanks in abundance to my children, Zelda and Zahir, for putting up with my irregular writing hours and tolerating the music I listen to while writing. It's too noisy, I know.

Motherlands are beloved, no doubt; sometimes they can also be exasperating and maddening. Yet I have also come to learn that for writers and poets for whom national borders and cultural barriers are there to be questioned, again and again, there is, in truth, only one motherland, perpetual and portable.

Storyland.

A NOTE ON THE AUTHOR

Elif Shafak is the acclaimed author of ten novels including *The Architect's Apprentice* and *The Bastard of Istanbul,* and is the most widely read female writer in Turkey. Her work has been translated into over forty languages and she has been awarded the prestigious Chevalier des Arts et des Lettres. She is also a public speaker, a women's rights activist and a commentator who regularly contributes to international publications including *The New York Times, Guardian* and *La Repubblica.* Elif has been longlisted for the Orange Prize, the Baileys Prize and the IMPAC Dublin Award, and shortlisted for the Independent Foreign Fiction Prize. She lives in London and can be found at www.elifshafak.com.

The weight of heaven

Trinity Umrigar